Shadowheart

Shadowheart

LEGENDS OF
THE RAVEN

James Barclay

The right of James Barclay to be identified as the
author of this work has been asserted by him in accordance
with the Copyright, Designs and Patents Act 1988.

First published in Great Britain in 2003 by
Gollancz
An imprint of the Orion Publishing Group
Orion House, 5 Upper St Martin's Lane,
London WC2H 9EA

This paperback edition first published in Great Britain in 2004 by
Gollancz

A CIP catalogue record for this book is
available from the British Library

ISBN 0 575 07544 9

Typeset at The Spartan Press Ltd,
Lymington, Hants

Printed in Great Britain by
Clays Ltd, St Ives plc

Acknowledgements

No surprises here, I guess. Tireless Editor and close friend, Simon Spanton was once again always there for debate, discussion and advice. And the odd beer. Arch publicist, Nicola Sinclair snared some great press exposure against the odds, and Robert Kirby, my agent, always looked forwards. Thank you for everything you do on my behalf.

And there's more. Thanks once again to Dick Whichelow and Dave Mutton for their support and healthy criticism. To David Gemmell and Peter Hamilton for valuable advice on the business side of being an author. To Ariel for sterling work on my website (particularly the gazetteer). To Rob Bedford, Gabe Chouinard and Sammie from sffworld.com for spreading the word. And once more to all those who took the time to email me about The Raven.

Cast List

THE RAVEN	*Hirad Coldheart* BARBARIAN WARRIOR
	The Unknown Warrior/Sol WARRIOR
	Thraun SHAPECHANGER
	Ry Darrick CAVALRY SWORDSMAN
	Denser XETESKIAN MAGE
	Erienne DORDOVAN MAGE
THE COLLEGES	*Dystran* LORD OF THE MOUNT, XETESK
	Ranyl CIRCLE SEVEN MASTER MAGE, XETESK
	Myx A PROTECTOR
	Suarav CAPTAIN, XETESKIAN COLLEGE GUARD
	Chandyr COMMANDER, XETESKIAN ARMIES
	Nyam SENIOR MAGE, XETESK
	Vuldaroq ARCH MAGE, DORDOVER
	Heryst LORD ELDER MAGE, LYSTERN
	Izack COMMANDER, LYSTERNAN CAVALRY
	Pheone HIGH MAGE DESIGNATE, JULATSA
THE ELVES	*Myriell* AL-DRECHAR
	Cleress AL-DRECHAR
	Rebraal LEADER OF THE AL-ARYNAAR
	Auum LEADER OF THE TAIGETHEN
	Evunn TAI CELL OF AUUM
	Duele TAI CELL OF AUUM
	Dila'heth ELVEN MAGE
	The ClawBound
BALAIANS, WESMEN AND A DRAGON	*Blackthorne* A BARON
	Devun LEADER OF THE BLACK WINGS
	Diera WIFE OF THE UNKNOWN WARRIOR
	Tessaya LORD OF THE PALEON TRIBES
	Riasu LORD KEEPER OF UNDERSTONE PASS
	Sha-Kaan GREAT KAAN

BALAIA
NORTH BAY
Sunara's Teeth
TERENETSA
Sethe River
Torn Wastes
PARVE
Baravale Valley
WESMEN HEARTLANDS (Uncharted)
Arch-Temple of the Wrethsires
Eye Lake
LEIONU
N
Sky Lake
Garan Mountains
W
E
Southern Force
S
SOUTHERN OCEANS

THE NORTHERN CONTINENT

Trivern Inlet

R. Tri

JADEN

RACHE

Blood Lake

JULATSA

DORDOVER

HAVERN

CORIN

Triverne Lake

Blackwing's Castle

LYSTERN

XETESK

Understone Pass

UNDERSTONE

Pontois Plains

DENEBRE

PONTOIS

Septern Manse

ERSKAN

HYLD

Grethern Forest

Triangle Castle

KORINA

Thornewood

GRESSE

The Buffs

GREYTHORNE

ARLEN

ERYTTE

Balan Mts.

BLACKTHORNE

Bay of Gyernath

GYERNATH

Arlen Bay

Mountains

Blackthorne

Yarhawk Crags

Chapter 1

The detachment of cavalry from the mage college city of Lystern wheeled and attacked again, charging hard at the defenders holding their positions outside Xetesk's east gates. Targeting the weakened left flank, they sped in, hooves churning mud, swords and spear tips glinting in the bright, warm afternoon sunlight. Thirty horses, sweat foaming under saddles, galloping under the steady control of crack Lysternan riders and led by Commander Izack.

'Come on, this time,' whispered Dila'heth to herself, watching the attack from a rise above the blood-drenched battlefield.

Down in the centre of the line, the bulk of the surviving Al-Arynaar and TaiGethen elves were engaged in a cat-and-mouse game, trying to lure the stubborn Xeteskians out of alignment. So far, their efforts had been fruitless. Protectors at the core of the defensive line, so disciplined, so deadly, remained unmoved.

A fusillade of spells erupted from the ranks of Xeteskian mages behind their warriors. FlameOrb, HotRain, DeathHail, homing in on the cavalry as they drove in. Lysternan shields glared and flashed, revealing the rich green depths of the mana-lattice that held them firm, deflecting the deep blue of the enemy castings.

Dila'heth could feel the pressure of the shields through the spectrum and respected their strength and the ability of the mages who rode while they cast.

Immediately, response came from the elven and Lysternan mages in the field behind the combat line. Yellow and green Orbs, burnished with flares of deep red and orange, soared over the warriors. Two dozen of them, wide as cartwheels, splashed down into the Xeteskian support. Shields creaked, blue light like sheet lightning seared the sky; but they held. It had been this way for twenty days. Probing, watching, feinting and attacking. The battle had barely moved.

'Keep up the pressure!' shouted Dila'heth, her words taken by runners down to the field command. 'Let's give that cavalry time.'

Izack's men struck, Dila'heth wincing at the impact. Horses snorted, men leant out left and right, swords and maces hammering down, their charge taking them deep into the defenders before they were halted. Even at a hundred yards and more, Dila's keen eyes could pick out individual suffering with grim clarity.

Leading his men, Izack, mouth open in a battle cry lost in the tumult, struck the helmet of an enemy, his blade crushing the metal. The foot soldier collapsed senseless and the hooves of the horse following trampled him into the mud. Further right, a lone Xeteskian pike skewered a horse's chest. The jolt threw the rider over his mount's head. The desperate, dying animal screamed, its hooves flailing. It fell, one shod hoof splintering the Xeteskian's ribcage, its body crushing its own rider. At the back of the charge, an enemy was knocked off balance by the press of horse flesh around him. He spun and staggered, his defence dropped and a spiked mace ripped off his face.

Swords flashed, horses reared, men roared. In the chaos, Dila watched Izack. The cavalry commander seemed to have so much more time than any of those around him. He pushed his horse through the throng, batting aside strikes to both him and his mount. She could see his mouth move as he tried to direct his riders to the point he sensed was weakest.

His horse kicked forwards, taking an enemy in the groin. Izack ignored the man's cries, fencing a strike away from his leg and cutting backhanded into his attacker's midriff. He was going to break through. The tide was with him and with those still in the saddle. Protectors were detaching from the centre of the line but they'd be too late. And waiting behind Izack, a hundred-strong reserve, made up of cavalry, Lysternan swordsmen and the Al-Arynaar. Enough to force the breach wide and open up the Xeteskian support mages to weapon attack. Dila's only concern now was the centre of the main fighting line. It absolutely had to hold.

Feeling sure the battle was about to turn decisively, she

swung round to call every able-bodied ally to arms and into the battle. At first, she thought the faintness and sudden nausea she felt was because she'd spun too fast. But she saw her condition reflected in the expressions of the Julatsan-trained Al-Arynaar mages standing by her and knew it was something infinitely worse.

'Oh no.'

The chain of focused mana cells holding together the powerful, elven, linked Spell- and HardShields collapsed. It was a sudden and violent shifting in the flow, as if every casting mage had simultaneously lost the ability to maintain the simple shape. But this was no mass error. Dila'heth had felt it. Every mage carrying the linked Julatsan construct was left helpless as the power in the spell scattered back into the individual castings, shattering them instantly.

Dila rocked with the referred pain of three dozen backfiring spells. Out in the field, mages, their minds threshed by flailing mana strands, clutched the sides of their heads, fell screaming to the ground or dropped catatonic from the shock. And two hundred swordsmen and as many in the support lines were left exposed to anything Xetesk could throw at them. There were nowhere near enough Lysternan shield mages to cover everyone.

A cataclysmic event had disrupted the Julatsan mana focus. It had been brief and the question of what had happened had to be faced, but right now hundreds of elves and men were terribly vulnerable. Dila'heth began to run down the slope towards the battlefield, calling mages to her, those that could still function at all.

'Shields! We must have shields!'

But the push was falling apart right in front of her. Nervousness had spread through the fighting force like cracks on thin ice. To the left, Izack hadn't broken through fast enough. He couldn't yet threaten the enemy mages and the Xeteskians had picked up on the crisis engulfing their opponents. Their warriors put more power into every strike, their arrows flew in tighter volleys and their mages . . . Tual's teeth, their mages cast everything they had.

Dila'heth tried frantically to gather the shape for a SpellShield while she ran but it eluded her. The mana wouldn't coalesce to give the shape its protective form, but was always

3

just beyond her grasp, like a butterfly on the breeze. Scared more than she dared admit, she slewed to a stop then started to reverse, simultaneously seeing Izack breaking off his attack and the arc of the first Xeteskian spells surge across the sky.

'Clear the field, clear the field!' Dila'heth shouted, half turning, almost running.

She could see knots of mages trying to cast, others helping confused and comatose victims. More mirrored her own fear, unsure of what to do. Xetesk's first spell impacts made the decision for them.

More FlameOrbs than Dila could count fell at the back of the allied line, detonating in the mud and splashing mage fire over defenceless men and elves. And where that fire touched a Xeteskian SpellShield, it flared brief cobalt and dissipated harmlessly. Safe behind their defence, the enemy just stood and watched.

A FlameWall erupted along the combat front and panic tore the allied line to shreds. Burning, trapped and terrified, the line disintegrated, men and elves scattering left, right and back, anywhere that the flame might be less intense. Here and there, pockets of Lysternan shields provided shelter for anyone lucky enough to get under their protection but the overwhelming reliance had been on the Julatsan-based elven construct and too few could find sanctuary.

Everywhere she looked, Dila'heth could see burning swordsmen running blindly away, heading for the camp and the help that would be too late for so many. Flaming corpses littered the ground and the air was filled with the screams of the dying, pleading for help and relief. But in places, field captains were beginning to call their men and elves to fledgling order. Dila shook herself.

'Come on, we've got to help them!' she yelled into the roar of flame and the shrieks of agony all around her. She ran to the nearest victim, trying to force the simplest healing conjuration into her mind. Anything that would extinguish the mage fire that burned his clothes and covered his bare arms, eating at his flesh.

The shape formed slowly, frustratingly so, but at least it was coming. But then, so did the HellFire. Columns of super-heated blue scorched from the smoke-filled sky, each one targeting a single soul. Scant yards away, one struck the central

4

figure in a group of mages. The deluge consumed his body in an instant, the splatter took the other five in a flood of flame and the detonation pitched Dila from her feet.

What little order there had been developing in the retreat was destroyed. With FlameOrbs still crashing to earth and HotRain beginning to tumble from the sky in fist-sized tears, the rout was complete.

Dila'heth lay where she had fallen, bleeding from a cut on her forehead. Beside her, the swordsman had died, his cries fading quickly as he succumbed. She raised her head to see DeathHail slashing across the field. It would be a miracle if anyone escaped alive.

Only Izack remained in control. Dila watched him lead his cavalry across the front of the Xeteskian line, blunting any move, the shields surrounding his men flashing deep green from repeated spell impact. But the enemy had made no effort to move forwards. Shorth take them all, but there was no need. They had already won the day. Chances were, the battle was theirs too.

Dila dropped her head back into the mud, tears of pain and frustration squeezing from her smarting eyes. Clouds of smoke billowed across the field, muffling the sounds of defeat and triumph all around her. Somehow, they would have to regroup but first they had to understand why their magic had failed so catastrophically.

Exhausted and aching, bleeding and strained, Dila pulled herself to her knees and began to crawl from the battlefield, waiting for the moment when the DeathHail ceased and she could run. Bodies lay thick on the ground before her. Some were moving, most were not. To her left, a further detachment of cavalry galloped out to support Izack. But on the rise in front of the camp she could see a line of men and elves just standing and staring in disbelief at the disaster that had swamped them all.

Yniss himself would have to smile on them if they were to turn the tide now.

The great hall at the top of Lystern's squat, wide college tower felt chill despite the warmth of the day and the sunlight streaming through the ornate stained-glass windows that over-looked the huge circular table.

In an arc surrounding the Lord Elder Mage, Heryst, sat the four mages who made up the law council. All old men, all trusted advisers of the relatively young college and city ruler. Opposite them, The Raven were gathered around Darrick, who stood at their centre while they sat, listening to the charges laid against him. Otherwise, but for fifteen college guardsmen and a gaggle of clerks and monitor mages, the hall was empty, its spectacular domed and timbered roof ringing hollow.

Hirad Coldheart couldn't shake off a fundamental sense of wrong. It pervaded his every sense and had settled like a cloying web over his body. He had already been reminded twice of court protocol and now The Unknown Warrior left a restraining hand on his shoulder, keeping him in his seat. He had been promised his say but he couldn't shift the notion that it would be after any decision had been made in the minds of those opposite him. Not Heryst, the law council.

Darrick, of course, had remained impeccably disciplined throughout. Former General of the Lysternan armies and now accused of desertion, treason and cowardice he had returned to the college of his own free will to answer the charges. And nothing The Raven could say about the timing of his decision, and which priorities they felt he should place higher, carried any weight whatever.

He was a deeply principled man and for him, clearing his name transcended any action The Raven wanted to undertake. Those principles were one of the things that made him such a valuable addition to The Raven. But they were also a frustration Hirad found difficult to bear. So much remained to be done and he felt they were wasting time. Events were moving fast and they couldn't afford to be left behind.

Heryst looked round from a brief whispered conversation with the law mages. Two were frowning, one shaking his head, the fourth impassive.

'At this juncture,' said the Lord Elder Mage, 'We will drop the charge of treason. It is clear that your intention was not to act against Lystern. Indeed your assertion that our alliance with Dordover at the time was the potentially more treasonable act is one we cannot counteract with any great surety. Endangering the men under your command by virtue of that treason is therefore also dismissed.

'But the charges of desertion and cowardice must stand and you will answer them.'

Hirad opened his mouth but The Unknown squeezed his shoulder.

'Ridiculous,' muttered the barbarian.

'I know,' said The Unknown.

'I laugh at any suggestion of cowardice,' said Darrick. 'But within the laws of Lystern, I am guilty of desertion. That is not in dispute.'

'That is not a clever opening to your defence,' said Denser.

Darrick looked to his right long enough to spear the Raven's Xeteskian mage with the stare that had sent a thousand raw recruits' pulses stuttering before he continued.

'It was desertion,' affirmed Darrick. 'But the circumstances mitigate my actions and indeed made my decision the only honourable one.'

'There is no precedence for mitigation,' rumbled one of the law mages, a heavy-jowled man with eyes sunk deep into fleshy sockets.

'Then precedence must be set by this hearing,' said Darrick, betraying no hint of his emotions. 'Because this was not desertion through cowardice or fear. Neither was it desertion that in any way increased the risk to the men in my command. In peacetime, it would have been considered resignation on principle.'

'But this was not peacetime,' continued the mage. 'And you were facing an enemy.'

'Even so, the circumstances will be heard,' said Heryst.

'You are swayed by your personal friendship,' said a second law mage, grey-haired and long-nosed.

'And by his previously unblemished record of service, courage and honour in battle,' said Heryst. 'We are not trying a conscript here.' He smiled as he turned to Darrick. 'Make this good, Ry. There's a heavy penalty attached to your unmitigated guilt.'

'I am only too aware of that,' replied Darrick. 'And that in itself is the first part of my defence – that I came here voluntarily to answer this charge. There was little chance of my being arrested with war at our borders. I need to clear my name so I can take my part without looking over my shoulder for college guards carrying warrants.'

'I'm sure you have all our thanks for offering yourself up without our needing to divert resources,' said the long-nosed mage dryly.

Hirad scowled and tensed. He wasn't happy with the atmosphere. The four old men were clearly intent solely on establishing guilt. Only Heryst seemed truly interested in the possibility that Darrick took the only decision open to him under the circumstances. The question was, did he have ultimate sanction in this forum?

'The docks at Arlen, those three seasons ago, were a place where not just I but every Lysternan was betrayed. It was where some of those empowered to determine control of the Nightchild abandoned their morals and put her under sentence of death. And not just her, but also her mother, Erienne, who sits at my left.'

'We are perfectly—'

'You will let me speak uninterrupted, my Lord Metsas,' said Darrick. There was no anger in his voice.

Metsas's face darkened but he said no more.

'As has been documented, I found myself commanding cavalry that, far from preventing a ship sailing at the behest of the Lystern-Dordover alliance, were in fact defending it from Xeteskian aggression. And that is because it contained Dordovan mages in cahoots with Black Wings. Black Wings, gentlemen. The ship also contained a hostage: Erienne.'

Darrick gestured to Erienne and Hirad saw remembered pain flicker over her features. She laid her head briefly on Denser's shoulder.

'Dordover was using her to get to Lyanna. Her daughter. And then the mages would have cast her to the Black Wings to be murdered while they did the same to the Nightchild. It was an inhuman tactic for which Dordover deserves nothing but eternal contempt. And if any here present were in tacit support, that contempt is yours too.

'I love my city and college, make no mistake. I love its principles, its morals and its ethics. And I could not lead a force that would see those values betrayed. It was a decision which broke my heart but I had no other option. Surely, as the men who uphold our ethics and principles, you must understand.

'But know this, too. I carried out my resignation correctly.

8

I handed command to Izack in the knowledge that he was fully capable of carrying out his duties as correctly as I was. He proved me right, of course. My men were not put at excessive risk and the burden of Lystern's actions was taken from them. It was I who received the orders; Izack and his men were merely dutybound to carry them out.

'Yet, at the same time, I gave them a choice. I did not incite mass desertion and, as the record shows, no such action was taken. The decision was left with each individual's conscience, but what choice did most of those men really have? They had families who relied on them. They had lives to lead beyond the conflict. And they had nowhere to go.

'I was different. I had The Raven.'

Heryst shifted in his seat, evading Darrick's steady gaze. Hirad watched the law mages too. None showed the slightest understanding of, or sympathy for, Darrick's dilemma. And the words spoken merely confirmed the shallow nature of their thinking.

'Indeed you did have The Raven,' said the long-nosed mage. 'And you fought alongside Xetesk while at the opposite end of the docks, your men were being killed by Xetesk. How do you equate that with responsible discharge of your duties?'

Darrick nodded slowly. 'Lord Simmac, if my duty was to protect murderers and witch-hunters, then I am happy to have failed. If it was to protect the innocent and deliver the best possible outcome for Balaia and hence Lystern then, with one glaring exception, I and The Raven succeeded. Though subsequent events have removed any shine from our success.'

'The exception being?' asked Simmac.

'That Lyanna died and so we will never know if she could have used her power for the good of us all.'

'Of course,' said Simmac, as if the fact had slipped his mind.

'Dordover wanted her dead the moment she escaped them,' said Hirad quietly. 'What was your desire, I wonder?'

Heryst looked at him squarely. 'Hirad, with all due respect, we are not here to debate Lystern's flawed alliance with Dordover. Ry Darrick is on trial here.' He allowed himself a brief smile. 'But since you have been desperate to speak ever since we began, perhaps now is the time, if Darrick is done?'

'For now,' said Darrick. 'Though I reserve the right to speak again.'

'Granted,' said Heryst. 'Hirad, the floor is yours.'

The barbarian stood, feeling the cold stares of the law mages gauging him.

'It's really simple,' he said. 'The events Darrick set going saved the elves from extinction. He saved so many lives by joining us. Still not quite enough, though.'

The Unknown squeezed his forearm. The Raven still felt it. They'd been too late to save Ilkar, the elf who had been with The Raven since the start. An elf they all loved and who, ironically, had feared watching them all grow old and die around him.

'And how exactly do you work that out?' asked Simmac, expression all but a sneer.

Hirad felt the almost overwhelming urge to cross the table and flatten his long nose. He took a deep breath.

'Because,' he said carefully, 'had he not organised the defence of the Al-Drechar's house on Herendeneth; and had he not fought with The Raven and alongside Xetesk in that house against the Dordovan and Black Wing invasion, not just Lyanna, but all the Al-Drechar would have been dead. And with them, as it turned out, would have died every elf. Only they had the knowledge to rebind the statue of Yniss and halt the plague.'

'I fail to see—' began Simmac.

'And where would your forces be now without the elves, eh?' Hirad raised his voice, hearing it echo into the rafters. 'Without their swords and their magic to back you and Dordover against Xetesk? Answer me that and keep sneering.' Hirad almost sat then but there was one other thing to say.

'Ry Darrick is one of the bravest men I have ever met. He is also without question the most moral and upright. Everything he does is for the benefit of Balaia, and that is something we should all be striving for, don't you agree? Removing him would remove one of our most potent weapons from the fight that is still to come. And believe me, we are on your side. The side that would see balance restored to our land.

'Remove him and you make The Raven your enemy. And you don't want that.'

Hirad sat. He felt his pulse thudding in his neck and was glad of the weathered tan on his face; he was sure he was flushed.

'Well done, Hirad,' said The Unknown.

Darrick turned his head and nodded fractionally.

'Does anyone else wish to speak?' asked Heryst.

'Hirad speaks for us all,' said The Unknown. 'Darrick is Raven. He was instrumental in saving the elven race and his honour and courage are beyond question. If you find Darrick guilty without redress, you must ask yourselves exactly what it is you are actually finding him guilty of.'

'Desertion,' said Metsas, the word snapping from his mouth. 'From Lysternan lines.'

'Or perhaps of doing his duty by his country.'

'If you believe that,' said Metsas.

'Oh, I have no doubt,' said The Unknown. 'But it is you who sit in judgement.'

'For the record,' said Heryst, 'and excuse the slight contradiction but I am both Darrick's judge and commanding officer, I must make mention of Darrick's unblemished record of courage and service to the city and college of Lystern. To list every event would take longer than we have, and that in itself should inform us of his character. They are all well documented but three stand out as shining examples of his loyalty, strength and ability.

'The sorties into Understone Pass in the years before the pass fell. How much more damaging would the Wesmen invasion have been a decade later had we lost the pass earlier?

'The battle at Parve six years ago. Darrick led his cavalry into the heart of Wesmen power to break their lines and allow The Raven through. Without him, would Denser have been able to cast Dawnthief and pierce the hearts of the Wytch Lords?

'Finally, the Wesmen invasion. Darrick's command of the four-college force was critical in delaying the Wesmen long enough for help, in the form of the Kaan dragons, to arrive on the closing of the Noonshade rip.

'Within those commands, acts of personal heroism and sacrifice were played out. In his time as Lystern's general, Darrick has, without question, been central to saving Balaia.'

Hirad could see the law mages' expressions. Their disdain for what they had heard was plain. These were mages of the old school, which taught that allegiance to Lystern and a love of Balaia were not necessarily linked. And Darrick had chosen Balaia.

11

'Are we done?' asked Simmac. Darrick and Heryst both nodded. 'Good.' The elderly mage snapped his fingers and a young woman detached herself from the clerks. 'The Sound-Shield, please.'

She nodded and began to cast. Her hands described a dome above the heads of the five who sat in judgement. She mouthed silently, cupped her hands and spoke a single command word, completing the simple spell.

'How long will it take?' asked Hirad, watching Metsas begin to speak and seeing him flick his hand at The Raven. Heryst frowned and shook his head as he replied.

'Not long, I fear,' said Darrick. 'I've only the one ally inside that bubble of silence.'

'But at least he's head mage,' said Hirad.

'I suspect that means little in the middle of a war that half of Heryst's council thinks Lystern should not be fighting,' said Denser.

'True,' said Darrick.

'You think Heryst may sacrifice you as a sop to the opposition faction?' asked The Unknown.

'It's possible,' said Darrick. 'He's not as confident as I remember him.'

'I don't see it,' said Erienne. 'Surely the salvation of the elves is enough.'

'To save my life, possibly. To free me, I don't know.'

To his left, Hirad heard a growl. He glanced across to where Thraun sat, eyes fixed on the law mages and Heryst. Thraun's face was pinched and angry, lips drawn back over his teeth.

'Blind men,' said Thraun.

'I know what you mean,' said Hirad.

They fell silent, watching the law council argue Darrick's fate while the tension soared in the great hall. Hirad felt sweat on his palms and, next to him, Darrick at last showed some emotion. His face was lined with anxiety beneath his tight brown curly hair and his fists clenched and unclenched by his sides. He swallowed hard and glanced round at Hirad, his smile terribly weak, his eyes small and scared.

Time stretched. The Raven couldn't look at each other, their gazes instead locked on the scene being played out in silence across the table. Metsas and Simmac had already revealed their hands and Heryst's allegiance was clear. It rested on the two who had not spoken a word during the hearing. Where would their heads and hearts fall?

The quiet dragged at Hirad's ears while he watched Heryst reply in obvious anger. His hand slapped the table, vibrations carrying around its circumference. The Lord Elder Mage jabbed a finger at Metsas and gestured at the two undecided mages. The law mage winced and shrank back in his chair but his expression hardly changed. Heryst asked a simple question. Metsas shook his head, Simmac made no move and the other two nodded.

'The decision is made on majority.' Heryst's voice was unnaturally loud, puncturing the silence once the SoundShield had dispersed.

If it was possible, Darrick stood a little straighter, his hands still once again.

'The findings of the law council hearing in the matter of Lystern's charges of desertion and cowardice against former general Darrick are as follows.'

Heryst's face was carefully neutral but his eyes couldn't disguise his discomfort. Hirad clutched the arms of his chair. He felt suddenly very hot and wished for just a morsel of Darrick's bearing.

'The charge of cowardice is dismissed. The charge of desertion, of leaving the men in your command to face a foe of unknown strength and of subsequently leaving the scene of battle to take up arms against an ally is upheld.

'The usual penalty for desertion is death without appeal. But these are not usual times. And there is no doubting your abilities as swordsman, horseman and leader of men.'

Lord Metsas cleared his throat but a sharp glance from Heryst stilled any further interruption.

'It is the decision of this court, therefore, that you, Ry Darrick, be redrafted into the Lysternan cavalry, there to serve under Commander Izack in the war against Xetesk. Your rank will be reduced to cavalryman second class but, as you are aware, the Lysternan armed forces have always rewarded clear ability with swift promotion, often in the field.

'You will leave for the east gates front at dawn tomorrow. Do you have anything to say now sentence is passed?'

Hirad didn't know what to think. Relief that Darrick wasn't to be executed was diluted with the knowledge he was to be taken from The Raven. And on the back of so much recent loss, Hirad couldn't shift the notion that somehow The Raven were being forced to share his punishment.

For a few moments, Darrick was still while the chamber awaited his reaction. It was not one that any of them expected.

'I accept the decision but not the punishment,' he said.

Lord Metsas snorted. 'You speak as if you have a choice.'

'I do,' said Darrick. 'I can choose to agree to your punishment or remain true to what I believe.'

Hirad was sure everyone could hear his heart beating in his chest, the silence was that pronounced. Heryst was completely confused; his face had fallen and he looked as if he was about to burst into tears. Erienne was shaking her head but The Unknown and Thraun were nodding. Hirad was with them.

'And what exactly is it that you believe?' Lord Metsas asked.

'That Balaia needs me with The Raven far more than it does at Xetesk's east gates. That we can right the balance if we're left to act and the allies hold Xetesk at her walls. That my return to the Lysternan cavalry is a sham.

'Gentlemen, you have to understand me. I am Raven. And that is all I will ever be now until the day I die.'

Across the table, Metsas and Simmac relaxed into their chairs. Heryst closed his eyes briefly and leant forwards, fingers kneading his forehead.

'Then I have no option,' he said. 'I've done everything I can for you. Ry Darrick, if you refuse to join the cavalry, the sentence of this court can only be one thing. Death.'

Chapter 2

The silence that had fallen over the largely rebuilt College of Julatsa had lasted for so long that now no one dared speak lest he or she voiced the fears they all harboured. None of them had suffered, for which the Gods had to be thanked, because none of them had been casting at the time.

But they had all been touched so deeply it had taken their breath and their strength, and had drawn them all to the gaping hole in the middle of the college. It was the one thing they couldn't put right because there just weren't enough of them, but it was the one thing they needed because without it the college would not function as a fully formed magical entity.

The Heart.

Buried to prevent its destruction by Wesmen and now lost until enough Julatsans could be gathered to raise it and allow its pulse to beat through the college once again.

They had thought the Heart's burial would merely cause it to lie dormant but that was not the case. And it was this dread realisation that had drawn them all, few that they were, to the jagged crater. Three hundred feet below and covered in impenetrable black, lay the Heart.

Burying it had toppled the Tower which had been built above it, entombing those few brave souls who had sacrificed themselves to save the college from ultimate destruction. Reversing the burial was far more difficult and the forty mages standing around the crater simply weren't enough.

Pheone stood chewing her lip, trying desperately to frame words of hope for them all, but her heart was as heavy as the pit in front of her was deep. They'd clung to the belief that though it was dormant, the Heart still kept their magic alive. This had given them the faith that one day, however long it took, they would be able to return their college to its former glory. Not now.

'It's dying, isn't it?' Pheone said, her voice carrying across the courtyard. No one answered her though the shifting of feet told her they'd all heard her.

What in all the hells was she supposed to do? They'd all turned to her when Ilkar had left to do The Raven's work three seasons ago. Expected her to take up where he had left off. Like it was that easy.

Gods, how she missed him. His strength, his touch, his kiss. Not a day went by that she didn't look to the gates, wishing for him to ride through them. He'd know what to do, where to find the mages they needed to raise the Heart before it was too late. Perhaps he would still come. But news was so hard to come by with so few Julatsans in contact with the college and she'd heard nothing of his whereabouts for over a season. And every day without word chipped at her belief a little more.

'That's not possible,' said Lempaar at last. The oldest mage amongst them, he was an elf who had stayed clear of a disease that had claimed ten of his race and a fifth of the already small mage population. Only now was news filtering through that the disease had afflicted tens of thousands of elves on both continents before apparently running its course.

'We all felt it, Lempaar,' said Pheone. 'We all know what it means.'

It had been relatively short-lived. An abyss had opened up in each one of them, giving them a glimpse of an existence without the touch of mana. It had been terrifying. A void of unfathomable depth, of unbridgeable loss.

Pheone let her gaze travel slowly across the assembly. They all, like her, were trying desperately to argue themselves out of the obvious. Every teaching any of them had received on the subject had been clear. The Heart, they said, was the centre of Julatsan power but was not the portal between them and mana in itself. Losing it would be a terribly weakening blow but it would not end Julatsan magic, just make it more difficult.

So said the teachings.

'But they're wrong,' whispered Pheone.

'Who?' asked Lempaar.

'Everyone who ever taught us anything about the nature of Julatsan magic.'

16

They were all looking at her. Waiting for her to tell them what to do next. It would have been funny had they not been facing catastrophe. She was unelected, leader only because she, like Ilkar, had a flair for organisation. It had been easy when there was so much work to do. But now the building and repair was done, bar the Tower, and they were facing a future that made weak roofs and dangerous structures insignificant issues. Now they faced losing the ability to interact with the mana spectrum. Julatsa was dying.

'We have to think straight,' Pheone said, trying to force her own thoughts into some semblance of order. 'There are steps we can take and we can't afford to give up. Not after all we've achieved.

'Lempaar, could you take as many people as you need and scour what texts we have for any hint of what is going on in the Heart? Maybe we can, I don't know, feed it or revive it in some way. Anything to prolong its life if indeed it is the Heart that is the problem.

'Buraad, Massentii, Tegereen, we need a clear plan to get out our plea for help. Every Julatsan mage must have felt this. Every one of them must come here to help us raise the Heart.'

'We need so many,' said a voice from across the crater.

'Then we'd better start getting them here now,' replied Pheone.

'Why do you think we'll be more successful this time than before? We've asked, you know we have. So few answered. And now there's a war going on out there.' It was the same voice, from a mage who looked like they all must feel. Washed out. Lost.

'I know. But we have to succeed. And at least the war has brought elves here from Calaius, though the Gods only know why. They are all Julatsan-trained and we have to make them understand what is at stake. What other choice do we have than to try? The alternative is unthinkable.

'Listen, we have to stand strong, support each other. Anyone not included in the library detail, probe the mana. Let's find out exactly how it feels to construct spells now. Can you shape as easily? That sort of thing. But be careful. We can't afford to lose anyone to a backfire.

'Is everyone clear?' Silence. 'Good, then let's get cracking. We'll talk again at dusk.'

Tessaya, Lord of the Paleon tribes of the Wesmen, looked down at the flowerbuds bursting through the earth at his feet, a smile unbidden on his lips. All around him, his village buzzed with activity. Water was being drawn from the wells, farmers were sharpening tools ready for the planting, dwellings were being re-thatched and strengthened. He could smell a freshness in the air. It was the smell of new life. It was the smell of hope, and hope was something his people craved.

Six years after the wars that had seen so many of the menfolk die fighting in the east, the mortal enemies of the Wesmen had sent more misery to haunt them, fractured as they were. To Tessaya it had appeared to be weather the like of which none had experienced in living memory. But his Shamen had smelled magic in the gales, the rain storms, the lightning that burned and in the earth that heaved and sucked the living down to hell.

Day after day they had been struck, and when the storms eased, they were roasted in hot suns. The crops had drowned or withered, the livestock had not bred and when winter had come, though the elements had ceased their battering, it was clear many would die.

Deep in the Heartlands, Tessaya had entrenched himself, calling surviving lords to him and pleading for a pooling of all they had. If, indeed, this was the work of the eastern mages, then their aim was to wipe out the Wesmen forever. Only by working together could they survive and come back stronger.

The lords had listened. Tessaya was the oldest among them and had survived wars with the east and tribal conflicts over two decades. He alone had gathered the tribes into a force strong enough to take on the east. And the lords, many of them new and scared, believed he could do it again.

But they had suffered through the winter. They had had wood to burn but nothing to cook above the flames. Animals had had to be kept alive to breed. Men, women and babes grew gaunt, and the weak and sick did not survive. Pyres burned daily on all the holy sites to remind them of their tenuous hold on life.

It was a time when the Shamen grew to a new stature. They preached the mercy of the Spirits and indeed, it seemed even to one as sceptical as Tessaya that they were not alone in their struggle. Perhaps the winter wasn't as harsh as they remembered. Perhaps the hunting parties found more wild game than they had a right to do. Perhaps the hardy berries and roots had spawned a naturally greater harvest.

Or maybe some force was giving them the tools to live.

Tessaya was happy for his people to believe what they wished. His pact with the tribal lords meant there was precious little theft of food, and that which took place was punished by staking and death. And as the days of cold crawled past, he could see a new determination growing within the Paleon. Where so recently he had seen the acceptance of weakness, now he saw the desire to live, and more importantly, to grow again. What the mages had sent, the Wesmen would turn into strength.

And now, with the new season upon them, and life returning to the hard soil in abundance, he could look forward again to a glorious future. While there would still be hardship until the next crops were gathered, at least there would be Paleon to take in the harvest. It would be a time of celebration like no other.

Tessaya grieved for all those he could not help. Those who chose to live beyond the Heartlands; and those already too far gone to live on will alone. But now his mind turned again, inevitably, to thoughts of conquest.

Because the Shamen had only been half right, if the stories he had been hearing these last days were true. Yes, the elements had been powered by magic. But they had not been sent by the colleges. And even more interesting, the destruction that had been visited on the east was perhaps even more severe than they had suffered in the Heartlands. What state were their enemies in? Good enough to fight and win?

He had heard rumours of Julatsa's failure to rise from its ashes and that the colleges were at war with one another, tearing each other apart. And even better, that the ordinary people, those not afflicted by magic, were turning against their would-be masters. And that these same people desired to rebuild their lives without the use of spell and chant. Very interesting.

Tessaya needed answers and he needed proof. He had made mistakes before, believing in the tales of others, and his people had died in their thousands because of it. This time he wanted to hear the truth from mouths he could trust. He knew the

Wesmen were weakened, that his armies would be small. But if the prize were truly there for the taking, and if much of the east no longer supported the colleges, there was hope. Hope that the Wesmen could finally claim their birthright and dominion over Balaia.

Lord Tessaya breathed deep. He would need to talk to his closest advisers and Shamen. This was a matter that would need particularly careful handling. He bent and plucked one of the early flowers from the earth at his feet and took it back in to show his wife.

The smoke had cleared from the battlefield; the spells and arrows had stopped falling. The pleas for help were fading echoes against the blank walls of Xetesk and the only sounds filtering across the space between the enemy forces were the taunts of the victors and the calls of carrion birds.

Dila'heth, her head thumping at the site of the gash she'd sustained, stood up from the dying Al-Arynaar elf she'd been tending and looked again over the battlefield. Bodies lay where they'd fallen. Scorched mud and shallow craters signified where FlameOrb and HellFire had landed. Scraps of charred clothing blew on the light breeze. Beyond the bodies, the Xeteskians had stood down their front line, leaving a handful of guards to watch while the rest celebrated in full view.

She felt someone moving up beside her. She glanced sideways.

'Why don't they attack?' she asked.

'They don't need to,' said Rebraal. 'All they have to do is keep us away from the walls and occupied while they finish their research of the texts they stole from us.'

The leader of the Al-Arynaar pointed to a group of Protectors and mages who were moving back towards the gates.

'And they aren't going for a rest, I guarantee you that.'

'Where, then?' asked Dila.

'Well, they were struggling to the south, so the messengers said, so it could be there.' Rebraal shrugged.

'But you don't think so.'

'No. If The Raven are right, they'll be looking to strike north as soon as they can.'

'North?'

'Julatsa.'

'Would they?'

Rebraal nodded. 'Why not? They want dominion, Julatsa's the weakest player . . .'

'But . . .'

'I know, Dila,' he said, touching her arm briefly to comfort her rising anxiety. 'Tell me what it felt like. Out there.'

'How could you understand?' she asked, unwilling to recall the void she had touched. 'I don't know, it was like the magic just . . . failed. For that time, it just wasn't there. I felt like you feel every day and you can't know how horrible that is for a mage.'

'Ilkar had been trying to explain.' Rebraal's smile was weak. His brother's death had affected him more than perhaps it should, given Dila's admittedly incomplete knowledge of their relationship. 'But what does it mean?'

Dila shook her head. 'We don't know. We need to get someone to Julatsa, find out. Whatever it was, they'll have more information, I'm sure.'

'The reason Ilkar came to Calaius was to recruit mages to take back there to raise the Heart. Perhaps he knew something was going wrong. Is that possible?'

Dila shook her head. 'I don't think so. Like all of us, I expect he just wanted Julatsa returned to her former position. And if you're right about Xetesk's intentions, then that has become an urgent consideration. How many mages did he think he wanted?'

'He wasn't specific,' replied Rebraal. 'Hundreds, I think.'

Dila's heart sank. 'Rebraal, we've barely got two hundred spread around Xetesk now.'

'I know,' he said.

'When will our reinforcements arrive?'

'Hard to tell. When we left Ysundeneth to come here with The Raven there was precious little activity. The word has only just gone out and the Elfsorrow has taken so many.'

'So what will we do?' Dila'heth felt a surge of desperation. And the sensation that, despite the open ground on which she stood, she was trapped.

'How many did we lose today?' asked Rebraal.

'Too many.'

'That's not an answer.'

Dila nodded. 'But it's still too many. There are one hundred and seventy-four bodies out there. And up here, seventy-eight won't be fit to fight or cast for ten days. Another forty or so will be buried where they lie.'

She looked into Rebraal's eyes, saw him doing the addition, the result making him wince.

'We lost over half of our Al-Arynaar warriors and mages in less time than it takes to boil an egg.' Dila gestured at the Xeteskians. 'They could snuff us out on this front right now, so why don't they?'

'Like I said, they don't have to. And actually, I'm not sure they could. Izack is still strong and they don't know the extent of our magical problems. Anyway, why lose men against an enemy not threatening you?'

'So what will we do?' Dila searched Rebraal's face for the answers she couldn't find.

'Wait and watch. Messengers have gone north and south. We'll get relief. And you must organise your message to Julatsa, either by horse or Communion. Until then, we have a border to keep until The Raven arrive. And Auum gets back.'

'Where is he?'

Rebraal gestured at the blank walls of Xetesk with his chin. 'Where do you think? They've got our property and we want it back.'

'Gyal's tears, how did he get in? More, how will he get out?'

Rebraal smiled. 'He's Auum. Duele and Evunn are with him. They'll find a way. They're TaiGethen.'

'I hope you're right.'

'Trust me,' said Rebraal. 'Trust him, too.'

'Rebraal?'

The Al-Arynaar leader turned at the sound of his name, Dila following his gaze. It was Izack. Armour dented and blood-streaked but still very much alive.

'Commander, we have much to thank you for. Without you, today could have been much worse.'

'It is worse, believe me.' Izack's face was grim and his eyes darted around, as if the facts he knew confused him.

'How?'

'I've had word by Communion from Lystern. You aren't going to like it.'

Chapter 3

Hirad flew from his seat as the guards closed in to take Darrick to the holding cell in the Tower, their swords drawn. His chair squealed across the polished wooden floor and Denser watched him trying to take in everything at once. The six guards striding towards Darrick from around the left and right of the table; the law mages who had stood as Heryst delivered his verdict; and the rest of The Raven, who had spread reflexively to defend the condemned man.

'Not one more step,' warned Hirad. He reached for his sword but of course, he was unarmed as they all were. 'You aren't taking him, so back off.'

'Hirad, this isn't helping,' hissed Darrick.

The swordsmen came on. Denser saw The Unknown turn towards Hirad as the barbarian switched his gaze to Heryst.

'Make a new decision. Don't let them make you murder him.'

Hirad's voice was a growl, his eyes were bulging and his whole body tensed for action. Muscles rippled in his neck and arms and his breathing had the natural depth of the ready warrior. Denser had seen the danger signs before; they all had.

'Stand aside, Hirad,' warned Heryst. 'You will not obstruct this court's officials.' .

'I'll do more than that to any man who tries to take him.'

The guards hesitated, looked to Heryst for guidance.

'Hirad, please,' said Darrick. 'Do as he says.'

'You're Raven, Darrick. And this isn't happening.'

At a nod from Heryst, the guards made another move. Hirad exploded. He took off at a speed Denser didn't think him capable of any more. But The Unknown was both ready and quicker. The huge shaven-headed warrior met the barbarian square on, wrapping his arms round him and shoving hard, legs braced, feet slipping on the wood floor. The slap of the impact echoing around the hall made Denser wince.

'Get out of my way!' Hirad pushed, trying to lever The Unknown's arms away.

'Gods' sake, Hirad, calm down!' The Unknown shouted into his face. 'Thraun, help me.'

Erienne was gaping. Denser made a half move and stopped. The guards kept on coming and Darrick stepped around Hirad's back and walked towards them.

'No!' Hirad forced one of The Unknown's arms back. 'Let go of me. They'll kill him.'

He pivoted and lunged after Darrick, threatening to break free, his rage giving him a strength to match even the big man's. But as he turned, Thraun caught his free arm and the two Raven men bore him backwards, cursing, spitting his fury and heaving against their grip.

'No, Unknown, you bastard. Don't let them do this. Let me go, now!'

'You are not helping, Hirad. Let it rest.'

The Unknown's face was red with exertion. The muscles in his shoulders were bunched beneath his shirt and the cords of his neck stood proud. Hirad's feet slithered, searching for purchase. But he had no answer to the combined power of The Unknown and the quiet, determined Thraun.

'Damn you, Heryst!' shouted Hirad as he was all but carried through a door and out into the corridor beyond. 'You're a murderer, you hear me? A fucking murderer. You should be the one dying, not Darrick. He's trying to save Balaia. What are you doing? Murderer!'

'Hirad! Enough!'

'And damn you, Unknown. Damn the lot of you bastards who stood by and let this happen.'

The voices started to echo as the unequal struggle moved away and out of sight. A curious calm descended on the hall. Darrick had given himself up to the guards who were flanking him but not restraining him. Denser was aware of Erienne's anxious breathing close by and he wrapped an arm around her shoulders. Across the table, Heryst and the law mages stood. Metsas and Simmac wore slight smiles while their clerks gathered around them, pale and frightened.

Heryst walked around the table to stand in front of Darrick. The Raven swordsman met his gaze squarely.

'I am sorry, Ry,' said the Lord Elder Mage. 'But you gave me no option.'

'I thought you a man of strength and vision. A man I could trust and be proud to serve,' said Darrick. 'But I saw it first in Dordover and here again today. You are weak. You would betray anything to cling on to power. What a disappointment. You are not the Heryst to whom I swore loyalty. I have nothing more to say to you.'

He looked away.

'Take him,' said Heryst. 'Give him anything he wants.'

'Yes, my Lord.'

Darrick led his jailers from the Great Hall.

'You're making the worst mistake of your life,' said Denser.

Heryst glanced over his shoulder; the law mages were watching him.

'You know, I've always respected The Raven,' he said, walking across to Denser and Erienne. 'You fight well, you're honourable and you've helped Balaia through some of her darkest days. But sometimes, I think you forget who you are and where you came from. At heart, you're mercenaries. You spent a decade fighting for money and glory. You're the best, I'll grant you that, but it does not put you above my laws. Not anyone's laws. Hirad would do well to remember that.'

'He's just trying to save his friend,' said Erienne. 'His only mistake was thinking you were doing the same.'

Heryst sighed. 'Ry Darrick refused my help and he is beyond salvation now. I cannot break the rules for anyone, and the Gods know I bent them as far as I could, or where would my authority be? I would be corrupt, favouring some and condemning others. That is not Lystern's way.'

'Darrick is Raven. Hirad isn't going to forget this,' warned Denser.

'Hirad is one barbarian. And a short-tempered one at that,' said Heryst. 'The best thing you can do for him now is calm him down, get him saddled and get him out of my college. In fact, out of Lystern. He's a nuisance that I don't need.'

Denser shook his head. 'Out of all of you, only Styliann ever really understood The Raven.'

'And look where it got him. Dead in another dimension. Dystran is in charge now.'

'Indeed,' said Denser. 'And the shame is that he, Styliann, is not here to explain to you what you should already know. Because then you would understand the gravity of your decision.'

'Like I say, sometimes you forget your place.' Heryst turned away. 'Be gone by dusk.'

Bedlam in The Raven's chambers. Denser could hear it as he and Erienne approached down the main stairs from the Great Hall and turned left through the tower doors to the senior mage and guest quarters. The Raven had been given three bedchambers leading off a high-ceilinged drawing and dining room.

Denser and Erienne shared a look of raised eyebrows before he pushed the door open. Hirad and The Unknown Warrior stood toe to toe, the former so furious he was sweating in the cool of the drawing room, his braided hair flying with every jerk of his head.

'You aren't listening to me, Hirad, you ca—'

'Why should I listen to you? We had a chance to save him then and there and you blanked me.' Hirad's finger jabbed into The Unknown's chest. Denser saw the big man's fists clench.

'Something wrong with your eyes, Hirad? Or is it the usual brain failure? I counted nine mages and fifteen armed guards. We didn't even have one dagger between us. They would have killed you. All of us.'

'I may not have your brain but at least I've got heart,' rasped Hirad. 'I'd prefer to die trying than look on like a scolded child. How about you, eh?'

The Unknown's left hand whipped up and caught Hirad's finger in mid-jab.

'Put that down or I'll break it. Don't treat me like some boy you can push around.'

'Someone's got to push or Darrick's going to die.'

The Unknown forced Hirad's hand down to his side, their gazes locked together.

'No one is dying today,' said The Unknown.

'No? Asked Darrick his opinion, have you?'

'You know better than this.'

'I know one of The Raven is about to be executed. What do you know? The sun's got to your fat neck, Unknown.'

The Unknown's arms moved in a blur. His hands gripped the barbarian's upper arms and he lifted Hirad clear from the ground, moved two paces and dumped him in a chair.

'Now you will sit there and you will listen.'

Denser recognised the chill in The Unknown's voice. Hirad didn't.

'So now I have to sit and wait for the killing cast, do I?'

The Unknown leant in, hands braced on the arms of the chair.

'You have tried my patience enough. If you want to take me on, feel free to try if it'll make you feel better. Think you can down me, do you, Coldheart?'

'Unknown, I—' began Denser but The Unknown snapped out his left hand towards him, palm raised.

'What's it to be, Coldheart? Use your fists or your head. It's up to you.'

Hirad stared at him, eyes bulging, breath hissing from his nostrils.

'Tell you what,' continued The Unknown, 'how about I get the deepest thinker of us all to tell you what you should have known from the very start? Thraun?'

The shapechanger, who had been watching the exchange in agitated silence, frowned.

'I . . .' he began. Denser could see the confusion in his eyes.

'If you wanted to rescue Darrick, when would you do it?' asked The Unknown.

Thraun tried to frame the words but as so often, the block between his thoughts and his speech remained obstinately in place.

'Now you listen to me, Unknown,' said Hirad, voice quieter but brim full of rage. 'I have just lost Ilkar and we were helpless. And if you think I'm just going to sit around here—'

'Wait,' said Thraun, instantly the centre of attention. 'Wait until the very end. Until they think we have given up.'

'What?'

'Think, Hirad,' said The Unknown, straightening, his voice pained. 'For once in your life, think.'

'What else do you reckon I've been doing?'

'Absolutely everything but,' said Denser. He walked over to

27

the cold fireplace on the mantel of which stood a pewter jug and carved wooden mugs.

'Wondered when you'd join in the fun,' growled Hirad.

Denser poured mugs of ale and handed them round.

'This isn't fun for any of us,' said Denser. 'Heryst wants us, or more particularly you, out of the city by dusk.'

'Well he knows what—'

'Hirad!' barked The Unknown. 'Drink your ale, take a deep breath and count to ten. Slowly. You have to calm down.'

Hirad opened his mouth.

'Just don't,' said The Unknown. 'Because right now, you are the second biggest threat to Darrick's life.'

'And how do you work that out?'

'It doesn't take a genius, Hirad,' said Erienne.

'What?'

Denser almost laughed but kept it in check. He could see Hirad's anger at them all crumbling in the face of his lack of allies.

'I want to assure you of one thing,' said The Unknown quietly. 'The Raven will not abandon one of their own. It's never happened before and it isn't going to start now.'

'I—'

'Hold on, Hirad,' said The Unknown.

He walked to the door and yanked it open, looking up and down the corridor. Satisfied no one had been listening, he closed it again, looking at Denser.

'Just in case, eh?'

Denser nodded. 'No problem.'

The SoundShield was a simple casting, done in moments. Denser nodded when it was in place. Hirad, still breathing hard, tried to take them all in at once, a frown across his face. He settled on Erienne who walked over to him and knelt by him, a hand on his cheek.

'Oh, Hirad, you react in all the right ways but at all the wrong times.'

'I have to do what I feel,' he said.

'Time and place,' said The Unknown. 'Show that passion later and we stand half a chance.'

'Later?'

'Yes, later.' The Unknown walked around in a tight circle. 'Erienne, how long until the execution?'

'Midnight is traditional in Lystern. The condemned is not supposed to witness the joy of another new day.'

'Midnight,' confirmed The Unknown. 'When we all come together in the Vigil for Darrick's passing. Hirad, are you getting this?'

'Sort of.'

'Gods falling, a sign of life!' The Unknown drained his mug and sat opposite the barbarian. 'And now, at last, we can plan.'

Devun had been a long time coming to Understone. For so many days he'd feared what he would find. But the faltering Balaian army the Black Wings just about commanded needed reassuring. Selik had promised he'd join them but he'd failed to materialise. And so the army of ordinary Balaians, united against magic, had stopped in its tracks, scant miles from the walls of Xetesk. Their goal was in sight but they were too scared to approach it without their leader.

So, belatedly, Devun had ridden with a group of ten to find him. Understone had been turned to nothing more than an open grave. He dismounted fifty yards from the garrison stockade and let his horse bend its neck to crop the burgeoning plains grass. He could smell the sick taint of decay on the breeze and could see the damage to the wooden stockade which Selik had made his headquarters. A few yards later and the first bodies were clearly visible, lying in the grotesque shapes of their deaths.

Devun sent his men on down into the town and carried on towards the stockade alone, already knowing what he was going to find. A numb feeling spread across his body. He tied a rag around his mouth and nose, to guard against the stench that grew with every pace, and drew his sword, just in case. But the scavengers had been and gone. The bodies in the main street had been stripped of weapons, armour and clothes. And he could see, up towards the eastern end of the town where his men were headed, that every scrap of canvas had been taken from the makeshift site that had housed much of the army of the righteous.

Swallowing bile, Devun pushed open the gates of the stockade, a gasp escaping his lips. The ground was covered in bodies. Clouds of flies feasted on the corpses. Carrion birds pecked and tore at the festering, decomposing flesh. Every body had been stripped, just like outside, but here he could chart more easily the course of the battle. Slaughter, more like.

There had been two conflicts. One right here by the gates where a jumble of bodies, unrecognisable in their putrefaction, lay in close formation. The other had been concentrated to his right. A clear area in front of the burned remnants of a collapsed rampart was bordered by a press of bodies. Beneath them, the ground was stained black with their blood.

Whoever had been here had presumably taken their own dead away, leaving the Black Wings and ordinary Balaians to rot where they fell. Devun was disgusted. He walked on across the compound; the smell in the still warm air was staggering. He fought back the nausea, waved his free hand in front of his face to fend off the swarms of flies and stepped between the bodies as best he could.

He stopped for a while in front of the door to the garrison offices and barracks. He knew what he'd find inside, he just had to see for himself. And if not inside, he'd have to look at every corpse lying behind him.

Devun pushed open the door and the savage odour hit him like a charging horse. He gagged and coughed, leaning against the door frame until his vision cleared and the cold sensation eased enough for him to move on.

Just ahead and to the right, was the office door and an answer to his question. Scratched into it was a symbol. It was rough but there was no mistaking it. He spat on it, watching the spittle dribble down across the eye and claw of The Raven's sign. He opened the door. The office had been ransacked. Papers were strewn across the floor. The table and shelves were all done for.

By the door in the left wall a rotting head lay separated from its stripped body. Devun walked over to it, knelt and grasped the hair that still covered the skull. So much of the face was gone, eaten by rats and insects, but the bone around the left eye socket was warped and the left cheek criss-crossed by dozens of tiny cracks. IceWind had done this but that wasn't what had killed Selik. It was The Raven.

Devun placed the head carefully back on the ground, stood and walked quickly from the building.

Later, sitting on his horse in front of his men, Devun

watched the flames consume the Understone garrison and give some belated respect to all those who had died within it.

'What will we do?' asked his new lieutenant. 'Without Selik, the army will break up faster than ever.'

'We have to bring new muscle and new energy to the fight,' said Devun. 'Captain Selik had always kept one idea back. Something he thought we could do if we were desperate. I think that time is now. It's risky but if we bring down the colleges, it'll be worth it. Follow me.'

'Where are we going?'

'To talk to the Wesmen.'

Devun turned his horse and trotted away towards Understone Pass.

Chapter 4

Dystran sat at Ranyl's bedside, where he had spent every hour he could since the Circle Seven Master, and his close friend, had felt the cancer take its death hold. By the old man's head lay a black cat, an expression of human desperation on its features. Dystran wasn't surprised. When Ranyl finally died, the demon familiar would perish with him. The two had been melded for more years than he could remember. Certainly for longer than his tenure as Lord of the Mount of Xetesk.

Dystran sighed. He seemed to have been doing so a lot lately. He'd never really believed Ranyl would actually die. And now he had to face ruling without the man responsible for putting him there in the first place. It would be like losing a limb.

'Stop mopping my brow and tell me what happened today,' said Ranyl, voice still strong though punctuated by gasping breaths.

Dystran dropped the cloth back into the bowl by his left hand and smiled. 'Sorry. I don't mean to mother you. I just wish you'd let me ease the pain for you.'

'I have eternity to feel nothing, my Lord,' said Ranyl. 'Let me feel what I can for as long as I can, even if it is somewhat uncomfortable.'

It was far more than that. Ranyl's drawn white face, pasty skin and feverish brow were evidence enough. But he had been quite determined that when he could no longer numb the pain himself, no one else was to do it for him. Not even the Lord of the Mount.

'So tell me, young pup,' said Ranyl, face softening when he used the over-familiar expression. 'What taxes the mind of Balaia's most powerful man today?'

'Well, old dog.' Dystran responded in kind. 'We have witnessed an extraordinary event today. Something happened to Julatsan mana control. Every spell deployed failed at once during the morning's fighting. Quite suddenly and quite without warning. I have people working on the spectrum now, trying to assess the situation though I understand it was only a temporary condition.'

'But you took full advantage?'

'Without wasting resources, yes,' said Dystran.

'Result?'

'I've been able to recall a significant number to prepare for the press north.'

'But you're unhappy?' Ranyl's breath caught as he felt a sudden sharp pain in his stomach. He closed his eyes while it passed. He turned his head on his pillow. 'What's wrong?'

Dystran couldn't hold the stare. He'd never been able to. He chuckled and stood, walking in a small circle, his fears plaguing him again. At moments like these he wondered how he had survived so long on the Mount. Surely true leaders had more conviction, more strength. All he felt were palpitations, the skin crawling on the back of his neck and the anxiety that descended when his vision tunnelled.

'Am I doing right? Is what we plan the best path for Xetesk and Balaia?'

Ranyl breathed deep. 'It is natural to doubt your path,' he said, his voice soft. 'Because only by questioning your actions do you ensure you choose the right ones. And you have, my Lord. Xetesk must rule and you must preside over that rule. Don't be anxious if you doubt so long as your courage never wavers.'

Dystran sat back down, squeezed out the cold cloth and mopped his mentor's brow. The old man worsened by the moment.

'Who will guide me when you are gone?' he whispered.

'You do not need a guide. You can see the path, you know you can.' Ranyl cleared his throat, gasping at new pain. 'Now, enough soul-searching for one day. I am tiring and I want to know about the research on the elven texts. And the latest from Herendeneth.'

Dystran relaxed. 'The Aryn Hiil is a treasure, a real treasure. We have hardly started to understand its most basic secrets but

33

it is clear the elves' linkage to all the elements is far more fundamental than any of us imagined. It is no myth, and one of those elements *is* magic. We were right. The Aryn Hiil has so much to give us. It's the central writing of elven lore and the words it contains are only part of its importance.'

Ranyl's watery eyes glittered with new energy. 'And how long before we have spells to exploit it?'

'I am awaiting an estimate,' said Dystran. 'But not imminently, unless the Aryn Hiil reveals information allowing us to adapt spell shapes we already know. You know the research time needed for anything we have to start from scratch.'

Ranyl managed a weak nod. 'But when you are not at my side, I suspect you are spending time with our Herendeneth team, yes?'

Dystran shrugged. 'The dimensions are where the power really lies. And what the Kaan and Al-Drechar have told us opens up so many possibilities. I can see a time when I could drown Dordover without having to leave the catacombs. But it is too far away for our current purposes.'

'Is anything useful now?'

'Oh yes. It is just a shame the One will die with the Al-Drechar. We will soon know about the realignment of the dimensions. On a whim I will be able to open a pathway and send Sha-Kaan home to his own world. On another, I could release all the Protectors. Or make more. The demons no longer have a monopoly on understanding.'

'Good,' said Ranyl. 'Then I can die confident.'

The familiar moved uneasily where it lay, half shifting to its repulsive demonic form. Dystran knew how it felt. Ranyl's time was near.

'Can we do this?' asked The Unknown, when The Raven reassembled at dusk to eat and talk.

The time since the verdict had been difficult and enlightening by degrees. Everything had hinged on Heryst accepting Hirad's apology for his outburst. And he had done so with little complaint, rescinding his earlier order for The Raven to leave by nightfall.

'It was strange,' Hirad had said, and The Unknown who had accompanied him had agreed.

'He wanted to apologise to us,' he'd said. 'His hands are

tied. He feels as badly about this as we do but anarchy is a heartbeat away in this city unless he is seen to be even-handed in this most delicate matter.'

The Raven had been given leave to begin their Vigil by the cell block, which was attached to the barracks, and would also remove Darrick's body. In the time left, each of them had visited Darrick under observation, Erienne and Denser had taken the chance to study in the library and The Unknown had tested the feeling of the remaining cavalry and guardsmen in the college.

'It's possible,' said Denser. 'But it depends on getting inside the cells without casting. They'll be watching the mana shield over the college very closely for sure.'

'Find anything useful in the library?' asked Hirad.

'The odd snippet,' said Erienne. 'But as you can imagine, there were archivists taking a great interest in everything we read. The only truly useful fact is that the cells are outside the very heart of the Tower's mana focus.'

'Well, that's a relief,' said Hirad.

Denser chuckled. 'You never studied.'

'Bloody right,' said Hirad. 'Too busy trying to find enough food to live on when I was young. Unlike you pampered mages in your warm colleges.'

'The point is,' said Erienne, 'that there's something I've become aware I can do almost without thinking.'

The Raven shifted uncomfortably. There was something about the entity of the One magic that Erienne harboured so unwillingly that didn't sit well with any of them. They had all grown up with college-based magic and accepted it even if they didn't understand it. But the One, a myth made real, that took its power not just from the mana but all the elements, was a force about which so little was known.

Two ancient elves on the island of Herendeneth, far out in the Southern Ocean, were its last practitioners. For them, Erienne was the last hope of perpetuating the original magical force in the Balaian dimension. But for Erienne, every time she touched the power, savage memories resurfaced. Because her daughter had been allowed to die to effect the transfer of the One entity into her mind.

And now she was trapped. Needing the Al-Drechar elves to help her control and understand the One lest it overwhelm her untrained mind, but hating them because it was they who had let Lyanna die. The Raven knew it, and they knew it was pain they could do nothing to ease.

'What is it?' asked Hirad.

'I can sense people. If the mana flow isn't overpowering I can sense their signatures because magic flows around them differently, not like it does around buildings and the world in general. We are like the elements coalesced, you see, concentrated. It makes us stand out against walls or trees, whatever. This side or the other side, up or down. And if I concentrate, I can tell if they are mages or not.' She paused, looking at Hirad. 'You don't understand, do you?'

'Not really,' he replied. 'But if you're telling me you can see through walls and floors, I don't care.'

'Only if the mana flow isn't too strong. In the Tower, I couldn't. At the cells, I probably can,' said Erienne.

'Probably?'

'Sorry, Unknown, it's the best I can do. According to the structural drawings of the college, the flows dissipate through the cells because it's not part of the main geometric structure. Trouble is, if they've repointed anything since the original building was done, it could have altered the mana map.'

'Why would they do that?' asked The Unknown.

'Broader focus for something like new lecture theatres or long rooms. Students need all the help they can get and part-focused mana is perfect when you're learning a new construct,' said Denser.

'Can't you tell by tuning into the mana spectrum?'

'Unfortunately not. We're not trained in monitoring. Put it this way. Dipping into the spectrum in a college is like standing in a rainstorm and trying to see if it's not as torrential fifty yards away.' Erienne shrugged.

'Any risk in this for you?' Hirad leaned forward.

Erienne raised her eyebrows. 'With the One, everything's a risk right now. But I think I can contain it. The Al-Drechar will help.'

'Right,' said The Unknown. 'Thank you, Erienne. We'll use that skill if we can but that leaves just Denser as cover. Once we're inside, SpellShield, all right?'

Denser nodded.

'Now, I understand there is to be a protest outside the cells and barracks,' said The Unknown, leaning across the table conspiratorially. 'It's exactly what we need.'

'Why?' asked Denser.

'Because I think it's going to give us our way in. Help yourselves to more food and drink, then Hirad and I will tell you all about it.'

Nyam had always been suspicious of the old women. Outwardly compliant they might have been; very willing to help and to explain the finer points of their considerable dimensional knowledge. But whenever he talked to them, he got the feeling that at least one of them was, well, elsewhere. Not physically, he'd explained to the others more than once, but inside her mind.

But apparently he was making far too much of it. They were old, he was told, borderline senile. Hardly surprising their minds wandered away now and then. He couldn't make them understand. They might be ancient but the light in their elven eyes was as bright as that in the eyes of the son he had left behind in Xetesk. So he decided to watch them. One day, something would give.

He smiled to himself as he ambled in the warm sun outside the house of the Al-Drechar. High up in the sky, the surviving Kaan dragon, with whom they maintained an uneasy peace, circled. It had threatened them all with death if they stepped out of line and none of them doubted its capacity to carry out that threat. They had seen all too clearly the results of its anger. That was why the five mages and fifty Protectors left on the island all wished they'd been chosen for the ship home thirty-odd days before.

Nyam walked a little way up towards the beautifully arranged terraces which housed the long dead of the Al-Drechar. There was Diera with the laughing little boy, Jonas. She was tending the Nightchild, Lyanna's, grave while he sat, face upwards, pointing at Sha-Kaan's circling.

Nyam smiled again and found a conflict of emotions running through him. He yearned for his wife and family; another part reached out and understood Diera's loneliness and yet he couldn't escape the fact that he was attracted to her. They all were. She'd been the subject of ribald conversation more than once but none of them would so much as touch her. You didn't try it on with the wife of The Unknown Warrior, no matter how far away he was.

That part of him that sympathised so much with the help-lessness of her exile was strongest. She cut a forlorn figure at times, standing on the rocks overlooking the channel into which a returning ship would sail, or spending hours wandering the little island with Jonas wrapped in her arms or experimenting with walking beside her.

Yet she wouldn't reach out. She shunned the Xeteskians completely, never spoke a word to any Protector and didn't seem interested in the Al-Drechar, whom she spoke to like old aunts rather than powerful mages. She ate with the few Drech guild elves who tended the dying mages but only really spoke regularly to Sha-Kaan so far as Nyam could tell. Outwardly bizarre but actually eminently reasonable. The dragon had a telepathic link with the barbarian, Hirad Cold-heart. All to do with the Dragonene order. He'd have to read up on it.

Nyam turned at the sound of his name. His turn to sit with the Al-Drechar again and see if he could get clarification on a couple of points, no doubt. Another smile. Perhaps today was the day something would give. He'd be waiting.

They began to gather at dusk. Heryst and his closest adviser, Kayvel, watched them from a window high up in the Tower. He had always known Darrick was incredibly popular but this, following his desertion, was surely unprecedented. Posts were abandoned, meals went uneaten, families didn't see their men-folk at the time they expected. With much of the army com-mitted to the north and east of Xetesk, it was never going to be a huge gathering, but its import was not lessened by that fact.

'There will be no one patrolling the streets or our walls,' said Kayvel.

Heryst nodded. 'But it's a respectful gathering. They all know the law.'

'They all love Darrick,' observed Kayvel. 'Don't expect their respect to extend to you.'

'We must have order,' said Heryst.

He glanced behind him. His personal guard, four senior soldiers, stood waiting. Not every member of the military shared the prevailing mood.

'So what action will you take against this?' Kayvel indicated the crowd which now numbered in excess of one hundred and was growing steadily.

'None,' said Heryst. 'They must be allowed to express their feelings. So long as the protest remains peaceful.'

'So you feel they are justified?'

'Of course I bloody do.' Heryst's voice was quiet. He turned his attention back on the cavalry and soldiers outside the barracks. He felt a sickness in the pit of his stomach. This was comfortably the worst day of his tenure. 'What choice do I have? He isn't the first to be executed for desertion in this conflict. You know the feeling in the council and out in the city. We're on the brink here. Our decision to ally again with Dordover is very unpopular.'

'And you think executing our most famous son will help you?'

'We must maintain the rule of law. None can be seen to be above it. That way lies anarchy.' Heryst sighed, searching for a way to change the subject. 'Where are The Raven?'

'In their chambers,' said Kayvel. 'Eating.'

'Good.' Heryst turned from the window. 'Keep them under close scrutiny. I won't have them whipping up the crowd. We can't afford that sort of disorder. And tell the watching mages they have to be vigilant.'

'You don't trust them?' asked Kayvel, his tone edged with surprise.

'The Raven?' Heryst smiled. 'Oh, I trust them all right. Enough to know they'll try something. Can you see them knocking meekly at the door to collect Darrick's body?'

'Then why did you not have them escorted from the college?'

Heryst breathed deep and sucked his lip, regarding Kayvel until understanding creased his features. He stepped in very close to Heryst and leaned so close their faces all but touched.

'You are playing a very dangerous game, my Lord,' hissed the adviser, voice barely audible.

'On the contrary, there is very little risk,' whispered Heryst. 'The Raven are not murderers. They are, however, very resourceful.'

Kayvel clicked his teeth. Heryst continued.

'I assure you I will do everything in my power to stop them

should they attempt a rescue. However, I don't believe I can spare the men for a pursuit.'

'You must order the gates closed,' said Kayvel.

'I cannot do that,' said Heryst. 'You know our constitution and there is no external threat to the college. We must and will remain open to all who need our help. That is Lystern's way.'

Kayvel shook his head and turned away, moving a step towards the window. When he turned, his expression was deliberately neutral.

'You are making a mistake,' he said.

Heryst moved to stand beside him again and looked down on the crowd which stood in almost complete silence in the courtyard.

'If it is a mistake to let The Raven pay their respects to one of their own with dignity, then it is one I am happy to make.'

'You know what I mean,' snapped Kayvel.

'Yes, I do,' whispered Heryst. 'Darrick is my friend. I owe him this chance.'

Kayvel's face softened. 'I hope you know what you're doing.'

'So do I, my friend,' said Heryst. 'So do I.'

Chapter 5

The Raven moved out of their chambers to join the silent crowd shortly after the last hour of the day was sounded. Some two hundred and more Lysternan soldiers, many of them Darrick's men, were gathered from posts in the college and across the city.

The Raven split up, according to The Unknown's design, interspersing themselves with those in the front arc by the door to the windowless cell block, which adjoined the barracks, while Hirad disappeared round the side to the stables. Positioned so he could watch the door to the cells and the base of the Tower from which Heryst would soon emerge, The Unknown didn't see Hirad return but he heard his voice as he passed without stopping.

'Stable's deserted. Everyone's out here. We're saddled and ready.'

The Unknown said nothing. The time was approaching. Agitation was running through the crowd that had been building ever since Darrick had been moved to the barrack cell block as dusk fell. A murmur of voices stilled with the creaking of a door. Every head turned towards the Tower. Six men emerged from the brazier-bright entrance and out into the lantern-lit, shadowy courtyard. The stride was measured and confident.

The Unknown could see Heryst and his adviser, Kayvel, walking in the centre of the quartet of swordsmen. Their weapons were sheathed but their eyes roved the crowd. The Unknown knew they were being monitored. It shouldn't matter.

Standing just behind the front rank of the loose crowd, The Raven waited. Heryst and his guard walked into the silence, the

41

crowd closing around them as they came, no more than two paces away. Not close enough for The Unknown.

Standing to the left of the guard-flanked barracks door and looking across at the approaching entourage, he signalled Thraun with a slight nod. The troubled shapechanger made no sign he'd seen The Unknown but his feral eyes glittered in the light of a nearby lantern and the half pace he took was more than enough.

He nudged into the pair of soldiers in front of him, forcing both to take a balancing step forwards and bringing them very close to Heryst. Denser's similar nudge ensured the ripple continued and Erienne's gave the move a momentum of its own.

'Shame on you!'

The Unknown heard Hirad's voice, turning the murmur of disquiet into more vocal opposition. Cries of 'Spare Darrick' and 'Crime' sounded and the crowd pressed in. Immediately, the guards upped their pace. Seeing the concern on Heryst's face, The Unknown moved.

He pushed hard into the backs of the two men in front of him, sending them stumbling into Heryst's guards. The reaction was as automatic as it was predictable. The soldiers were fended off roughly, sent spinning left and right and into the gap came The Unknown. He allowed himself to be helped by the agitated group behind, his shoulder thumping into the first bodyguard who sprawled backwards, arms cartwheeling and striking another man who lashed out instinctively.

The jostling took on an edge, the atmosphere firing to tension in an instant.

'Get back, clear the path!' ordered one of the bodyguards.

The Unknown stepped round to face him, fist slamming into his gut. The guard's eyes widened. The Unknown's head connected sharply with the bridge of his nose. He fell.

Turning, The Unknown saw Hirad and Thraun closing in at the back. Denser had confronted another guard. He couldn't see Erienne. He forced his way towards the barracks door, meeting Heryst's eyes on the way. The Lord Elder Mage opened his mouth to shout but a hand clamped around his neck and dragged him back. The Unknown ploughed on, shoving soldiers aside, hearing the anger reach boiling point. The guards at the door had only just seen the danger

42

to their Lord through the confusion of bodies in front of them. One had his sword half out when The Unknown straight-punched him in the face. His head hit the wall behind him. He sagged.

The other faced up, fists raised.

'Sorry,' said The Unknown and laid him out with a strike to the point of his jaw.

He headed for the door, sensing a change in the atmosphere. Behind him, Heryst called out for assistance and he heard Hirad's gruff voice.

'Bodyguard's changed, big man.'

The Unknown opened the door quickly. It bounced against the wall. He ran in, knowing The Raven would be right behind him. The small hall was empty, so far. He swung round. Erienne had followed him in, Thraun and Hirad were forcing a protesting Heryst across the threshold. Denser came in last, already casting.

The barracks door was slammed shut, the fizzing of a Ward-Lock echoed in the enclosed space and the sounds of the angry crowd were muted. There were a few thumps on the door but to no effect.

'Welcome to your new home,' said Heryst.

Hirad put a dagger to his throat. 'Don't try casting. You aren't quick enough to beat me.'

Heryst's face was flushed with anger and embarrassment. 'You won't get him out.'

'Just watch us,' said Hirad.

'How long will that lock hold?' asked The Unknown.

'Hard to say. They'll need magic. Good magic. But this is a college.'

'Point taken.'

The Unknown faced forward. Ahead of them, the stone-flagged hall had two doors either side, one straight ahead.

'Erienne?'

She was leaning against a wall as if to stop herself falling. Her eyes were closed and a fist clutched at thin air.

'Difficult,' she murmured. 'Men below. Swords and magic. Can't feel anything up here.'

'There's too much focused mana,' said Denser. 'We need to get down to the cells.'

'What—?' began Heryst.

'Time for quiet,' said Hirad. 'Let us show you what we can do. Stairs?'

Heryst eyed him briefly before gesturing ahead. They moved off, hurried by a heavy impact on the door behind. The Unknown strode ahead, Thraun hard on his heels. He slapped the door back.

It was a guard room. The Unknown made instant assessment. A desk stood against the far wall, weapon racks were right and two guards flanked a downward spiral stair left. Both men drew swords immediately. The Unknown raised a hand.

'We have Heryst and we've come for Darrick. You can make this easy or difficult. Your choice.'

The Raven and Heryst came in behind. Sword points dipped. 'My Lord?'

'Idiots,' muttered Heryst. 'Guard the prisoner!' He shouted. 'We're attacked. We—'

Hirad's hand covered his mouth and jerked his head sharply back.

'We'll carry you if we have to,' he said.

The Unknown's eyes did not stray from the guards. 'Weapons down. Please.'

They hesitated. Thraun growled. It was a sound from his wolven past, chilling as it echoed from the walls. The Unknown smiled thinly. The two guards dropped their swords, metal clattering against stone.

'Good choice. We aren't going to hurt you, that isn't why we're here. Denser, Erienne.' The two mages stepped up. 'But you can't take any further part in this. Like I say, you can make it easy or difficult.'

Two short incantations and the guards were cushioned to the floor.

'Right,' said The Unknown. 'Hirad, you're first. Heryst goes in front of you. I'm behind with Erienne so let me do the talking, all right? Denser, Thraun, you get the rear. Let's go, Raven.'

Hirad pushed a resigned and unresisting Heryst ahead of him, dagger ready, free hand on the Lord Elder Mage's shoulder. 'Not too fast. I'd hate you to fall.'

The spiral stair was wide and lantern-lit. No sound came from below.

'There is no one at the base of the stairs,' Erienne said.

'Further on, I don't know yet. The stair ends in two more full circles.'

The Unknown nodded. 'Hirad, keep a tight grip on him. This is where it gets interesting.'

The spiral stair unwound into a long corridor lined with blank walls and heavy wooden doors. A single iron-bound door stood at the end some sixty paces distant. The Unknown spoke for the benefit of the hidden guards.

'Lord Heryst is in front of us. You don't want him hurt any more than we do so I suggest that you stay wherever you are hiding. No one needs to be a hero. We're all on the same side. But we've come for Darrick and no one leaves here until we get him.'

Silence.

The Unknown smiled. At least they had some discipline. The Raven, Heryst at their head, moved slowly along the corridor, footsteps echoing loud from the dark stone walls and low ceiling. The cell block smelled damp and vaguely rotten, as if the filth of ages had pervaded the stone where no amount of scouring could remove it.

'Cheerful place.'

'Shut up, Hirad,' hissed The Unknown.

They passed the first doors, the cells they fronted dark and quiet. By the number and spacing of doors, the cells were very small.

'Stop,' said Erienne suddenly. 'Left and right, second cells. Swordsmen. Two each side.'

Heryst drew in a sharp breath.

'Not a word,' whispered Hirad.

The Unknown considered briefly. He indicated Thraun and Denser to the left door, moving to cover the right himself.

'Let's move on,' he said loudly enough.

Heryst opened his mouth but Hirad's dagger pushed into his neck, pricking the skin.

'I will bleed you,' he said, voice low. 'I don't want to but I will.'

He pushed Heryst on towards the end of the cell block, their footsteps slapping echoes off the walls.

The Unknown waited, watching Erienne closely, uneasy at the split forced on them but needing to take the gamble. She walked slowly in Hirad's wake, body tensed, her mind straining to keep a rein on the power sluicing through her. The walkers

45

passed another two sets of doors before Thraun indicated noise. Simultaneously, Erienne stopped and looked sharply left. Doors seemed to open everywhere.

'Damn!' spat The Unknown, already moving down the corridor. 'Hirad, keep Heryst moving.'

Behind him, he heard the sound of metal-shod feet on stone. Ahead, two figures emerged from a cell left and one from the right.

'Erienne!'

Lost in the One, Erienne was slow to react. A leather-clad warrior ran at her, lowering his sword and thumping into her with his shoulder and sending her sprawling against the opposite wall. She cried out in surprise and Hirad turned, began moving towards her but found his way blocked by the second soldier.

'Hirad! Behind!' shouted The Unknown. But Heryst was already moving, running towards the end of the corridor. The Unknown could see his hands describing arcs in the air as he went. 'Trouble.'

He charged up the corridor, his pace fast despite the stiffness in the hip damaged on Arlen's docks. Fast enough to surprise the lone figure who stood in front of the open cell door right. Without pause, The Unknown whipped a fist into his cheek and chin, spinning him round and hard into the wall. He fell senseless. The Unknown hurdled both him and Erienne to chase the casting Heryst.

As he passed, Hirad swore, moving to attack the threat to Erienne. He stepped smartly inside a round arm strike, blocked the sword arm away with his left hand and thudded the hilt of his dagger into the soldier's temple. The man sagged under the blow and Hirad helped him down with a double-handed strike to the back of his neck.

The Unknown closed the gap fast, footsteps ringing in his ears, the shouts and sounds of hand-to-hand fighting behind him that he couldn't afford to let distract him. Heryst slowed and turned, eyes widening a little at the sight of The Unknown's huge frame coming at him. He held his hands wide, encompassing his targets. The Unknown dropped and slid in, feet first, boot buckles striking sparks from the stone. Heryst's mouth moved. The Raven warrior ploughed into him, sweeping his legs from under him.

The spell was lost. Heryst crashed heavily down, half on, half off The Unknown who was already shovelling sideways and coming to his haunches. He rested one hand on the back of the struggling Heryst's neck.

'Enough, Heryst.'

Back down the corridor, Erienne was in trouble. Overpowered by her attacker, he had her in a neck lock, his short sword close to her midriff.

'Back off!' shouted the soldier. 'I'll kill her.'

Hirad advanced another pace. Out of the soldier's view, Denser and Thraun were closing in, leaving four still figures behind them. The Unknown could see blood on Denser's face and Thraun's knuckles but the floor had none of the slick that told of mortal wounds.

'We have your Lord,' said The Unknown, coming to his feet and dragging Heryst with him. 'No one is killing anyone in here. Least of all you.'

'You don't want her to die,' said the soldier, fear in his voice.

He retreated, his back to a wall. The Unknown saw him swallow hard as he watched The Raven close in but focused his attention principally on the door behind him. Darrick was beyond it, that much was sure, but how many others? Mages. Prepared and ready to cast. And an honour guard of anywhere between two and six. Not great odds and they had little time before the door above them was breached, trapping them.

Erienne was calm, waiting for what she expected to be the inevitable. In front of the soldier, Hirad and Thraun obstructed his view of Denser. The soldier was naïve. And in a magic college, that was unforgivable.

'Idiot,' hissed Heryst, his voice choked by The Unknown's powerful grip.

'Shame,' muttered The Unknown.

'When you're ready,' said Denser.

Thraun and Hirad parted. Denser cast. He was a very accurate mage. His tightly wound spell snapped out, catching the soldier square in the face. Blood spattered from his broken nose and in his surprise, he dropped his weapon, both hands clutching at his face. Hirad moved in and put him on the floor.

'Good work,' said Hirad. 'ForceCone, was it?'

'You're learning,' said Denser. 'Are you all right, my love?'

'Never better,' said Erienne but she was pale and a deep

47

frown pressed on her eyes. 'Bit of a headache, though. Too much focused mana in here to do what I was trying.'

'Raven, let's step it up!' ordered The Unknown. 'Denser, SpellShield; Hirad, come take your charge back. Thraun, you're with me. Erienne, stand down, we'll take what comes through here.'

The room beyond was proofed against sound from without. It was to protect both those inside and those in the cells awaiting their fate. Not that a condemned of Darrick's calibre would cry out for mercy. But even he would wish to enjoy his last moments in peace. The Raven, though, had no intention of letting these moments be his last.

The Unknown drew his sword.

'Everyone inside signed up to Darrick's sentence. Kill if you have to.'

'Unknown, the Code.' Hirad had his sword drawn but he was uneasy.

The Code: to kill but never murder. It had guided The Raven for more than fifteen years. Raised them above mere mercenaries. Earned them a respect they had never abused. Made them legend.

'They would murder an innocent man,' said The Unknown. 'A Raven man. They forfeit their right to life within the Code. But remember. Only if you have to. The Gods know we need everyone we can get for the fight against Xetesk.'

'I don't understand,' said Heryst.

'No,' said Hirad. 'You don't.' He turned and faced the door. 'Raven. Time to take our man back.'

It wasn't a cell door. Thraun and The Unknown shouldered it simultaneously, the timbers cracking under the sudden, brutal force. Denser followed them as they tumbled in, scattering wood and heavy drapes, his SpellShield covering them. Behind them came Hirad and Heryst, the Lord Elder Mage bowed and humiliated.

Thraun rolled to a crouch and sprang at two soldiers standing opposite the door. Neither had a weapon drawn. The Unknown moved smoothly to his feet. To his left, two mages from the law council sat behind a table. Darrick sat in a plain, hard-backed chair to the right, writing in a book. He was flanked by guards who dragged swords from scabbards and paced towards The Unknown. Across the room, Thraun clattered his fist into the face of one soldier, stood and threw the other man at the advancing guards, a growl escaping his lips.

The Unknown put his sword's point to the neck of a still seated law council mage.

'Enough,' he said into Thraun's echoes.

The standing guards lowered their swords, taking in The Raven, Heryst and their senseless comrades.

Darrick completed his thought, scanning the words he had just written before looking up, a rare smile edging over his features. He closed his book.

'I was wondering when you'd get here,' he said, standing up and straightening his shirt.

'Not even you can be that cool,' said Hirad.

Darrick grinned. 'Well, I must admit, I feel you cut it a little fine.'

'And we're not out yet,' said The Unknown. He took in the room, its dark candles on tall iron stands, the dark drapes hanging from every wall, the chill in the air. Every bit an execution chamber. His gaze came to rest back on the law mages. 'Let's get these men into cells. Weapons stay here.' He pushed the point of his blade a little harder. 'My Lord Simmac, if you'd be so kind.'

'You will all die for this,' he sputtered.

The Unknown sighed. 'I doubt that, Simmac. What we will do is rejoin the fight against Xetesk. We've already lost two days. Time you saw the bigger picture, little man.'

Thraun picked up unconscious soldiers by their jerkin collars, one in either powerful fist and dragged them from the execution chamber. He moved at a loping run, the men's boots rattling across the stone flags. Denser encouraged the two remaining guards down the corridor with a meaningful wave of his sword, and The Unknown ushered the law mages along right behind him.

The Raven worked fast, splitting the soldiers and mages between cells, Darrick helping Thraun clear the corridor of men, both still and stirring. With a set of keys taken from a guard, the cells were locked down one after another but before locking the final cell door on Simmac, The Unknown paused.

'I know you can break this door down in a heartbeat. That's

why Heryst is coming with us. Any noise from down here and he dies. You do understand me, don't you?'

The Raven set off at a run, taking the stairs at speed and reaching ground level to find the pair of guards still down under Denser and Erienne's spells. From the main door, there came the sounds of furious activity and heavy impacts. But the door was still holding.

'They're getting close,' said Denser.

The Unknown saw the slight shake of Heryst's head as he turned to face them.

'So, mighty Raven,' he said. 'I've been waiting for this. Escape through that angry mob of loyal Lysternans is going to be a challenge.'

'Yes,' agreed Denser.

'I can't wait to find out how you plan to get away. I can hardly be a shield for all of you.' He smiled, enjoying himself a little.

'Oh, Heryst,' said Denser. 'You've been out of the game too long.'

'I beg your pardon?'

Denser indicated the wall opposite the main barracks door. 'The stables are this way and we have no intention of using the door.'

'I—'

'Watch and learn,' said Darrick, voice cold. 'Like I did.'

'Stand away,' said Denser.

'No,' said Erienne. 'Let me do it.'

'Can you?' he asked.

She nodded. 'I'd better, I think. Quieter my way.'

Heryst's eyes had narrowed in confused suspicion once more. The Unknown ignored him.

'Don't take on too much.'

But Erienne was already lost inside her mind, standing absolutely still, facing the wall, her arms by her sides. The Unknown watched her in profile, mesmerised by the movement of her lips, the narrowing of her eye and the rapid movement of its pupil. A wind blew through the guard room, ruffling papers and blowing through clothing. Heat, like the summer sun bursting through cloud, surrounded them. Smoke poured from the wall, which cracked and moved. A glowing red line, rough but shaped like a doorway, etched and burned

50

in the stones. Beneath the red line, stone became dust, dropping to the floor with a sound like spilled grain, leaving an opening into the night.

The Unknown gasped, feeling the power surging through the elements around him. He glanced at Heryst. The Lord Elder Mage's face was taut, his eyes wide. Erienne swayed and fell into Denser's arms.

He looked down at his wife then back at the opening she had created.

'Bloody hell,' he breathed.

'Not seen that sort of thing for a while, then?' asked Hirad.

'Hirad,' said Denser. 'No one has seen or done that sort of thing on Balaia for hundreds of years.'

Hirad shivered and glanced at Thraun and Darrick who moved carefully over to the smoking opening which overlooked the stables and paddocks beyond. Outside, the way was clear and quiet but the sounds of the crowd filtered round the sides of the building.

'We should go,' said Darrick. 'Quickly.'

'Come on, Heryst,' said Hirad. 'We need you to order the gates opened.'

Heryst made no move. 'We never close our gates,' he said vaguely.

He shook his head, trying to clear his thoughts, his gaze tearing from Erienne to The Unknown.

'She possesses it,' he said. 'Everyone will want her and what she carries.'

'Not if they don't know,' said The Unknown.

Heryst gestured behind him. The sounds of spells impacting the door to counter Denser's WardLock had ceased.

'I felt it. So did Denser and every mage in this college. The Gods only know how far the ripples will spread through the spectrum. We all know what it means. It was no college-based casting because there was so much more involved than mere mana. The Nightchild told us that much.'

'But her identity need not be known,' said The Unknown.

'The connection will be made.' Heryst shrugged. 'She will be safer here. You all will.'

'Except Darrick,' said Erienne weakly.

She was still clinging on to Denser. Her face was white and drawn and she was shivering.

'You know we can't stay here. We have made a promise to Ilkar. Julatsa's Heart must be raised and Xetesk has to be stopped. That isn't going to happen if we sit here under your questionable protection,' said The Unknown. 'The question really is, are you going to make it difficult for us to ride away from here now?'

Another spell struck the outer door. Timbers heaved. The sound of angry voices grew louder.

'Darrick is under sentence. I can't change that,' said Heryst. 'But Erienne must stay. Xetesk must not be allowed to take her.'

'She's Raven,' said Hirad. 'And Xetesk, nor Dordover, nor you will ever own her. Let's go.'

Heryst was going to be a hindrance.

'He stays,' said The Unknown. 'Denser?'

Denser nodded, released Erienne into The Unknown's arms and turned on the Lord Elder Mage of Lystern who stiffened. Hirad's sword point rested gently on his heart.

'It doesn't hurt,' said Denser.

'Pain I can handle. The stain on my reputation will take longer to clear.'

'You opposed us. You pay the price,' said Hirad.

'You'll be hunted out there,' said Heryst. 'At least I offer you life.'

'Life?' said Hirad. 'Hear that, Darrick?'

'I hear.'

Denser spoke his short incantation. Heryst slumped backwards, Hirad cushioning his head. The main door splintered.

'Run,' he said.

The Unknown swept Erienne up and followed Thraun and Darrick across the short space to the stables. The shapechanger hurdled the paddock fencing and ran in through broad, open doors. Darrick pulled open a side door and disappeared inside.

The Unknown ran in after Darrick with Denser and Hirad right behind him. One man lay on the ground, groaning and clutching at nose and groin. 'Thought you said it was empty.'

Hirad shrugged and pushed past him, leading the way through the tack room, past the saddle bars and on into the stables themselves. The pungent smells of dung and wet straw filled the air; the sounds of agitated horses mixed with the calls to arms from outside. Thraun's silhouette was framed against the night sky as he worked in the dark stables, unlatching gates and pulling horses out, his eyes piercing the shadows easily.

'Hirad, take the spare. I'll carry Erienne, she can't ride. Let's go, let's go!' said The Unknown, turning his head as he ran.

Lysternan soldiers were moving quickly through the tack room. Ahead, Darrick had vaulted into his saddle the way only a cavalryman could and had snatched up a rake. Hirad was climbing aboard and Thraun had opened the last stable gate.

The Unknown switched Erienne from his arms to over his left shoulder, put a foot in the stirrup and heaved himself on to his mount, pain flaring in his hip. He moved Erienne to sit in the saddle in front of him. An arrow thudded into a timber by his head.

'Ride, Raven. Ride!'

He yanked hard at the reins, turning his horse to the entrance. He dug in his heels and the animal sprang forwards. Darrick rode back down the stables, whirling the rake in his right hand. He heard the whistle as it whipped through the air and the dull thwack of wood on leather.

The Raven surged out into the paddock. Next to The Unknown, Denser was preparing. Just behind, Hirad hunched low, his left hand clutching the reins of Erienne's horse. Thraun came to The Unknown's right-hand side and he heard Darrick yelling his horse to greater effort.

In front of them, the low paddock fence neared. Beyond it, the walls of the college loomed above. Buildings rose on either side. From between these buildings, soldiers and mages ran to try and cut off their escape.

'Hang on, Erienne,' said The Unknown.

'I've got nothing better to do,' she said.

Denser had cast a SpellShield which flared deep blue under attack from Lysternan mages. The Unknown hadn't seen a cast and that meant a ForceCone or mind attack. While relieved they weren't going for the kill, he knew there was only one way to stop what could quickly become a barrage that Denser, on his own and riding, would find difficult to repel.

'Let's get amongst them!' roared The Unknown.

He kicked his heels into his mount's flanks again, gripped Erienne tight and jumped the fence, landing and turning left immediately, heading straight for a line of soldiers forming across the path to the gates. He looked quickly behind left and right. Denser and Hirad were in his wake. Thraun and Darrick had taken the flanking positions. The former Lysternan cavalry general veered far left, the rake now in his left hand and sweeping out, scattering soldiers unwilling to strike one of their own.

Ahead the soldiers, who included no archers, began to move. The Raven were not going to stop and their horses were trained and experienced at facing men on foot. They would veer to avoid contact but they wouldn't pull up.

'Clear the path!' yelled The Unknown. 'Stand aside!'

And then they were in the midst of the crowd. Without orders, the defence was non-existent, with no soldier willing to put himself in the way of a charging horse. Arrows and spells were no longer an option.

The Raven bore down on the gates which were open but blocked with carts too high to jump. Denser knew what to do.

'Don't fail us now, Denser,' said The Unknown to himself.

The mage straightened in his saddle, dropped the reins and pushed his arms forwards, palms facing up and outwards. The ForceCone roared away, catching one of the carts square on. Wheels shrieked on cobbles, wooden sides buckled inwards, canvas coverings tore. The cart tumbled away, soldiers diving for safety.

'Come on!' yelled Denser triumphantly.

The Unknown laughed and chased him out into the streets of Lystern.

Chapter 6

Auum edged a little further back into the shadows while the college guards, three of them, walked past. They didn't stray far from the walls of Xetesk's college of magic, walls that burned bright with the light of torches, lanterns and spells, but their eyes were forever on the murk at the edge of the light. They knew a threat was near but had never laid eyes on it and wouldn't until the time was right.

It was Auum who had to decide that time, yet he had to admit to himself and his Tai that gaining useful access to the college was going to be very difficult. His and four other TaiGethen cells had been watching the college for five days. The elite elven hunter-warriors had remained undetected for the whole of that time, looking for any gap, any way in and, just as importantly, any way out.

But Xetesk was on high alert. Ever since the theft of the Yniss statue fragment by one of their own, the Xeteskian college guard had been stung into action. Gates and doors had been reinforced, patrols had been doubled and trebled and the lights on the walls left little in shadow. Mages had joined the archers on the ramparts and the four main gatehouses vetted everyone who approached them, only opening for the minimum time needed to let people in.

Auum watched the guards walk past. They were young men, scared and uncertain. His Tai could have killed them all before they knew they were under attack but it wasn't necessary and might only draw unwanted attention to them. He had no particular desire to kill, despite what the Xeteskians had stolen. Most of the men he had seen walking past were the same. Recruits who had little idea of the crimes their superiors had committed.

Inside the college, it would be no different. All he, as leader of the TaiGethen, desired was to recover the sacred texts stolen from them. He wanted to take them back to Aryndeneth, the temple of Yniss deep in the rainforests of Calaius. He wanted the mages inside to be unable to use them, as they currently were, for research into ways to dominate the elves. Revenge on those who had perpetrated the sacrilege could come later.

He turned to his Tai, the elves he trusted with his life every day and who trusted him without question. Both Duele and Evunn were painted in the deep greens and browns of their forest camouflage. It worked equally well here in the stinking alleys and quiet, cramped back streets of Xetesk. An alien landscape to Auum but one he could use. They had prayed to Yniss, the God of the Harmony and Tual, Lord of the Forest Denizens. More than once, Auum had wondered what the gods of the elves would think, looking down on their people.

The city was foul. It made him shudder. It closed in on him, an offence to his senses. The TaiGethen were far from home, as far as they could get from the embrace of the forest and the calls of its animals, the scents of its flora and fauna and the feel of the rain on their heads.

'This place gets under my skin,' said Auum. 'We must reassemble outside the walls and pool our information.'

'We will need all the Tais to get in and Al-Arynaar mages to shield us,' said Duele.

'There is very little in our favour,' said Evunn.

'We are the TaiGethen,' said Auum. 'And we will prevail. We do the work of Yniss and he will not discard us.'

The Tai became utterly still at a sound from behind them. The alley in which they were hidden, fifty yards from the walls of the college, was narrow and led between squalid tenements and warehouses to the central cloth market. It was not a thoroughfare used by anyone but thieves. Two who had made the mistake of running across the Tai earlier that night lay in thick weeds twenty yards into the gloom.

Auum signalled Duele to unsling his bow. He and Evunn drew short swords and unclasped jaqrui pouches. The sound came again on the light breeze blowing along the alley. Looking back down the alley, Auum could see no one. Black tenements stared back, desolate and oppressive. The air was still and cool and he could smell nothing above the stench of the city all around them. Yet someone was approaching and doing nothing to mask his progress.

He was singing.

It was a broken tune, half-remembered and sung in a mumble that would surely have been incoherent even to a local. Auum's limited grasp of the eastern Balaian language gave him no chance of understanding it.

The drunk stumbled into sight out of a side passage about thirty yards away, steadied himself against a wall, considered his direction for a moment and began weaving towards them. The Tai held its collective breath and pressed hard into the deepest shadow. Duele squeezed Auum's shoulder but the Tai leader shook his head. Yniss forever punished the murder of innocents.

The drunk's passage up the alley was tortuously slow, the song discordant; now barely audible, now a gravel-throated low roar. Auum checked the college walls. So far, he had drawn no attention but approaching from the left was another foot patrol. Auum cursed silently.

Another stumble and the drunk was upon them, choosing that moment to lift the roof, his song reaching an incomprehensible crescendo. He caught Auum's bleak eye as he loomed from the shadow and the alcohol-induced exuberance caught in his throat. He half choked. Auum watched the man look him up and down then, as if sensing others, turn with comical slowness and repeat the process with Duele and Evunn.

He pointed at Auum. 'You—' he began.

'Go,' hissed Auum. 'Away.'

All thoughts of drink and song forgotten, he hurried out of the alley, bounced off the corner and turned left, heading towards the guards and glancing behind him every other pace less death strike him down unawares.

Halfway to the patrol he had a change of heart and veered away but they were quick to intercept. One grabbed an arm, another asked a question and the drunk pointed back towards the alley.

'Fall back,' said Auum. 'Be ready.'

The Tai retreated into the black of the alley, back to and just beyond the bodies of the thieves. Light approached the mouth of the passage and the patrol peered inside. Duele tensed his bow.

'Let them come if they will,' whispered Auum.

And they did. Cautiously, holding a lantern well out in front and with swords gripped in nervous hands. Two were in front of the third. It was a formation that would save none of them.

Auum and Evunn crouched in front of Duele. They prayed as they waited that Shorth, the god of the dead, would take these men swiftly and silently.

The lantern's spread was maybe ten yards. It was a poor, smoky flame and the glass was dirty. Behind it, the patrolmen were picked out in ghoulish yellow light, their faces stark and scared, unsure. Auum waited. Like watching a hunted animal cross the point of no return, he scanned every movement looking for the sign that he had been sensed.

The moment they were too far into the alley to be seen from the college walls, the Tai struck. Duele's bow thrummed, the arrow bisecting the two and taking the third through the eye. Immediately in its wake, Auum and Evunn powered up from their crouches, covering the short distance with frightening speed.

Distracted by the fall of their comrade, the two had stopped and half turned. Auum planted his left foot and kicked up and straight out at his target, catching him in the throat as he swung back just too late. His windpipe crushed, he choked and fell, clutching uselessly. Auum pounced, his short sword delivering the killing blow.

Left, Evunn had downed his man. Blood poured from a gash in his neck and the light faded from his eyes, his cries muffled to nothing by Evunn's hand across his mouth. There had been barely a sound bar the lantern glass breaking when it hit the ground.

Auum nodded, gave brief thanks to Shorth for answering their prayers, and stood.

'They will be missed and found,' said Duele.

'Yes,' said Auum. 'But with these.'

He stopped and dragged one of the thieves' bodies from the scrub.

'Overpowered by enemies of their own kind,' he said. 'We'll place a blood trail for the one who got away.'

They worked quickly and then were gone, like whispers on the wind.

*

Heryst became groggily aware of his surroundings. He was in his chambers near the Great Hall. Trimmed lanterns cast a gentle light. The sweet smell of curative herbs bathed his nose and throat, clearing his mind like water washing away loose dirt. He stretched on his pillows and widened his eyes. At the foot of his bed, Kayvel came into focus.

'How long?' he asked.

'Exactly one hour,' said Kayvel. 'It was a remarkably accurate casting. Denser, I presume? Xeteskian, certainly.'

'Who else?' said Heryst.

'Anything hurt?' asked Kayvel, walking around the bed.

'You expect me to answer that?' Heryst almost smiled. 'You'll have to try harder.'

'Like The Raven, you mean, my Lord?'

'Sarcasm is poor humour. Especially at this hour of the night.' Heryst swung round and put his feet on the cold stone floor. He enjoyed the sensation. 'Make yourself useful and pour me a glass of water.'

Kayvel turned to the jug and crystal glass sitting on a tray by the bedside. 'It was too easy.'

'No, no,' said Heryst. 'They made it easy.'

'You let them stay here, my Lord. You let them carry arms on college grounds.'

'Which they used for nothing but threats. Effective threats, but just that. Even so, I didn't see that move in the courtyard. I thought I had it all covered but that was smart. Once they were inside, it was easy enough. Getting out, though, should have been well nigh impossible . . .' He trailed off, the events replaying in his head. He drained the glass Kayvel gave him on one and wiped a hand across his mouth.

'I saw it,' he said. 'And I felt it. Tell me you felt it too.'

Kayvel's face told its own story. 'Like someone dragging a hook down my spine.'

'I want them followed,' said Heryst. 'And I want you to contact our delegation in Dordover and the lead field mages. I want to know how far the effects were felt. You might also talk to our Dordovan guests. No doubt they are already in Communion.'

'Much of what you ask is in hand. But following will prove difficult. We have already lost them; however we do know with some certainty where they are headed. We can be waiting.'

'She's the ultimate weapon in this war,' said Heryst. 'I will not lose her to Xetesk. Nor Dordover. Right. See that our forces are alerted to The Raven. Use Darrick as the reason for their recapture.'

'What about Izack?'

Heryst raised his eyebrows. 'Put it this way, I don't think we can rely on the cavalry to be available to help.'

'But if it's a direct order—'

'Oh, he won't actually refuse or hinder our efforts. But we're a long way from the battlefield. Expect him to be otherwise engaged.'

Darrick brought The Raven to a halt in a quiet side street deep in an area of warehousing. He slid from his saddle and marched up to Hirad, dragging him into an embrace.

'Thank you,' he said pulling back, a surge of relief flooding every cell of his body.

Hirad shrugged. 'You're Raven. Leaving you wasn't an option.'

'We've done well,' observed Denser, moving across to Erienne, who The Unknown had handed down from his horse. 'We've turned you from respected general and hero of the people to deserter and now outlaw. Good going.' Erienne clung to him. 'Are you all right, love?'

'Course I'm not bloody all right. I've just been passed about and flung around like a bag of rags after casting a spell I probably shouldn't have tried.'

'Why not? The Al-Drechar were there, weren't they?'

'Sort of.'

'Erienne?'

'Look, they didn't think I was ready. They said my casting wouldn't be honed enough and that it would take too much out of me. They were right.'

'What did you do, exactly?' asked Denser.

'I removed constituent elements. Just left dry dust in simple terms. Unpicking the physical lattice, mind you, that's difficult.'

'Impressive, though,' said Darrick. 'And I am forever in your debt, Raven or not. Now, can you ride, Erienne?'

'So long as it's not too far. I'm exhausted.'

'We have to get out of the city and well away before dawn. I know a place a few miles east of here where we can rest. We're heading for the Al-Arynaar, I take it?'

'Let's get ourselves going and talk on the way,' said The Unknown. 'We'll take it easy until we hit open ground, give Erienne a chance to catch her breath a little. Anyone carrying an injury? No? Then let's get moving.'

They mounted up, The Unknown and Hirad riding forward with Darrick, the horses at little more than a walk, through the quiet early morning streets. They could hear no pursuit.

'They won't bother,' said Darrick. 'They'll guess where we're heading. We haven't got any other realistic choice.'

'This complicates matters,' said Hirad.

'Every non-elf can now be assumed a potential threat – barring Izack perhaps but even he will have orders.'

'You think they'll come after us aggressively?' Hirad looked across at Darrick.

'You heard Heryst,' said the former general. 'He wants to control Erienne and more than that, he'll not want her taken by Xetesk or Dordover.'

'Hmm.' The Unknown chewed his lip. 'And if the ripple has been felt elsewhere we'll find ourselves hunted by everyone when they work out what it means.'

'I don't understand,' said Hirad. 'It's a different magic.'

'But it draws on mana first,' said Erienne. 'The real power of the One is what else you can bring to bear.'

'I believe you,' said Hirad. 'Just take care of yourself.'

'Don't you worry about me,' said Erienne, but Darrick could hear the affection in her voice.

Hirad turned in his saddle.

'It's my job,' he said.

The Raven rode out of Lystern.

'Tell me what it means,' demanded Dystran.

He was standing in an archive room just above the catacombs, and all the laboratories and research chambers they contained. Like every mage in the college, he had been rudely awakened by the ripple in the mana, coming to with a sense of déjà vu. He had wrapped a cloak around his night shirt and run barefoot to the archive room where his spectrum guards spent their days and nights. He was tired but excited and, little over an hour after the incident, impatient for answers. One answer.

'It is difficult to be certain. The effect was only faintly visible in the spectrum though even that was strong enough to wake us all,' explained the middle-aged mage, a man whom Dystran had never come across before.

'But it came from Lystern,' said Dystran.

'Undoubtedly, my Lord.'

'Humour me now,' said Dystran. 'And take your best guess. I understand your desire for exactitude but I have to plan. I, after all, am in charge. What do you think caused this ripple or polarisation, whatever the term you prefer to use?'

'It felt familiar, my Lord,' said the analyst. 'Unpleasantly so. If you pressed me, I would say, and I must beg leave to verify, but I would say we had experienced a casting of the One magic. All the signs that we learned so well from the Nightchild's devastation were there but this was ordered. Under control.'

'Yes!' Dystran clapped his hands together. 'Correct answer. Verify away. Don't sleep until you have the proof you need and don't fear being wrong. I need the truth more than I need lies dressed up as good news.'

Dystran called his advisers to him and strode from the room.

'Get me whoever it is that's in charge on Herendeneth. I need to know why the hell the Al-Drechar haven't revealed there was another practitioner. And get me Chandyr and Myx from whatever front they're defending. The march on Julatsa might have to be postponed.

'Oh, and get me an update on our dimensional experiments based on the information those two women supplied us. Gods, there's so much to do.'

He turned a corner and took a spiral staircase, going up two steps at a time.

'Ranyl,' he said to himself. 'You'll have to postpone dying. I need you more than the darkness does.'

In Dordover, the night's rest was over for every mage capable of reading the signs in the spectrum. Vuldaroq had received powerful and urgent Communion from Lystern shortly after midnight. The news had sent him surging from his bed, his overweight body sweating as he ran, wiping a cloth at his puffy red face.

Even in his dreams he had felt the unease that had whispered through the mana spectrum and on hearing the report from his delegation and his experts, knew his feelings were grounded in truth.

'Be absolutely sure,' he instructed the research team. 'But be quick about it. I want to know how this is possible. And at first light, I want to see the Lystern delegation. In the meantime, I want every spare man hunting The Raven. I think it's safe to assume, as our delegation suspects, that Erienne carries the One, if indeed we are facing that power again. I want her here, where she belongs, as a child of this college.'

He sat back in his chair. 'Dear Gods falling, The Raven. Praise the day when they stop making my life so bloody difficult.' He sighed and looked around him. 'Come on, we've got work to do.'

Chapter 7

In contrast to the dawn weather, the mood was distinctly cool in the Al-Drechar's reception room on Herendeneth. Myriell joined Cleress as usual in their preferred location by the kitchen, their elven helpers shadowing every uncertain, arthritic step. No one would dare disturb their sleep but a trio of tired-looking Xeteskian mages was waiting for them as they awoke. She recognised them all; Nyam, Leryn and Krystaj.

'To what do we owe this pleasure?' asked Myriell, having spent an inordinate amount of time having her cushions and blankets precisely arranged by her Guild elf attendant, Nerane.

She could feel their irritation growing but ignored it and the increasingly frequent 'tuts' coming from Cleress. But then Cleress had spent so much more time defending Erienne's mind of late, including her rather rash use of a creation she wasn't quite ready to use. Understandably, she was tired.

Myriell, on the other hand, had enjoyed her best night's rest for ages and felt energetic enough to indulge in mischief-making.

'You have not been straight with us,' said Leryn. He was their leader and a fool. All slimy smiles and political intent.

'I think you'll find we have answered all your questions to the best of our ability,' said Myriell evenly.

'You did not tell us there was another practitioner of the One.'

'You didn't ask.'

'So there is.' Krystaj this time, a bored and ineffectual student. A poor mage.

'That is your assumption,' said Cleress, finally connecting with Myriell's train of thought.

'And we wouldn't dream of questioning the assumptions of Xetesk,' added Myriell. Looking Leryn square in the eye.

'So tell us,' said Nyam, the only smart one among them. 'Is there another practitioner?'

Myriell smiled. 'We were a widespread order at one time. There is a chance that others have survived like we have.'

'That is surely untrue,' said Nyam. 'You two are over four hundred years old and have survived this long only because you've been here and have had daily care. We have detected the One magic on Balaia. We suspect a student and you are the only teachers.'

Myriell and Cleress were silent.

'Tell us,' said Nyam. 'Is there a student with whom you have contact?'

We cannot tell them, pulsed Cleress.

They know already. All we can do is divert them.

They will guess.

This was always inevitable.

'I would remind you that we are not under your control, merely your protection, such as it is,' said Myriell. 'And we are happy to help with your researches. The state of our order is, and will remain, our own business.'

'Your evasion confirms our suspicions,' said Leryn.

'And your assumptions. Is the knowledge useful?' Cleress employed her best patronising smile.

'You will tell us the name of the practitioner,' said Leryn.

'Ah,' said Myriell, holding up a finger in admonishment and beginning to really enjoy herself. 'Definitely a mistaken assumption. No we will not, even assuming we know.'

Leryn snatched up the neck of her dress beneath the blankets, dragging her almost upright.

'You are testing my patience, Myriell. Tell us what we need to know or we will extract it.'

Myriell felt no fear and displayed nothing but calm. 'Fascinating. Don't you agree, Cleress?'

'Fascinating,' she agreed.

'We were wondering how you propose to do that,' said Myriell.

'Pain is a great loosener of tongues,' said Leryn.

Myriell nodded. 'How original.'

She gripped Leryn's wrist with her right hand, her meditation quick and sure. Erienne's chosen construct would be admirable. Short, sharp and very, very hot.

Leryn cried out in sudden pain, leaping backwards and dropping Myriell who released his wrist and settled back into her chair. Leryn looked at his blackened arm, the smell of his toasted skin in the air, the thin tendrils of smoke mesmerising.

'Do not make the mistake of thinking you can threaten us, Xeteskian,' said Myriell, all traces of humour gone from her voice and face. 'We have power you can only guess at and while our bodies may be frail, the One sustains us and guides us until our last breaths. We are in charge here and you will not demand anything of us. Now, the audience is over. Cleress and I wish to talk. Leave at once.'

Myriell signalled Nerane to rearrange her blankets. Nyam opened his mouth but Cleress stayed his words.

'We will not repeat ourselves,' she said.

Nyam looked at Leryn who nodded, his pained expression a picture of shock and humiliation. The three mages left the room in silence.

It is dangerous to stoke their anger, said Cleress, still choosing to speak mind to mind.

It is time they knew their place, countered Myriell. *When we were protecting poor Lyanna we had no strength to protect ourselves. Now it is different, if only by a small degree but they will not know that. We are the Al-Drechar. I will not have them think we are helpless.*

Well, you've certainly achieved that.

Myriell relaxed further back into her chair, feeling a little tired. Her arthritis was flaring badly. *But they will guess soon enough and it will make them desperate. Let's not forget that friends and loved ones of The Raven are our guests here. I think we should have a quiet word with Diera.*

Devun didn't have Selik's courage and belief. That fact had hit him hard as he rode through the damp chill of Understone Pass. He'd sent three of his men back to the righteous army to urge patience and begin to explain why they must seek the aid of the Wesmen, leaving a guard of six making the journey to the sworn enemy of Eastern Balaia.

None of them had travelled the Pass before. None had experienced its oppressive closeness, its deep darkness and its extraordinary majesty. To think it was only part natural. That so many had struggled and died for its construction only to unleash a conflict that had rumbled on for hundreds of years, occasionally exploding into bloody and destructive life.

It was an incredible feature that demanded respect but that wasn't why Devun and his men took so long to travel a distance which would take a galloping rider a little over four hours. He knew that it was because he was scared. That he had no idea how he would approach the Wesmen they would encounter at the western end of the pass. And so he and his men moved with exaggerated care, and stopped more and more frequently the nearer they came. Their lanterns threw shadows in front of them that made their already nervous horses unwilling to move and they needed no second bidding to halt. Though who it was that needed calming more was open to debate.

Devun lost all track of time but thought they must have travelled through the night, given the exhaustion that descended on them all. It did at least allow him to formulate some sort of plan but he couldn't shift the knowledge that Selik would have been far better equipped to face the Wesmen.

All Devun could do was adopt the sort of confident air he knew Selik would have exuded and hope that whoever stopped them failed to see through to the frightened man behind it. Assuming, they weren't simply killed out of hand.

The answers came very suddenly. They had been anticipating the end of the pass for some time. There was more movement in the air. It was less dank and every now and again, the faint smell of wood smoke added to the mix. Their pace had slowed still further and, riding abreast, all seven of them were squinting to the furthest extent of their lanterns' throw when a shout from ahead stopped them.

In moments, dozens of torches were alight ahead of them, stretching from ground level to the natural vaulted roof of the pass above. They illuminated a gated wooden barricade, strengthened with iron strips and punctuated with slits through which Devun could well imagine arrows pointed.

Immediately, he dropped his reins and raised his hands head high to signal peaceful intent, indicating his men should do the same.

'No sudden moves,' he said, breathing deep and slow while his heart pounded in his chest. Seeing the structure ahead of him, he was acutely aware of the folly of their position. Just seven men who could so easily be snuffed out. And who would miss them? Few barring those trying to hold the army together near the walls of Xetesk. How in all the hells did he expect to persuade the Wesmen into alliance?

'Tough it out,' said one of his men as if hearing his thoughts. 'Act like Selik would have done and we'll ride back heroes.'

Just what he was thinking. Carrying it out, now that was something else.

A crack appeared in the doors, and daylight flooded into the pass followed by the sweet smells of spring. Devun shielded his eyes. Three men stood silhouetted in the glare. They began walking when the gates had opened fully, revealing many more behind them. They walked with total confidence, one slightly ahead of the others who both carried unsheathed swords. Moving as slowly as he could, Devun dismounted to meet them.

He faced a shortish man, heavy set, bearded and dressed in light furs. His small eyes scowled from his face and his voice carried no warmth.

'Who are you?' he asked in heavily accented western Balaian.

'I am Devun, leader of the Black Wings. I would know your name.'

'Lord Riasu. You are far from home,' he replied, struggling for the right words.

'I need your help,' said Devun simply, trying to pick terms Riasu might know. 'I come to offer a deal to the Wesmen.'

Riasu raised his eyebrows. 'A deal? We want nothing from you.'

'You want what I can offer. But I must speak to Lord Tessaya. He is your leader still, is he not?'

Riasu shrugged. 'Yes. But I can tell him what you tell me.'

Devun shook his head. 'It must be face to face. Talk to him. Ask him. I will await your reply.'

'I will think on it.'

'Thank you,' said Devun.

Another shrug from Riasu and he turned to go.

'Lord Riasu,' said Devun, and waited until the Wesmen lord looked back at him. 'We are hungry and thirsty. Can you spare food and water?'

Riasu barked out a laugh. 'You should be dead. This is our land. Be happy you still breathe.' He paused. 'I will think on it.'

Devun watched him go, seeing the gates close on him before blowing out his cheeks and turning to his men.

'Well, what do you think?'

'I think we're still alive and that's as much as we could hope for,' said one. 'What now?'

Devun scratched at his head. 'We have no choice. We wait.'

Pheone awoke with the sun streaming through her unshuttered window in the newly built room in the south of the college of Julatsa. If she chose to look out she could see much of the college spread out before her but the last thing on her mind was enjoying the view despite the brightness of the new day.

She felt nauseated. Her head felt thick and heavy and her stomach churned like she'd eaten something bad the night before. She knew it wasn't food and a wry smile dragged briefly across her face. For the first time in her life, she was wishing sickness on herself because at least it would mean the problem wasn't infinitely more serious.

Pheone tried to relax and focus inwardly, switching into the mana spectrum. That was where the source of her nausea was, she was sure of it. For one terrifying moment, she couldn't tune in at all but then there it was before her mind's eye. The gentle flux of focused mana that was the signature of the spectrum at the core of a college.

Yet it was far from right. The flux was weak. She could see that as clear as day. There was a random edge to the overall focus and that was indicative of the failing of the Heart. She frowned. They'd been seeing the slight breakdown for a while now and that wasn't why she was feeling off. There had to be more. She followed the flux focus into the deep core of concentrated mana that flowed around the Heart. The pulsing core of the college, the centre of its power. Buried from normal sight but visible on the mana spectrum.

It was there as it had always been but displaced by its burial those few years before. Years that had seemed like an eternity. A displacement that had stopped the college in its tracks. Julatsans were no longer called to the college because the pulse was not loud enough. But those that remained had kept faith that the pulse still beat as strong. Not true. Not any more.

Pheone searched harder, probed the core and soaked up the

mana streams that to a mage were like standing in a warm spring breeze. She felt comforted for a moment but it was false.

A chill shot through her body and her eyes snapped open. The Heart was losing its colour. Julatsan mana was a glorious warm yellow. Gold if you were romantic. It was the colour of life, of vibrant, exuberant pure magic.

Or it should have been.

What Pheone could see through her experienced attuned senses was dulled. Tarnished. Just slightly but there. If a shadow passed across the land it dulled the beauty of its colours. So it was with the Heart of Julatsa. A shadow was across it, dulling its beauty, hiding its power. It hadn't been there yesterday but it was there this morning. Hardly noticeable.

But if it grew it would take their power from them. Hide it behind impenetrable shade. And then the college would surely die. She couldn't allow that. Not while she had breath in her body. Dammit, if only Ilkar were here. How she needed his strength right now. At least their message should reach the battle lines outside Xetesk soon. The Al-Arynaar would have to help them, surely they would. Their mages stood to lose just as much.

She tuned back to normal light. The nausea was subsiding now she had its cause. She sat up and began to pull on her clothes, wondering if others had felt and seen what she had. She hadn't reached the door to pull it open before the first shout of alarm reached her ears.

Chapter 8

Hirad relaxed and let Sha-Kaan's dominating presence into his mind. He noted a resignation in the great old dragon's feelings. Acceptance of fate, perhaps. Weariness, certainly.

'I am lonely, Hirad Coldheart,' he rumbled. 'Lonely, old and tired.'

'I'm doing everything I can,' said Hirad, heart skipping a beat at the melancholy edge in Sha-Kaan's voice.

'I need my own kind. I need the healing winds of inter-dimensional space. I need my home.'

He sounded so old. The will was waning. Almost six years in exile since the violent realignment of dimensions following the closing of the Noonshade rip. Six years with his life energy ebbing away, day after tortuous day.

'What's happened, Sha-Kaan?' There must be something to force this change for the worse.

'The Kaan birthing season is now. Our greatest joy and our time of greatest risk. They have looked to me for so long to protect them.' Sha-Kaan grumbled deep in his throat. 'And this time I will not be there. If I was, I wonder if I would have the strength to truly help.'

'I feel your loss,' said Hirad. 'But please have faith in us. I made you a promise and I will keep it.'

Warmth flooded Hirad's mind. 'You are my friend, Hirad, and I trust you. But you are a rare breed of man, it seems to me. Most of your race are without honour or true soul.'

'Lucky I'm on your side, then,' said Hirad, both moved and embarrassed by the unbidden compliment from the most unlikely source.

'Listen to me, Hirad. There is danger here. Erienne has employed the One magic, has she not?'

'Yes.'

'Xetesk felt it. They have passed their knowledge here through the Protectors and their mages are pressing the Al-Drechar for answers. So far Erienne's identity remains a secret but these men are strong and I cannot stop them all, should they choose force to uncover it.'

'Diera?'

'Safe so far. She is the wife of Sol and the Protectors will not harm her or her son. It is the mages that concern me. Work fast, Hirad. Xetesk must be weakened and its attention drawn elsewhere. I must have my home and I can bring help. The One must survive to build a stronger world but I fear bloodshed.'

Sha-Kaan left Hirad's mind abruptly, leaving the barbarian momentarily confused. He sat up gingerly and looked around the dilapidated barn to which Darrick had brought them. Its roof, such that remained, clung to damaged timbers and only one wall was anything more than glorified splinters. Still, it represented shelter and that was some comfort.

The Raven were circled around a small fire. Erienne was asleep in Denser's arms, no doubt in contact with the Al-Drechar. Darrick too was sleeping, though his was an emotional tiredness. The Unknown was awake, lost in his thoughts and staring at the blaze. Thraun was outside. He would guard them while he prowled the overgrown fields and sniffed out scent-marked territories. Still so much the wolf. Still so much lost inside himself. Hirad doubted the Thraun he remembered would ever fully reappear.

'How's my family?' asked The Unknown, seeing his eyes open.

'Unharmed,' said Hirad evenly. 'I don't think you're going to like this much.'

'He calls it administrative guidance,' explained Hirad to Darrick.

It was an hour before dawn and The Unknown had urged them be on their way, his face severe in the light of Hirad's report from Herendeneth. He had said little as he pushed them to clear the camp, saddle up and go but there was no doubting the fire within and his renewed desire to get inside Xetesk. And quickly.

The city was two days' ride at best and their situation was far from ideal. Lysternan and Dordovan supply chains were everywhere on the principal routes, their security augmented by college horsemen and mercenaries not willing to fight for the besieged Xetesk despite the higher wages.

Not so long ago, The Raven would have contracted themselves to Lystern or Dordover too. Their desire for balance in the colleges would have stopped them joining Denser's home college. That and Ilkar's determination never to work for Xetesk. How different it all was now. Once feted, The Raven were now effectively outlawed and hunted by all but Julatsa. And yet they were still Balaia's best chance of lasting peace if they lived long enough to make good on all their promises.

'It's an interesting use of language,' said Darrick.

'He used it first when threatening Styliann, would you believe. Funny how Xeteskians always seem to be on the receiving end.'

'And who do you think will be getting the benefit of his advice this time?' asked Darrick.

Hirad shrugged. 'Could be Dystran, though I don't think that particular Lord of the Mount will be available to us. Put it this way, anyone who can affect the safety of Diera and Jonas is in the target area.'

'Got to get in first, though,' said Darrick.

'The TaiGethen will help,' said Hirad. 'Should be fun.'

Darrick eyed him oddly then and Hirad knew all over again why he would miss Ilkar so much. The Julatsan elf would have lost no time commenting on how only Hirad would describe invading the Dark College as 'fun'. Something to make him laugh and make him believe even more that they would succeed.

No one could do that now. Denser tried but he had a lot to learn. Ilkar was irreplaceable. But at least Darrick could read Hirad's mood and thoughts right now.

'That's why we're doing all this,' he said. 'To make Ilkar's sacrifice meaningful.'

'Yeah,' said Hirad, voice gruff. 'Can we talk about something else?'

The agreement to a daily Communion had seemed a small price to pay and a sensible measure in Lystern and Dordover's latest military alliance against Xetesk but there had been times when Heryst rued sense. Today was one of those days. He'd had no sleep since The Raven's audacious liberation of Darrick and he'd known that Vuldaroq, High Arch Mage of Dordover, would have questions, if not outright accusations. It didn't help that it was his, Heryst's, turn to seek Communion, so depleting his mana reserves further in a contact he had no wish to make.

'At least you do me the honour of contact at the appointed time,' said Vuldaroq, his tone cold, saying everything about his assumed knowledge.

'There is no reason why I would not,' said Heryst carefully, sensing already so many echoes of their past conversations.

'Really? I had thought you might be engrossed in the search for a common enemy.'

'I have people I can trust to conduct necessary investigations.'

'Are they as good as your jailers?'

'Vuldaroq, you will not tax me about events wholly within the legal compass of my college,' said Heryst. 'We have more pressing matters to discuss. Particularly the situation at Xetesk's east gate.'

It was a deflection Heryst had assumed would fail but he had to try it anyway.

'That situation, while unfortunate, is static and no more of our forces are currently at risk from further failures in the Julatsan magic system. What is surely a risk to us all, however, is the use of the One magic within your college borders last night and the escape of the likely practitioner. An escape you did little to oppose.'

'And this view was given to you by men watching from windows how far away . . . a hundred yards? Perhaps a little less if I'm generous.' Heryst felt ready for a fight. Dordover deserved nothing less.

'Are you disputing The Raven escaped from your college around midnight last night?' asked Vuldaroq.

'No.'

'And Erienne was with them.'

'She was one of The Raven last time I checked,' said Heryst.

'Don't get clever, Heryst, it does not become you when you are on the defensive.' Vuldaroq's voice in his head was full of righteous indignation. 'I know the One magic was cast in your college grounds around the time The Raven escaped. My analysts have pinpointed the area closely enough. Gods burning, man, it wasn't very difficult. I also know that The Raven were in your college and that Erienne is the only likely suspect as someone able to perform such a casting.'

'And how do you work that out, Vuldaroq?' Heryst clamped down hard on his irritation. 'Recent history has informed us that the reason Erienne and Denser conceived the child was precisely because Erienne, in particular, had no way of casting such magic but wanted to produce an offspring that could. Perhaps you'd like to enlighten me as to how you know different. Is there something pertinent to our alliance that you have accidentally omitted to tell me?'

Silence in Dordover. Vuldaroq considered his response. Had Heryst not seen Erienne's casting with his own eyes he would not have believed it possible she could harbour any knowledge of the One. But she did. The question was, given Vuldaroq had already guessed her to be the practitioner, as Heryst had thought he would, how would he back up his claim. What exactly did Dordover know that he was prepared to share?

'It is the only logical explanation,' said Vuldaroq carefully. 'I was on Herendeneth when the Nightchild died. Erienne was with her as were the Al-Drechar. Something must have been passed to her or else she has somehow been able to use some knowledge of the Al-Drechar's teachings. Heryst, I am not an expert. No one is. We have to work together.'

'We are working together,' said Heryst.

'Damn you, we are not!' snapped Vuldaroq. 'You know something and you are not telling me. What did you see?'

'I was too busy attempting to stay alive. Hirad Coldheart had a knife to my throat.'

'That they could escape with Darrick from under your nose.' Vuldaroq chuckled, returning to his preferred line of provocation.

'Well, you'd know all about defeat at the hands of The Raven,' said Heryst. 'Remind me how many men you committed to the offensive on Herendeneth?'

'It is hardly the same order of magnitude as being outwitted in your own college grounds.'

'You still lost. One thing we can agree on. It hurts.'

'So help me, Heryst, damn you. Did Erienne cast a spell of the One?'

'I don't know,' Heryst replied. 'The One was used but by whom, why and to what effect we are still investigating. In case it is The Raven, we have them under observation. We know where they are headed. They are only six. They cannot evade us forever, should we wish to stop them.'

'I would have thought that your main priority. After all, Darrick is with them.'

'That is an internal matter I am dealing with separately,' said Heryst coolly. 'You will not intercept them. You don't understand.'

'Oh, I understand, my Lord Heryst. I understand that you know Erienne performed the casting in question. I understand that you were not strong enough to stop her escaping you and I understand that my forces are all ordered to arrest The Raven on sight.'

'Vuldaroq you—'

'And before you protest, I understand something else too. If I were Xetesk, and I had pinpointed the One casting, I might be taking a detour on my way north, to ensure Julatsa never rises. Care to guess where that might be if I believed the ultimate weapon resided there?'

Heryst had no answer. There was none that left him with any credibility in this debate.

'Lucky, then, my dear Heryst, that we are friends and allies, isn't it? With me at your side, you might just stop them destroying your college. I think it's time you were completely straight with me, don't you?'

Thraun pointed away to their left and up on to the ridge along which the supply wagons had passed earlier that morning. Heading for Xetesk and heavily defended, the train had rattled past with a cloud of dust, squealing axles and hard-driven horses. Seeing the signs from over a mile away, The Raven had simply ridden further from the trail and rested their mounts while they watched it go by.

But now, galloping hard away from the Dark College, horsemen were approaching fast. The Unknown dragged his reins right, turning his horse on the canter and digging in his heels, demanding more speed. The Raven followed him, angling away from the ridge and trail, hoping to hide themselves in the folds of land. Here, the ravages of Lyanna's uncontrolled elemental power had wreaked terrible damage. Barely a bush or shrub stood tall. Trees lay broken and rotting. And criss-crossing like whip scars across the back of the land, the top soil was torn away, leaving dark slashes in the green of spring grass.

Hirad urged his horse on in the wake of The Unknown and Thraun, sparing a glance behind to reassure himself that the others were keeping up. The sound of hooves hitting soft earth filled his ears, clods of mud churning into the air in the wake of their passage.

The Raven rode down a shallow incline, heading for a cleft between two rises that would take them back towards the ridge and beneath the sight of any riders. But they were not going to be fast enough. The dust from the ridge signalling the oncoming horsemen was already too close and while Hirad watched, the heads of the leaders appeared on the skyline no more than a hundred yards from them.

Forcing a reckless pace along the trail, Hirad clung to the hope that they wouldn't see The Raven below them. But with a shout, the whinnies of horses pulled up sharply and a sudden change of direction, that hope disappeared. Whoever they were, they split into two groups, of at least six each. One began edging down off the ridge in direct pursuit, the other wheeled about and galloped back down the trail, looking to head them off.

'Keep moving!' yelled The Unknown. 'We can beat them on open ground.'

He hunched over his saddle, Hirad mimicking him, the strong smell of horse sweat in his nose and mouth. And then Darrick was by him, riding easily as if he were out for a training gallop. He caressed his horse after The Unknown, eating up the ground between them, leaning over and pulling at the big man's shoulder.

The Unknown turned his head. Darrick drew a finger across his throat, pointed front and back and with barely a flick of his reins, swung his mount right and began charging directly away from the path, heading for a steep-sided gully. The Unknown followed him, Hirad doing likewise, frowning, not understanding for a moment. Yet the reason for the move soon became apparent.

Darrick dragged his horse to a stop in a cloud of dirt and loose stones, ten strides from the gully edge. The Raven pulled up around him, the sounds of their pursuers loud in the sudden lull. As one, they turned. Left and right, riders came on, angling in at them, one group over a hundred yards distant, the other perhaps twice that, having picked its way down from the trail ridge.

'Listen to me,' said Darrick. 'We couldn't afford to get trapped between them on the gallop. They knew they had us there, they know the terrain.'

'Whatever's in your mind, tell us fast,' said Hirad.

Darrick twirled the now headless rake he'd taken from the Lystern stables in his right hand as he spoke, Hirad acutely aware of how vulnerable the ex-general was, garbed only in his dress uniform.

'Couldn't you have picked up a sword?' he said.

Darrick shrugged. 'Without armour, I'd rather keep them a little further away. Right, we'll go at the closer group on my mark. Let me lead. Don't flinch. Denser, ForceCone at the far group if they close. Anything to slow them when they wheel as they will to follow us. Swords, everyone, Erienne centre for protection, casting SpellShield. Anyone ever wanted to be in the cavalry?'

Blades hissed from scabbards, free hands held reins loose. Horses, heads up, ears pricked, stood ready, shifting slightly. The nearer group came on. They weren't flat out. Darrick waited and Hirad saw what he must have seen immediately. These weren't cavalrymen against them. They didn't have the form or the relaxation in the saddle.

'Waiting,' said Darrick. 'Waiting, let's have them wondering.'

'Mercenaries,' said Hirad. 'You'd think they'd know better.'

'Shield up,' said Erienne.

'ForceCone ready,' murmured Denser.

Ilkar's voice never came and Hirad's heart missed a beat.

At less than thirty yards for the nearer group, maybe ninety from the other, Darrick spurred his horse.

'Note their blade position. They'll chop down, trust me. You know what to do. Come on! Close form. Ride, Raven!'

His mount sprang away, the rake handle held a third of the way down and pointed straight along the animal's neck. The Unknown was after him, Thraun on the right flank, leaving Denser partnering Erienne in the centre while Hirad defended the rear quarter. He felt his pulse race and a grin split his face as the wind rushed into him. He roared his energy, Thraun taking up the call. The Raven rode.

Oblivious to the vulnerability of his unarmoured body, Darrick galloped directly for the centre of the mercenary charge. Deep green light splashed across Erienne's shield from a mage rider, the casting dissipating harmlessly.

Darrick twitched the rake handle in his grasp, the wood now held horizontally away from him. He kicked his horse's flanks again, closed the gap to engage, feinted low then whipped the pole through head high. His target had already begun to defend low and couldn't readjust the heavier weapon in time. Darrick's rake caught the top of his head, knocking him senseless. His blade fell from nerveless fingers and he slumped back. Darrick didn't pause to look, ducking low in the saddle as an enemy to his left struck out, missing his back by a whisker.

A stride behind him, The Unknown and Thraun drove in. The big man's sword whined through the air, striking right and out, plunging into the undefended body of Darrick's left-side attacker. On the other flank, Thraun clashed metal with a fast-armed swordsman, carving his own blade round and riding on unharmed. His opponent was not so lucky. Hirad was following up, his blade straight and true and his grip strong, the man dead before he hit the ground.

The Raven punched a hole clear through to open ground. Darrick fended off more blows, his rake splintering in his hands. The Unknown dragged his blade through the thigh of the mage rider and Thraun nicked another on the way past but they weren't finished. Denser rotated in his saddle, ForceCone cast with a single word. Without a SpellShield the surviving enemy were defenceless. The Cone slapped into the backs of them, catapulting riders from saddles, fracturing bones in men and horses.

'No!' shouted Darrick. 'Too early.'

He pulled up and turned.

'Wrong,' said Hirad, seeing the faltering gallop of the second group. 'That was cavalry, this is Raven. Kill but never murder.'

'Form up!' called The Unknown. 'Darrick my left.'

They trotted into a single line abreast, still under Erienne's shield. Loose horses milled in confusion, the injured limped or lay, their cries echoing mournfully from the ridge. Dead and wounded mercenaries were scattered over an area of twenty yards and Denser kept a weather eye out for mindless acts of bravery. Ahead of them, the centre rider of the group raised a hand. His five colleagues reined into little above a trot.

'Shouldn't go attacking The Raven, Tolmek,' said The Unknown, commanding voice crossing the twenty yard divide. 'And you can have the same but it is not what we want.'

'There's a high price on your heads, Unknown,' replied Tolmek. 'And those are my men you've killed and wounded.'

The mercenary leader had modelled himself and his team on The Raven. He was an experienced fighter, scarred from battle, his sharp blue eyes bright beneath a fluted helmet which crushed his untidy black hair to his head. If The Raven admitted to respecting any others in their trade, he'd be high on the list. Right now, though, he was a potential enemy. He understood that.

'We have the right to defend ourselves.'

'I have the right to try and fulfil open contracts,' replied Tolmek.

'I'm sure,' said The Unknown. 'Yet we're all fighting on the same side. You want Balaia saved, you turn and ride away.'

'What I want is money enough to retire before I'm too weak to hold my sword.'

'Then fight with Xetesk. They'll pay you more,' said Hirad.

'I think you know me better than that, Coldheart.'

He nudged his horse on ahead of his men, closed until The Unknown's mount nuzzled his and spoke quietly.

'Everyone is looking for you,' he said. 'I can understand Lystern's anger but there's more, I know it. Dordover is way too keen to see you taken. All of you alive, not dead. What's going on?'

'Time you were leaving,' said The Unknown. 'You don't want to force us to fight you.'

Tolmek half smiled. 'Tempting though it is to try and earn the reward . . . maybe another time.'

'We won't strike first against you,' said The Unknown. 'But force our hand and we won't hesitate.' He gestured to the mess surrounding them. 'See to your wounded then go.'

Tolmek nodded. 'Be lucky, Raven. I—' He paused and frowned. 'Where's Ilkar?'

Hirad's heart dropped at the sound of his name. 'He's dead, Tolmek. Elfsorrow took him. Xetesk is to blame.'

Tolmek raised his eyebrows and began to turn his horse. 'I'm sorry to hear that. And perhaps I can make Xetesk sorry too.'

'Just leave us alone, don't follow us,' said The Unknown. 'Tell the trade. Don't try to stop us. It isn't worth it.'

The Raven moved to let Tolmek take his surviving men to their fallen.

'I wonder how big the reward is,' said Hirad, The Raven gathering to leave.

'Huge, I would hope,' said The Unknown.

'I'd be insulted by a small one,' agreed Hirad.

'So why didn't you ask?' Darrick, like all of them, was dismounting.

'Best not to know,' said Hirad. 'After all, however big, it could always be bigger.' He put an arm round the general's shoulder. 'Now, while Tolmek is sorting out the mess you organised, why don't you see if there's anything round here you like. It's your right, after all and besides, that rake of yours has seen better days and I think we should avoid bloodying your uniform any further.'

Chapter 9

'All right, what have we got?' asked Dystran, once seated around the dining table with his elven archivists and dimensional research teams. Ranyl was on his way, apparently. But it would, as with anything in these last painful days, take him some considerable time.

To Dystran's left, an old master dimensional mage was about to begin when Dystran held up his hand for further silence.

'I realise my last question may have given you the impression that I am merely after a quick update on our current state of research. Let me disabuse you of that particular notion.

'In case it has escaped your attention, we are at war. There are thousands of souls beyond our gates whose express intention it is to nail me to the walls of my Tower. Probably upside down. We may have won a recent victory but the tide is still against us. Our people live in fear of invasion. Hundreds clamour every day to leave.

'In this war, either Xetesk triumphs or we become a husk, never to reclaim our rightful position. Now, in order for the former and not the latter to be our fate – and let me assure you, if it is the latter you will all experience your fates before I do – there are certain things we must do, and do right. For that, I require your individed attention and assistance.'

He paused and looked around the table. Eight men between the ages of thirty and eighty had lost their appetites for the vegetable stew and bread before them. Wine and water settled in glasses.

'So let's start with the easy one. Was it the One magic cast in Lystern last night?'

'Yes.' Kestys, that was his name. Dystran had never been good at remembering names. But he remembered faces all right. And this man's, unremarkable and slightly reddened as it was, was utterly familiar.

'And the caster?'

'That we have not yet ascertained.' Kestys looked for help to either side of him. It was not forthcoming.

'I see.' Dystran sucked in a breath slowly and carefully. 'Stop me if I make a mistake here. We still have Protectors on Herendeneth, meaning we have muscle and we have the means to communicate between there and here, correct? Yes. And you have presumably requested that the Al-Drechar be questioned about the identity of our mysterious practitioner?'

'Of course, my Lord,' said Kestys, shifting in his seat, a light sweat on his brow. 'But they have not been forthcoming.'

Dystran pushed his hands through his hair. 'On that island, our people face one dragon with no fire, one woman and a baby, half a dozen servant elves and two old mages. How is it they have been allowed to be "not forthcoming".'

'The Al-Drechar retain considerable power.'

Dystran smiled thinly. 'They do. They are also very, very old, and dying. They spent themselves trying to protect the Nightchild from her own power and they have never fully recovered. Two of them died. Pressure them further. And if they resist, threaten someone else. The baby, for instance . . . any latent talent there that could scare five Xeteskian mages? I think you understand me.'

'My Lord.'

A door opened behind him. Dystran turned to see Ranyl shuffle in. The cancer-ravaged mage was leaning heavily on two sticks but still refusing the aid of the mages trying to cluster around him. The room focused on him while he dragged himself to his chair next to Dystran and sat down, propping the sticks against the table. His face displayed his pain, his eyes his undimmed determination.

The Lord of the Mount poured him a glass of chilled water. Ranyl drank deeply.

'Thank you, my Lord.'

'Any time,' said Dystran. 'We will continue if you are ready.'

Ranyl smiled. 'Make no allowances, my Lord. I am here, therefore I am capable.'

A dry chuckle ran around the table. Ranyl commanded enormous respect from every mage in Xetesk but there was

83

more to it than that now. Every senior mage knew that Dystran would respect Ranyl's wishes on his successor to the Circle Seven.

'So that we don't delay you any longer than necessary, we will deal with the progress of our research into the elven writings. I was hearing about a breakthrough?'

'Small but very significant,' said Gylac, the chief archivist and the only man truly capable of deciphering the ancient elven writings. Another man whom Dystran feared would die before his work was complete. 'I have found a common thread in all the pieces we recovered from Calaius. It speaks of the encasing of all elven people in a sheath of magic that sustains them in the tasks laid down for them by their gods.'

'The key to their longevity?'

'It is the closest we have got so far, my Lord,' replied Gylac. 'What I find interesting is the similar language we have found in the admittedly vague references to the Elfsorrow.'

'Oh yes?'

Gylac gestured at Ranyl. 'My Lord Ranyl has theorised on the subject to a greater extent than I. I am concentrating on translation.'

'Gylac is being rather modest,' said Ranyl, inclining his head. 'This is not a small breakthrough. If we are proved correct and can understand fully the interaction between elves and mana, we should be able to create a spell that disrupts this sheath. Synthesise Elfsorrow, if you like. The construct is already in development but we have too many unknowns to complete it thus far.'

Dystran's heart rate was up. It was more than he could have hoped at this stage. 'How long?'

'I cannot say,' said Ranyl. 'Gylac's team are working as hard as they can but some of the language is so arcane it defies translation. I suggest we increase our efforts to capture an elf or two who could help us.'

Dystran nodded. 'I am meeting our military commanders shortly and will discuss that option with them. Thank you. All of you. This is good news. But only as far as it goes. We must have new weapons or we will eventually lose this war.' He paused. 'Now, our dimensional experiments.'

'Complete,' said Ranyl. 'We have re-established full contact with the demon dimension; the Al-Drechar's information has allowed us to redraw our map of inter-dimensional space and calculate dimensional alignment events. When they occur, our full range of dimensional spells will be available for the event's duration. We are ready. We are back in control.'

Dystran smiled again. 'I want the alignment information passed to the army so we can factor it into our attack plans. When will the first helpful event occur?'

'Three days,' said Ranyl.

'Then that informs our timetable.' Dystran jabbed a finger at Kestys. 'You need to do more work. Get me the identity of the One caster on Balaia and get it for me in three days. Given that we are again linked to the rest of dimensional space, we can send that damn dragon home. Perhaps you should offer a deal. Actually, I don't care. If I catch you sleeping before this task is complete, I will feed you to the demons.

'Eat quickly. This meeting is closed.'

To his credit, Riasu had despatched a fast rider towards the Wesmen Heartlands immediately he'd taken Devun in. To Devun's irritation, he hadn't advised the new Black Wing leader of the fact for over two days. They were two days when Devun alternately feared for his life and saw the potential of Selik's plans open up for him.

Riasu wasn't a particularly difficult man but he was suspicious. And his grasp of standard eastern Balaian was fragmented, though still far better than Devun's tribal Wes. His suspicion was well founded and explained his initial hostility.

He had been tricked by eastern devils before, he had said, and he would not be again. One mage and his army of walking dead, blank-faced men had promised the Wesmen help in destroying all the colleges bar Xetesk six years before. He had been a liar, like all easterners. Many brave Wesmen warriors had gone to the Spirits because of him. He, Devun had discovered after more difficult questions, had been Styliann, former Lord of the Mount of Xetesk; and killed by a dragon in an alien dimension.

Still, it gave Devun his first glimmer of hope. Riasu had been very pleased to hear of Styliann's demise. But it had still taken Devun two days of fragmented discussion to persuade Riasu first not to kill him and second, to take him to meet Tessaya.

And so to this. Devun and his few Black Wing guards, riding

unarmed under the hostile gaze of ten times their number of Wesmen warriors. None of their hosts bar Riasu had horses but they seemed unconcerned by hours of jogging, leaving Devun impressed despite himself.

There had been a glint in Riasu's eye when he revealed Tessaya had already been contacted and that a meeting point had been arranged. Devun had firmly gritted his teeth and consigned the memories of fear and uncertainty to the back of his mind. All that mattered was that he was making progress and Riasu could have his little victory. He was acutely aware, though, that Riasu was one hurdle, Tessaya another entirely.

The terrain they travelled was spectacular if bleak. Great shale and rock slopes fled away to the north while ahead a line of scrub-covered hills promised difficult conditions for man and horse.

'Tell me, Riasu, did your people suffer under the bad storms?' asked Devun, keeping his language deliberately simple as he referred to the elemental destruction wreaked across the continent by the Nightchild.

Riasu turned a harsh face to him as they rode together. The dark, unruly hair that surrounded his gruff, wrinkled face was shot with grey. His lips were small, his nose bulbous, having seen too much wine over the years, and his eyes were buried deep beneath his brow.

'Warriors died with no enemy to fight,' he said. 'Children's bellies swelled though no food was inside. Elders perished early to join the Spirits. We suffer still but nothing breaks the Wesmen.'

'I am giving the Wesmen that enemy,' said Devun.

He paused, fighting the urge to speak more quickly. Conversation had been little short of torture at times.

'So you say.' Riasu shrugged.

'Do you not believe me?'

'I believe you hate magic,' said Riasu. 'But can you give us our enemy? They will hide within their walls and cast their evil. Are they really broken or do you lie like all your kind? The Lord Tessaya will say.'

Riasu still hadn't properly understood. Devun felt as if he expected the Black Wings to march the mages from the gates of Xetesk in chains. He hadn't even tried to fully explain the ramifications of the war now consuming the colleges, nor his support from the non-mage Balaian population. It would have been pointless. Fortunately, the man he was being taken to meet was possessed of a far higher intellect.

Lord Tessaya had been the first Wesmen leader to unite the warring tribes in over three centuries. First, it had been under the banner of the Wytch Lords, and fear as much as respect had driven the Wesmen to a single purpose. They had so nearly succeeded too, their ultimate failure a combination of the sheer strength of the combined colleges and their magic and the extraordinary intervention of The Raven. So few, yet responsible for so much.

But the mark of the Tessaya's true influence was the maintenance of tribal unity in the aftermath of defeat. He was still their leader, still their greatest hope of victory. And the only man worth talking to in the whole Wesmen nation. He was not to be underestimated. That was why Selik had hatched plans to ally with him.

They travelled all day and well into the early evening, covering a great deal of stark and barren ground, endlessly climbing and descending slope after slope, but still Devun felt frustrated. A rough calculation of the mid point between the Wesmen Heartlands and Understone Pass had them riding for at least three days before the first possibility of a meeting.

It was with great surprise then that, late in the evening, a glow emanating from behind a hill resolved itself into a camp lit by a ring of what smelled like dung fires and crisscrossed by braziers. A palatial tent was pitched at the camp's centre and around it in clusters of two or three, a dozen smaller, circular tents were grouped by campfires, standards flying over each one.

Approaching closer, Devun could see that the standards were all identical, depicting the bear's head and claws of the Paleon tribes. Fifty yards from the pool of light, Riasu halted them in the shadow.

'Dismount,' he ordered. 'None may approach the Lord Tessaya on higher seat.'

'What?' Devun blurted out. Riasu looked at him askance, demanding he explain. 'Tessaya is *here*?'

He'd been prepared to believe a camp could have been constructed but not that the Wesmen leader could have travelled here already. Riasu simply nodded. Devun signalled his men to dismount but his mind was racing. He walked round the front of his horse.

'How can he be here? Is this where he lives?'

'No,' said Riasu, that sparkle in his eyes again. 'He lives in the Heartlands.'

'But he is here to meet me?'

Another nod. 'Yes.'

'So how can he be here already?' Devun gestured at the camp. 'I mean, how fast was that rider?'

'The rider ordered the camp built,' said Riasu.

'So how . . . ? Did Tessaya fly or something?'

'Horse,' said Riasu. He laughed. 'You think us savages. But those touched by the Spirits are closer to the Gods than you will ever be.'

'I don't understand,' said Devun.

'No,' agreed Riasu. 'You are not Wes.'

Devun was desperate to know how they'd communicated. Would a bird have been fast enough? Possibly. He knew they used them but still the distance was significant and the method uncertain. It was clear, though, that Riasu was happy to perpetuate the mystery.

'What happens now?' he asked.

Riasu smiled at his next small victory. 'Your men will stop here with my warriors. They may move no further into our lands. You will come with me.'

'Sir?' said Devun's deputy who had overheard the exchange.

'We'll do exactly as he says. Just keep yourselves quiet, demand nothing and you'll be fine. Don't let them provoke you.' Devun indicated their empty sword belts; all their weapons were being held at the pass. 'Remember our circumstances.'

'Yes, sir.'

Devun turned to Riasu and pulled his cloak close, feeling an unseasonable chill in the evening air.

'Lead on,' he said.

'Good luck,' said the deputy.

'If I have to rely on that, I think we're in trouble,' said Devun, a wry smile on his face. 'But I appreciate the thought.'

Riasu led him towards the camp. At each fire stood a quartet of warriors. Around each tribal tent and fire group, men and women busied themselves cooking, eating and checking weapons. Around the palace tent, guards stood watchful. Tessaya was taking few chances. Just beyond the ring of fires, Riasu stopped him.

'Wait. I must seek permission for you to enter.'

Devun watched him go, walking proud and tall, nodding curtly to the guards who stood aside for him to pass before turning to glare at Devun with undisguised malevolence. He stared back, becoming aware of his vulnerability. If things went awry, he would be dead very quickly.

While he stood waiting, the scents of the camp drifted over him. Wood smoke and cooked meat, rich herbs and even a hint of canvas wax. It was a very well ordered camp but he expected nothing less. Lord Tessaya was an impressive man; and that was before Devun actually met him. He felt a nervousness he hadn't experienced since he was first introduced to Selik.

Riasu wasn't long, walking quickly back to the camp perimeter and waving him in.

'Come,' he said.

Devun strode by the guards, hearing one of them mutter something. Though he couldn't understand the words, the tone and intent were clear enough. He stopped and looked deep into the eyes of the Wesman who was a head shorter than him.

'Say what you will,' he said pointlessly. 'But we will be allies. You will respect me one day.'

'Devun!' snapped Riasu. He uttered a stream of angry Wes and the guard paced back, hand moving from the hilt of his sword. 'No games.'

Devun walked over to Riasu and the two men passed by the six-strong guard at Tessaya's tent entrance. Down a short canvas hallway, another guard held aside a gold trimmed, deep green and tasselled curtain.

'Show respect to the Lord Tessaya,' warned Riasu.

Devun smiled at him, feeling his anxiety growing. 'I had never thought to do otherwise.'

He walked into the grand single room of the palace tent, taking in the netted four-posted bed that stood at the far wall, the fine carved table and six chairs to his right and the plain woven rugs that covered every inch of grass. And he took in the group of three low, dark red plush sofas arranged around a rectangular table on which stood a jug, two metal goblets and a spread of meat and bread.

In front of the sofas stood Tessaya. He was a broad-shouldered man, his shoulder-length hair tied in a loose pony tail. His weathered, pitted face carried the scars of countless battles but his eyes were chips of pure energy. He was dressed in loose-fitting grey robes, cinched at the waist with a tri-coloured plaited cord. He paced forwards. He didn't offer a hand but his face wore an expression of welcome not hostility.

'Captain Devun of the infamous Black Wings,' he said in faultless standard eastern dialect. 'A shame neither Selik, nor his predecessor, Travers, had the wit to seek my help. I congratulate you on your good sense. Come, eat and drink with me. We have much to discuss.'

Chapter 10

It took The Raven almost three days to reach the periphery of the war zone. Three days in which The Unknown's growing concern for the safety of his family was only tempered by his determination to see The Raven reach their destination capable of making a difference. That was the difference between them, Hirad decided. He would have hurtled down the trail, taking his chances because time was everything. The Unknown knew they would achieve nothing by being caught.

It hadn't made him any easier to live with, though. Whenever they rested, hidden in a cleft, river valley or one of the few surviving stands of trees, the emotions he kept in check for the good of The Raven surfaced. He prowled, biting his nails. He irritated Hirad for more and more contact via Sha-Kaan and he snapped at Darrick, who had suggested a faster route.

Now, a mile and more from any supply trail and travelling over tricky ground in the dead of night in a direction designed to take them into the Al-Arynaar camp without crossing allied patrols, Hirad felt he should speak to Darrick.

'This is us,' he said. 'The balance we strike between emotion and practicality is one of those things that makes us who we are. Or so Erienne says. She calls me the heartbeat and The Unknown the brain.'

'And what am I?' asked Darrick.

'A friend with a lot to learn about us.'

'But I could have helped. Selected a better route.'

'The Unknown didn't agree and we believe what he says,' said Hirad. 'But in this case it's personal too. And if The Unknown wants us to be cautious, that is what we'll be. He only turned on you because you didn't understand that. We do it our way and you're one of us now but we all have our key strengths. Yours are things like tactics, on and off horseback. One of The Unknown's is always, always doing things the right way. Question him and you question his ability.'

'I would never do that,' protested Darrick. 'The thought is ludicrous. I just wanted to help.'

'And you'll learn the ways. Believe me, Ry, he holds you in high regard. But this is his task we're helping him with and we must let him do it his way. When he needs help, he'll ask.'

Darrick blew out his cheeks and threw up his hands. With a mercenary sword at his side and an oversize leather jerkin over his uniform jacket, he at least looked more like a member of The Raven. But his youthful face wasn't scarred enough for a long-term mercenary. Too pretty. Like Sirendor Larn. Hirad smiled to himself remembering his old friend. A long time dead and gone from The Raven but never forgotten.

In front of them, the way was suddenly full of figures blocking their path. They had melted from the night and were practically close enough to strike. Bows were bent back and the crouched stance of others carried threat and intent.

The Unknown held up a hand and The Raven halted, seeing themselves hopelessly outnumbered. The Unknown kept his hands away from his weapons, Hirad staying his initial reaction and doing the same. A heartbeat later, he heard laughter ahead and saw two figures moving through the line of archers.

'I knew I was right,' said the voice in accented, slightly clumsy Balaian. 'And you are predictable.'

Hirad slid from his horse and trotted forwards, clasping Rebraal's shoulders.

'Only Ilkar's brother would have guessed our route,' he said, relief gladdening his heart.

'I can't take all the credit,' said Rebraal indicating Auum, who stood beside him, not a flicker of emotion on his green-and-black camouflaged face. 'He has an eye for the land not shared by our – uh – allies, if we can truly call them that.'

'Oh, we can still call them that,' said The Unknown, dismounting and walking to stand by Hirad, the rest of The Raven climbing a little more slowly from their horses. 'We are still after most of the same things. And don't take any credit, Rebraal. Why do you think I brought us this way?'

Auum wrinkled his nose at that though Hirad was unsure how much he really understood. Behind him, Thraun growled and crouched. A ClawBound panther loped from the shadows and nuzzled him. Its elven partner, face painted half black, half white, impassive, walked close.

'We aren't safe here,' said Rebraal. 'We have made a secure area near our camp. You can hide there. We must be quiet on the way.'

Leading their horses, The Raven followed the Al-Arynaar and TaiGethen elves in silence. It was a walk of over two miles, close to the Lysternan and Dordovan encampments, but Hirad didn't feel under a great deal of threat. TaiGethen scouted ahead and on the flanks, ClawBound ranged in the deepest shadows. Any inquisitive ally would be turned away. Any enemy wouldn't live to report back. What the elves did beyond fighting at the gates of Xetesk was their business.

The main elven camp was quiet as the early hours passed. The only fires were for cooking and they were positioned in a single area close to the Lysternan forces. Beyond them, and further into the shrub and trees that the elves preferred to the open camps of their allies, The Raven were shown into the secured area, patrolled by Al-Arynaar. Their horses were unsaddled before being led away to the central picketing area.

A small fire lay at the heart of this camp within a camp. Above it dangled two cooking pots and surrounding it, logs had been dragged in for seats.

'Been expecting us?' asked Hirad.

'We have tracked you for a day,' admitted Rebraal.

A single figure sat poking at the fire. He stood quickly and stepped forward, straightening his clothing. Hirad couldn't quite see his face but Darrick knew exactly who he was.

'Take a wrong turn off the battlefield today?'

'No, General. I just heard you might be making an appearance.'

Darrick and Izack embraced, slapping each other on the back. Izack showed Darrick to a seat, turning and waving the others in.

'Don't worry,' he said. 'I'm acting on my own.'

Hirad shrugged and moved into the glow of the fire, The Unknown at his shoulder.

'Do we trust him?' asked the barbarian, voice low.

'If Darrick does, I do,' said The Unknown. 'Let's eat and talk.'

He seated himself the other side of Izack, Hirad next to him. Denser and Erienne sat across the fire from them. Hirad was worried by them both. Erienne had been so quiet since casting the One spell and her silence had affected Denser. There was more to it than the concerned husband. He didn't want to think they were keeping something from The Raven. Surely Denser had been warned enough about that.

Last into the firelight was Thraun. His face carried a deep frown and he shook his head, troubled in the depths of his mind. If it was possible, the frown deepened when he saw Izack. His agile frame slid quickly around the fire and he dropped to his haunches in front of the Lysternan cavalry commander, blond hair flying briefly. He studied Izack's face the way a predator studied prey before striking.

'Thraun, it's all right,' said Darrick. 'We can trust him.'

'Risk,' said Thraun, focusing on Darrick momentarily.

'I won't betray you,' said Izack. 'Hear what I have to say.'

'Heryst's man,' said Thraun.

He straightened up but, before turning away, pointed to Izack and then to his right eye.

'What's got into you, Thraun?' asked Hirad.

'Later,' said Thraun, his tone so low it was little more than a bass rumble.

A little less confident than when he'd greeted Darrick, Izack ladled out strong herbal tea for them all and pointed to the soup, bowls and bread.

'Report,' said Darrick. 'Please,' he added, remembering himself.

Izack chuckled.

'A pleasure, General, though it makes grim listening. The siege is still secure but we are certain some supplies are reaching Xetesk. We suspect underground passageways but we have found nothing so far and, to be frank, can't spare too many men to look. We suffered heavy losses here on the eastern front as a direct result of the first Julatsan mana-flow failure. This has left—'

'Whoa, whoa,' said Denser, holding up a hand. 'What failure?'

Both he and Erienne were staring at Izack as if he'd just told them the world was about to end.

'You don't know?' Izack gaped.

'In case it has escaped your attention, our Julatsan is dead,' said Hirad gruffly. 'And your glorious leader told us nothing about events elsewhere.'

'I'm sorry,' said Izack. 'Stupid of me. Look, I don't know the technicalities, you'll have to ask the Al-Arynaar mages. The effect was a multiple backfire of the shield net over our front line. The Xeteskians took full advantage. We lost hundreds.

'Right now, we aren't even attacking on this front. The northern gate forces are only just holding because Xetesk have reinforced from here. South and east, it's pretty much as you were but we've taken all their reserve to ensure Xetesk can't punch through here. Not that I think they want to. They're just happy to occupy us.'

'Erienne, Denser?' The Unknown was staring across the fire. 'How could this failure happen?'

Both mages shook their heads. 'It's absolutely unbelievable,' said Denser.

'I can answer that,' said Izack. 'Julatsans arrived here at the east gate lines this morning to talk to the Al-Arynaar. They say the Heart of Julatsa is failing.'

For a time, all that could be heard was the crackling of the fire and the breeze through the leaves above.

'How can that be possible?' asked The Unknown eventually.

'It isn't,' said Erienne. 'At least, that's what we've all been taught.'

'But assuming it is, what's the result?' asked Hirad.

Erienne shrugged and spoke plainly not really believing what she was saying. 'Julatsan magic dies and the balance of magic on Balaia shifts irrevocably.'

'That's not happening,' said Hirad. 'No way.'

'All right, Hirad, let's keep it calm,' said The Unknown. 'Izack, presumably the Julatsans are here to get help from the Al-Arynaar, being Julatsan-trained initially.'

Izack nodded. 'Absolutely. They say that only the Al-Arynaar can help raise the Heart because they have the knowledge of Julatsan magic. And raising the Heart is the only way to stop this failure becoming permanent. Does that make sense?'

Denser blew out his cheeks. 'Sort of. Bringing the Al-Arynaar to Julatsa to raise the Heart was something Ilkar wanted to do. It's why we went to Calaius in the first place, before the Elfsorrow struck. As for this failure of Julatsan magic, I don't know. Like Erienne says, this goes against all our teaching. Burying a Heart will stop development because the core power can't flow and that's why you'd only bury one if it would otherwise be destroyed.'

'Which is what Julatsa did when the Wesmen invaded.'

'Exactly, Hirad. But it should still beat. The power should never falter. There's no reason why, that's what we don't understand.'

'So we get the Al-Arynaar mages and go to Julatsa. What are we waiting for?' Hirad spread his hands.

'Hirad, please,' said The Unknown. 'I know you're anxious but we have to do this right. Where's Rebraal?'

'I am here.' Ilkar's brother, leader of the Al-Arynaar, walked from the shadows where he'd been leaning against a tree.

'We need to talk to one of your mages. Well, Erienne and Denser do. Find out what timescale we're dealing with here.'

Rebraal nodded. 'Of course. Our lead mage is Dila'heth. I'll bring her to you.'

'Thank you. Now, Izack, what have you been told about us?'

'The official line is that you're outlaws and General Darrick is a condemned man wanted for his execution. But it doesn't add up. We are told not to harm any of you but to bring you back to Lystern alive and well. And the Dordovans have been told the same thing.' Izack smiled. 'Heryst and Vuldaroq may dislike each other but we fight side by side. We're friends, mostly, and we talk.' The smile faded. 'But everyone here knows there's more to it. Unknown, every mage here felt the casting. The elves rejoiced, Lysternans and Dordovans were troubled. And everyone knows the timing of the casting and your escape from Lystern. It's too coincidental.' Izack looked square at Erienne. 'People have drawn their own conclusions. That's why you have to be so careful.'

'And what about you?' asked Erienne, meeting his gaze.

'The General believes in you so I believe in you too.'

Erienne said nothing but raised her eyebrows a fraction in acknowledgement. Denser put a hand on her knee and she returned her gaze to the fire.

'So tell me, have the TaiGethen completed their scouting?' asked The Unknown.

'Yes,' said Izack. 'But I think they're still worried about how to get into the college itself.'

'That's where we come in,' said Denser. 'Or more particularly, where I come in.'

'You're planning on going in with them?'

'Think we're safer out here among our allies, Izack?' said Hirad.

'Surely in the elven camps—' he began.

'We've business to attend to,' said The Unknown. 'And we're not sitting out here hiding our faces and watching the action.'

'I take your point,' said Izack.

'One more thing, Commander,' said The Unknown. 'Just how would this front hold up if the elves were to leave it?'

'Simple. It wouldn't.' Izack shrugged.

'You do know that once we've finished inside Xetesk, the elves won't stay here,' said The Unknown.

'I am well aware of their reasons for joining our fight thus far,' said Izack shortly.

'Then you have to be ready for them to leave – mostly to march north to Julatsa to help raise the Heart.'

'Then the siege of Xetesk will collapse. They can rout us from the east gate at will, and every other front will be compromised as a result.' Izack sighed heavily. 'They know why we're fighting this war. They will benefit from our victory. Gods, I've fought so hard to establish what we have and lost so many doing it. Don't leave us defenceless. You'll be handing the victory to Xetesk.'

'Want to know what I think?'

'About war, Darrick, absolutely everything,' said The Unknown.

Rebraal and an exhausted-looking elven woman who had to be Dila'heth, walked into the camp. The Unknown pointed them at Denser and Erienne and, after brief introductions, the four engaged in fervent conversation.

'The moment we retrieve the elven writings, as we must, keeping us at bay will become unimportant to them. Surely they are doing nothing more than keeping us from the walls because they are researching what they have learned from the Al-Drechar and those same writings,' said Darrick.

'Well, I like to think our forces are keeping them from surging north to destroy Julatsa, which I take to be their first goal,' said Izack.

'Let me ask you something, Izack,' said Darrick, now every inch the general of the armies. The position in which he so excelled. 'What is the purpose of your engaging the Xeteskians in this combat?'

'To probe for that weak point. To try and make the breakthrough. Turn the battle in our favour.'

'Wrong. That is the Dordovan command holding sway over you, if that is what you really believe.'

Hirad leaned forward, rapt despite his tiredness.

Izack stared at the floor. 'We have to beat them,' he said. 'Time is short. I've always known the elves would leave one day.'

'In a siege you're just wearing them down,' said Darrick. 'Bit by bit. Otherwise, why engage them at all? Why risk your own men? What you have to believe is that they will crack under the pressure, living in the prison you have created for them. This siege is being fought just as much in the mind as it is on the battlefield.

'Now your defeat the other day was damaging. It allows Xetesk to rest because you can't afford to fight them on this front. If he's clever, Dystran will be making sure his generals are rotating duty on all fronts now.

'His men are fresh out there in front of you, aren't they?'

Izack nodded, mute, sucking in his top lip.

'You won't break them,' said Darrick. 'That isn't where we will beat Xetesk. Whatever Vuldaroq and Heryst believe, we can't win here.'

'So what the hell am I doing!' Izack bit down on his temper. 'General?'

'You're showing them we won't be beaten and you have bought us and the elves the time we need. You've weakened them, make no mistake. And when we get out of Xetesk with the writings, having done whatever damage we can to their research, they are going to come after us. And not just because of a few ancient texts.'

'How so?' asked Hirad.

'There is more they will want. The power of the One, which they surely crave will be lost unless they break the siege. And if the Al-Arynaar succeed and raise the Heart of Julatsa and we can protect it while it strengthens, they will be on the brink of losing the war.' Darrick raised his eyebrows.

'And what makes you so sure they can break the siege?' asked The Unknown.

'They're keeping plenty in reserve, I can feel it,' Darrick said. 'They have made no move to break out because they don't need to. Not yet. But mark my words, they will be mobilising for a move north soon. If they start to push at all four gates you'll know it's imminent because they'll be striving to occupy every enemy they can. What we can do by getting in and out of Xetesk is force their hand. We don't want them ready, believe me.'

'So what do we do?' asked Izack. 'How do we stop them?'

'Now's the time to be fighting harder than you ever have at every gate. Every one of them that dies or is forced to fight until exhaustion is a victory. I know we'll suffer losses too but we'll have the psychological edge. And when they try to break through the north gate as they will, we need to have enough men and mages in reserve to chase them. Don't forget, we can't abandon the siege or we'll be just inviting more Xeteskian warriors to chase up to Julatsa. We cannot allow them to know we are reinforcing the north gate lines. We must make them fight to keep their city even while they run to attack Julatsa and reclaim the writings and, if they're lucky, Erienne, when they guess her identity.'

'But that's the trick, though, isn't it?' said Izack wearily. 'How do we manage our resources to manufacture a meaning-ful reserve? How can we take most of our men from the fight east, south and west and still keep the pressure up on Xetesk?'

Darrick smiled. 'Well, that's why I'm here, talking to you now.'

'Good,' said The Unknown. 'Then I suggest we leave you two to it. We're going in tomorrow night so work to that timescale. I'm sure Auum will agree we should wait no longer. Meanwhile . . .' He stood up, his eyes on Thraun who had remained completely still, staring into the shadows beyond the fire. 'Thraun, come and talk to me. I want to know what's wrong.'

The shapechanger fixed him with a sullen look.

'Now.' The Unknown's tone brooked no dissension.

Hirad watched The Unknown put an arm round Thraun's tense shoulders and firmly but gently guide him from the fire. Deciding to get himself some soup, Hirad brushed himself down and ambled over to the cook pots. He caught Denser's troubled gaze.

'How bad?' he asked, stirring the thick broth. 'Want some of this?'

Denser shook his head. 'Very bad. Very bad indeed.'

'How long have we got?'

Denser half shrugged and glanced at Rebraal who was translating for Dila'heth.

'That's the problem,' he said. 'We can't know. They've had one instance of mana-flow failure and the focus around the Heart isn't complete. They say it's like a shadow, leaching colour from the Julatsan mana spectrum. One day, soon probably, that shadow will deepen enough to stop the Heart beating and even now it's spreading out, weakening every casting they make. Put it this way, the longer we delay, the harder it will be to reverse. It's terrifying.'

'Is it?'

'Yes, Hirad, it is. To a mage, losing contact with the mana spectrum is the worst thing that could possibly happen. It would be like a living death. Like living in a Cold Room the rest of your life. How can I make you understand? I don't know . . . for you the closest thing would be like losing the use of your sword arm. It would be hanging there, you'd know it *was* there but you just couldn't use it. Send you mad, wouldn't it?'

Hirad nodded. 'Well, let's not spend too much time in Xetesk, eh?'

'I'm with you there.'

The Unknown Warrior didn't take Thraun far. Just beyond the firelight and into the trees. He'd looked anxious; perhaps the woodland, such as it was, would calm him.

'Thraun?' The Unknown stopped and turned the shapechanger to face him. 'What's bothering you? Even for you, this is quiet and withdrawn. We need you with us all the way inside Xetesk. It's going to be tough in there.'

'We can touch our enemies,' said Thraun, leaving The Unknown momentarily at a loss.

'No, Thraun,' he replied. 'These aren't our enemies. They still want what we want but with regard to us they're misguided.'

'He will betray us,' said Thraun, nodding his head toward the camp.

'Izack? You've got that wrong. He's as loyal to Darrick as we are to each other. He's—'

Thraun gripped The Unknown's arm hard.

'He won't mean to,' he said, and The Unknown could see him struggling for the words that just refused to come. His green eyes, yellow-tinged, shone with moisture in the dim flicker of the fire to their right and his face was pinched, angry. He swallowed. 'He won't mean to, but he isn't Darrick.'

'What? Thraun, please. Try to explain what you mean.'

But the shapechanger was looking away towards Xetesk, sniffing the air, tasting its quality.

'I see what the wolf sees,' he said.

The Unknown started. It was the first direct allusion to Thraun's acceptance of his other self that he'd uttered in years. Somewhere inside his mind, another wall had fallen.

'You've lost me,' he said.

'The air is not good here,' Thraun continued, turning back to The Unknown. 'I will fight with you. I am Raven. But wolves do not hunt where they will find no prey, only rotten meat. Do you see any other wolves here?'

Chapter 11

Dystran, Lord of the Mount of Xetesk, heard the distant roar of men and the impact of spells. He smelled the faint tang of smoke on the wind through his open windows and knew it was morning. But there was a different quality to it this morning. He dressed hurriedly, ignored the breakfast tray that had been left on his side dresser while he slept and headed down the stairs of his tower, which sat in the centre of a ring of six similar towers.

He snapped his fingers at his personal guards on the way to the stables and waited impatiently while their horses were pulled from stalls and saddled. He knew he could have asked for opinion but he didn't want it. Too much in this war was going on without him seeing it first-hand. At least the delay gave him time to issue a few orders, the only words he was going to utter until he stood on the ramparts above the east gate.

'Bring Chandyr to me at the gate. Bring him quickly. I don't care if he's lying in a pool of his own blood, I want to talk to him. Second, I want an assessment of Julatsa's strength in my briefing chambers when I come back and a man of substance to discuss it with me. Third, I want to know to the hour when we will have a dimensional alignment that will enable us to cast DimensionConnect or something similarly destructive.

'Now, clear me a path to the walls, I'm a busy man.'

One of his guards ran back towards the tower circle to pass on Dystran's instructions. Two others mounted up and led off at a gallop towards the east gate of the college and out into the streets. The remaining three rode around Dystran as he put heels to flanks and cantered away into his city.

He'd not ridden out for too long. It was so easy to feel that the war was going largely according to plan when safe in the cocoon of the college. When those gates closed, shutting out reality was simple, but in the streets, his people were not at ease. Businesses were dying, people were slowly but surely going hungry as his rationing measures bit harder. It was the middle of spring and at a time when the farms that supplied food to Xetesk should be green and yellow with burgeoning crops, most lay idle and overgrown or, worse, supplied his enemies.

Dystran needed his people to understand that they'd come too far to turn back now, to surrender to the old order that would remove Xetesk's power. Remove him. He needed them behind him, believing in the greater glory of Xetesk. For the first days of the siege, support had been so solid. His attempts to engage every citizen in the effort, make them feel involved in a struggle for their survival, had appeared to work. From stretcher teams to water carriers, soup-kitchen cooks to weapon sharpeners, everyone had been designated a task. The sense of togetherness had been extraordinary.

How quickly that support was waning. Barely forty days into the battle and they were losing faith. The eyes turned to him were scared, angry or both. He could understand the fear. None of them was allowed to witness the fighting unless directed for support duty and that meant, for most, that all they had was what they could hear, and the rumours that came back day by day. Most were exaggerated, some verged on being lies. Yet there was little Dystran could realistically do. In the absence of obvious signs of victory, minds naturally turned the other way and doom was easier to share over a few drinks.

It had been such a hard path to walk. Trying to keep his people believing in him but not letting them know why they had to suffer the torment of war outside their walls. War they couldn't see but that could engulf them, should the tide turn against them.

How could Dystran tell them that all they had to do was wait a few more days? If he did, his enemies would know too and that he could not afford.

'Just hold on,' he whispered as he passed faces turned to him in desperation. 'Just hold on.'

He rode through the military positions behind the east gates, positions mirrored at all four portals into the city. Waved through guard posts and directed down cleared channels he made towards the great closed gate itself. Seventy feet high, iron-bound doors in frames of stone, sweeping a hundred and more feet into the sky to meet at the apex of the grand east gate tower. The spired tower boasted three ornate arches from which his generals would be directing the battle half a mile away on open ground, safe above multiple oil runs and reinforced ramparts.

Either side of the gate tower, the dun-coloured city walls ran away, a mile and more, studded with archer turrets and guard posts, quiet now with so much of his force concentrated around the main battle sites. But the walls themselves were surely deterrent enough. Founded deep in the earth and with internal buttressing, the walls sloped very slightly outwards as they rose some seventy feet tall, as high as the gates. They had never been breached and it gave Dystran great comfort to imagine the sheer size of any force that could genuinely threaten the sanctity of the city.

But, like any walled settlement, the gates were the weak points.

He dismounted, the noise assaulting his ears as he did so. Of hundreds of feet rushing everywhere in pursuit of orders; voices raised to bellow new instructions; forges hammering out new weapons, horseshoes, and repairing battered armour. The temperature had to be twenty degrees higher than in the college. To his left, steam covered the entrance to a kitchen and behind it, Dystran knew his men lay dying, dragged from the field every day.

But many more lay ready, fit and waiting for the order to advance. That day was close but not even his generals knew how close. Only Dystran and Ranyl knew. Any card he retained he had to guard with care.

Dystran double-stepped up the spiral stairways that curved around the gate turrets, his feeling of unease growing. He ran along the first rampart tier and up the central stairways into the tower proper. Reaching the central arch, he found Chandyr already there . . . and saw for himself the sacrifice being made in the name of Xetesk and its Lord of the Mount. He leaned on the uncomfortable but beautifully carved balustrade and stared out at the battle, what little he could see of it.

The recent dry weather had dried the topsoil and a cloud of

dust hung over the scene of battle, thickened by smoke from fires and spell impact. Dystran could just about make out the opposing fighting lines in the fog. The Xeteskian line, some five hundred yards wide, was laid in a disciplined curve held firm by Protectors at ten points.

The huge masked warriors led the defence, provided communication along the entire fighting line at the speed of thought and fed confidence into his men. Dystran could imagine the Soul Tank, deep in the catacombs of the college, boiling with activity. Even though they fought individually, the Protectors operated with one mind, those close to brothers engaged in combat directing attention towards threat and opportunity. It made them the awesome force they were. So difficult to break down, so damaging to enemy morale.

Behind the front line, reserves stood waiting, shouting encouragement, pulling away the injured and plugging gaps in the line. Further behind, mages stood or sat in knots, with guards in close attendance. Some directed offensive spells across the lines into enemy support, others maintained the shield lattices against spell and missile attack.

Completing the picture were his archers and cavalry, both mobile, both with their own mage defence, and deployed tactically. The archers kept enemy mages busy with spell defence, the cavalry were in three loose groups, left, right and centre, positioned to counter surges by enemy swordsmen and cavalry, or take advantage of any weakness in the enemy line.

Dystran watched as the centre of the enemy line pushed hard, dragging men into the swell of battle. Steel glinted through the smoke and dust. The roar of voices increased. From behind the enemy warriors, spells arced into the sky. FlameOrbs, green- or yellow-tinged and trailing steam, the superheated mana balls rose and fell into the mage and archer lines behind. Deep blue shields repulsed, sheeting light over their charges. The power of the enemy spells dissipated into the ground, kicking up spats of dirt.

And behind the barrage came the arrows and, with a flash of weapons and thunder of hooves, the cavalry. They forged in heavy on the left flank. It was a thrilling sight. Dystran winced as the Xeteskian cavalry surged forward to meet them between the two main lines.

The opposing forces met, breaking into small groups with

individual battles fought out in the mass of men and horses. And, riding across the back of the attack, came the Lysternan commander, plugging a weakness with an individual charge of breathtaking ability, weaving through a gap Dystran didn't even see from his distance and striking a Xeteskian cavalryman from his mount.

He could have been Darrick. In fact, the whole attack could have been masterminded by the former general, so classically was it executed.

The Xeteskian mages and archers responded. The air thickened with arrows. DeathHail hammered onto metal, ground and shield. HotRain fizzed into existence, each drop trailing smoke. HellFire thrashed from the clear skies, its brief roar eclipsing every other sound. The Lysternan shielding flashed green, repelling what it could. Choking smoke billowed afresh into the air. At the periphery of the lattice, a SpellShield failed, telltale black spots rippling as HellFire hit it with too much force to be contained. With a clap like thunder, the Xeteskian spell drove through. Beneath it, the knot of archers had no chance whatsoever.

Dystran watched on a few more moments, happy that this latest enemy surge would be turned away. But, just as when he awoke, there was a nagging in his mind that something significant had changed. He hadn't seen enough of the fighting to put his finger on it. Fortunately, he was standing next to a man who had.

'Tell me, Commander Chandyr. What is it that is different about today?'

Chandyr smiled and turned briefly from the battle to look at his lord. He was an experienced soldier, weathered face crossed with scars from the skirmishes that were a fact of life for any career soldier. Dark circles around his eyes told of his overlong hours on duty but still they retained their energy.

'I could have done with you in the army, my Lord,' he said. 'Most of my advisers have noticed nothing.'

'But you have.'

'Several changes and I should tell you that this is happening on all fronts and I have been forced to bring up some reserve, for the morning at least. First, they are pushing harder than at any time in the last ten days, leading me to think they suspect we'll be launching an offensive soon. Second, the elven mages are few and far between, telling me they are either resting, unsure of their ability to cast, or both. Third, right now I can't see enough elven fighters. And that is the strangest of all since there are more in the front line than I've seen since the siege started.'

'Reinforcements?'

'Where from?' asked Chandyr. 'And given that they want to break us, why haven't we seen them in tandem with the elves before now?'

Dystran chuckled. 'My dear Chandyr, you are the military mind. I rather think I should be asking that question of you.'

'Apologies, my Lord, I'm thinking out loud.' Chandyr cleared his throat. 'I can only surmise that they have found some new mercenaries or perhaps that one of the Barons has been persuaded to lend his support. Whatever, it has given the bulk of the elves time to rest and regroup and I think that is significant. They are waiting for us to act and they will be ready.'

'Your thoughts?' asked Dystran.

'There is little open to us, my Lord. Whatever your time-table, I suggest you stick to it. We also should not change our plan to attack through the north gate; any other leaves us in the open for long enough to lose the effect of surprise. I don't think the elves are planning an assault, that would be futile but we had to expect them to expect us to force the pace at some stage.'

'Thank you, Commander,' said Dystran.

'My Lord?'

Dystran turned to be faced by an anxious-looking youth wearing the armband of a messenger.

'Speak up,' said Dystran.

'I am ordered to tell you from your college guard captain that he has found something you need to see urgently.' There was an uncertain smile.

Dystran nodded. 'Very well. Go and get some food from the kitchen and get back to your post. Well done.'

The messenger bowed and ran back the way he had come. Dystran shook Chandyr's hand.

'Keep me informed. Anything out of the ordinary and I must know it. Our time is close. Be ready.'

'Always, my Lord.'

A canter back through the city and Dystran was intercepted at the college gates by Captain Suarav, the most senior college guard soldier. Like Chandyr, a career in the military had left him cynical and scarred, older than his forty years, but his sense of duty and loyalty shone out. He was a man Dystran instinctively liked and trusted. Dystran smiled to himself. Ranyl would remind him of his like and trust of Yron, hero turned betrayer. He wondered briefly what had happened to him. Dead, he presumed, and probably at the hands of an elf. Fitting.

'My Lord, I wouldn't normally bother you but I felt you should see this in person before it was cleared.'

Dystran jumped from his horse and handed the reins to a waiting stable hand.

'What?'

'This way, my Lord.'

Suarav indicated around the college walls and led the way. They walked quickly across the open space between the college and the rest of the city, heading for drab tenements and blank-faced warehouses. The guard captain walked down a stinking, narrow alley into gloomy shadow that gave a lie to the brightness of the morning. A buzzing sound up ahead revealed itself to be a cloud of flies underneath which, three guardsmen stood, swatting ineffectually.

'This isn't a time for a walkabout view of social deprivation in Xetesk,' said Dystran, without a clue why he was being dragged down here.

'I can assure you it is nothing of the sort,' said Suarav. His tone was not encouraging.

They walked down the alley in silence. Thirty odd yards in, Dystran was presented with five bodies. The rats had got to work in the time since the men had died. Two of them were dressed in rough clothes and Dystran couldn't care less about them. What concerned him greatly was the patrol of three that lay with them.

'How long have they been dead?' he asked.

'A day, maybe more,' said Suarav. 'We knew they were missing but didn't suspect this. As you know, we have had the odd attempted desertion.'

Ignoring the stench of death and the mass of flies swarming about the corpses, Dystran and Suarav knelt for a closer examination.

'At first we thought this was a fight gone wrong between thieves and our men, but it can't be that.'

'Why not?' asked Dystran, who had assumed exactly the same. He turned his head to one side to try and breathe some cleaner air.

'Just look at the wounds,' said Suarav. 'These two bastards don't have a mark on them but their necks are broken. Our men have been taken down by a clean arrow shot here, and a crushed windpipe and a single thrust here. The third's had his throat torn out. I'm afraid these men have all been killed by the same foe. We've seen it before in these alleys.'

'Elves,' grated Dystran. 'In my city. *Again.*'

Last time, with Yron's help, the elves had taken back the ancient elven thumb fragment from under Xeteskian noses. It had stopped the elven plague in its tracks and swung the war away from Xetesk. Dystran wasn't about to allow that sort of thing to happen again. He straightened quickly and strode from the alley, Suarav in his wake.

'Double the number of patrols, treble the guard on the archives, use any spare men to watch the entrances to the catacombs. No one who can use a sword or a spell sleeps tonight in my college, understand?'

'My Lord?'

'There aren't many elves in the battle today. Chandyr thought they were preparing for a breakout by us but they aren't, are they?' Dystran shook his head. 'Some of those bastards are coming in here tonight. Perhaps all of them.'

The trouble was, he reflected on his way back to his Tower, with almost all the remaining Protectors banished from the college grounds because of their questionable loyalties – Dystran suspected but not could not prove, yet, their complicity in the theft of the thumb fragment – he didn't necessarily have the men to keep the college secure from the elves. Any normal strike force, yes, but these people were way too clever, way too fierce. One thing he had to do was put watchers on the city walls.

There was a great deal to be done.

In the end, Tessaya and Devun hadn't spoken much that first evening. The Wesmen Lord had seen the Black Wing's tiredness, had apologised for their treatment while insisting on its necessity and had seen Devun and his men to a freshly pitched tent outside his camp boundaries.

He hadn't been recalled until after midday the following day, by which time he and his men were rested, refreshed and well fed, if still nervous at their position. Returning to Tessaya's tent at the sullen request of a Wesmen warrior with the most halting Balaian, Devun breathed in the scents of steaming bowls of flower petals and incense candles, relaxing perceptibly.

Tessaya was dressed much as he had been the previous night and he showed Devun to one of his sofas, offered him food from the platter of bread, fruit and meat on the table between them, and sat down himself.

'So, where did we leave it last night?' he asked 'You had told me of the appetite for war being displayed by the colleges, the continuing troubles of Julatsa following our own successful occupation there, and the siege currently in place around Xetesk. Lystern and Dordover in alliance, you said?'

'Yes, my Lord,' said Devun.

'Please.' Tessaya held up a hand. 'I am not your lord. To you, I am Tessaya, as to me you are Devun.'

'Thank you,' said Devun, disarmed in spite of himself by the charm of this man, whom he had heard to be little more than a savage. 'And they are aided by elves from the southern continent of Calaius.'

'Yes, fascinating,' said Tessaya. 'Very capable, you said.'

'Extraordinary,' replied Devun. 'I myself was witness to an attack of theirs when three elves killed fifteen of my men. A match for Protectors, I've heard it said.'

Tessaya raised his eyebrows. 'Now that would be worth seeing. But to business. You came here looking for my assistance. I am at a loss as to how to give it. I can hardly join a siege perpetuated by my sworn enemies and I do not see the point of attacking them and letting Xetesk, the worst of them by far, off the leash.'

He sat back, having grabbed an apple from the platter, and now bit into it, washing down the fruit with a goblet of wine. Devun felt himself being pierced by Tessaya's startling gaze, which blazed from beneath heavy brows.

'I agree with what you say, and I am not asking you to join the siege alongside the colleges. Before Selik was murdered by The Raven, he had built an army of the righteous. Ordinary

Balaians who, like you and me, want to see an end to the evil that is magic.

'He wanted to attack Xetesk on a new front, bring down its walls and in doing so, allow Lystern and Dordover in to pull down its towers. But our army has faltered in sight of the walls and needs fresh energy. The Wesmen could provide that as our friends and allies.'

Devun hoped he'd set out the argument as Selik would have wanted. He poured a goblet of thick red wine with a slightly unsteady hand and tried to relax tense shoulders.

'The Wesmen are not used to being a mere distraction,' said Tessaya. 'And it remains our sworn intention to stand in the centre of Xetesk and pull down its towers ourselves. Tell me, do you think that Xetesk is surviving the siege well?'

'So far, it seems, and very well. While they have not threatened to break it, their lines in front of their gates have not been seriously tested by all the reports I have received, though I must admit my intelligence is incomplete.'

Tessaya drained his goblet, refilling while he spoke. 'You are not a natural military tactician, Devun. I mean no disrespect by that. I, on the other hand, have studied the ways of eastern warfare as it has developed over the centuries our scribes have been recording events. The Spirits can tell us much too, if you know which questions to ask.

'From what you have said and from what I know from other sources, I think one of two things. First, the siege is not intended to lead to the overthrow of Xetesk but to negotiated surrender. Lystern, to my knowledge, has no desire to see Xetesk die but clearly wants to change its leadership. About Dordover, I know little, though they are more combative. Second, Xetesk may be waiting its moment. Do not mistake lack of action for lack of ability to act.'

'Why would they not wish to break the siege at the earliest opportunity?' Devun was both confused and embarrassed.

'Who knows the minds of mages, Devun?' smiled Tessaya, and Devun felt as if he was being gently chided by his father. 'And I may be wrong. What we must do, though, is think very clearly. And what I think is this. If I was to emerge as the head of an army and march towards the college lands, I would instantly unite the colleges against a common enemy.

'It is strange you and Selik failed to consider this possibility and a more suspicious man than myself might wonder at your real motive for coming here to invite me into the war.'

He paused and Devun felt the colour drain from his face. He thought about protesting but if Tessaya considered him an agent of some unification arm of the colleges, he was as good as dead already. So he decided to take a long drink instead.

Tessaya chuckled. 'Good. I am glad you feel no need to defend yourself. And I know the beliefs of the Black Wings and share them. I think your only crime is naivety. So, assuming this is not an option, we must hope that the Xeteskians will strike out. Assuming they want to gain dominion over magic as we must, where would they go?'

Devun knew the answer to that one. Selik had told him. 'Julatsa,' he said. 'To finish the job you started.'

'Precisely. And so help us in our aim and, in the process, take much of the siege army away from their walls to stop them. In that circumstance, I might be persuaded to strike.'

'So, what must I do?' asked Devun.

'Go back to Xetesk. Watch for their move if such they make. Remember. If no move is made and they are weakened by invasion or surrender, this helps us as much as them marching to Julatsa would. Indeed, if they do surrender, I would propose that Julatsa be our first strike.'

'You seem very well informed already,' said Devun.

'No,' said Tessaya. 'But I can read the military mind. It is why I am still alive.'

'I have heard about your heroics,' said Devun.

'Just necessities to keep my people from extinction.' Tessaya waved a hand. 'Now, the other thing we must discuss before you leave is what the Wesmen will gain from any alliance. I have to be sure you have the authority to grant me what I want.'

'Tell me what it is and I will do everything in my power to see you get it,' said Devun.

'Ah, but there's the problem. How great is your power? And please do not make the mistake of thinking we will simply melt back to the west of the Blackthorne Mountains when the colleges are thrown down.'

Another chill stole over Devun. He hadn't thought through the consequences and now Tessaya knew everything about the weak state of eastern Balaia. Too late to put the djinn back in the bottle.

'The force of the people is with the Black Wings whom I control. With magic gone, east and west can live side by side. We can take Balaia forward to a future of prosperity for us all. We would welcome your people into our lands to live alongside us. Over time, of course. People will be suspicious and even my words might not be enough, should others be seen to be taking advantage.'

'Indeed,' said Tessaya and his smile split his face. 'Now, drink up and go and talk to your men. I have plans to make, a council to call and an army to raise. All in very quick time. I will call you back tonight. Then you will tell me what you offer the Wesmen and I will respond with our guarantees.

'Don't disappoint me.'

'You need not fear that,' said Devun, getting up, his heart heavy and his stomach churning. He tried not to think about what he might have just begun.

'Oh, one last thing, just to humour me,' said Tessaya. 'You mentioned The Raven. Whatever happened to them?'

With anger replacing his nausea, Devun related everything he knew.

Chapter 12

It was early evening and the cloud was thickening appreciably overhead. It was going to be a fortuitously dark night. The Unknown Warrior, Izack, Darrick and Baron Blackthorne sat around their fire. The latter was a reluctant but welcome addition to the siege army, his normally stern, dark features deepened still further by his enforced decision.

All around them, the elven camp was alive with quiet activity. The Al-Arynaar prepared, the TaiGethen prayed and Claw-Bound stood sentinel while more of their kind travelled the ground to Xetesk and their planned entry point.

The Raven too, readied themselves. Armour straps were buckled and swords sheathed in silence. Strips of cloth were wound into buckles and cinches, hilts tied down hard, scabbards bound in thicker weave, chain links greased and darkened.

'Second-guessing Xetesk has never been easy,' said Blackthorne, one hand smoothing his impeccably trimmed, grey-flecked black beard.

'True, but we have no choice but to assume a successful raid tonight will hasten their decision to attempt to break the siege,' said The Unknown.

'But how ready are they?' asked Darrick.

'Our view is that they could move any time they wanted to. The TaiGethen have been inside Xetesk every night for the past ten. They've seen the cycling of soldiers and mages, they've seen fresh units training in the streets. They've reported forges pressing more weapons than can possibly be used on the siege fronts and they're building supply. Damned if I know where the food is coming from but it's getting in. Importantly, we've seen an increase in activity following the Julatsan mana failure.'

'So, do we assume they'll attempt to break siege immediately we escape with the writings?' asked The Unknown.

'I do admire your confidence,' said Blackthorne.

'Never been wrong so far,' replied The Unknown.

'I think there's every likelihood Dystran will mobilise immediately,' said Darrick. 'We know he wants to destroy Julatsa first; that's why the siege is in place, after all. Second, he knows the elves won't leave here until they get their sacred writings back from him. And third, he knows we have to use the elven mages to help us raise the Heart of Julatsa. Hence, he's happy to perpetuate the siege. We force his hand, he'll come after us, mark my words.

'But when we make the run for Julatsa, he'll want to break us before we can establish a defence. He can't do that if he's two days behind us. If the TaiGethen are right, we may only be a couple of hours ahead of him when we start to move north.'

'That leaves the allied forces with a dilemma.' Blackthorne stretched out his legs.

'How so?' asked Darrick.

'We are not of one accord regarding our field positions to await Xetesk's expected attack,' said Izack.

'What's not to agree? We're in position aren't we?' Darrick let his shoulders slump. 'You'd better explain.'

'It's another reason the Baron has joined the Lysternan lines,' said Izack. 'We've been in discussions with Dordover's military command for days now and reached an impasse very early on. It all rests on where Xetesk will focus their breakout.'

'The north gate, presumably,' said The Unknown.

'Exactly. And defended by Dordovans, as is the west gate. And so far there has been little activity there by the way – no probing, no attempts to get scouts into the field, Cloaked or otherwise. The Dordovans feel their forces at the north gate are going to be hit hard if not routed when Xetesk tries to break for Julatsa and it's hard to disagree with them.'

'So what are they proposing?' asked Darrick, voice a little weary.

'That the siege is lifted and we make battlefield preparations north of Xetesk. Take them head-on, all of us,' said Izack.

Darrick was shaking his head. 'When?'

'General?' queried Izack, slipping easily back into his old place in the chain of command.

'When are they planning to start dismantling their camps and shifting their forces to wherever this mythical battlefield is? And, might I add, I can think of few places where we could use our possibly – and I repeat, possibly – superior numbers to our advantage.'

Izack shifted on his seat. 'Well, as soon as we apprise them that the elves are going in to raid.'

'Gods burning, they are more stupid than I thought,' said Darrick.

'But they could be slaughtered,' said Izack.

'So what?' snapped Darrick. 'This is a war. Sacrifices have to be made for the greater good. We cannot risk Julatsa's demise. If we lose them, balance is lost forever. Don't they understand that?'

'They understand they are in the front line,' said Blackthorne. 'They are just men.'

'In war, no one is just a man,' said Darrick. 'He can be greater than his dreams or another passive victim of the conflict.' The Unknown felt a slap on his arm. 'You understand.'

'Yes I do,' said The Unknown. 'But we are no longer dealing with soldiers here. Or not just soldiers.'

'I appreciate that.'

'Do you, Darrick?' The Unknown raised his eyebrows. 'I don't think you do. Many of the men out there have had their spades, rakes and brushes taken from them and swords thrust in their hands. They aren't soldiers. They will fight but they will fear. They aren't like us. We are born to fight. These men will bake your bread tomorrow. Do you see?'

'I see they are defending their freedom.'

'But understand they see it through different eyes than ours,' said Blackthorne. 'Heap responsibility on them as high as you like but one man in every two facing both HellFire and Protectors outside that north gate was not a soldier even a season ago.'

Darrick was silent for a while. Beneath his lank curls, his face creased while he fought to get his thoughts into order. It was clear he was struggling.

'It makes no difference,' he said. 'They have a role to fulfil. And that role is stopping Xetesk marching an army north for as long as they can. To the last man if they have to. And before you break in, there are two factors here.

'Firstly, I can't believe the Dordovan command believes it

has a better chance of marshalling its bakers' boys out in the open field in a battle line a mile long than it does here – with or without Lysternan assistance.

'Second, the moment they pull back from the walls, they announce their intentions good and loud to Xetesk. They hand the Dark College the initiative and sentence all of us inside at the time to death – let's not fool ourselves. Dystran is clever and well advised. He'll know what we're attempting and all attempt at secrecy will be lost.

'And remember, when the soldiers pull back, they ease pressure at two gates, allowing reinforcement of the others, probable resultant victories east and south, and therefore a lessening of our strength.'

'Assuming we don't pull back with them,' said Blackthorne.

Darrick ignored him, standing and pacing.

'What are they thinking of? Keeping Dystran's forces split is the only way. The consequences of defeat in open field are staggering. He would march unopposed all the way to Julatsa. And that would be just the start.'

'They are thinking of self-preservation,' said Blackthorne gently.

'By abandoning their most defensible positions? By dismantling siege coordination? They are panicking. If it were Lystern, we would stand and face them, outnumbered or not.'

'But it isn't Lystern,' said Blackthorne. 'And that is the point.'

'I should talk to them,' said Darrick. 'They have to see sense.'

'Sit down, Ry,' said The Unknown. 'You're under sentence of death, remember?'

Darrick paused in his pacing. 'But there's—'

'No,' said The Unknown. 'You are not the man to negotiate. You're Raven now. Sit down.'

Darrick sat reluctantly, unused to taking orders but unwilling to challenge The Unknown's authority.

'We're trying the same arguments,' said Izack. 'All they can see is their north gate forces being overrun and Xetesk still having clear run north.'

'What can be done?' asked Blackthorne. 'This is no longer purely a military decision. Politics is involved and relative strengths of surviving college forces. No college will leave themselves open to future attack at their own gates. Nor should they.'

'I know, I know,' said Darrick, waving a hand in a resigned gesture. 'Remember when we were all together against the Wesmen? That's the template and it kept us alive. Right.'

Darrick lapsed into thought. Around him, the triumvirate of senior Balaian warriors watched on in silence. He wasn't long in reaching a conclusion.

'All we can do is appease the Dordovans. What we can't do is let Xetesk know we're anticipating a breakout – and that's what a reformation to the north will do. It will also leave them with no doubt in their minds. They will attack and hope to end it there and then. Effectively win the war for Balaia at a stroke.

'Here's what I suggest. And it's a risk worth taking. We strip all the reserves from the south and east gates and move them north, leaving just a skeleton Lysternan fighting force here, supported by Baron Blackthorne's men and the Al-Arynaar now they've had a day's rest. We can do that quietly and over the course of the night. Izack, you know how it's done so I won't lecture.

'Baron, I think it's down to you to talk to the Dordovan command and make our case. They will respect you and, most importantly, if you can take an idea of numbers to them, it'll mean that Lystern and Dordover are truly standing together to counter Xetesk. You have to make it stick, my Lord.'

Blackthorne smiled. 'I can be very persuasive.'

'We're all counting on it,' said Darrick. 'Meanwhile, the sooner we can get in and get out of Xetesk, the more chance we have. I suggest we don't waste time.'

'No doubt the TaiGethen will agree with you. Right, are we all set and clear?' The Unknown looked around the fire, saw the nods in response. 'Baron, Izack, do the best you can. Darrick, let's go.'

The quartet stood up and shook hands, wishing each other luck and strength. The Unknown walked over to the Raven, sitting together at the edge of the firelight. All had been watching and listening intently.

Hirad stood up as he approached and strapped his sword belt around his waist. The talking, the resting, the frustrating watch of the day's battle was done.

'Our turn now,' he said.

The Unknown nodded. He'd felt like a caged animal all day, anxious to get over the walls but knowing he had to wait his time to begin the process of protecting his family, hundreds of miles to the south across the Southern Ocean.

'Everyone's clear about everything, aren't they,' he said.

'We could be little else,' said Denser. 'But however tight our plan, I can't stress enough how dangerous the college will be. Dystran is not stupid. The Protectors may all be outside but he'll have considerable defence in there.'

The raiding party was gathering as dusk gave way to night. The TaiGethen had been resting and praying all day. Four cells of the elite elven warriors would be taking part, along with Rebraal and six Al-Arynaar mages to supply shield and offensive support. ClawBound pairs were approaching the city to assess the strength on the walls, using the cloud cover that had prematurely darkened the sky. They would direct the elven warriors where to scale the walls and provide what diversion was needed.

'There's something else,' said Denser. 'Though I may be speaking to the deaf in the case of the TaiGethen. And that is that we aren't looking to destroy Xetesk and its mages tonight. We need them in the future if there is to be any balance.'

'I'm not running in there just circling my fists,' said Hirad. 'It was bad enough in Lystern.'

'That's not what I'm saying,' said Denser. 'And I will spare no one who threatens our lives. Just nothing indiscriminate, that's all I ask. Xetesk is still my college.'

'A college that would see you dead in a heartbeat,' said The Unknown Warrior. 'As they would all of us.' His face was grim in the firelight. 'Don't expect mercy from me.'

The big man checked the edges of his long sword and daggers yet again, walked slowly to Thraun and Erienne while he rebound the weapons in their sheaths. 'Erienne? You're quiet. Tell me.'

'I'm scared,' she said, her eyes confirming it.

'So you should be,' said The Unknown. 'We're about to break into the Dark College.'

'No, it's not that . . . well, it is but that fear I can deal with. It's what's inside me. Every day I have to fight to stop it dominating me and it's tiring. Consuming. Because one day I might fail.'

'But the Al-Drechar help, don't they?'

'Without them, the power would swamp me,' admitted Erienne. 'But they're so weak. Only one can help me block the One's force while the other rests. What if one of them dies. Or both?' She shuddered.

The Unknown frowned. 'But it will ease, won't it?'

'It gets harder and harder to believe that,' said Erienne. 'Right now, the One is a barely contained power in an uneducated mind and body. I have so much to learn. Dordover awakened the One prematurely in my daughter and all of us may still pay the price of that stupidity. If the Al-Drechar can't teach me how to restrain the One on my own before they die, I dread to think of the consequences.'

'Shouldn't you be with them, then? The Al-Drechar, I mean.'

A smile touched Erienne's lips. 'And be away from the only people who keep me believing there's an end to it? Look, Unknown, the Al-Drechar do what they can before I fall asleep, before I get up, and they talk to me in my dreams. It's enough. It'll have to be. Anyway, The Raven never work apart.'

'Music to my ears,' said Hirad from across the fire. 'Glad someone listens to me.'

'We rarely have a choice,' said Denser. 'That voice could knock holes in solid rock.'

Erienne put a hand on The Unknown's arm.

'I'll be all right,' she said. 'I can suppress the One and cast Dordovan magic. I won't let us down.'

'I never doubted you would,' said the Unknown.

'They will have watched,' said Thraun abruptly. 'They will know we're coming.'

'Not the Raven, the elves maybe,' said Hirad. 'We've thought of that.'

'No.' Thraun growled. 'Beware.'

Around the periphery, the TaiGethen were waiting for them. Two figures moved into the firelight.

'Are you ready?' asked Rebraal. 'We need to leave as soon as we can. The cloud cover is breaking to the south already.'

'You are sure you must come?' Auum had been unconvinced of The Raven's participation all day. Despite his rather grudging respect for them, he hadn't changed his opinion that they would be a liability, particularly in climbing the walls.

'Yes,' said The Unknown. 'With us, you are stronger.'

'And we have business to attend to inside,' said Hirad.

Denser chuckled. 'A couple of trifling matters, that's all.'

Darrick cleared his throat. 'It's not a laughing matter.'

'Ilkar wouldn't have agreed with you,' said Hirad.

'No,' said Darrick. He smiled quickly, embarrassed.

'Come on Raven, time to go,' said The Unknown.

The Raven moved to join the elven raiding party. Hirad paused by Blackthorne.

'Glad you dropped by, Baron.'

'This conflict threatens us all now, Hirad,' he said, eyebrows casting his eyes into deep shadow. 'There is no strength in neutrality. Not any more. Any of us strong enough must fight to stop Xetesk achieving dominion.'

'Remember there is more than one side fighting Xetesk,' said Hirad.

'I'll continue to forgo the considerable bounty on your head if that's what you mean.'

The two old friends clasped arms.

'Be lucky,' said Hirad.

'Be careful,' responded Blackthorne.

'Hirad, move it.' The Unknown's voice came from the gloom.

'Duty calls.'

Hirad trotted out of the camp. Ahead of him, the TaiGethen had broken into their cells of three. All but Auum's cell were disappearing fast into the night, making no sound, leaving no clue as to where they had just been. Hirad couldn't help but be impressed by their grace and speed. And when he turned to Auum, Duele and Evunn, he caught in their eyes exactly why they were so extraordinary, even among the ranks of exceptional elven hunter warriors like Rebraal.

From their black-and-green painted faces burned belief and determination, mixed with supreme confidence. Their faith in their Gods and in their own abilities precluded the notion of failure. And tonight, the Al-Arynaar and the Raven were similarly masked, all pale flesh covered in dark paint. But there the similarity ended.

'Your weapons are secure?' asked Auum, his accent thick, his command of the language uncertain.

'Nothing will move,' said Hirad. 'We'll be as quiet as you.'

A smile flickered on Auum's face. 'Do as we do. No talk until we are inside the city.'

He turned and set off at an easy trot, Duele and Evunn his shadows, The Raven following in their wake.

Chapter 13

They had travelled for around two hours, hidden in low brush and scrub and always at least half a mile from the walls of Xetesk. Hirad had kept up an easy stride. Being neither as fit nor as fleet as the TaiGethen he had accepted that he, like the rest of the Raven, would fall slowly but steadily behind.

Periodically, one of Auum's Tai cell would appear to direct them or run with them. Their faces would betray nothing but Hirad could guess what they were thinking just the same. He smiled to himself. It was true, The Raven weren't used to running any distance. But they had other strengths and he was determined to make them very apparent.

Now, they were facing the first major risk to the enterprise. Underneath the blanket of heavy cloud, which had just disgorged one heavy shower out of an almost constant mist of fine rain, they sat looking out at the four-hundred-yard wide stretch of open ground that ringed the walls of the Dark College. They had travelled slowly and quietly into the edge of the rough scrub and now all that kept them from a mage with augmented sight was patchy thigh-high grass and the night itself.

A ClawBound panther padded into their circle and nuzzled Thraun before eyeing the rest of The Raven with something verging on contempt and moving to its partner, who squatted next to Rebraal and Auum. Animal and elf gazed deep into each other's eyes, their silent communication flowing between them. Hirad watched them intently, seeing nothing but the occasional flicker of their eyes. The ClawBound elf, the white half of his painted face unnaturally bright, turned his head to Rebraal and Auum only when he was ready.

Both warriors asked him questions, their elvish rapid and incomprehensible. Mostly, the ClawBound would reply with a nod, shake of the head or a hand gesture. Very occasionally, he would utter a single word, voice rough and unused to speech. And finally, he stood abruptly and led his panther away.

'So what's the verdict?' asked Hirad.

'There are more guards patrolling the walls than on previous nights,' said Rebraal. 'We will not get in without confronting some.'

'That's not good,' said The Unknown. 'We can't afford our cover blown until we're inside the college.'

'We don't see a choice,' said Rebraal. 'The TaiGethen will handle it. At least then we can ensure silence.'

Auum began to speak, lost his words and asked Rebraal a question which the leader of the Al-Arynaar translated.

'Denser, your entry point to the college. Does it involve travel near the walls?'

'It does not,' said Denser. 'I'll show you the best route when we get inside, just like I said. If we die getting in, at least you know where you're headed. Just as we agreed.'

Rebraal held up his hands. 'Auum just wanted to know. In that case, our entry into the city being discovered at some point before we reach the college may work in our favour.'

'You've lost me there,' said Erienne.

'No, he's right,' said Darrick. 'If they know we're inside the city but not yet in the college, they're bound to increase patrols on the streets and strengthen guards around the college walls. Only we aren't going in the front door and all those men will be outside.'

'To begin with, at least,' added Denser.

'Any advantage we can gain is good enough for me,' said Hirad. 'So what's the plan?'

'You wait here with me until the TaiGethen have cleared passage to the base of the walls,' said Rebraal. 'There'll be a diversion as well and we'll make a run. If you get seen and challenged it's down to you.'

'And what about you, Rebraal?' asked Hirad.

The elf shrugged. 'I'm Ilkar's brother. I owe it to him to help you get there unharmed.'

'Thank you.'

'Believe me, I'd rather not have to. You are putting your-selves in great danger and risking our mission.'

Hirad bridled but the Unknown spoke up quickly.

'We understand your feelings but we have to do this as much as you do. Those we love are at risk.'

Rebraal nodded. Next to him, Evunn and Duele had come to Auum's sides. The cell bowed their heads in prayer, acknowledged Rebraal with the briefest of hand contact and ran away into the dark towards the walls of Xetesk.

Hirad sighed. There wasn't even going to be anything to see. Right now, all he could do was wait.

Auum led his Tai into the thick stalks of the plains grass and dropped immediately to his haunches. Evunn was five yards to his right, Duele the same distance left. The rest of the Tai cells were spread in a loose arc with Auum as the centre point. All had the same brief. Reach the walls unseen, unheard. Once there they were temporarily safe; the outward slope of the walls ensured that. It had made climbing a little more tricky but nothing a TaiGethen elf couldn't deal with. About certain members of the Al-Arynaar and the Raven, Auum wasn't quite so sure.

While he wouldn't normally give chance any credence, Auum confessed to himself that they had been lucky thus far. Tonight was as perfect a night for the raid as they could have wished. Above, the cloud was deep, lowering and unbroken. The rain that fell light but steady added to the gloom and a breeze ruffled the grass around him, further masking his progress from watchful eyes on the walls.

He became still and listened to the sounds around him as he knew his Tai would be doing. He tuned into the low ambient noise that surrounded him; the rustle of the wind through the grass, the movement of animals within it, the buzz of night's insects. He concentrated on the movement of the grass itself, the waves that spread across it, their frequency and scale.

And then he began to move himself, matching his low crouched steps with the grass, and stopping as it stilled. All the time, his eyes never left the walls as they grew closer, rearing into the sky, bleak and tall. He could see the light from torches and lanterns hung on their parapets or carried by guards. Away to the left, one of the dozens of small guard towers that studded the circumference was lit up by braziers within, luminescence spreading out from the narrow arched windows and the open door, picking out the mist of rain.

The ClawBound had been very accurate in their summation of the extra presence on the walls. He could see lights moving at intervals more regularly than at any other time. There was no doubt that there would have to be an entire stretch cleared to allow them all enough time to lower themselves to the other side and get to the relative safety of the muster point which was an empty house crushed between a bakery and a small disused stable block.

Closing on the base of the walls, Auum slowed still further. His pin-sharp eyes could make out the features on the faces of the guards walking seventy feet above. He could hear snatches of conversation above the susurration of the grass all around his head. And he could smell the stone and the city beyond. It was a mix of age and smoke, cold and fire, life and death. Ahead of him, shapes moved against the dark grey stone. ClawBound. The panthers padded noiselessly up and down the base of the wall, their partners shifted minutely, noses sampling the air, eyes sweeping the grass, watching the TaiGethen approach.

Soon, Auum was standing with them. They had briefly acknowledged his presence. Two of three pairs had set off along the walls, one left, one right. The third remained, the panther now sitting, licking its paws, growling quietly in its throat. Evunn and Duele emerged from the grass.

'Climb,' said Auum. 'You know where the fastenings are.'

Duele moved immediately to the base of the wall. He took the coil of rope from his shoulder and tied one end to his belt. Pausing only to check his route, he began to climb.

Auum watched him go, seeing his sure movements make nonsense of the seemingly smooth surface of the wall. Age had forced small cracks in the stone cladding. Most were covered by moss but Duele's fingers found them all, digging in and holding firm. His feet did likewise, fine leather boots edging their way into tiny crevices. One toe was enough to give him purchase enough to push further up.

Of course it was a climb he'd made many times before but Auum enjoyed watching him. Tual, lord of the forest denizens, had blessed him with a skill few could match. Auum had never seen him so much as hesitate.

The coil of rope unwound steadily. Evunn dropped to his haunches and bound his own length to Duele's. It was the best they could do. The Balaian rope was coarse, thick and heavy.

Strong enough, but cumbersome. Two lengths of something over thirty feet left enough play to loop it over the fixings they'd driven into the base of the overhang on previous visits and leave the bottom end at around head height. Simple for an elf to climb but Auum wondered, not for the first time, how the humans would fare.

Above him, Duele clung to the walls like a lizard on the underside of a branch. He was at the steepest angle of the overhang now, one move from the nearest hook that they'd had fashioned by Lystern's battlefield smiths. He said a quick prayer to Yniss to keep Duele safe. He need not have worried. Duele untied the rope from his belt with one hand, swung deftly out to the fixing, looped the prepared rope end over the hook in the same motion and lowered himself easily to the ground.

'Well done,' said Auum. 'We'll use three ascent points to-night. Check your weapons again now. You won't get another chance.'

The Tai tested blade edges, bowstring tension, arrow feathers and jaqrui throwing crescents, ensuring the whisper blades were foremost. Every heartbeat, more TaiGethen appeared from the grass, emerging as if from underground tunnels, the movement in the open was so slight.

Duele and Evunn took ropes from four Tais, Evunn binding the lengths, Duele attaching ends to his belt. Swiftly, he climbed the first rope, hand over hand, his movements strong and smooth. A few feet below the fastening, he stopped. Locking his feet on to the rope from which he was hanging, he took the free end of another rope from his belt and leant out at arm's length, balanced like a dancer. Below him, Evunn began to swing the rope like a pendulum. In total control, Duele swung closer and closer to the next hook, looping the rope end over on the fourth pass and switching ropes to repeat the process. He finished on the furthest right of the three ascent points and hung there, waiting.

Auum turned to the assembled Tai cells clustered under the overhang out of sight of any Xeteskian guard.

'Climb in Tai order,' he said. 'Wait for those above you to clear the rope and only complete your climb when you are cleared from above. You know your moves. The walkway will be secured left and right before we begin our descent to the muster point. Tonight, we go to reclaim the Aryn Hiil.

Tonight the wrongs that have been done to us will be avenged. May Yniss keep you safe, Tual guide your hands and Shorth take your enemies quickly.

'Tais, we move.'

Auum swarmed up the centre rope, Evunn to his left. From the hooks, it was an arm's stretch to the edge of the overhang. The architects had indulged themselves with a narrow ridge and simple carvings which rested below the crenellations. They were a great help.

Auum led the way, pushing off from the wall and establishing a finger grip on the stone ridge. He let go the other hand and hung for a heartbeat over the seventy-foot drop before swinging to double his grip and immediately hauling his body upwards. He reached up and grabbed a carved motif with one hand, one foot now on the ridge. His other foot joined it and he straightened, hugging the wall tight, waiting for Duele and Evunn to join him. Looking right, he saw Duele had beaten him to it. He smiled.

And now it began.

Not six feet from him, Xeteskian guards walked by, their voices soft, their boots echoing off the stone walkway. Between them and the TaiGethen was a last pull up onto the battlements, a slide across the outer wall, four feet thick, and a drop down to the parapet.

Auum could not deny he was tempted. Surprise alone would probably be enough. But he was a born rainforest hunter and instead employed one virtue that above all others kept him alive and ensured his success. Patience.

As though hanging from strangler vines high above the forest floor, the Tai waited. Each prayed to Yniss, each to Gyal, to keep the rain falling and the cloud dark. And each counted the patrols as they passed. The density of footsteps, the distance between them, and their direction.

Experience told them that the walls were sectioned for patrol between guard posts but tonight there was much increased activity. Whereas before they had had enough time to cross the walls and lower themselves down the other side between patrols, tonight, Auum counted three on their section alone. Two each of two men, one of three. And with the distance between the guard posts only a little over two hundred yards, their attack would have to be without error. So be it.

The Tai were ready. A patrol of two walked by, left to right. Auum counted thirty in his head and moved on to the top of the wall between two battlements. Evunn was beside him and both elves crouched hidden between two battlements, invisible from both sides of the walkway.

The second two-man patrol approached from the opposite direction. Auum could hear them talking. They paused to look out over the darkened land. Same place as before. They walked on, strides out of step, passing the two TaiGethen.

Now the shadows moved. Auum and Evunn dropped to the walkway, took a single running stride and grabbed their victims. One hand went over the mouth, the other clamped to the side of the head. They pulled back hard, heads snapped round, necks cracked and bodies fell limp.

They dragged the corpses back to the wall, boots dragging on the stone. Auum listened hard. No alarm. Not yet. Behind them, the two-man patrol walked on unconcerned, while ahead, the three-man patrol continued on towards their guard post and the end of their section. Along the well-lit walkway, he could see they had just a few yards to go. This was going to be close.

Duele waited for them on the sloping wall, grabbing the collars of both dead men while Auum and Evunn leapt up beside him. They arranged the bodies as best they could in the moments available, torsos leaning on the wall, legs straight and arms laid on the wall, hoping to project the illusion of two men looking out into the night. While Auum and Evunn hung onto the corpses, Duele unslung and nocked his bow.

The wait was long but it was always so when the trap was baited. They heard the voices before the footsteps. Auum could make out the odd word but the tone was jocular, at least to begin with. The urgency came when the dead men failed to reply or to make any move.

An order was barked. Pace increased and angry words were exchanged among the patrol. They were scant paces away. Duele tensed his bow. Auum and Evunn readied themselves, knives in their hands.

A hand clamped on the shoulder of Auum's dead man. The TaiGethen leader blurred, swinging round the battlement and plunging his blade into the throat of the guard in front of him, bearing the man down and out of line of sight. Evunn leapt too, knife catching the torchlight as it whipped home. Duele stood and fired, his arrow taking the third guard through the mouth. There was the chink of metal on stone as he fell.

Immediately, Auum and Evunn took off after the last patrol. Still oblivious, the wind over the wall and their own words masking what had happened behind them, they were about to make their turn expecting to see their comrades walking towards them. How different it would be. Auum unclasped his jaqrui pouch and plucked out a whisper blade. In his other hand, his knife dripped blood. The patrol paused at the open door to the guard post, taking a cursory glimpse inside before turning.

Auum's jaqrui flew, cutting through the night air, chopping over the smoke from a bracketed torch, the sound of its passage sibilant and menacing. Simultaneously, Duele threw his knife, the blade twirling end over end.

Fifteen yards away, the guards only had time to raise their hands in defence. Duele's knife flew true, striking his target in the chest, piercing his loose-tied leather armour. He grunted and stumbled forwards. Beside him, his companion lost three gloved fingers to the jaqrui which chopped into his cheek.

For an instant, both were silent, disbelieving eyes locking with their assailants who were coming on at frightening speed. The fingerless man began to emit an agonised wail, the sound choked with blood and fear. The other made a grab for his sword. Duele drop-kicked him in the chest, driving the knife through his back. Auum cut off the wail with a blow to the throat and a hand clamped hard over the enemy's mouth.

Silence again. Auum waited over the bodies, straining for any sign that they had been heard. At a nod, Duele edged to the guard post and looked inside. He closed the door and stood guard, shadowed from any casual glance up from the streets.

Auum trotted back down the walkway, waving Evunn to the other guard post. Only now did he consider the city. The walkway was perhaps five feet wide with a sheer unprotected drop to the black streets and buildings below. Across the city only watch fires and a few house lanterns burned against the darkness but he could easily make out the shapes of Xetesk's college towers against the clouded backdrop.

The stench of the city was much stronger here and would be worse once they'd descended to the muster point, which had been chosen for its relative lack of surrounding population, sleeping or otherwise. The cloying odours of packed humanity mixed with the reek of fires, sewers and foundries. It was an affront. Only by turning away could Auum smell the open ground and distant trees. How these people could live this way was beyond him.

He crouched for a while at the edge of the parapet. Nothing untoward could be heard. He rose and ran to the access point on the wall. Ahead of him, Evunn had reached the other guard post. Again, the door was closed and his Tai stood sentinel. Auum tapped his knife on the stone and waited for the next Tai cell to join him on the walkway. Each elf carried a coil of rope.

'Marack to the ropes; Ataan, put the bodies over the wall; Uvoll, I need these lights doused. Work fast.'

The cell split. Auum knew darkening the wall section would eventually draw attention but he couldn't risk being seen from the streets now. Soon, the parapet would be full of elves. He tapped the wall again. The next cell joined him.

'Ropes,' he said. 'Quickly.'

A third strike and the fourth cell made the walls.

'Down to the streets. Secure the muster point.'

Auum turned back to the open ground and struck the wall a fourth time. The second stage was about to commence.

Chapter 14

'Thank you,' said Tessaya, raising his goblet high and draining it off in one long gulp, spilling wine from the sides of his mouth.

Beside him, Riasu laughed, refilled both their cups and the two Wesmen lords clashed them together before draining them again.

From the door of his tent, Tessaya watched the flames climbing high into the clear night sky. He could smell the ash and the burned flesh on the breeze. He could hear the terrified shouts for help and the screams of pain. And he could see burning men stumble outside their flaming tomb to be cut down by his warriors before they had gone two paces.

He felt nothing for those he had ordered killed. Not for the men he had never met, nor their puffed-up and astoundingly foolish leader, Devun. A man who had been so happy to tell everything he knew and make himself utterly dispensable.

'What a treasure to have fallen into our laps,' said Tessaya. 'Thank you Devun, and thank you Lord Riasu for bringing him to me.'

He turned and strode back into his tent, an arm around Riasu's shoulders.

'Can we do it?' he asked, dropping into one of the plush sofas. 'Do we have the strength of arms and do we have the will?'

Riasu remained standing. 'That we have the will is certain. It is in our blood to conquer. And the war council will sit here tomorrow. Then you will know if we have the strength.'

'I would know more than dead Black Wings or the Spirits can tell me,' said Tessaya. 'Send scouts to Xetesk. Tell them to count everyone they see. Tell them to memorise the state of the siege. And, Riasu, tell them to be careful.'

Out beyond the plains grass that surrounded Xetesk, The Raven waited. Despite his convictions, Denser was experiencing mixed feelings. Sneaking into his home city and the college that had nurtured his talent so expertly was making him uncomfortable. Beside him, Hirad was itching to get going. The barbarian could barely contain his energy. It was a good sign. Inside, they would need a Hirad who was unstoppable and who would drag all of them beyond their limits. Never would the heartbeat of The Raven be needed more.

Erienne leaned into him.

'Gets to you, doesn't it?' she said softly, one hand squeezing his knee.

'Eh?'

'Remember how we all broke into Dordover a few years back?'

Denser smiled. They had been after one of the Dawnthief catalysts and had only just escaped with their lives. Erienne had risked everything.

'This is a different situation,' he said.

'Not really. The feelings are the same whether they are declared enemies or not, and whether we are stealing or reclaiming. Makes you feel a traitor, doesn't it?'

Denser nodded. 'Sort of.'

'Don't feel guilty about it, that's all I want to say,' said Erienne. 'It's only natural. I will forever love Dordover. It is the actions of a few people who have destroyed my loyalty but I have my memories and the hope the leadership will change for the better in the future. You're the same. You grew up under Styliann, Laryon and Nyer. Remember them, for all their faults, and try not to fix on a loyalty you feel you should have but can't recall.'

Denser looked into her eyes, saw the battle going on inside her and smiled.

He leaned forward and kissed her cheek, stroking her hair beneath the hood of her lightweight cloak. 'I love you.'

'What I understand is that you can't afford to think of any of those bastards in there as your people,' said Hirad.

'Your tenderness is overwhelming,' said Denser, turning his

attention to the barbarian. Hirad's eyes were bright and fierce, shining from the darkness surrounding them.

'They will feel none,' he said. 'And you are Raven. We are your people. You no longer belong to Xetesk and you can't afford to wonder why.'

'No, that's not it,' said Denser.

Hirad shrugged. 'Doesn't matter what the reason, if you hesitate once, you're dead and perhaps we all are. If you go in there with anything less than total belief, you won't come out. And I am not losing another mage. Understand?'

Denser chuckled, patted Hirad on the shoulder. 'You know I do. Don't worry about me.'

'I have to worry,' said Hirad. 'Like I've said before, it's my job.'

Near them all, Thraun stood up quite suddenly, staring towards the walls. Next to him, The Unknown and Darrick made to grab his arms to haul him down but he was too quick, taking a couple of paces out into the grass. He growled, sniffed at the air, crouched and turned.

'They talk,' he said.

'Who?' asked The Unknown.

'Listen.'

It was ahead of them towards the walls but left and right, not where the TaiGethen and Al-Arynaar mages were clustered. It was a sound they had all heard before but in the depths of the Calaian rainforest. Growing in volume, everything from low-throated growls to high-pitched yowls and whines, the Claw-Bound panthers let rip, bringing an alien resonance to the heartland of Balaia.

It seemed to echo from the clouds themselves, reverberate through the brush and bounce from the walls of the city. It was at once beautiful and terrifying, carrying with it the mournful quality of lands lost and the taste of great age and reverence. It sent a shiver through Denser's body and Erienne reflexively tightened her grip on his knee.

Hirad added a growl of his own. 'Didn't they think we were playing fair?' he demanded into the noise. 'So they thought they had to announce we were coming, or something? Make sure everyone was waiting for us once we got inside to make a fight of it? Gods burning, have they no idea of stealth?'

Rebraal appeared by his left side, speaking for them all to

hear. 'Inside the city, that sound is clawing at every door. Let me ask you, would you rush outside, sword in hand, or make sure the bolts were across and keys turned in every lock? And those few ClawBound are doing something for you right now. They are diverting every eye on the wall. Now run and don't stop until you can slap stone.'

Hirad chewed back his retort and stood. 'You heard him,' he said. 'Raven! Raven with me!'

The Raven ran in fighting formation, The Unknown at the head of the uneven chevron, Hirad and Darrick to his right, Thraun to his left with Erienne and Denser behind the warriors. Streaking away in front of them was Rebraal, the Al-Arynaar skipping through the thigh-high grass as if it barely covered his feet while The Raven struggled behind, forcing the sinewy stems aside as they came on.

For all it was an effort and he felt as if he were running headlong into the teeth of death, Denser felt exhilarated. The damp air was fresh and chill in his lungs, the sheen of rain on his forehead cooled him and the rush of the grass around him, the breeze in his ears and his friends charging on ahead lifted his heart. He would have shouted but for the folly that would have been.

Panting and out of breath, he made the relative safety of the walls. The last TaiGethen cell was climbing a trio of ropes that dropped from the overhang high above, and the only people left were Rebraal, the Al-Arynaar mages and The Raven themselves.

'Stealth,' said Rebraal. 'When you have learned what stealth means, Hirad Coldheart, then you can question how we do things. The tracks you have made through the grass could be followed by a blind man.'

The ClawBound communication was dying away to echoes on the wind. Denser looked back and saw the dark trails slashed in the grass.

'Hardly matters,' said Hirad. 'Your ClawBound saw to it that they know we are coming.'

'They already knew,' said Thraun, voice a hiss.

'You keep saying that,' said Hirad, his voice quieter now the panthers were silent. 'What do you mean?'

'They saw the battle,' said Thraun. 'They knew we would be coming.'

'He's right,' said Darrick. 'If their commander's anything like a tactician, he'll have seen the change in plans today. Nothing we could do about it. We had to test them. But the mere fact of more guards on the walls tells us all we need to know.'

'Yeah, but they won't be expecting us. Only elves,' said Hirad.

'I'm counting on it,' said Denser.

The Raven looked up at the ropes disappearing into the deep shadow under the overhang. While they watched, the ropes stilled momentarily, signalling the Al-Arynaar to begin their ascent. Not hesitating, three elves hauled themselves up the ropes, making a nonsense of the effort, their lithe bodies ideally suited to the task.

Denser frowned, feeling his heart beat a little faster. Beside him, Erienne shuddered.

'Bloody hell,' she whispered.

'Now at the top, there's a slightly tricky move,' said Rebraal, as if describing a walk along a beach containing the odd slippery patch of rocks. 'You'll have to swing out to grip the decorative ridge then pull yourselves up. There are people waiting to help you so you should be all right.'

'Should,' said Erienne.

'Hmm,' said Denser. He breathed deeply. It did nothing to calm his nerves and the obvious option was already in his mind. 'Sure is a long way up.'

'And down,' muttered Erienne.

'Fair enough,' said The Unknown. 'Here's the order. We'll follow the last of the Al-Arynaar. Hirad, you go with Thraun and me. Darrick, you'll guard the base of the wall until we're clear while you two,' he turned to Denser and Erienne, 'are flying. We can't risk you.'

'You're saying you don't trust us to make the climb?' Denser bridled in spite of the relief he felt at The Unknown agreeing with his thoughts.

'I'm saying you aren't sure you can. Tell me if I'm wrong.'

Erienne shook her head. 'No, you're not.'

'Denser, once you've carried Erienne, bring up Darrick. He should be light enough, unlike the rest of us.'

'I can climb,' said Darrick.

'That's not the point,' said The Unknown. 'We can't spare the time.'

'Whatever you say.'

Denser felt a strong hand clamp around his shoulder.

'Never mind, Denser,' said Hirad. 'We can't all have the muscle and guts.'

'Fuck off.'

Hirad chuckled.

'I'm letting you fall if you slip, Coldheart,' added Denser.

'More pull-ups,' said Hirad. 'Build your upper body and arms a little.'

'In fact, I'm going to cut the rope above you.'

'Just leave him,' said Erienne. 'Don't let him get under your skin.'

'He's already there. Has been for years.'

Denser tuned himself to the Xeteskian mana spectrum, pausing to see the multiple points of focus all over the city, from healings to wards to Communion. One more casting wasn't going to be noticed. He drew in the simple shape for Shadow-Wings. The basic planar structure, feathered along one edge, was complete in moments.

'Ready?'

Erienne wrapped her arms around his neck, he swept up her legs and they rose up the wall. Denser found his heart hammering in his chest. He kept looking up and could see elves on the ropes, swinging out into nowhere to grab the narrow ridge. Not for the first time, he was glad to have alternative means at his disposal.

He flew slowly, breasting the battlements at snail's pace. TaiGethen were waiting there. Erienne unlocked her arms and was helped onto the wall. Denser descended again to watch The Raven climb.

He found them a little under halfway up. They were all very strong men. Thraun looked like he was born to it, Hirad's teeth were bared as he surged up, hand over hand, and The Unknown, typically organised, used his feet as a brake on the rope while his hands found new grips.

Denser smiled to himself and twitched his position to fly next to the barbarian.

'All right, muscleman?'

Hirad glared at him. He was forty feet from the ground now and the exertion was beginning to show.

'Absolutely fine,' said Hirad between gasps for air.

'I had every confidence.'

'I know,' Hirad grinned. 'I'm me.'

'Yes you are,' muttered Denser. 'The Gods save us all.'

There were no alarms. Denser plucked Darrick from his unnecessary guard duty and deposited him on the wall next to Erienne before watching his friends swing out to the ledge, elven hands helping them as they pulled themselves up.

He landed next to The Raven on the walkway. It was darkened and almost empty of elves. Auum and Rebraal were seeing the last of the Al-Arynaar down the ropes to the muster point. The TaiGethen leader looked over to them and nodded.

'Quickly,' he said. 'There is an alarm further along the wall.'

Denser took one look at the panorama of his city. A place he had loved, still loved, but now he had to class it as an enemy. He shook his head, picked up Erienne and stepped over the wall, dropping steadily. Slowly, the sights were lost to him. The market square, dark and silent; the Park of Remembrance, lawns now surely turned over to crops or grazed by livestock; the iron foundry, still belching smoke and flame; the grain stores, huge and solid and the reason Xetesk could survive famine and now siege. And finally, the seven towers of the college, their target for the night. They could not have chosen one more difficult.

At the base of the ropes, Rebraal was waiting with a TaiGethen elf. Denser was directed to the muster point, floating quietly past the bakery, cold and lifeless, a victim of the war.

Inside the empty house, the raiding party gathered. Denser dismissed his Wings and set Erienne down, moving slowly while his sight adjusted, the assembled elves resolving gradually from the gloom. Twelve TaiGethen warriors, six Al-Arynaar mages, Rebraal and The Raven. About to take on the Dark College.

'Dear Gods preserve us,' he whispered.

'What was that?' Erienne's voice too was barely audible.

'Sorry, love,' he said. 'I'm just imagining what we could face in there.'

If anything, the quiet in the house deepened still further as Auum walked in. He spoke briefly with Rebraal, translating for The Raven.

'One final time, here is what we know from our nights of scouting. The Protectors are outside the gates. Most of the college and city forces are stationed outside the walls of the college. We expect those walls to be heavily defended, leaving little sword strength but much mage strength on the ground. Secrecy for the maximum time is therefore critical.

'But, my brothers and sisters, never forget that we face a powerful adversary. Keep within the Al-Arynaar shield whenever you can. Let Tual guide your senses. We know what we must do and what we must find. Keep your Tais close. This is a jungle like our own; it will show you no mercy.'

While Auum led the prayers before battle, The Raven gathered together.

'Think we'll die in there?' asked Darrick.

'If we pretend we are up against anything less than we are, I think there's every chance.' said Denser. 'And if the Julatsan mana flow fails again while we're inside, the TaiGethen will be defenceless.'

'Not sure you can ever call them defenceless,' said Hirad.

'You know what I mean.'

Around the house, the elven prayers finished. Denser looked into Auum's eyes and nodded.

'You know where to go,' he said.

The TaiGethen led them out into the Xeteskian night.

Chapter 15

Denser thought he knew his city like the proverbial back of his hand. Gods falling, but the walls had prevented much new building for centuries. But he was shown alleys he'd never seen before, walkways he'd thought too narrow to travel, and ways across the city he hadn't known existed.

The playhouse had tunnels beneath it. There was a network of accessways built around the edge of the central market. The north grain store had an outer skin providing gap enough to inch along. And the fact that the city was under curfew proved a gift because the TaiGethen were *so* quiet. Patrols might have littered the streets but the sound of their passage was like a klaxon from three streets' distance.

It was eerie, Denser decided. Not real somehow. Xetesk was dying. Slowly, but it was dying. Yet beneath the apparent quiet acceptance of that fate, there would be barely suppressed energy. Neither the college nor the city would go down without a fight. The question was, when would that energy erupt?

The raiding party moved carefully, placing quietness above speed. There had been no further alarm from the walls and they could only conclude that the shouts they had heard pertained to something other than their incursion. That was not a state that would last very long. Soon, the guard would change, or someone would open the doors of the guard towers and find the darkness, the blood on the stone, and the disappearance of seven men. If they were lucky, that discovery would not be made until they were inside the college itself.

Denser glanced round at The Raven while they travelled, seeing care and determination on every face and in every step. They studied the ground before every pace, moving in the footfalls of the TaiGethen wherever they could. They walked across mud and weeds rather than stone and gravel, hugged the shadows of every alley they travelled and held their collective breath when forced to cross a major thoroughfare. Not even the TaiGethen had a way around every obstacle.

They almost made it undiscovered too. Auum had led the raiding party to the warehousing that bordered the artisans' quarter he knew so well. Despite himself, he'd been impressed with The Raven's ability to move silently. Moving up the alley where they'd killed the guards the night before, he saw that their bodies had gone, though the thieves' corpses remained.

'They know we were here,' he said to Duele at his shoulder.

'It was inevitable,' said Duele.

'Unfortunate, nevertheless. Pass the word.'

He crept up to the mouth of the alley and looked over at the college. The effect of the discovery of the guards' bodies was clear. On the cobblestones in front of the college, patrols marched with purpose. Auum watched them long enough to know that the density of men meant that one patrol could always see their comrades ahead. It was the same up on the walls themselves. Lanterns and torches lit the entire length in front of him. Guards moved in pairs, lookouts stared out into the city and archers stood by them, ready and waiting.

He was beginning to back away when the alarm went up. Light bloomed away to the south as a warning fire was lit. Men started running along the walls. Shouts rang around the college. The south gates swung open and a detachment of soldiers trotted out and disappeared into the streets ahead of them. On the cobblestones, the patrols ceased their circular walks and fanned out, heading across the apron, some directly for them.

Auum fell back faster, seeing shapes flitting into the sky from inside the college. Like large birds but without the grace. His eyes tracked them as they flew. Wings like bats, heads like bald monkeys, their calls like diabolical laughter mixed with broken speech. He shivered, turned and trotted back to where the raiding party were waiting.

'They are coming,' he said, hearing Rebraal translate for The Raven. 'We must move. Denser will lead us now.'

There was no debate. Denser, surrounded by his friends, turned and moved quickly but quietly away along the back of the warehouse. Auum signalled Evunn and Duele to hang back, keep any guards from their backs. At the far edge of the squat, low building, Denser paused and The Unknown Warrior checked left and right before leading them across a narrow path and into the passage the other side, along between another two warehouses. The sounds of alarm and search rang out to their left, closing but not too fast.

The second set of warehouses was different in character. Made of stone and slate rather than wood, they soared three times as high and had identical heavy, iron-bound wooden sliding gates facing each other. Denser stopped at a low, flat-roofed building just beyond, attached to the warehouse facing the college walls. Beyond it, the landscape of the district changed, becoming less uniform, studded with chimneyed workshops, dwellings and fenced yards.

Auum breasted through the TaiGethen for a closer look. Denser was standing square in front of a padlocked door set into a featureless wall.

'This is it,' he was saying. Auum looked to Rebraal for confirmation he had understood. 'Give me room. If this goes off, I don't want anyone hurt.'

At a gesture from Rebraal, the TaiGethen and Al-Arynaar fell back a few paces.

'Marack,' said Auum, getting the attention of a cell leader. She was a Tai that Auum respected as much for her strength of mind as her warrior's abilities. Her original cell had been taken from her by the Elfsorrow but still she kept faith with the Gods and her new cell already admired and trusted her. She was an example to them all. 'Take your cell, secure the next crossway. Porrak, your cell behind us. Strengthen mine. Wait for my call. If you have to kill, kill silently.'

He focused his attention on Denser and watched the mage at work, attempting to circumvent what he assumed were magical traps of some kind. He could hear Erienne talking to him and edged closer to Rebraal who began translating.

'It's not a trap,' said Denser. 'The entire door is an illusion and a particularly good one at that. You can touch the padlock if you like but it isn't actually there. It's a piece of shaped rock fused into a sheet of solid metal. Even a good thief can't pick stone. The locks are all set into the door. There are three of them and all are operated by magic. I need to work out if they have changed since I was apprised of their key constructs.'

'Why isn't the illusion just one of flat wall?' asked Erienne.

'Because it has to reflect all the other workshop entrances around here. The people who constructed it maintain this work on the basis that hiding a door in plain sight is part of the art of illusion. It's worked for years.'

'What happens if you don't divine the key constructs?'

'A very loud noise and my death,' replied Denser. 'You should stand aside.'

But none of The Raven moved. Auum smiled inwardly.

'Just describe what you're seeing,' said Erienne. 'I might be able to help you.'

Denser relaxed his body and reached out his hands towards the door, touching various parts of its surface. Auum looked hard for the break between reality and illusion but couldn't see it.

'The three locks engage a single WardLock casting that covers the entire doorframe. It's well maintained and skilfully cast. No chance of setting off the traps by accident which I would say was unusually thoughtful if it weren't for the fact that this entrance is meant to be a secret from almost everyone and to stay that way. Each lock has a different construct code linked to an explosive and alarm-ward combination.

'I have to form the three key constructs that temporarily block the lock and alarm mechanisms, so disengaging the WardLock.'

'And these are constructs you have been taught, are they?' asked The Unknown from behind Denser.

'Yes. There is no clue in the lock constructs, which are just flat squares of mana each about the size of my hand. Each square has a keyhole described in it, for aesthetic purposes, I assume, because the key constructs have to cover the entire lock to unlock it, and don't penetrate it as such. All very pretty.'

'So, can you sort it?' Hirad's whisper was gruff. 'Our elven friends are getting nervous about rapidly closing patrolmen and I'm getting old.'

'It'll take as long as it takes,' said Denser. 'I have to assume the key constructs are unchanged. And you have to hope so too or this'll be the briefest raid in the history of Xetesk. Now let me be. Erienne, there's nothing you can do for me except to stand away from any blast area. Please.'

Watching on, Auum felt the unusual desire to be able to see

what Denser was seeing. But he could watch the mage's intricate hand and finger movements as they teased mana into the shapes he wanted, the silent mouthing of words as commands augmented the structure formation, and the tiny beads of sweat on his brow as the effort gained momentum. That there was an element he could neither feel nor see that could affect them all so profoundly was a source of eternal discomfort to Auum. For him, it was an omission that Yniss had made when the world was created. He took it as a challenge to be overcome. To be quicker than cast magic. For the TaiGethen, it was the only way.

At the mating call of a motmot, faint and carried on the breeze, Auum turned. Evunn drew fingers across his eyes, pointed down an alley towards the college and held up three fingers.

'Get him to hurry.' Auum told Rebraal. 'We have company.'

He ran to his Tai. The search net was expanding. He could hear men to their left and right now, some carrying lights, some moving without. He edged his head around the corner of the warehouse and saw them coming. Two were soldiers, one a mage by the look of him.

'We don't want blood or noise near here. Not now,' whispered Auum. 'Why didn't you see them earlier?'

The patrol was only about twenty yards distant, approaching with exaggerated care and holding a lantern ahead of them.

'They came from a side path,' said Evunn. 'I am sorry.'

'You cannot know this place like them,' said Auum. 'Porrak, your Tai watch ahead. Bows ready. We will take the mage alive if we can.'

Porrak's cell unslung bows and took a few paces back, fading into the shadows to give Auum's trio room. A sense of déjà vu came over Auum, waiting while the glow from the lantern grew as it neared. The Tai were standing perfectly still in the lee of the warehouse. Auum would be happy if the patrol walked right past them but one glance and shout was all it would take to bring the might of Xetesk down on them.

The Xeteskian patrol were not talking. Auum could hear their steps, measured and deliberate, in time with each other. And while he listened, they slowed, as one, on closing to less than ten yards from the crossway. He frowned. This was not a conscript patrol. He hadn't been able to see much of them beyond vague dress; the lantern had obscured their faces. But there was no aura of anxiety, no whispered fear. These were experienced professionals. That they would walk past the alley without at least scanning down it as far as they could see was inconceivable.

Auum held up three fingers. He bent first the middle finger, then those left and right in order. Duele and Evunn knew their targets and he knew they would not wait to attack. The lantern light intensified, spilling into the alley. Auum waved Porrak's cell further back. He tensed his body, plucked his knife from his belt and reversed it in his hand.

The patrol was on them. He could hear the individuals' breathing. One caught a breath, sensing something out of place. They paused. One could be heard inching up the warehouse wall, the others presumably just behind him. The plan changed again. Auum held up a single finger and pointed at himself. Next he gestured Duele and Evunn to follow him in an arc into the passage. Finally, he closed his fist.

The Xeteskian slid along the wall. Auum waited, hands poised, ready to pounce. His being was centred. He could all but smell the rainforest and every sound came to him as clear as cicadas in the evening. His enemy's leather armour making the barest scratching on the stone. The man's regular breathing, his boot tracing through stiff weed grass.

Three fingers of one gloved hand gripped the edge of the wall, first knuckle showing. Either a mistake or a calculated risk. Whatever, Auum ignored it, holding for the prize which came immediately after. A head began to emerge, eyes straining round, hair covered by a metal and leather helmet.

Auum wagged one finger. Duele and Evunn began to run. The TaiGethen leader took a half pace away from the wall and snapped out his right hand clamping onto the Xeteskian's face. Startled, the man dropped back but he couldn't break Auum's grip. The elf's left hand whipped round, the dagger hilt in his fist hammering into the soldier's temple. He sagged, Auum pulling him forward into his chest.

Duele and Evunn were shades across the lantern light, movement hard to track against the blank walls. Duele hit the mage carrying the lantern. He'd backed away reflexively before gathering himself to try and cast but he never stood a chance.

The elf clamped a hand over the lantern handle, jerked the mage off balance and cracked his right fist into his jaw. Evunn had no need of such restraint. He ducked under a flailing fist and jabbed straight-fingered into his enemy's throat, crushing the man's windpipe.

'Get these men away,' hissed Auum.

Porrak's cell ran to help and, two to a body, they trotted back to the raiding party. Denser was still working on the locks, Erienne in close attendance. He was looking calm and in control. Hirad and The Unknown Warrior were standing apart, ready to run to assist. The other elves hadn't moved a muscle. Auum hadn't expected them to.

'Well?' he demanded.

'Nearly there,' assured Rebraal.

'There'll be more. We need in now.'

Denser must have heard him.

'Got it,' he murmured.

There was no sound but the mage straightened and pushed the door open.

'In,' said Auum.

The Raven, led by Denser, moved in first. The Al-Arynaar followed them and finally the TaiGethen, Auum last, making sure all his people were safe. He pushed the door closed behind him, hearing the faint fizz and crackle as the WardLock reset. A LightGlobe was set to hover, illuminating a blank chamber about thirty feet on the longer side and fifteen on the shorter. A door was set into the far wall. The room was empty of any furnishings.

'Tell me again what this is.' Hirad was looking around him, nonplussed.

'Come on, Hirad, mages have not always been the most popular rulers in Xetesk,' said Denser. 'Boltholes were inevitable for the chosen few.'

'Yeah, but you were never in the Circle Seven. How did you find out about it?'

'I was the Dawnthief mage,' said Denser. 'It was felt I should be given the information. My mentors showed me the path and gave me the key constructs. I couldn't tell you if they sought the permission of the rest of the Circle.'

'And how would you get away from here?' asked The Unknown.

'Fly,' said Denser. 'In the event the college was surrounded and archers were positioned around the rooftops, the Circle could have disappeared into the artisans' quarter and away.'

'It's a coward's way out,' said Hirad. 'Fairly typical of Xetesk.'

'Who cares? It gets us in and no one will suspect we'll come this way because not even Dystran thinks The Raven are here, let alone that I'd know the combinations.'

'Good,' said The Unknown. 'Now what about them?'

He walked over to the Xeteskians, Denser following him. The two soldiers had been dumped to one side of the door, Auum having snapped the neck of the one he'd knocked cold. But the mage, under the watchful eyes of Duele and Evunn, was showing signs of coming round.

'Well, well, well,' said Denser. He knelt and shook the mage, slapping his cheeks. 'Wakey, wakey, Arnayl. You need to answer us some questions.'

Arnayl's eyes flickered open and a hand moved to rub his chin while he stretched his mouth. Middle-aged, his light hair was streaked with grey and his square face was lined, eyes red-rimmed. He blinked in the gentle light, frowned while taking in the faces of elves and men around him and started violently when he focused on Denser.

'What the f—'

'No time for that,' said Denser. 'There are things we must know.'

'Where am I?'

'Somewhere you never believed existed,' said Denser, smiling. 'Now, what's the current mage and college-guard strength inside the walls?'

'Find out,' said Arnayl. 'You'll get nothing from me.'

He tried to raise himself on his elbows but Denser shoved him back, his head cracking on the packed ground. He grunted.

'Let me remind you of your position.' Denser's tone hardened. 'There are more than twenty people in here. All of them would be happy to end your life. All of them have lost precious things because of Xetesk's actions and your life is forfeit, as is anyone's who stands in our way. Now I might be able to persuade them to let you live but you've got to help me out. Right now.'

'I will not betray my college,' said Arnayl. 'You cannot ask that of me.'

'The more we know, the fewer Xeteskians will die,' said Denser. 'But we are going in and we will get what we came for. You can help us save your fellow mages or you can die, knowing many will join you. Answer me.'

Arnayl stared back, closing his mouth deliberately. The sound of a sword being drawn echoed thinly in the small chamber. The point of that sword pressed against Arnayl's throat. Hirad spoke.

'Your people triggered Elfsorrow. You would have presided over genocide. Thousands died, including my friend Ilkar. Because of you—'

'I had nothing to do with that decision.'

'You are Xeteskian, sworn to your college. You are to blame.' The swordpoint drew blood. 'Don't think I won't kill you in cold blood.'

'Please.' Arnayl's voice was choked and the colour had drained from his face. He spread his palms in supplication.

'Tell Denser what he wants to know. And don't try to cast. You aren't quick enough to beat me.'

Arnayl swallowed and closed his eyes. 'I can't tell you anything. Surely you understand.'

'I understand,' said Hirad.

He drove the point of his blade through Arnayl's throat. Blood fountained into the air. The mage juddered and died. Denser shot upright, jumping away from the mess.

'Gods, Hirad, what are you doing?'

'He would have told us nothing,' said the barbarian, dragging his blade clear and wiping it on Arnayl's cloak.

Auum nodded. 'He is right.'

But there was something in Hirad's eyes that wasn't right. Like he'd lost his focus. Denser had seen it too. So had The Unknown.

'Hirad, what is it?' asked Denser.

Hirad was shaking. He fought to steady his arm to sheathe his sword and when he turned his face back, there were tears standing in his eyes.

'I could have saved him,' he said. 'And now all I can do is avenge him.'

'No one could have done that,' said The Unknown. 'Ilkar

said it himself. When he contracted Elfsorrow he was already dead.'

'No!' shouted Hirad. 'All that time we wasted. We let Yron escape into Xetesk and lost days. *Days.* And being here and listening to that bastard just makes it so real. I could have ridden after him. Gone round the Protectors and caught him, made him give us the thumb fragment. I stopped.' He turned away from them. 'I stopped. And he died.'

'It wasn't like that,' said Denser. 'You aren't counting right. Even supposing we'd caught Yron, Ilkar would still have caught the disease and died on the voyage.'

But Hirad was shaking his head. 'We could have made it to Calaius,' he said, voice dropping to a hoarse whisper. 'Back to the rainforest. We would have found a way.'

Rebraal walked over to him, the eyes of every elf and The Raven on him.

'We must all take some responsibility,' he said carefully. 'I could have stopped them at the temple but I didn't. The TaiGethen and ClawBound could have found him in the forest but they didn't, not soon enough. We can't go back and correct what has gone but we can shape the future, make Ilkar's death mean what it should – the start of the return to balance in magic. And for that we need the Aryn Hiil and our other writings. We need that strength to go to Julatsa with the confidence to succeed.

'Don't lose it in here. We need you.'

Hirad breathed deep. He managed the briefest of smiles in Rebraal's direction. 'I'm sorry.' He took them all in now. 'All of you. This is very difficult.'

'We all know what his friendship meant to you,' said Erienne. 'Do right by him and help us all get out of here alive.'

The barbarian nodded, a very definite gesture. He looked squarely at Auum.

'Let's go get your books,' he said.

Chapter 16

Dystran hadn't really slept at all. At best, a few hours' edgy rest, broken by those damned elven-controlled panthers. There was something about the noise they created. Unearthly, somehow, it drove shivers to the core of them all. Broke their dreams. They were the enemy's most potent psychological weapon though they didn't seem to realise it. Dystran would have have had them calling all night. As it was, the alarm, when it came in the early hours of the morning, was almost a relief.

He'd agreed the defence plan with Commander Chandyr on the city walls and Captain Suarav in the college guard during the previous day and so dressed unhurriedly before leaving his tower and descending the long spiral stairs, past his guards and disabled static alarms and blocks.

Myx was waiting at the base of the tower. The huge Protector, like fifteen of his brothers, was being used more for city-wide and battle communications than protection. Dystran knew the humiliation they felt but he had no time for guilt.

'News,' he demanded.

Myx fell into step next to him. 'The walls have been breached. There are enemies in the city.'

Dystran sighed. One failure already. 'How many?'

'It is impossible to say.'

'Oh, right,' Dystran smiled. 'You're going to tell me that no one saw anyone, I suppose.'

'Correct, my Lord.'

Dystran stopped. Make that two failures. 'I was joking.'

'Yes,' agreed Myx, uncertain how to respond.

'You're telling me that no Xeteskian guard or mage has laid eyes on the enemy even though they are inside the walls?'

'Some will have, my Lord. We have not yet found the bodies.'

'Was that a joke?'

'No, my Lord.' Myx was surely frowning beneath his mask but Dystran couldn't see it.

'Stupid question.' Dystran waved a hand and set off again.

His mind boiled, the acerbic comments he might deliver churned away. He shook his head, muttered to himself and scratched his hair, unruly from his disturbed rest. He was halfway across the spectacular domed hall which lay at the centre of the tower complex and high above the Heart of the college.

Passages ran away towards the chambers at the base of each tower as well as to banqueting and reception halls, guest quarters and administrative offices. It was a maze for the unwary and the design was entirely deliberate. Ways to the real power of the college were not easily discovered and no senior or circle mage wanted the uninvited venturing into catacombs or tower.

Dystran's sandals slapped on the exquisitely patterned marble floor as he headed for the intricately carved main doors. The left one opened and a soldier hurried in.

'Ah, Commander Chandyr, how good of you to come before I called. I expect you'll be bursting to explain to me how an unknown number of highly skilled elves are running loose in my streets.'

Chandyr's momentary confusion cleared when he saw Myx.

'You've heard,' he said.

'Evidently.'

'Sorry, my Lord.'

'So, would you care to enlighten me? I understood that no section of the city walls was to be unguarded at any time. I also understood that patrols would always be in sight of one another as they are outside the walls of my college. Given these two parameters, I fail to see how anyone got in without tunnelling. Difficult through our foundations, I would suggest.'

Dystran kept a firm grip on his anger. He knew Chandyr was a competent soldier but he was better suited to the open field, on the back of a horse. Circumstance, though, had conspired to install him to the city's most senior military position.

'No, my Lord, they scaled the walls. I have no explanation for it. I came here to report on our search and to offer my apologies.'

Dystran waved a hand. 'Apologies later.' He sighed again. Seemed he'd been doing a lot of that. 'What do you know and what's happening right now?'

'Seven men are unaccounted for, presumed dead. We found three ropes leading down from an area of the south wall by the Darin bakery. There were no other signs. We have been unable to track them and have begun a spread search of the streets. We have cast the net from both their point of entry and the college walls assuming they intend eventually to gain entry here.

'We will find them.'

Dystran chuckled. 'You know, somehow I doubt you will but I wonder whether that matters.' He paused. 'You haven't removed any of my guard from the college walls?'

'No, my Lord.'

'Good, see that you don't. Here's what I suggest because they have only one target and that is this college. They will not kill the common man, they will not spoil our grain, poison our water or fire our buildings. And do not think that they have not been pressured to do just that on any of the innumerable nights we may assume they have already run free in these streets. It is what I would have demanded.

'They are a singular race. That much I have learned from men like Yron, and those incredible texts we guard so jealously. They seek that one prize and then they will go. So why don't we let them come, now they have gained entry so effortlessly? They cannot gain our walls unseen. They do not have the magic to threaten us. Julatsa fails more by the day.

'Rest your men, Chandyr. Guard my walls and guard my cobblestoned yards. And when we see them at our gates, we can call two hundred of the reserve from their bunks to fight them and fifty mages to burn them. They will not enter this college.'

'My Lord,' acknowledged Chandyr.

Dystran turned away and wandered back towards his tower, a complete calm descending on him. 'Now why didn't I think of that before?'

'Because until now you were unsure of their sole intent.'

'It was a rhetorical question, Myx,' said Dystran.

'Yes, my Lord.'

'Stand outside my door tonight. Wake me should the elves be spotted. The sport should be worth watching.'

'I will, Lord Dystran.'

'One more thing,' said Dystran as they entered the base of his tower and headed for the stairs. 'I would know the exact time we are able to cast the first of our new dimensional magics. And I would know which of our castings is the better prepared for use.' He smiled at Myx and patted his shoulder. 'Just in case.'

Hirad led The Raven along a passage hacked out of packed clay, shored up with timbers along its length. It bore the signs of considerable age and, here and there, despite the holding spells, timbers had fallen away and the tunnel threatened to cave in.

Beyond the door in the blank warehouse office, a flight of wooden steps had run down for more than thirty-odd feet before levelling into the slightly meandering damp and reeking passage. They'd run all the way, the LightGlobe never far from Denser's shoulder, guiding them, the rats scattering before them, feet splashing in puddles.

The barbarian's mind was a riot of conflict. It had fallen on him so suddenly though he knew it had been there, waiting for a moment of weakness to present itself. He couldn't afford to let his guilt cloud his judgement but he couldn't push it aside either. This place. This filthy passage led to the heart of everything and everyone he blamed for Ilkar's death besides himself. No one was innocent. And the thought that they had come to steal and not mete out justice was one he found hard to bear.

He knew what they had to do. Knew their success could ultimately make sense of Ilkar's wishes but within the walls they ran beneath, those who had casually signed away his life had live blood in their veins. How desperately he wanted to let it drown the entire college.

The Unknown had run beside him in the narrow passage all the way, talking, keeping him with them. Without Ilkar he was the only one Hirad would hear.

'Don't let it consume you,' he said. 'Control it. Master it. Use it to help us do what we must. Revenge can come later.'

But Hirad knew there would never be a better chance and

enough of him hoped they would be discovered by those capable of facing him, to feed his desire.

'Remember you are Raven. Remember what that means.'

He ran harder.

It was Denser's voice that stopped him, stopped all of them.

'Slow. We are sloping up. Quiet now.'

The pace dropped to a walk, breath pulled more easily into lungs, pulses slowed.

'All right, let's orient ourselves,' continued Denser. Rebraal's murmur could be heard, elven ears tuned to him. 'This slope ends at a door beyond which is a store room for the Mana Bowl. The other side of the door is a basic illusion. The door is unlocked from this side but is locked and alarmed on the other. Once we go through, no one step back or you'll trigger the bell ward. That's very important.

'The Mana Bowl sits just to the north-east of the tower complex and butts on to an administrative block. It is diagonally opposite the library, which also connects at one corner with the complex. I've explained to you the ways we can get in. Here is where we meet when we're done. You'll recognise the fallback positions if we encounter trouble. Let me remind you they are the banqueting halls which run south from the complex and the reception hall of the dome itself. Is everybody clear?'

Hirad scanned the TaiGethen. There was no doubting their readiness.

'We won't get in and out without encountering anyone so kill quietly,' said The Unknown. 'We only get one chance at this.'

Hirad walked to the end of the passage. A wooden door and frame were set into the stone surrounds of a building. There was no handle.

'How do I—?'

'I said it was unlocked, I didn't say a non-mage could open it. Stand aside. I'll have to lose the LightGlobe, sorry.'

The sudden dark was disconcerting. Hirad put a hand on the wall to steady himself. Next to him, Denser muttered under his breath. He could hear water dripping behind them, the scuttle of rodents and the ominous creak of the weaker timbers.

The hand on his shoulder had him jumping almost clear of his skin. He felt breathing by his ear and a voice spoke low, menacing and in elvish. It was Auum.

'What did he say?' Hirad's voice sounded loud in the nervous quiet. 'I presume you're there, Rebraal.'

'He said he will not let you risk his success. He says the TaiGethen are doing the work of Yniss tonight and any who threaten that work will be killed.'

Hirad bristled. 'Well, you tell him his inspirational words need work. Tell him, The Raven do not make a habit of failure. And tell him if he threatens me again, he can have his fight.'

'Hirad—' warned The Unknown from close by.

'He saw how you reacted,' said Rebraal. 'Your loss of control. He doesn't believe emotion should guide you. He thinks that is weak.'

'If I had no emotions driving me on, you couldn't pay me enough to raid the Dark College. Don't any of you ever presume to tell me how I should or should not act. I have nothing to prove to you, him or any elf, bar Ilkar.'

'That's not—'

'Just leave it, Rebraal,' said Erienne, somewhere to the left. 'You don't understand.'

Thraun growled his agreement. Hirad jumped again. Sometimes the shapechanger was so quiet you could forget he was there. It didn't used to be like that.

'Quiet!' hissed Denser. 'We're in.'

A wan light washed down the passage from somewhere, soaking them all in grey, misty illumination as the door swung inwards. Hirad paused to lock eyes with Auum before a push from The Unknown sent him on to creep into the chamber beyond. It was small, too small to take them all at once. Shelves ran down two sides, forcing Hirad to edge sideways past ordered stacks of plain blue robes, simple sandals and cord ties.

'Robes for the Mana Bowl,' explained Denser.

'Very nice,' said Hirad, moving into the narrow gap between the shelves and looking up at windows in the ceiling through which the grey light was shining. He nodded at a door opposite. 'What's through there?'

'A corridor leading to offices, other store rooms, changing rooms, a contemplation and relaxation chamber and the entrance to the Bowl itself.'

'Thanks for the full tour,' said Hirad. 'Now, will there be anyone outside? We need to move ourselves.'

'The Bowl doesn't operate after dark, the focus is never right, strange as that may seem for the Dark College.'

'I've no idea what you're talking about,' said Hirad. 'I'm going out. Bring The Raven. We're leaving first.'

Hirad marched to the door and put an ear to it. Behind him, the message was relayed back into the clay passage. Out came the rest of The Raven, Rebraal at their rear, keeping communication as smooth as he could.

'Note these skylights,' Denser was saying to the elf. 'The library has the same ventilation and natural light source. If you're going in from the top, that's what you have to prise open.'

Hirad could hear nothing from the corridor. He laid a hand gently on the handle and pulled. The door swung open easily. Outside it was dark. Nothing moved. The barbarian moved out. The Unknown was immediately behind him, going left as he went right. Denser and Erienne followed them, spreading away either side with Thraun and Darrick in their footprints.

'Hirad, head up the corridor. Door at the end. That's our way out. We'll be in the shadow of the Mana Bowl and follow it round to the tower complex offices. We break in, the elves carry on. Got it?'

'Got it,' said Hirad.

There was the unmistakable smell of age and reverence in the darkened corridor. Hirad didn't feel he could have made a loud noise even if he'd wanted to. The atmosphere was oppressive, reminiscent of the rainforests of Calaius but without the humidity. He shook his head and paced on. The corridor had no windows, no skylights. Its only illumination came from behind and from under the doors of the rooms he passed.

He could feel the Mana Bowl to his right. It had a power all of its own. It was the place where initiate mages went to accept the mana or have it wreck their minds. A harsh but necessary test. Who'd be a mage?

At the door, Hirad stopped. The corridor was full behind him. Denser waved him on.

'It's all right. No alarms and no locks. We save those for the Bowl itself. That, the uninvited cannot be allowed to see.'

Hirad cracked the door and felt the dampness of the night air on his face. It smelled beautifully fresh after the underground passage. Orders were being shouted around the college. He could hear the sounds of running feet but felt they were above him, on the walls. He held up a hand and all movement behind him ceased. Rebraal came to his shoulder. They waited, listening, watching what they could through the crack in the door, which revealed nothing but a stone path, a hedge and a few manicured small trees.

Hirad turned to Rebraal who shook his head.

'No one is near,' whispered the elf.

'Well, it's now or never,' said Hirad. 'Come on, Raven.'

As he was instructed, Hirad opened the door just far enough and slipped out to the right. His heart was beating fast and reality hit him hard. He was standing in the grounds of the Dark College.

He closed his eyes momentarily, commended his soul to any God that was listening, and shifted crab-like along under the deep shadow of the Mana Bowl towards the towers of Xetesk.

Chapter 17

Lights burned in each of Xetesk's seven towers. Six in the outer circle soared upwards one hundred and fifty feet, with the central, dominant tower's peak at least a further fifty feet above them. A figure moved around that tallest tower, staring out from a balcony before disappearing from view.

Auum signalled that they could move again. All around them, the college was humming. Guards thronged the walls, walking their beats or staring out over the city. The two gate houses, east and west, were bright with lantern light, which spread pools over the courtyards within and, presumably, without. Up in the residential halls, light shone from many windows, indicating students losing a night's sleep, ready should they be called upon.

But no one moved across the ground. Not by the quartet of long rooms in the south-east corner, not around the lecture theatres to the north or through the ornamental gardens that bordered two sides of the tower complex.

Complacency was an enemy. The elves had learned that to awful cost. Xetesk clearly had not. Not yet. While they covered every inch of ground outside the college walls where they believed their enemies had to come from, they had ignored the space under their very noses; safe in the assumption that their spells would defend their critical structures.

Moving in heavy shadows around the back of the shrouded and shuttered banqueting halls, Auum made his decision the moment he saw the library. There was no point risking a casual observer noticing that the soldiers guarding the library's single entrance were missing. He nodded to Duele who began to climb at the junction of banqueting hall and library walls.

The architects had enjoyed their designing and the sculptors had given full vent to their talents, producing an extraordinary structure. In the context of the college, the library was a huge building, dominated only by the towers in whose shadows it stood.

Ornate buttresses climbed up the sides of the building, punctuating the three levels of grand arched windows of stained glass. The flat roof they knew to be studded with skylights and it was adorned along its edges and, so Denser said, its surface, with gargoyles and statues. The single set of double doors were set into the western end of the rectangular building.

Every stone was carved. Murals depicted the gathering and writing of texts. Scribes looked up in wonder from their work as mages conducted castings. Early scholars gazed down on the college, huge solemn faces lined with age and conveying knowledge and learning. Denser had assured them that in the daylight, it was a stunning sight. Auum cared little for that. What it meant to him was an easy climb, hidden for the most part from the eyes of his enemies.

Duele made short work of the climb. Evunn followed him at the same pace, with two Al-Arynaar mages in his wake. Next he signalled Marack to take her cell up. The two cells led by Porrack and Allyne would stay to be the eyes and ears on the outside, hidden in the shadows. Auum climbed up after Marack. He found the roof exactly as Denser described it. Impressive carved statues of demonic shapes, flying gargoyles and even piles of books and scripts.

Moving across to Duele and Evunn, he nodded to the rest of his charges, signalled them to wait hidden. There was no need to remind them to keep alert. Every eye scanned buildings or ground.

'We move.'

Auum and his Tai spread to three consecutive skylights, lying flat on the roof to look but not touching them. The small windows were set into raised and sloped stone casements. Auum's sight pierced the gloom below easily enough, helped by the fact that the library wasn't in complete darkness. From somewhere on the ground floor, light was edging out, probably from under a closed door.

Directly beneath him, Auum could make out row after row of wall-mounted or freestanding bookshelves and glass-fronted cases, their strict order dominating the floor. Towards the main doors, a shelf-free area was home to small desks, larger tables, book stands and a scattering of chairs. Some of the tables had books and parchments on them and Auum could make out lantern stands, quill-and-ink sets and paperweights.

To his right, and east along the length of the library, Auum followed the central carpeted walkway to a grand staircase that wound up to two landings. Each landing swept around a wide balustraded oval that overlooked the floor below. More bookshelves lined the outer walls and where the floor widened, more desks and tables covered the space. It was an ordered arrangement, undoubtedly airy and bright in the middle of the day. A good place to study but nevertheless alien to him.

He lifted his head and glanced left and right. Both Evunn and Duele were waiting for him, shakes of their heads indicating they too had seen no one. A whisper barely more than a breeze around the statues reached his ears. He turned his head to the source. Marack and her Tai were deep in the lee of a gruesome demonic effigy. She raised her right eyebrow. Auum followed its direction.

A man stood on the highest parapet of one of the outer towers. The swirling rain might have deceived him but Auum felt sure the man was gripping the rail as if he would otherwise fall. Something flitted around his head. Not a bird but winged all the same. Denser had mentioned these creatures. They were a danger. Part of a world from which Yniss protected them. They had no place here.

He watched, knowing he was exposed but hoping that his stillness would make him appear little more than a shadow on the stone. The creature landed on the rail and looked into the man's eyes. It reached out one hand and gently stroked the old man's cheek. Auum frowned. It was a display at odds with its appearance and origin.

Leaning heavily on a stick and bracing himself on the rail then the doorframe, the man edged back into his tower, the pain in each step obvious.

Something nagged at Auum. It may have been just one old man but he had chosen that moment to stir himself from rest and his apparent agony had not stopped him determining to take the air. Perhaps some of the enemy sensed what the guards on the walls plainly did not. The TaiGethen would not delay.

He beckoned over one of the Al-Arynaar mages. She was called Sian'erei, of the same broad family as the Drech Guild elf who had recently ridden with The Raven and died in their service. Sian was fiercely determined and a talented mage, both factors that had made her an obvious choice for the raid. But, like all of them, her expression was chastened now with the fear that another mana failure could happen at any time.

'We must be sure there are no traps on this glass. Work fast.'

Sian closed her eyes, Auum watching her eyes flickering beneath their lids and her mouth move soundlessly. She ignored the rain whipping into her small face and over her cropped dark-haired head while she probed the skylight for traps. The search was brief.

'Nothing,' she said. 'And the spectrum is steady.'

'Yniss keep it that way,' said Auum. 'Back to the shadow.'

She retreated and Duele took his cue, slithering across the roof.

'Opinions?' asked Auum.

'The fixings are weak,' said Duele after brief probing. 'We must guard against the glass falling inwards. Hold here.'

Auum gripped the frame where Duele indicated while his Tai levered up the tarred waterproofing that surrounded the casement. Beneath it, the brackets which held the window in place were revealed. Auum nodded for him to continue. Duele worked his knife under the first bracket. The wood squeaked as the bracket bent back, the sound piercing so close but lost in the wind and the hubbub of orders echoing around the walls. Inside the library, they would surely have been heard.

Duele looked to Auum who raised his eyebrows.

'We have little choice. Take your time, but be quick.'

A smile flashed across Duele's face. 'You have spent too much time with The Raven,' he said, bending to his task.

'We agree there.'

Four brackets held the window in place. Auum could feel it move easily in his hands after the second was removed. Shortly after, they were able to lever the window up and free, though he held it in place.

'Bring rope,' he said. 'One length.'

It came immediately, one end tied around a stone horse's leg. Auum removed the window, looking anxiously down to see the funnel of air playing delicately across loose pages. He grabbed the free end.

'Lower me,' he ordered, hanging his legs over the edge.

Duele and Evunn took the strain and he dropped through the small opening, feeling the change as the misty rain and breeze ceased and the atmosphere warmed and quietened. Once clear of the frame, he swung his body and descended head first, his legs balancing his body at an angle. There was no sound from below him. Indeed all he could hear was the strain on the rope as it bore his weight and turned slowly, affording him a comprehensive view.

He was coming down towards the third-level balustrade. It was a carved marble rail, as wide as his foot was long, off-white in colour and shot through with natural flaws in darker tones. Six feet plus from the woven rug-covered floor, he stopped, the rope played out to its full length. He pivoted again and dropped, landing lightly and crouching, eyes scanning the floor beneath through the balustrade rail.

Duele and Evunn joined him, splitting left and right and beginning to circle the floor. Marack and her cell came down behind Sian'erei and Vinuun, the other Al-Arynaar mage. Above them, the gap to the sky whistled and Auum spared it a look before moving off after his Tai towards the stairs.

Somewhere in here was the Aryn Hiil. Xetesk could keep the other writings if only they could reclaim that which contained so much that man should not discover about the elves and their genesis. Understanding of the Aryn Hiil would give Xetesk weapons against them. One had been unleashed unwittingly already. The others had to remain hidden.

Slipping silently down the stairs at the head of his people, Auum could feel the power of the work that surrounded them, as if each leather-bound volume, each protective parchment case and each glass display cabinet fought to contain the knowledge within. So much of Xetesk's history was here. So much havoc could be wreaked by its destruction.

But that was for men to decide. Once the Aryn Hiil was retaken, the elves had but one more task on Balaia before they left it forever.

The Raven, bolstered by Rebraal and two Al-Arynaar mages, moved quickly through the block of administrative offices that bordered the Mana Bowl on one side and were accessed through doors set into the eastern arc of the central dome of the tower complex.

Rebraal had made short work of a locked window, allowing them into the building, and, with Denser able to advise on the position of locks, wards and alarms progress was fluid. Soon they were gathered by a door into the dome itself. In their wake lay a short corridor and six offices for the use of the Circle Seven's private secretaries. Nothing useful had been gleaned from them, despite Denser having hoped they might gain clues as to who was in residence. Unfortunately, given the lights they'd already seen, it was likely every tower was currently occupied.

The Unknown Warrior took a moment to collect himself. He knew exactly what lay through that door. Last time he had seen it, it had been from behind the mask of a Protector. It was a majestic place. The bases of the six outer towers bordered it, the column of the central tower drove straight through its centre and down to the Heart. Its alcoves held statues of great masters long gone, the tower columns were carved with murals and warnings, the floor was spectacular tiled marble. And winding passages radiated out to a maze that led to the doorways to the towers and, ultimately, the catacombs.

He couldn't help it, he shuddered. Down there, lost in the network of chambers, tunnels, caverns and hallways was the Soul Tank. Every Protector was taken there to see for himself where his soul was held and why his thrall was binding until death. He winced as a hand touched his arm.

'Suffering, big man?' asked Hirad.

The Unknown nodded. 'I can feel them. No Protector likes to be this close to the Soul Tank. Standing outside your own prison brings a pain I cannot describe in here.' He touched his chest above his heart.

'And tonight the means to release them can be in our hands. We know it must exist,' said Denser.

'I don't share your confidence,' said The Unknown. 'And I don't know if we should release them, even if we discover how.'

'That's a question for later,' said Denser. 'There's much for us to do here. One thing at a time, eh?'

Another nod from the Unknown. He swallowed, unable to

162

push the visions from his head. He focused hard on what they'd agreed.

'Go, Denser. Let's get this over with.'

Hirad grunted. 'Time to strike back.'

Denser crouched by the door. There was no conventional lock. What held the offices from unwelcome visitors was what Denser described as a magical door wedge. It was moved at dawn every day and replaced every night by the tower master, a mage with influence only bettered by the Circle Seven themselves. Not a difficult spell to overcome but, like everything in Xetesk, it could link to a hidden trigger that might do anything from setting off an alarm to firing a disabling spell.

'Nothing here,' said Denser. 'No. Hold on.' He fell silent again. 'Ah. Clever. Very clever.' He chuckled. 'Hold on.'

He drew in a deep breath and held it. The Unknown looked on, brow creasing deeper and deeper. Denser was working his fingers at an extraordinary rate. All the movements were minute but there was an order and complexity at which he could only wonder. The casting, or teasing of mana as The Unknown suspected it was, went on far beyond the time Denser should surely have taken a breath. His face displayed no discomfort and his face defined his level of concentration, eyes screwed tight, jaw clenched, neck muscles corded.

At the last, he shuddered. 'Release,' he muttered and rolled onto his back, to exhale and heave in a fresh breath. They gathered above him, looking down as he recovered himself.

'What the hell was all that about?' asked Hirad. 'You mages make things so difficult for yourselves, you know. Keys. They make sense.'

'The whole point is that the Tower Master should be alerted if someone tries to break in,' managed Denser.

'I expect they'd just come in through the window like us, wouldn't they?' Hirad held out a hand and helped Denser to his feet.

'Thanks. You see, what you don't know is what we've triggered, coming through the windows and the office doors. It's a clever system and I'll explain it to you some other time.'

'So what did you do this time?' asked The Unknown, happy to be distracted.

'The Tower Master had a single strand of mana attached to the holding spell on the door. I suspect releasing the spell would have the effect of a ringing a bell in his chambers. I had to put in a lattice that would keep the strand at the right focus – that's tension to you, Hirad – and for that I had to calculate the focus. Not simple but not insurmountable.'

'And you reckon you got it right?' asked Hirad.

'No, I'm just killing time until the Tower Master gets here.' Denser shook his head.

Hirad suppressed a laugh. 'Not bad, Denser. Not bad.' He sobered almost immediately. 'But not Ilkar. Not yet.'

'Let's form up, Raven,' said The Unknown, taking the cue. 'Hirad, with me, Rebraal, your bow behind us. Mages centre, Thraun, Darrick you get the rear. And no debate. We see someone, we kill them. With one exception. Everyone understand? Denser, we'll do best with a SpellShield from you, I expect. Erienne, you and the others remember, no casting unless we're caught. We can't afford to be discovered through the mana spectrum.'

The Unknown indicated to Hirad to open the door. He stood to one side as the barbarian edged the gap wider. The domed hall was chill. Lanterns and braziers hung from wall spurs, the arcs of the outer towers and around the circumference of the dominating central stack that was Dystran's seat of power.

It was a huge chamber. The dome wrapped the towers some thirty feet above their heads. Directly ahead and mostly hidden by Dystran's tower, the massive gold-embossed arched wooden and iron doors kept out the night, reflecting the brazier and lantern light. Far left, a more sedate set of red-curtained doors led into the banqueting area while to the right, reception rooms were similarly shrouded, closed and empty.

But it was the unlit openings that set The Unknown's pulse quickening. There were seven. They twisted around and down, led to blind alleys, wards, alarms and, for the mage or guard trusted enough to know, to the base of spiral stairs and the top of the entrances to the catacombs. Seven up to the towers, seven down to where, historically, the seat of Xetesk's learning lay.

'Ahead,' whispered Denser. 'Skirt Dystran's tower to the left; we're headed for the curtained passage to the left of the dome doors.'

The Unknown led them out, his footsteps muffled by the

cloth still wrapped around his boots but torn and wearing thin. The marble would give them away if it could. So would his breathing, the creak of his armour, the heat from his body or the call of his soul. Gods, he was prepared to believe anything would. The trouble was, if one Protector was near enough, they would be discovered through him.

A knife was in his hand now and he indicated to Hirad to keep an eye right while he took left, knowing those behind him were doing the same. It was a walk that went on forever beneath Xetesk's most secure quarters. Every pace could bring doom so quickly. Each footfall might reveal those that surely waited for them.

The Raven crept gradually around the base of Dystran's tower. Pace by pace, their target passage was revealed and, inch by inch, he began to believe they would reach it without incident.

Footsteps. Echoing. The direction hard to tell but the sound was growing. The Unknown clenched his fist. The Raven stopped, the Al-Arynaar half a pace slower. Rebraal's bow tensed. Hirad gestured left, the other side of the tower. The Unknown nodded, pointed either side of the tower and shrugged. Hirad shook his head. Denser pointed left and raised his eyebrows. Mouthed 'trust me', and began to edge back the way they had come. Right now they were visible from the dome doors. Whichever way the enemy came around the pillar, that was bad.

The footsteps were from more than one person, walking briskly, and clearly now from one of the tower entry passageways. The Unknown locked eyes with Rebraal. He nodded his readiness. All they could do now was to wait.

Men came into the dome. The muffling of the echoes gone as a curtain was pulled aside. The footsteps clattered across the marble, steelshod toe-caps and heels tapping out counter-rhythms. Soldiers. That was something.

There were two of them. Cloaked, helmets under one arm and marching purposefully towards the dome doors. They were talking, one plainly disagreeing with the other. The Unknown recognised the profile of the older one. The younger, the angrier one, he didn't. He held up a hand, putting it in front of Rebraal's arrow. The Raven watched the men through the doors, which opened and closed for them, the guards on the outside not looking in as they pulled the slick-hinged and counterweighted halves together.

'Well, well,' whispered The Unknown. 'Still alive.'

'Who,' said Hirad, voice dead quiet.

'Suarav,' said The Unknown. 'Must be the oldest soldier on the staff if he trained me, eh?'

'And the other was Chandyr,' said Denser. 'Reporting to Dystran, the pair of them no doubt. Well, Raven, that's the heads of defence of city and college introduced.'

'I could have had them,' said Rebraal, bowstring relaxed once more.

'Not both of them and not without risk,' said The Unknown. He stared squarely at Hirad. 'We aren't here to kill unnecessarily. Come on. We've work to do.'

For Ranyl, rest was elusive. A new pain had been growing just beneath his ribs above his stomach and he feared that very soon even the thin soups he was currently able to take in would prove too much.

Now, even his familiar was asking him to submit to spells to numb the agony. He had seen the referred pain in the creature's eyes but was still determined that he would not allow others to cast on him that which he could not cast himself.

Having abandoned all hope of sleep, Ranyl had retreated to his most comfortable and supportive upright chair. His familiar had added logs to the fire, before curling up in his bed as a feline to sleep. Burrowing under the covers for warmth, his vitality was fading as his master slipped slowly away.

Ranyl knew he wouldn't be seeing too many more dawns. It was an abiding sadness. From his highest balcony, he had seen the most spectacular fire-red dawns when the season was right. But autumn was more than a lifetime away.

Perhaps worse, though, was that he was unlikely to see the outcome of the war or the final fruition of either the elven or dimensional researches. He allowed himself a smile. Good of Dystran to give him so much involvement. Further sign if it was needed that Dystran had become a worthy and wily Lord of the Mount. After all, he had only allowed Ranyl access to such potential influence in Xetesk after discovering early that the cancer would be terminal.

Before Ranyl had, in fact.

Still, at least he would witness the first use of the adaptable dimensional magics gained from the understanding of the ageing Al-Drechar and the dragon, Sha-Kaan.

And there was another regret. How he would have loved to have met them, elf and beast alike. Again, though, he conceded he should really be grateful. He had, after all enjoyed a key decision-making position in these central affairs.

He must have dozed off momentarily because he felt the cool air on his face without seeing the door to his bedchamber open and close to admit whoever it was who had come to see him. He sighed and opened his eyes, his vision swimming slightly as it always did. Another messenger, was it? Or perhaps Dystran. That would be comforting. He had a sudden urge to know what was going on and how the hunt for the eleven raiders went.

The room was darker. It was because two figures were standing in front of the fire. He could sense others in the room too but he focused on the nearest. Strange there should be so many and he felt a menace that unnerved him.

'Our apologies for disturbing you, Master Ranyl,' said one, the smaller of the pair. He could make out a beard but the finer features were still blurred. The voice he recognised but couldn't place. At least it was human, not elven and he felt himself relax. He blinked and his vision cleared further.

'But we have messages to pass to you and the Circle Seven, and we have information to collect and you know where it is.' This was the other man. Huge, shaven-headed and deep-voiced.

Ranyl's calm deserted him. He knew these men. And a glance told him he knew nearly all in the room. His bedchamber. His heart was racing and pain flared in his stomach.

'Dear Gods burning, how did you get in here?'

Chapter 18

The TaiGethen fanned out from the base of the stairwell and ran across the ground floor. Two cells, six elite hunter-warriors armed with short blades, jaqruis and bows. Silent through the grid of shelves and cases, feet caressing stone, wood and carpet, their eyes missing nothing.

The Al-Arynaar mages walked in their wake, drinking in the mass of Xeteskian knowledge all around them, calm in the certainty that while the TaiGethen hunted in front of them, they had nothing to fear.

Auum ran at their head, with Duele and Evunn to his left, flitting in and out of his peripheral vision between the shelves. Marack and her cell mirrored them to the right. As on the upper floors, they expected to find no one. Their sweep took them through the desks and tables and all the way to the doors closed against the night and a threat that had already bypassed them.

Auum paused at the doors and the TaiGethen gathered about him. The library was a welcome change from the city outside and its filthy cloying odours. The air smelled of ancient paper, treated wood and the mustiness of age, mixed with traces of lantern oil. He breathed it in deeply before he spoke, voice low.

'You have all seen the five doors we passed on our left. These are the archive chambers of which Denser spoke. If the Aryn Hiil is here, it will be in one of those. You have all seen the light from beneath two of the doors. Split by Tai cell, one mage to each. Remember Denser's warnings and let Tual's hands guide yours. We move.'

Auum led his Tai back into the library, heading past tables and around bookshelves to the row of five doors that led into the secure archive chambers. He stood back to let the mage move to the door. She stood directly in front of it and tuned to the mana spectrum. Beside Auum, Duele held his bow, and Evunn, two short swords.

Two doors along, Marack was ready. Auum nodded. The mages got to work.

Nyam's curiosity was undimmed. And he had no doubt the Al-Drechar were shielding a One mage despite their obstructive comments. Ever since their arrival, they had been kept from the most private rooms in the old house. The few remaining elves from the Guild of Drech were most insistent that their mistresses be afforded quiet and rest much of the time, so limiting the Xeteskian interrogation and, importantly, observation.

It was also clear that they were friendly enough with Diera who in turn had the ear of Sha-Kaan. And the dragon, weakened and without fire though he was, had let it be known that he didn't see the roof and walls of the house as a barrier to killing those who stepped out of line.

There came a time, however, when a mage had to make his move. Had to be noticed by the Circle Seven for initiative, ability, courage and loyalty. Gods drowning but on this small rock buried in the Southern Ocean that was difficult but Nyam had always been taught to grab opportunities, and he saw one now.

Let the others lick their wounds and remain scared of two old women and a dying dragon. He had listened to the messages passed via the Protectors through the Soul Tank. He knew the growing anxiety over the reality that the One still blossomed outside Herendeneth and not in Xeteskian control. He had heard the rumours of the identity of the practitioner; and in so many ways it all made sense though their research hadn't revealed how The Raven mage, Erienne, might have developed the talent following her daughter's death. Best guess was it arose coincidentally but the fact remained that there were two people on this island who knew the truth. Nyam had the chance for quick promotion sleeping not thirty yards from him. He wasn't about to let his colleagues take it first. He had to gamble on the rumour being true and he had to do it now.

The night was humid and, as ever, still. Stars scattered the night sky delivering nothing in the way of light and the house

169

itself had few lanterns burning. Nyam walked through the damp-smelling corridors to the wing where the Al-Drechar, Diera and Jonas slept. Two Guild elves stood guard at its entrance, barring his way.

'I apologise for the unpleasantness of the hour but I have news concerning The Unknown Warrior that Diera must hear.'

'She is sleeping,' said one of the elves in heavily accented Balaian.

'I know, and I would normally keep news until the morning but this she must hear now. He is in serious danger.'

'You would worry her this much about things she cannot influence?'

'She has always said she would know everything,' countered Nyam. 'Please. Come with me to her. Ask her yourself before I even see her. At least give her the option.'

He knew they had no choice. He knew he looked innocent and sincere. One shrugged, the other nodded and the door was opened for him. He was accompanied the short distance down the corridor by the elf who had spoken to him, arriving at Diera's door where he was told to wait. Further down the corridor, more Guild elves stood guard in front of the Al-Drechar's private rooms. Shortly, the elf reappeared and beckoned him in. As they passed, the elf caught his arm.

'Do not wake the child. Do not betray our trust,' he said. 'You are here but we do not want you here. Remember that.'

Nyam nodded and walked inside. Diera was sitting on the side of her bed, a light shawl draped over her shoulders and covering the top of her nightdress. One hand stroked her sleeping son's head. A lamp, wick turned low, was enough to reveal her anxious face and knotted hair. Gods but she was so alluring. A woman just woken. How sweet it would be if she were to beckon him to her.

Of course, she did not. She stared at him with a mixture of trepidation and contempt.

'Tell me about my husband,' she demanded. 'And make it quick. I may need to talk to Sha-Kaan.'

'Of course,' said Nyam. 'And I am truly sorry for the intrusion.' She waved away his apology. 'And I am sorry for worrying you but it is not your husband who is in danger. It is Erienne.'

He held his breath for her reaction. There was none barring a coldness across her face.

'If my husband is not in danger, then neither is Erienne. I suggest you provide better reason for this unwelcome visit.'

Beside her, Jonas stirred. She stared at Nyam meaningfully.

'The power the Al-Drechar help her contain,' he said, all the time studying her face. 'They are not strong enough any more. We can help. Xetesk wants the One to grow.'

'I don't know what you're talking about,' said Diera, but there was no irritation in her voice and a flicker across her eyes gave her away.

'You do,' said Nyam gently. 'I know you do.'

'Go,' said Diera. 'I can't help you.' She pulled the shawl tighter around her.

Nyam leaned forward and grabbed her upper arms roughly. 'Damn you, woman, you will help,' he hissed, seeing her moment's shock give way to fear. 'We cannot afford to have her running around unprotected by us. If the Al-Drechar were to fail, Balaia would be devastated all over again. My reports are it is already starting. Why do you think I am waking you now? Whatever it is the Al-Drechar are doing right now, it isn't enough. I must be allowed to see them, observe them, so we can lend our strength.'

'Then why not talk to the Guild elves or the Al-Drechar themselves if you are so genuine?' she asked.

'Because without you with me, they won't believe me. They will deny everything fearing what we will do. But all we want to do is help Erienne live.'

'Let go of my arms.'

He did so. 'I am sorry. Please Diera, for all our sakes?'

'You must think me very stupid, deaf or both,' she said, meeting his gaze. 'Do you think I talk to no one? Do you think I know nothing of Xetesk's desires? I am not the dim wife and mother you clearly think me to be. I am the wife of The Unknown Warrior. And you are in more trouble than you can possibly imagine.'

Nyam knew that already. A sense of calm had descended on him. He shrugged.

'The time for such fears is past. Xetesk has a war to win. Control of Erienne will bring us that victory.'

'She's just one Dordovan mage.'

171

Nyam smiled. 'Diera, I do respect you and your strength. Sol could not have chosen better. But respect me too. Erienne is very much more than just one Dordovan. Deny it all you like but we will prove it. Now, are we going to visit the Al-Drechar together?'

'Why should I move? All I have to do is shout.'

'Diera.' Nyam's lips thinned with his patience. 'My actions might bring about my death, I'm not sure. One thing I am sure of is that if you don't help me now, they will certainly bring about yours.' He reached a hand down to Jonas. 'Such a lovely boy. He needs his mother. Don't you think?'

Gylac knew he was close to the breakthrough. It could see him to the Circle Seven on Ranyl's death. The prospect excited him more than it should but he couldn't help it. He'd begun to notice the links in the elven texts two days before. Amongst the partially translated passages and the tracts of so far indecipherable script, there was a pattern emerging.

This Aryn Hiil was so much more than the history and practice of a religion expressed in ancient elvish. He was sure of that now though in truth, Dystran and Ranyl had always suspected it.

His initial theorising had been backed up by independent research from another member of his staff. It built on the centuries-old notion that the elves were inherently and dependently magical. All of them. The Elfsorrow had proved that beyond question but had run its course before they could synthesise it as a spell.

Now it looked as if they wouldn't have to worry about the loss of that opportunity. Because if he was right, and the magical theory supported him, there was a way of unpicking an elf from the mana that made him vulnerable. The elven nation would become Xetesk's new thralled race. Never mind Protectors, this would be a weapon infinitely more powerful. And it would be infinitely less risky than making pacts with demons.

He wouldn't sleep 'til he had the answer. After all, Ranyl didn't have long to live.

Gylac heard the door behind him open. He turned in his high backed chair, placing his quill on his note book.

'So, have you—'

What he saw in front of him was impossible. Laughable almost. He wasn't sure if he smiled or not. He felt a hot, incredibly hot, lancing pain in his throat. His body was flung back, connecting with the edge of the table. He scrabbled at the pain, trying to look down. He saw the shaft of an arrow and felt the hot pumping blood on his hands. There was a roaring in his ears.

They were all around him now, soundless like spirits. He was pushed aside, heard a short exclamation. They had the Aryn Hiil. His prize. His safe passage to power. He grabbed at an arm.

'You can't,' he gurgled, or thought he did.

A face stared down at him, so cold. The eyes held a hatred that made him shudder. He heard some words.

'Shorth awaits you.'

His grip slackened.

Ranyl barely had the strength to be scared, the pain in his stomach had intensified and his breath shortened. But even he could not help but respect the tenacity of this most deep of the thorns in Xetesk's side.

'You are persistent, I grant you that,' he said. 'We had thought you hidden outside Lystern somewhere.'

'Hiding is not in our nature,' said The Unknown Warrior.

Ranyl nodded and craned his head. 'Why don't you all come round here so I can see you. It isn't often one is confronted by The Raven in its entirety.'

'This is not the entire Raven. Ilkar died because of you.' Ranyl felt the touch of steel on his neck. 'Don't try anything. You aren't quick enough to beat me.'

Ranyl chuckled. 'Oh, Hirad, I am long past casting spells. I cannot muster the focus even to numb my own pain.'

'Gods' sake, Hirad, put it away,' said Denser.

'No,' said Hirad. 'No chances. Not in here.'

'My Lord Ranyl, we mean you no harm—'

'Right . . .'

'Hirad!' snapped Denser.

'He is Circle Seven. He is guilty of Ilkar's death. Mean him no harm if you like. I feel different.'

'We should have factored you in,' said Ranyl. 'Never ignore The Raven, eh?'

'My Lord.'

'Denser, yes, I'm sorry. What is it you want?' He felt for the bond with his familiar but it was weak. The demon was lost in sleep. He tried to pulse it awake, cursing his fading ability.

'Your dimensional researches. Tell us where they are,' said Denser. 'We need them.'

'Why?'

'That's our business.'

'Hirad, please,' said Denser. 'We have a friend to send home.'

'Ah, of course,' said Ranyl. 'The great Sha-Kaan. He will be repatriated when we have the capacity.'

The blade pressed harder 'Wrong,' said Hirad. 'Every day, he dies a little more. If you can do it, you'll help us do it now.'

Ranyl waved a hand. 'It is a fairly simple casting. We just don't have the time. Now if you could persuade your friends to lift their siege, we could help you.' He pulsed again. The familiar didn't respond.

'Where is the research held? And who is in charge of it?' demanded Denser. 'I know you. Nothing is left unrecorded. Which catacomb houses it?'

Ranyl shrugged. 'I haven't been down there for sometime, Denser. It could be anywhere.'

'He's stalling,' said another voice. Female.

'Erienne,' he said. The prize had walked into his bedchamber. 'I grieve for your loss.'

'Liar.'

'But a greater loss to the world would be you,' said Ranyl. 'You have such potential. Stay with us.'

'I've had enough of this.' The Unknown Warrior stepped in and grabbed Ranyl's jaw in one huge hand. He squeezed. 'No more games. No more delay. Let's get one thing straight. We can get in here undetected any time we want to so I suggest you take what I am about to say very seriously.'

The Unknown's face was very close to Ranyl's and he could see in the ex-Protector's eyes, the truth behind his words. There was more to this than capturing research. The warrior continued.

'Already, the Aryn Hiil will have been taken by its rightful owners but that isn't the only crime of yours we are halting here tonight. You will tell us where the dimensional alignment research is held so that we can end Sha-Kaan's imprisonment on Balaia, a trivial action unworthy of your urgent attention or not.' The grip on Ranyl's jaw tightened and The Unknown's face darkened further.

'There's something else. You and the rest of the Circle Seven will see to it that no harm comes to my wife and son on Herendeneth. They are there to keep them from the wreckage of this country. They are not your pawns. You will not suffer them to be threatened, used as any kind of ransom or even allow them to be touched by any Xeteskian.

'Do not fool yourself I will not find out. You know we are in contact. If anything . . . anything . . . happens to my family through one of your power games, you will wish your sickness had taken you earlier. And the Circle Seven will wish fervently that they had listened to you relating my words.

'Do you understand me?'

Ranyl was silent. No one had ever talked to him that way. His first reaction was to counterthreaten but he was in no position right now.

'I—' His mouth would barely open, such was the pressure from The Unknown's hand.

'Do you understand me?' He relaxed his grip.

'I hear you.'

'Good.'

'What a shame, though,' said Ranyl.

'I beg your pardon?' asked Denser.

'You could have been so much more.'

'Who?'

'You, Denser. The Circle Seven needs you. And you, Sol. You could have been the leader of the Protectors.'

The Unknown leaned in further, his smile carrying no humour.

'I already am.' He straightened. 'So talk. The research.'

Ranyl breathed in deeply. They had handed him control though they appeared not to realise it. Anything to keep them here a little longer.

'We are testing our theories night and day in the catacombs below my Tower. I am the Circle Seven mage sponsoring dimensional research. Kestys is my lead man.' He shrugged. 'You know where to go, Denser. Take it, if you think you're able.'

'Do we need to know anything else?' asked Hirad.

Denser shook his head. 'No. He's telling the truth.'

'Why would I do otherwise?' said Ranyl. 'I have so little still to lose.'

'Let's go,' said The Unknown. 'Denser. Ranyl looks tired.'

'No problem.'

Denser began to cast. Ranyl knew he would. There was no point in raising an objection and, in truth, a large part of him looked forward to a few hours of blissful, pain-free rest. He felt a twitch in his mind. He smiled.

The Raven prepared to leave. Their big, blond, silent and clearly troubled warrior put an ear to the door and shook his head. Lystern's greatest loss, Ry Darrick, went to his shoulder, others followed him.

'Ready for this?' asked Denser, voice a little faint with the effort of sustaining the casting, simple though it was.

'I am,' said Ranyl.

The spell was never cast. Ranyl's bed exploded in torn cloth and feathers. His familiar screamed its fury, taking the air on leathery wings, mouth slathering, eyes burning with hatred of the invaders.

The reaction was instantaneous. Denser turned, dismissed the sleep spell and began to prepare again. The Unknown's sword was out of his scabbard, pointed towards the familiar, his free hand pushing Erienne behind him.

'Fly!' shouted Ranyl. 'Ignore them, fly!'

'Block the window!' Hirad was already running for the open windows on to the balcony. 'Thraun, we've got to stop it.'

The blond warrior, Thraun, growled. Ignoring his weapons, he ran to the centre of the room, putting himself between the familiar and the window. Around him, the elven mages were preparing too. Darrick kept his attention on the door, another elf had a bow ready, arrow nocked, looking for a clear shot.

The familiar flitted above their heads, circled the small chandelier. It flew at Thraun, raked a claw across his face and laughed as the blood began to flow.

'Denser, we need you!' Hirad's voice cut across the laughter.

Thraun made a jump, quick and powerful, catching the familiar by surprise and closing a fist around its trailing leg. It squealed. Thraun dropped back down, dragging the creature with him.

'Hold it, hold it!' roared The Unknown. 'Denser.'

'Time,' gasped Denser.

Ranyl kicked out a foot. It caught Denser in the back of the leg. He flinched. It was enough.

'Damn you!' he grated. 'Rebraal, keep this man quiet.'

Thraun was struggling with the familiar. The size of a monkey, it had a strength far greater than its stature. It swivelled in his grip, head biting down, jaws clamping on Thraun's wrist. The warrior yelled, fingers uncurled.

'No!' spat Hirad.

The demon flew back into the air, screamed again and dived for the balcony window. Hirad launched himself at it. It balled a fist and lashed it into the barbarian's face, snapping his head back. Hirad still laid a hand on it but it was too strong, flying out into the night, chittering and screeching, calling the college to arms.

Hirad dragged himself to his feet, a hand feeling the side of his face below his right ear. He stared out after the familiar before turning to meet The Unknown's grim face.

'Oh, shit.'

The alarms began to sound.

Chapter 19

Auum ran back out into the library from the archive chamber, the Aryn Hiil inside his tunic, its comforting presence had brought a glow to his whole body. He had felt energised, vindicated. Every elf would benefit. They had taken back something so precious and could return home to talk about what might come next.

But so quickly, his mood had evaporated. Outside the library, alarms were sounding. Even through the thick walls and the cloying quiet, they could hear the shouts of men and the chilling call of demon familiars in the sky. The college was awake, it knew the raiders were inside and TaiGethen were at risk out in the open grounds. Perhaps it was they who had been discovered. Somehow he doubted it.

He couldn't afford the time to get back to the roof and led his people towards the doors.

'Answers,' he said as he ran. 'Windows?'

'Not viable. Fixed, large and spell-maintained,' said Sian'erei from behind him.

'Door, then. Check quickly.' Sian and Vinuun paced away. 'Marack, defend our right. Eye to the sky. You cannot kill the demons but you can hold them off. Duele, Evunn, bows. Yniss save us.'

'Trouble,' said Sian. 'This door is locked by metal and spell. Those men we killed were in here for the night. The spell is a WardLock, timed to release at dawn. We can't counter it.'

Auum cast his gaze to the heavens. The area above the doors caught his eye. Five richly-coloured circular windows ringed the portal. Decorative, probably telling a story judging by the depictions upon them and definitely a weakness.

He snapped his fingers and Duele followed his gaze.

'We can all climb there,' he said. 'Tais, we move.'

Dystran cast around for something to punch. Not confident about the state of his knuckles if he threw one at Myx, he chose instead to smash his glass in the grate of his dying fire.

'How? By all the Gods drowning, how?'

'We do not know,' said Myx. 'We will discover. Mages are investigating.'

'Well, bugger that for now,' said Dystran, grabbing his cloak and swinging it around his shoulders. 'Come on. And pass on these instructions as we go.'

'My Lord.'

'Ranyl is available, I suppose?'

'I do not know,' said Myx.

'Of course you don't.' Dystran hurried out of the office in his tower and took the stairs at a trot, knotting his cloak as he went. 'I want the reserve in here, combing the ground. I want every available Protector back from the walls. Get me the Circle Seven in Ranyl's tower quicker than they've ever moved before. And get every guard off the damn walls. Blind as they are, they might as well help look, even if it means they pat the ground with their hands.'

'Damn those bloody elves!'

Dystran simply could not believe it. What had he missed? How long had the elves been inside? Ranyl's familiar had been apoplectic with rage. Unable to answer anything coherently and beside itself with anxiety about its master, Dystran had dismissed it before starting to break the glassware. All he really needed to know was that the raiders had got into Ranyl's tower. And if they'd got there, they could have breached anywhere.

'Last thing. Double the library guard. Do it now. Oh, and get me Suarav. He has some explaining to do.'

'Go!' shouted The Unknown. 'Get out, now. We can still make the escape.'

'What about him?' Hirad pointed at Ranyl.

The Unknown grabbed his arm. 'Hardly matters now, does it?' He glared at the dying Circle Seven mage. 'What I said about my family? Remember it and believe it.'

'You aren't getting out of here,' said Ranyl.

179

'No?' The Unknown turned and spread his arms. 'Raven! Raven with me!'

He led the charge from the top of Ranyl's tower. Long sword in his right hand, he took the stairs two at a time, ignoring the pain in his hip and bracing himself on the outside wall, the spiral unwinding in front of him.

'What about the wards?' he called over his shoulder.

'Straight through,' said Denser, puffing at the effort. 'What's another couple of alarms, eh?'

'What indeed.' The Unknown ploughed on, hurdling the bodies of Ranyl's personal guard on the second and first landings. 'Hirad, you there?'

'Right behind you.'

'Hit anything that comes at you. I think it could be interesting in the dome.'

'No problem.'

They were a few strides from the base of the tower. The wards would start tripping the moment they moved into the curving corridors that led to the centre of the complex.

'Ready, Raven,' warned The Unknown. 'Rebraal, your mages need to deploy shields. Erienne, anything you like; Denser, something like a ForceCone?'

He heard the answers and focused ahead. His boots, still wrapped by strips of cloth, made muffled slaps on the stone. He spun off the base of the spiral stairs, up a short rise to a sharp left and into a longer, tight curve upwards. At the end of the curve, the way down to the catacombs, now denied them in the chase to escape. The Unknown didn't spare it a look, running by, triggering an alarm ward which shrilled painfully in his ears.

He burst through the curtained alcove, the second ward sounding, a flat tone repeating again and again. The Raven surged out into the dome behind him, Hirad taking up station to his right, Darrick and Thraun left, the Al-Arynaar in a loose group behind Denser and Erienne.

'Down!' snapped Denser.

Hirad and The Unknown ducked. A ForceCone played over their heads, knocking two Xeteskian swordsmen from their feet. The Raven ran into the gap left, heading for the dome doors. One of the Al-Arynaar split off, aiming for the office entrance they'd come through.

'No,' shouted Denser. 'We can't go back that way! Stop.'

'Rebraal, call him back,' ordered The Unknown, not taking his eyes from the doors. They were opening. 'Do we have a SpellShield?'

'You do,' Rebraal confirmed before shouting in elvish.

'Keep it tight, Raven.'

The Unknown tapped his blade on the ground in front of him as he advanced. The first of the Xeteskian guard spilled in, seven forming up with more filling the space behind them, expecting to be confronted by elves. What they saw, for those who recognised The Raven, was worse.

'One pace and duck,' said Erienne.

Tried and tested, the warrior line did as instructed, barely pausing while the IceWind howled over their heads, slicing into the oncoming soldiers. A shield flared deep blue, feeding the power of the Dordovan spell over its surface and away into the floor. Even so, the line faltered. Rebraal's bow thudded, an arrow found its mark and the first guard died.

'Tight form, Raven, let's go,' called The Unknown.

Using the central column as a pivot, The Raven spaced to the outer wall and moved in, Darrick the man on the flank watching for the expected flanking moves. Denser was with him, a second ForceCone poised.

'This needs to be quick!' Hirad's voice echoed off the dome ceiling.

The Unknown brought his blade up and parried a heavy blow from a huge guardsman whose eyes peered from beneath a metal helm, his hands engulfing the hilt of his sword. Beside him, Hirad lunged straight forward, weight to the left, anticipating the block and maintaining his balance.

But it was the left of the Raven line where the damage was most quickly wrought. Darrick was far too fast for his opponent, feinting left by the tower base and striking right, his blade piercing chest armour and ripping into ribs and heart. And Thraun didn't bother with subtlety. Clearing his head with a howl from his wolven side he swung overhead, one-handed, crushing the skull of his first attacker and moving on a pace to pile his left fist into the face of the next, flattening nose and driving him back into his comrades.

'Come on!' yelled Hirad, seeing the carnage to his left. He battered his blade in across his body, seeing it parried away but leaving his attacker open. The barbarian moved into the space and shoved the man back and off balance with a push to his chest, following up with a strike into his left leg, chopping deep into flesh and bone. The man went down screaming.

'HardShield up,' said Erienne.

'Rebraal, how many more can you see.' The Unknown was happy to keep the big man in front of him quiet while he marshalled the move. He dropped in a low strike left to right, saw it parried but clumsily. The man might be powerful, but he was slow. 'Any time,' he whispered.

'Five in front,' replied Rebraal. 'Five behind.' The sound of another arrow. 'Four. Mage down.'

'Denser!' called The Unknown, blocking another massive overhead blow, turning the blade aside and slashing in with his dagger, forcing the enemy back. 'Round left. Darrick, watch him. Rebraal cover. Pushing Raven.'

The Raven moved. Denser turned and ran away around the base of Dystran's tower, Rebraal right with him. Darrick pressured forwards, engaging two opponents with Thraun by him, powering in strokes that drove his targets further and further back. And The Unknown stared the massive guard in the eye.

'Time to die.'

Before his hip was smashed, The Unknown had been the fastest man in Balaia with a two-handed blade. Now without the core balance to trust himself with the heavier blade, his switch to the long sword and dagger had increased his strike rate even further. He already knew his enemy couldn't follow him so he waited. Dully, the guard tried to get in first, unwinding a scything blow across his chest. The Unknown simply ducked beneath it, came up moving forward and, with his dagger parrying away left to block any return, stabbed clear through the guard's throat.

The Raven stepped up again and now the Xeteskian mages responded, spells clattering into the Al-Arynaar's shield. The Unknown held his breath. Julatsan magic wasn't as sure as it had been. FlameOrbs splashed harmlessly away, DeathHail following, again repulsed. From the opposite side of the tower base, Rebraal found another victim and Denser's ForceCone hit the enemy immediately after.

Without their mage shield, the Xeteskian guards were helpless. The Cone caught them flank on, tumbling men into each other and driving them across the floor towards the outer wall.

Denser kept the pressure on, the shouts of the guards weakening as they fell to unconsciousness, crushing them together against unyielding stone. Some would never rise again.

In front of The Raven, the path was almost clear, with any Xeteskians left standing in disarray. Hirad drove his blade into the midriff of one attacker, The Unknown thundered his through, waist high, following up with a killing blow with his dagger. Rebraal's bow let loose again, this time the shaft skittering off the far wall and falling harmlessly.

'Go Raven!' Hirad's call sent The Raven running through the broken line towards the doors.

The Unknown turned to the two mages, beckoning them on. 'Rebraal. Keep your mages up. We can't afford them to lag, this is going to be tight as it is.'

'Right at the doors!' Denser's voice rose above the turmoil of shouts of pain and warning coming from the Xeteskians and the sound of The Raven charging for the outside. 'Follow the dome to the Mana Bowl.'

'Raven!' roared Hirad. 'Raven with me!'

Dystran heard the impacts of spells, felt a faint vibration through his tower walls. He increased his pace, Myx stepping in front of him to lead the way.

'What the hell is happening in my bloody college!'

'Protectors are moving from the walls. Suarav has been summoned. The Circle Seven are gathering themselves to be with you in Lord Ranyl's tower,' replied Myx smoothly.

'Damn that. Gods burning, Myx, who the hell is tearing up my dome! Right under my bloody feet!'

'It must be the elves, my Lord.'

'Yes,' snapped Dystran. 'Yes. Hurry up.'

'My Lord.'

They made the base of the tower and Myx led them unerringly through the maze of corridors and passages beneath the dome that led to the other towers, to the banqueting halls and to the catacombs. Since the incident with Captain Yron, Dystran had insisted alarm wards be reinstituted and guards be doubled for all the Circle Seven. Not that they had stopped the raiders reaching Ranyl. He had also closed off the known route to the reception chambers from his tower. Too many people knew about it. Too many chances to be betrayed.

The two men chased up the stairs, Dystran muttering at the sight of the bodies they passed on the two landings.

'Worse than bloody useless. What have I done to deserve this?'

'My Lord?'

'Never mind. Let me through.'

Myx paused and Dystran passed him. Ranyl's bedchamber door was open and he could hear low voices. He strode in without bothering to knock.

'My Lord Ranyl, are you hurt?'

'Only my pride.' Ranyl was sitting in his favourite chair by his fire. The familiar, much calmer now though veins stilled pulsed anger in its bald head, sat on the back of the chair, stroking the old master's head.

'No injuries? What did they want?'

'The research of course. They want to send their dragon home, same as ever.'

Dystran paused, frowning. 'The what . . . ? What do elves care about Sha-Kaan.'

Ranyl laughed. 'Oh no, my Lord. The elves already have what they came for, or so I'm told.'

'So who . . . ?'

'Who else? The Raven.'

Dystran started violently. 'What?' For a moment, he couldn't believe what he was hearing and then the thoughts started to cascade through his head. 'Gods falling, the bolt hole.'

'My Lord?'

'Denser knows it exists. Think, Ranyl, he was the Dawnthief mage, he had to know.' He spun to Myx. 'Drive them away from the Mana Bowl. No wait.' He swung back to Ranyl. 'And she is with them?'

'Of course she is,' replied Ranyl.

'Where's Suarav?'

'On his way, my Lord,' said Myx.

'Can't wait for him. Look, get this word around,' said Dystran. 'I want the Mana Bowl sealed up so tight a mouse couldn't squeeze its arse in. And when you find The Raven, it's very, very important that Erienne is not harmed. Is that crystal clear?'

'Yes, my Lord. And the others?'

'No one leaves here. Not an elf, not a Raven,' said Dystran. 'And since Erienne is the only one I want unharmed, if I'm not mistaken that means every other enemy of Xetesk dies. Got it?'

Myx shifted uncomfortably. 'I understand your desire.'

Dystran passed a hand over his face. 'And if you and your questionable alliance of Protector brothers don't feel you can fight against your dear departed colleague, Sol, don't. There are plenty of elves out there, I am sure.'

'Yes, my Lord.'

'One more thing,' said Dystran. 'Get me a Protector on Herendeneth. I want to talk to one of my mages. Time to turn the heat up, I think, see if our all-but-caged bird really is the one we think she is.'

The windows were opaque with age and the shifting lantern and torch light did nothing to help Auum see what was immediately below him. He didn't have time to worry. One TaiGethen elf stood on the wide and ornate frame surrounding each of the library doors. All weapons were stowed, each elf held a heavy book.

'You know what to do, you know where we are spreading. Al-Arynaar, care. Shield us if you can. Tual will see us from this place.' He nodded. 'We move.'

Auum straight-armed the spine of the book hard into the window. The ancient glass and lead fell outwards in large pieces. Another strike and the window frame was clear. He dropped the book, grabbed the base of the window and turned a tight roll through it, straightening his legs when they cleared and landing in a crouch, hand already unclipping his jaqrui pouch, the other grabbing at a short sword.

Directly ahead of him, Xeteskians were running towards the library along the side of a long low building. Far enough away for now. He spun on his heel, taking in the Tais, all of whom had landed and moved. There were three guards in front of the library doors, already dragging swords from scabbards and forming up a defensive trio. He ran at them, Duele and Evunn were with him.

The TaiGethen cell tore in. Auum flicked out a jaqrui. It keened through the air, the ghostly sound echoing from the library walls, and ripped into the sword arm of a guard who grunted and clutched at the wound. Both Duele and Evunn favoured dual short swords. Evunn surged up the steps, ducked a blow, spun a roundhouse kick into the chest of his target and followed through with twin chopping strikes, left to right, biting deep into neck and shoulder. Immediately, he turned and backhanded the next guard, Duele burying his sword deep into the same unfortunate's chest. Before Auum could finish off his wounded man, his Tai had completed the job.

'Go,' said Auum.

The Tai sprinted left around the library walls, across the way of the soldiers closing in. They would be on Marack quickly. Auum increased his pace. The gardens where Porrack and Allyne were hidden were close by.

'Tais, move!' shouted Auum. 'We are discovered.'

The enemy were closing on them from ahead and right. Perhaps twenty swordsmen and crossbowmen appearing from around the sides of more of the long rooms in which their mages' spells were tested. Ahead, he could see his brothers move fluidly to their feet and begin to run. Like spirits rising from the ground they came and he could hear the whine and whisper of jaqruis and the thrum of bowstrings through the growing clamour bouncing from the walls of every building.

Auum's Tai split, creating a wide front and narrow targets. Auum whipped out two more throwing crescents. Left of him, Duele hugged the walls of the library in deep shadow, closing on men who could barely see him approaching through the gloom. Right, Evunn had sheathed a short sword and his jaqrui howled away. The enemy were scant yards distant and the crossbow bolts started to fly.

Auum zig-zagged into the centre of them, diving forward to turn a roll across the ground, coming to his feet and driving his blade into the groin of an enemy. He leapt away, Duele now in the melee with him, drop-kicking into a face and carving a deep cut across a throat.

Now, Porrack and Allyne hit the rear of the Xeteskians, taking the crossbowmen apart. Auum ducked a blow, raised his sword to parry another and smashed the base of his left palm up into the face of his attacker, punching him off his feet. He danced backwards, assessing his next target. Three men rushed him. He grabbed out his other short blade, backed off a pace and let them come. To the right, one crumpled and fell, a jaqrui thrown by Evunn buried in his mouth, blood pouring from his ruined face.

Auum whirled his blades in front of him, feinted to strike, dropped to his haunches and swept the feet from the nearest man. Ignoring him, he drove upright, blocked two quick strikes from the remaining guard and whipped a blade into the man's chest, sending him stumbling back, leather armour slit and blood welling from the wound.

The man on the ground was back on his heels. Auum lashed a kick into his head, laying him out cold. In front of him, Porrack was surrounded and took a deep cut in one arm. He responded, kicking high and straight into the head of his attacker. The man's head snapped back with a sickening crack. Auum stepped in, his blade burying itself to the hilt in the lower back of another.

It was enough. The Xeteskians ran, disengaging and running back to the south of the college and relative safety.

'Leave them,' ordered Auum. 'Tais, with me.'

The glow of spells bloomed to the north side of the library, deep blue and orange. The TaiGethen and their Al-Arynaar charges turned back to help Marack and her cell. Auum led them right around the library, seeing Marack backed up the steps of the building and against the doors. One of her Tai was down but moving, the mage was casting and a dozen men were moving in, swords, crossbows and magic.

Duele and Evunn took up the call of the spider monkey, the guttural sound distracting the attackers, some of whom turned. Orders were barked, warnings called and the line changed formation. The TaiGethen threw jaqrui crescents. The Xeteskians answered with crossbows. A bolt grazed Auum's left arm. He heard a grunt behind him and someone stumbled. They would be helped, it was the TaiGethen way. He ran on.

Ahead, the Al-Arynaar mage loosed a spell. Deep yellow Orbs flew out into the enemy line, striking them dead centre. The SpellShield held, dazzling the night sky with sudden bright blue. And beyond the battle, the noise of more fighting.

The Raven.

They may have been to blame for their discovery by the Xeteskians but, true to their word, they were covering the agreed escape route. Auum let the smallest of smiles cross his face and stepped in to grace the field of battle once more.

Chapter 20

Nyam looked on, his mouth moving soundlessly. Surely, here was the evidence he needed. But whether he should take action was something else entirely. To his left, Cleress slept, so deep that nothing of the past few moments had disturbed her. In front of him, Myriell sat bolt upright in a chair, her head cushioned, tended by a Guild elf. Her eyes were closed but she was not asleep. He could see her eyes moving beneath their lids. Her hands occasionally teased at the air and, like him, her mouth was moving and her brow furrowed deeply but with concentration, not confusion.

He had misjudged Diera badly. The woman was far stronger than he had thought and that had led to the stand-off in which he now found himself. The moment he had threatened her life, she had snatched up her child and screamed for help, bringing the Guild elves into the bedroom. Almost immediately, Protectors had forced their way past the guards.

And now, Protectors ringed the entrance to the chambers, keeping the rest of the Guild elves away while Nyam studied the Al-Drechar. But more Protectors guarded the door to Diera's bedroom too, underlining their split loyalties and the fine line Nyam was treading. His colleagues, he noticed were either unwilling or unable to join him. Perhaps they were giving thought to the morning and how they would save their own pathetic lives when Sha-Kaan inevitably came to exact his retribution.

'Why did you do it?' asked Nerane, the elf mopping Myriell's brow. 'We were helping you every way we could. We answered your questions.'

'Not all of them,' said Nyam. 'And now I have the answer I need for my masters in Xetesk. You should not have hidden the fact that another One mage was alive and under your protection. We want to perpetuate the order, see it grow again.'

'You would take it for yourselves.' Myriell's voice was cracked and exhausted. 'We will not allow that.'

Nyam looked at the old elf again, saw her eyes open and staring at him with unfettered disgust.

'That assumes you have a choice,' said Nyam.

'We always have a choice.'

'You are protecting her now?'

'I am doing what I must. You risk what you covet by your intrusion,' said Myriell, her eyes closing again.

'You must let us help you,' said Nyam.

'We will never let our secrets fall into the hands of any college,' she said, voice faint. 'Get out.'

Nyam felt torn between his respect for the Al-Drechar and his need to exert his authority. Threats weren't working. He heard footsteps behind him and turned his head to see a Protector approach.

'You must hear me, my mage,' he said. 'I stand in communication with Myx.'

Myx. Dystran's personal Protector.

'Speak.'

Nyam listened and his heart began to charge in his chest.

Rebraal took up a position in the lee of one of the two pillars that flanked the entrance to the dome complex. As The Raven ran out in their trademark angled chevron, with the mages in a quartet just behind them, he stretched his bow again and assessed the state of the college defence.

Ahead of them, the ornamental gardens opened out into the courtyard before the west gates of the college, currently closed. Men were running towards the gatehouse from either side along the walls. More were gathered in the courtyard itself and The Raven were facing about four times their number of swordsmen, mages and archers.

To his right, the way they were planning to run, there was activity by both stables and barracks. Again, soldiers were gathering, some running away east in the direction of the Mana Bowl, others forming to move up to the tower complex. They would have to fight fast, keeping the path open for the TaiGethen who should be advancing from his left, having swept through the library. Assuming they hadn't encountered too much trouble, of course.

Spells arced out to strike both forces as they closed. Rebraal searched the enemy for the shield mages. Light glared. Al-Arynaar Orbs flashed against the Xeteskian shield, which dipped under the pressure. Denser followed up with an Ice-Wind. Clouds of supercooled air banked against the deepening blue of the enemy defence. From within it, Xetesk's reply flashed hard against the Al-Arynaar barrier. Again, he could see it flex but hold firm, keeping The Raven safe.

The fighting lines came together, The Raven with typical force. The Unknown flicked his blade inside the guard of his first attacker, splitting his face from chin to forehead. He followed it with a dash to the side of the head to cast the man aside, giving him space to fight free. Beside him, Hirad switched his sword grip at the last moment, confusing his enemy, who tried to adjust the strike that was already on its way. Succeeding only in unbalancing himself, the guard watched helplessly while Hirad swayed left and whipped his sword into his undefended left flank.

Rebraal's bow tensed. Xeteskians were rushing up from the courtyard to flank. There were archers and swordsmen, five of them in a tight squad. He loosed a shaft; it tracked slightly right, taking the front swordsman in the shoulder, spinning him round and dumping him on the ground. The others ignored their fallen comrade, running on. Hirad was going to be in trouble.

The Al-Arynaar leader plucked another arrow from his diminishing supply and nocked it even as he headed down the steps at a dead run to join the barbarian. He lined up another target, tensed and fired on the run. He missed the swordsman, the arrow nicking the cheek of an archer and doing nothing but drawing attention to himself.

Time to fight. He crouched low a pace, laid his bow on the ground and came on, drawing his short sword as he closed on The Raven's line. Hirad hadn't seen the risk to himself, caught up as he was with a skilful and quick opponent.

'Hirad, your right! Guard your right!' he called.

Arrows flew by him forcing him to duck reflexively. He needed to get under Erienne's HardShield fast. Elsewhere in the line, Darrick and Thraun were forming an excellent partnership, the raw bludgeoning power of the shapechanger counterpointing Darrick's slick swordplay and solid defence.

'Flanking right!' shouted The Unknown, taking up Rebraal's warning and thrashing his blade at the guard confronting him. The man blocked the blow but staggered back under the impact. The Unknown saw him to the ground with a blow from the hilt of his dagger.

Hirad swept his blade in hard and low, his opponent blocking it aside, twisting away and licking his blade into the barbarian's left arm, slicing leather and flesh. Hirad growled and sent in a riposte, chopping a cut high up on his enemy's thigh. He backed away a pace and the move saved his life.

At the very last he saw the pair of swordsmen bearing down on his right flank, and wrenched his sword out to drive away the first strike though for the second time in quick succession a blade nicked his arm, this time his right. He ducked under a wild sweep from the other flanker but was helpless in the face of his original attacker. The quick man lashed in a killing blow but found The Unknown's blade blocking his way and the big man's dagger punching into his temple.

Rebraal took off in his last three paces and planted a two-footed kick into the chest of the second of Hirad's flanking attackers. He landed atop the man, heard ribs crack and turned to get the barbarian's grateful nod before the pair of them carved into the last standing swordsman, putting him down in a heartbeat.

The archers backed off in a hurry, taking the defending mages with them towards the courtyard. From around the side of the library, Auum led the TaiGethen into view right on cue.

'Raven, let's go!' called The Unknown.

But from across the college to their right, from the barracks and stables, came more of the enemy. And simultaneously, the western gates of the college swung open and men poured in, heading straight for them.

'Oh dear Gods,' said Hirad, breathing hard, the muscles in his arms protesting, his thighs burning with exertion.

The Raven's move faltered almost before it started, the TaiGethen gathering around them. From everywhere, it seemed, Xeteskian forces converged on foot and even on horseback. Arrows and bolts filled the air, clattering against Erienne's HardShield.

'We aren't going to make it,' said Darrick. 'They've got us trapped.'

'Ideas?' demanded The Unknown. 'We're out of time.'

'Only one place we can defend,' said Denser and he was already moving back towards the tower complex. 'Follow me.'

'Back to the dome, back to the dome!' yelled Hirad. 'Rebraal, bring your people.'

The raiding party turned and ran headlong for the steps up to the open doors and relative safety. The shadows shortened right in front of Rebraal, Xeteskian spells rushed through the air, crashing down on the rear of the group. He heard Gireeth scream in pain, turned his head and saw the mage's shield go. There was a wash of heat, hard cobalt light flashed and the lone FlameOrb burst on to the TaiGethen below.

Elves, burning and dying, were driven to the ground, their cries lost against the fire that rushed up the steps, biting at all their heels.

'Faster!'

Hirad, breathing in gasps, upped his pace in front. The doors were within a couple of paces. Auum led his Tai cell in, The Raven charging in behind, the survivors of the collapsed shield in their bootprints.

Thraun and The Unknown bent their shoulders to the doors, shoving the well-oiled and counterbalanced side fast closed, hearing arrows rattle against the wood.

'Denser, WardLock now,' ordered The Unknown.

'Ahead of you there.'

The casting was quick and efficient. Pale blue light crackled across the lock and through the veins of wood-and-iron binding. Rebraal slid to a stop in the blood of the fight so recently played out. He turned and took them all in, elf and Raven alike. Three TaiGethen and two Al-Arynaar mages hadn't made it. And alive though the rest of them might be, the same thought ran through all their minds.

In the centre of the Dark College, they were trapped.

'Ah, gentlemen, so glad you could all make it on this quite unbelievable evening.' Dystran smiled thinly from his seat in Ranyl's dining chamber on the second landing of the tower.

The dying lord himself was upstairs resting. The remainder of the Circle Seven were seated at the table.

'You'll note there are no refreshments,' continued Dystran. 'You'll also note that despite my request, Captain Suarav has so far been unable to join us. Would you like me to summarise why that is?'

He looked around the table, seeing the group of men, all of whom were at least twice his age. None of them would look him in the face. There was a phrase concerning ivory towers. He'd have to look into ways of seeing they saw more of the world beyond their noses.

'It is because this college is under attack by a few ageing mercenaries and some extremely impressive elves.' No meaningful reaction. He slammed his fist on the table. 'They are tearing up my college! Surely even you heard the odd shout or the odd spell marking our once pristine walls?'

'My Lord,' acknowledged someone though Dystran was barely listening.

'Tell me, Myx, where are The Raven and their elven friends at this moment?'

'They have just run into the dome, my Lord,' said Myx. 'The doors have been WardLocked.'

There was a stirring around the table.

'Yes, gentlemen, they are scant feet below us. Fortunately, there is a small bright spot I can apprise you of. On Herendeneth, a proactive young mage by the name of—' He clicked his fingers.

'Nyam, my Lord,' said Myx.

'Nyam has confirmed beyond reasonable doubt that the Al-Drechar are shielding a One mage. As you know, we feel that mage to be Erienne of the same Raven who are currently trapped beneath us. Here is what we will do.

'First of all, we need to send a message to some old friends. Then, I intend to prove that Erienne is that mage, and you must be ready to act on the mana spectrum the moment that proof is clear. We have always said that we should be able to adequately protect a One mage from his own mind while the awakening process completes, then school that mage in the art as laid down in certain of our more precious texts.

'It is time for us to make good on that assertion.' He turned to Myx. 'Your brothers, how close are they to their positions outside the Tower complex?'

'Before the hour turns, they will all be ready, my Lord.'

'Good. In that case instruct our new friend Nyam that when the hour turns, he is to kill the Al-Drechar currently shielding Erienne.' Dystran turned back to the table and examined the ends of his fingers before looking up into the blank faces of his Circle Seven. 'That should give us our proof, don't you think?'

'We can't stay here,' said Denser.

'No, really?' snapped Hirad. He rubbed a bloody hand through his hair. 'And there was me thinking we'd set up camp here, wait for the trouble to die down.' There was an impact on the doors. Timbers creaked but it seemed half-hearted, an act of frustration more than a serious attempt to break in. 'Gods this is just like Lystern, except we don't have horses waiting saddled and this city has walls.'

'Quiet, Hirad,' said The Unknown. 'Denser, facts and quickly. What do you have in mind?'

'This is an indefensible position, despite how it might look. Outside, they'll be waiting for instructions from the Circle Seven who will be in here somewhere. Look, it's grim. Our escape route is blocked. Right now, I don't think there's a way out for us. At least in here, or rather, in the catacombs, we can achieve something and hold out longer.'

'Like what?' asked Hirad.

'Got a dragon to send home, haven't you? I know where the research is held. Maybe we can last long enough to effect the casting. Depends how simple it is.'

'You aren't confident about our chances, then?' said The Unknown.

Denser shook his head.

'It's the best plan we've got,' said Hirad. 'Rebraal, you hearing this?'

The elf nodded. 'I've relayed it to the TaiGethen. We all knew it was a risk coming here. We're with you.'

'And the Aryn Hiil?' asked Denser.

'It will not fall back into their hands. We'll destroy it first.'

'Good, then let's go,' said the dark mage. 'One last thing, Unknown. Where we think this research is, and the lead mage. It's near the Soul Tank. I'm sorry.'

The Unknown nodded. 'I'll be all right. Just don't ask me how I'm feeling, any of you. You already know.'

'Follow me, then,' said Denser. 'I—'

A high-pitched sound flashed round the dome. Loud and piercing, it dug at the ears and vibrated through heads. Hirad clapped his hands to the sides of his head, grunting involuntarily. Across the dome, swords clattered to the floor and the elves were dropping to their knees, their pain written on their faces.

Abruptly, the sound ceased, leaving behind it the impression of great space. A voice, amplified by every surface and clear as a bell, filled the space.

'Now I have your attention, I have a proposal for you. You can hear me, can't you, dear Raven, dear elves?'

The voice echoed away. Hirad picked up his blade and scanned around, looking for the source. He saw Thraun breathing hard, his eyes closed, face pale. The elves were faring no better. The Unknown was glaring at the ceiling, chest puffed out, sword once again in his hand. Darrick was rubbing at his ears, face carrying that expression of irritation that was becoming a trademark, while Erienne stood close to Denser, looking to him for an answer which he duly provided.

'Dystran, how unnecessarily loud to hear your voice.'

'I rather thought you'd be impressed by it. You should be. You have gathered in the most perfect place for Intonation. Bear that in mind. I can be much, much louder.'

'Yes we are all duly impressed by your ability,' said Denser, his tone bored. 'What do you want?'

'I want to end the bloodshed,' said Dystran. 'You have proved your prowess fighting my people but that's over now. You are caught, you know you are. But you need not die. I have a deal for you. Surrender yourselves now and none of you will be harmed. The elves we will guarantee safe passage back to Calaius once this siege is broken, assuming they let us have back what was taken from our library. And The Raven will remain here as our guests until this unseemly conflict is over. General Darrick, as a man under sentence of death in your own college, I should think that a very happy solution. Denser, you can reacquaint yourself with the place that made you. Sol, you can be sure your family are safe, talk to them through your Protector brothers whenever you like and Erienne . . . Erienne, with us you can fulfil your potential.

'It is tempting, I know. But you'll want to discuss it so I give you a short time to do so. Then open the doors. The other way is pain and suffering, believe me.'

Dystran's voice echoed away to nothing. Hirad opened his mouth but saw Denser put a finger to his lips and point up. Then he spread his arms wide, asking the question. Every head shook. Denser smiled, put the his finger back to his lips and beckoned them all on, pointing to Rebraal to come close.

'They'll have the entrances to the catacombs guarded. Perhaps Auum could do the honours,' he said into the elf's ear.

Rebraal nodded. 'We will see to it.' He walked over to Auum and relayed the message.

Led by the TaiGethen, The Raven entered the catacombs of Xetesk.

Pheone walked alone around the crater that hid the Heart of Julatsa, her mind torn between grief and hope. Her people had reached the Xeteskian siege lines and contacted the Al-Arynaar. Communion had confirmed what she wanted to hear. They would come but had a mission to perform before leaving the lines and heading north. The news had filled her with an optimism she had never thought to feel again. But so quickly, her heart had been crushed again.

The Raven were in the game, it seemed, though their location was a closely guarded secret because of trouble with both Lystern and Dordover. But she hadn't really listened to the reasons why. Because when she had asked after Ilkar, she had been told of his death. The Communion had broken then and there, and the loss and emptiness had swept through her like a gale that had no end.

She had run from her friends, where they had been conducting the linked Communion, and they had been respectful in turn, leaving her to herself and her thoughts.

She had cried long for Ilkar, his smile, his energy and his sheer presence. The touch she would never feel again, the pain that must have accompanied his death from the Elfsorrow. She thought of The Raven too. Such a close friendship now destroyed by something they couldn't fight. Helplessness. She knew how that felt all right.

Finally, she pushed the images of the elf she had loved from her mind and tuned in to the mana spectrum. The shadow was there, covering the Heart, smothering its colour, dulling its power. And the effect they'd noticed in the last couple of days was there, and growing too. The shadow was sending out flares of gloom like spears into the mass of the spectrum. She wondered what that meant. So far they had come up with nothing.

At least it hadn't led to any further failures of the Julatsan focus. But it was inevitable that some would come. Every spell they cast took so much more effort, left them that much more drained than they should be. And the problems would be amplified for those casting outside of the college and city.

Pheone stopped walking and gazed down into the perfect blackness that the moonlight could not penetrate, letting her tears fall into its depth. Like the dark below, the shadow was intensifying, little by little, day after day. And every day, the chances of being able to raise the Heart when the elves arrived diminished a little more.

She prayed they would not arrive too late but the abyss was yawning wide.

Chapter 21

The most feared place on Balaia without question, the catacombs beneath the towers of Xetesk were told of in legend and myth, in dark tales and to keep children in bed. They inspired extraordinary exaggeration based on ignorance but some of the invention was shot through with truth.

Here was where the research to which the students weren't privy was carried out. Where experiments on human subjects dragged there by Protectors had been carried out in years gone by. Where contact with the demon dimension was first established and the power of Xetesk enhanced. Where the Circle Seven had exclusive run with their teams of talented adepts in the neverending race for political influence through spell development. And where the Soul Tank lay.

But as they hurried past the guards so easily killed by Auum and Evunn and on into the labyrinthine passages designed to confuse the unwelcome walker, Hirad noted that the descriptions of jagged rock tunnels, narrow and dripping with water feeding underground pools stocked with hideous monsters were far from accurate.

'What do you think we are, savages?' said Denser. 'Left here, Rebraal. Take the stairway down, then left again.'

'Well no, but still. It's a bit smart, isn't it?'

Denser shrugged and followed Rebraal and Auum down the stairs. 'I don't know. I've never known it any other way. Just because it isn't the way you heard it was . . .'

Far from the dank, rough underground horror he'd been led to expect, Hirad was walking through carefully constructed passages the quality of which wouldn't have been out of place in a mansion house. Wide enough for three people walking abreast, the roughly circular corridors had been smoothed with plaster and painted in pastel colours. There were even a few paintings hung on the walls.

The whole place glowed with a gentle blue light and air circulated, keeping the passages fresh.

'Mind you,' continued Denser. 'We haven't reached the depths yet. This is just the upper level. Rebraal, straight on, then hard right. More steps. Wait at the bottom. That's where the fun starts.'

'How do you mean?' asked The Unknown.

'Hold on. Wait until we reach the bottom of these stairs.'

'Ever the man of mystery,' muttered Erienne.

'Yeah,' said Hirad.

The base of the stairs marked a change in the catacombs. Although the light remained, gone were the pleasant decorations, replaced by stark murals and smooth, unpainted rock faces. They stood in a domed chamber, the ceiling eight feet or more above The Unknown's head. Passages led off it in four directions and the air was cooler. It was the first open space they'd encountered since they'd entered.

'We need to stop,' said Denser.

'Why?' asked Hirad.

'Because you all need to understand how this works as far as you are able.'

'So talk,' said Rebraal.

He stood at the head of a group of confused and irritated elves. They were uncomfortable here below ground, beyond anything they could readily recognise.

'I think we've bought ourselves a little time. It's best spent here,' Denser said. 'Rebraal, please relay this as best you can.'

'Whatever you say.' His face betrayed some anxiety.

'All right, listen,' Denser said instead. 'You have to understand the nature of the catacombs. They've been built over fifteen centuries, no one knows exactly what area they cover because there's never been any organisation to their building. Generation upon generation of Circle Seven mages have built as they saw fit, extending their predecessors' areas, digging their own, sealing off what they don't want. Where I have brought you now is the full extent of my knowledge.

'This is what we call a hub room. It's the central point of a Circle Seven mage's catacomb chambers, in this case, Dystran's. Looks to me as though he hasn't spent too much time on decoration recently. There are hub rooms all over the catacombs, dozens. Some mages own several. Dystran undoubtedly does.

'Right, directly ahead of us is the place we want to be. You can expect alarm wards across most passages in the hub areas but we may not have time to look for them all and disarm them. Doors we need to worry about. Traps are as common as mistrust down here.'

'Isn't there a map of the catacombs at all?' asked The Unknown.

'There's a map room where we're going but it's incomplete because Circle Seven mages are unwilling to admit to everything they've developed. It's like a different country down here. There'll be mages researching down here who barely ever see the light of day. I'm sure Kestys is among them right now and he won't be undefended, though whether it's by magic or muscle, I don't know.

'I just want to get across to you what it's like. We could be attacked from any direction, it depends on the knowledge of the mages sending forces against us.'

'Sounds completely ridiculous to me,' said Hirad.

Denser shrugged. 'It's just the way it is in Xetesk. The way to the top is through influence and influence comes from new magical knowledge. That's the currency of political power. Dystran is top dog because he has always been central to the development of dimensional magic and chosen his aides because of their limited life expectancy.'

'I like nothing more than a history lesson, as you know,' said Hirad. 'But right now, all it means to me is that we have to secure whatever area it is you say we have to and keep it secure until you do whatever it is you do. Then we fight our way out.'

'What could be simpler?' said Denser. 'This way.'

He trotted over to the passage directly opposite the stairway, The Raven gathered around him with the elves spreading naturally into the space behind, watching and listening. He held up a hand and crouched, closing his eyes to tune to the mana spectrum. While he waited, Hirad looked up the corridor.

He could see half a dozen ways off it, up to what looked like a junction a couple of hundred feet away. It looked so harmless but the atmosphere that poured from it felt anything but; he turned to mention it and was confronted by a set of expressions that chilled him to the bone.

Thraun was staring straight ahead down the passage, his pupils huge in his yellow-tinged eyes. Sweat stood out on his forehead and he looked tensed to run. Beside him, The Unknown Warrior had a hand to his head. His mouth moving slightly, his eyes screwed tight shut. He was swaying. And Erienne, like the big man, was clutching at her head, her frown deep and her eyes, boring into the barbarian's, small and scared. Only Darrick looked anything like himself.

'Gods under water,' breathed Hirad. 'Darrick, see to The Unknown. Thraun, hold on there.' He stepped up to Erienne and cupped her face in both hands. 'Erienne? What's wrong?'

'It's Myriell. They know, Hirad. Xetesk knows about me. It's not a bluff any more. They've seen her shielding me. I'm the only one it can be. Hirad, there are Protectors in her chambers.'

'Oh no.'

'What are we going to do?'

'It's worse than that,' said The Unknown.

Hirad swung round. The Unknown's face was drawn and pale, as if he had a pain right behind his forehead.

'How?'

'I can hear them, Hirad. This close to the Soul Tank I can hear everything. They've been ordered to kill Myriell when the hour strikes. That's any time now. A mage will order it; he's standing in front of her now.'

'Tell them not to, Unknown. You've got to stop them,' said Hirad.

Next to him, Denser was moving his hands in an intricate motion, like picking strands of a web on each finger and moving them against a breeze.

'I can't, Hirad, I can't speak to them. I can only listen,' he said. 'They've been recalled from the siege too. They're coming here to the catacombs. They won't fight us but they will fight the elves.'

'The TaiGethen can take them,' said Hirad.

'There's over fifty of them. Down here they are more awesome than anywhere else, despite how badly they'll all feel. Believe me, it won't go well for us. We are threatening the Soul Tank.'

Hirad drew breath, thinking for a moment. 'One thing at a time. Thraun. Snap out of it. Thraun!'

'Up there,' said Thraun, indicating the corridor with a jerk of his chin. 'It's rotten. I can smell it, like ten days' dead flesh.'

'Not now, Thraun. Look after Erienne, you know you can help. I'm going to talk to Sha-Kaan, see what can be done. Unknown, Darrick, you've been here before. We need a defence tighter than a rat's arse. Rebraal, we're in trouble. Be ready. Darrick will have instructions, please don't let Auum question them, we're good at this. Denser, are you through?'

'Almost there,' said Denser, and Hirad respected the man's concentration, given what he must just have heard. 'Can't trigger it. It would blind and deafen us all. Just for a while but long enough, if you know what I mean. Don't rush me.'

'We're running out of time.'

'I heard.'

Hirad smoothed Erienne's cheek. She was badly frightened. 'It's all right. Sha-Kaan will stop them and Cleress is still there.'

Erienne shook her head, tears forcing themselves from her eyes. 'She can't do it alone, Hirad. My mind. They're going to destroy my mind like Lyanna's was destroyed. Please don't let them.'

Thraun pushed Hirad aside firmly. 'Talk to your dragon,' he said, pulling Erienne to him. 'I am here.'

Hirad dropped down to sit with his back to a wall. He closed his eyes and felt the presence of the great dragon deep in his mind. He was resting, unaware of the potential disaster unfolding before The Raven.

Great Kaan, I must disturb your rest.

I am tired, Hirad Coldheart. Tell me good news. Hirad could feel the dragon's irritation.

I have none, Sha-Kaan. Please listen. Xetesk threatens us here and on Herendeneth. Mages on the island have been ordered to kill the Al-Drechar. It would leave Erienne unshielded.

Sha-Kaan's growl reverberated through Hirad's head causing him to gasp in pain.

I warned them, said the dragon. *I told them the consequences of such action. I will attend to it. Tell me your position, your mind is in turmoil.*

We are trapped inside the catacombs. Xetesk's forces are coming for us but we are close to the research that can send you home. We want to hold out for long enough but if Erienne is hurt we will struggle.

Then don't delay me. Tell The Unknown Warrior I am mindful of his family.

The contact was broken. Hirad shook himself and simultaneously felt a huge fist grab a handful of his leather armour and drag him to his feet.

'Hirad, time to go.' It was The Unknown, eyes fierce with new determination though deep within, the suffering under the tumult of voices from the Protectors dragged at his mind. 'There's been a change of plan.'

'There has?'

'Yes, there has. Now move.'

'Sha-Kaan will keep your family safe,' said Hirad as he was propelled towards the corridor down which Denser and the TaiGethen had just vanished.

The Unknown paused enough to nod his thanks. 'The Protectors will be there for them too.'

'What's the change of plan?'

'We're going to release the Protectors.'

Nyam stood at the threshold of greatness. Or folly. He had heard the whispered words related to him by his Protector, Ark. He had stepped away from elven ears when the import of what was being discussed became apparent. But he had not for one heartbeat guessed what Dystran's next move would be. And so he stood in the corridor outside the Al-Drechar's rooms and his hands shook and the sweat dampened his armpits and face.

'He cannot ask that of me,' said Nyam. 'The devastation that could be unleashed. We've learned that much, surely.'

Ark was quiet for a moment, relaying Nyam's words and receiving Dystran's next utterance.

'He assures you the power resides in Xetesk to counter the threat of devastation. He demands your compliance.'

'Please, it is an unnecessary risk, Ark. Impress upon him that capturing the girl will give him what he wants. He doesn't have to do this.'

Another pause. 'He feels it is time to exert his authority over this island. If you will not do his wishes, one of us will.'

'Ask him to reconsider, please. There's still time.'

Ark's blank mask faced him. 'He asks you to remember who is Lord of the Mount. His decision stands. He will give the word.'

Nyam nodded wearily. 'Tell him it will be done on his word.'

'My mage.'

Nyam waited until Ark focused on him again, hating himself for his cowardice. 'Ark, you will carry out this deed.'

Ark merely nodded. After all, he didn't have a choice.

A roar split the air, shuddering windows in their frames. Nyam winced.

'Oh dear Gods burning, he knows.'

The Unknown Warrior tried without success to shut out the voices in his head. They spoke of confusion, of anxiety but through it all of purpose. They were advancing towards The Raven, they were sheltering Diera and Jonas and one, Ark, was standing by to murder Myriell. He didn't feel he had any choice. His brothers concurred but the situation was causing unsettling currents in the Soul Tank.

It brought all the memories crashing back for him yet again but this time so much more acutely. The view through the mask; the hand of a demon hovering ever near his soul; the knowledge of the pain the creatures could cause him on a whim; the strength of the Soul Tank; the depth of brotherhood that he could never experience again and could never explain.

The Unknown breathed deep and looked left and right. Two of the remaining three Al-Arynaar mages moved slowly up the passage, tuned deep into the mana spectrum, looking for any hint of further Xeteskian wards as they moved towards the junction ahead. Behind them walked Marack and her surviving cell member, Harroc. Indeed all the Tai cells bar Auum's had now lost a member following the piercing of the shield outside the tower complex.

Porrack and Jaruul, Allyne and Lisaan were guarding a left-hand passage opposite him and just beyond the catacombs' map room in which Auum stood with Thraun and Erienne. The former two were trying to understand the three-dimensional mana model of the network of passages, chambers and openings, the latter trying to gather her broken concentration.

Hirad, Darrick, Rebraal and Auum's Tai were covering the

hub room they'd so recently vacated, waiting for the onslaught they could hear echoing through the catacombs.

Everything was ready. He and Denser were outside the door to the research room, Denser trying to divine the solution to the trap ward cast over its surface and just a few yards away, the place he'd never thought to see again but now knew he would. The Soul Tank.

'Hurry, Denser,' he said. 'This is unbearable. They are closing. Please, I don't want more to die.'

'It's complex, Unknown,' whispered Denser. 'I can't see the solution.'

'Dammit, I don't have the time,' growled The Unknown. He stepped across to the map room and beckoned Auum out. 'Rebraal!' he hissed. The Al-Arynaar elf ran back up the passage. 'Are they closing?'

Rebraal nodded. 'On us any time. Our mage is ready.'

'Good. We're getting nowhere fast here. I need that door opened and the trap triggered. Is he fast enough? Denser says flesh contact will trigger it.'

'I'll see to it.'

The conversation was short. Auum sized up the door, handed his boots to Rebraal and sprinted away about twenty yards.

'Denser, move. Can't be waiting for you.'

The Unknown motioned anyone in the potential target area aside. Denser saw Auum coming, muttered under his breath and stepped smartly aside. The TaiGethen leader came up the corridor at a pace The Unknown could never have matched, his legs a blur. By the research room door, he stepped around side on, snapped into a cartwheel and lashed out a foot as he travelled, connecting solidly with the heavy bound wood.

He was past it as the ward triggered. A rectangle of flame seared out from the door, scorching the wall opposite and billowing heat along the passage.

'Gods burning!' The Unknown put his hands in front of his face for a moment then dragged out his sword and marched to the door. 'Unlocked? Good.'

He twisted the ring handle and kicked the door in, striding through in the same movement and running around the long table that dominated the floor space. Two mages had spun round from the blackboard they'd been sketching on, jaws slack.

'Which one of you bastards is Kestys?' demanded The Unknown bearing down on them.

One pointed to his comrade who, bravely enough, pointed to himself.

'Lucky for you,' spat the Raven man.

He grabbed the other and rammed his sword through his gut, the blade rasping on his backbone, and let the body drop to the floor, blood gushing over his boots. The dripping blade was against Kestys's throat in the next instant.

'Do exactly what I say, exactly when I say it, and Denser might just persuade me to leave you alive.'

'Who—?'

'Just pray you can do what we think you can or they'll be mopping you up too.'

'Unknown!' called Hirad. 'We've got company.'

The Unknown Warrior smiled at Kestys unpleasantly, saw the drops of urine puddling around his shoes and grabbed his collar.

'The sand timer has started so I hope you're really good. Because you've got even less time than we have.'

Chapter 22

The thud of spells pressuring the Al-Arynaar ForceCone protecting the open end of the corridor could be heard, heavy, regular and with an air of inevitability.

'I need another mage here now!' yelled Hirad. 'Rebraal, get one of them, Sian can't hold this on her own.'

A shout in elvish and the sound of feet slapping past but The Unknown could barely lift an eyebrow to care. Here it was. In a plain room, hung with darkest blue hangings. No pattern lifted the sombre atmosphere, nothing but the gentle blue light offered any life at all. The chamber was no more than a cell, fifteen feet on each side with a waist-high stone dais in the centre. And on top of the dais sat a carved stone block only the height of his dagger and twice as long. So physically diminutive but the ancient Xeteskian language and screaming faces carved on its flat surface told the knowledgeable everything about that which it contained.

It was the Soul Tank. It had no lid and the hollow inside was governed by the demons. Their deal with Xetesk meant that they linked each soul to its host Protector body; and in return for the control they exerted in the name of Xetesk, they leached life energy from the souls at their mercy. For The Unknown, it oozed power and evil. It was a prison with no windows and no air. One in which the essence of so many Xeteskian men had been trapped from puberty to death and one from which only he had escaped alive.

Until tonight. The Unknown laid his hands on its surface. He could hear the voices so loud now. In concert while they organised themselves around the tasks their masters had set and unsettled because they knew where The Raven were. And he was sure they could sense a change. The Unknown would see to it that change was effected or he would die in the attempt.

He turned to Kestys. The mage, with a dagger held to his throat by Denser, was quite white. He shivered and looked with wide, terrified eyes at the big warrior.

'You know who I am,' said The Unknown.

Kestys managed a nod. 'You are Sol.'

'So you know what I want.'

Kestys dragged in a tremulous breath and swallowed hard. 'I can't do that. Please. Don't ask that.'

Denser slammed the hapless mage back against a wall, ruffling the blue cloth hanging. 'You will, Kestys. This abomination must end and it must end now.'

'I can't—'

'You can!' snapped Denser. 'Think I am without sense? I saw what was in that room. I know you can realign the dimensions and I know you have solved the script for undoing the Protector deal with the demons. I've been to Herendeneth, Kestys. I understand the depth of the knowledge they will have passed to you.'

'It's not that easy,' protested Kestys.

The Unknown slapped the top of the Soul Tank. He pushed Denser aside and put a hand round Kestys's throat. 'I don't have the time to debate this. I expect Denser can work it out. But I don't want to risk that just in case my friends out there can't hold on against your bastard master for long enough. And let me assure you, if he does break through, you will die before I do.' He ignored the choking sounds the mage was making, instead gripping a little harder, lifting him from the ground. 'I can hear them in my head right now. All of them, don't you understand?' He pointed behind him at the Soul Tank. 'I feel them. I feel their pain and I know their desire to be free. But I can't tell them I know because they can't hear me. But you, Kestys, you will free them. You will allow them to take off those masks and live as men, not slaves.

'Don't miss this chance to do one thing of worth in your pathetic life. Because, believe me, if you don't there will be no other chance to do anything. Your choice. Give my brothers their lives or drown in your own blood.

'Which is it to be?'

*

Auum and Thraun had gone to stand behind the ForceCone, ready in case it should fail, leaving Erienne alone in the map room. She was trying to drag her thoughts together such that she could be of some use in the fight if it came to it. But it was so hard. She felt an axe poised behind her neck. Gods, she could feel its edge, hard and true.

And the One entity fed off her fear. She could feel that too. The mental mass that she tried so hard to repress was working so hard against her and Myriell. Trying to overwhelm her and release itself. She realised that in some fundamental respects, she didn't understand the One entity at all. That it could destroy its host so deliberately and surely wither itself. She had to remind herself again that it was not sentient.

She shook her head but the conflict wouldn't fade. Outside, she could hear Hirad exhorting the elven mages to more effort to keep back the barrage of the Xeteskian mages. Through the mana spectrum she could sense the weight of the battering they were taking. She and Denser needed to be there to help them but she couldn't summon up a candle flame to save her life right now. And Denser was with The Unknown. She could hear them both shouting. Gods drowning, everything was falling apart.

She took a deep breath and held it, her eyes closed. Breathing out, she focused hard on the map hanging in the air. Like the light that caressed the entire catacombs, the map was a magical construct, sustained by the focused energy in the mana stream caused by the centre of Xetesk's Heart. It was impressive too. Denser said that Dystran had sent a mana trace through the passages and chambers to try and create the first complete map of the catacombs. The resultant model was an extraordinary construction which grew that little bit every day. And it was vast.

Picked out in shades of blue and red, it covered between one and seven levels depending on which area of the catacombs you were standing in. It had to sprawl underneath the whole college and way out into the city beyond, perhaps even further. Erienne could understand why the walls of the map room were covered with sketches of small sections of the mana map. It was terribly difficult to discern locations. She had no idea which passage and rooms represented where they stood. The only positive thing she could take out of it was that they could surely lose themselves in here forever, far beyond the widest search.

Ridiculous. A tunnel complex of which no one truly knew the extent. She wasn't at all sure that Dystran would find his answers from this bird's nest of tiny mana trails. Erienne frowned. A tiny flash caught her eye. She leaned in close. Right at the base of the map and far to the left-hand side, beyond the furthest extent of the catacombs proper, the mana trace had found a rogue passage. Actually, now she looked, there were a few of them, stretching out further than the central mass.

She watched for a moment, saw the map growing minutely. She almost smiled but a sharp stab of pain within her head dragged her rudely back to reality. She gasped at its sharpness, deep in her mind.

Myriell, are you there?

I am, child, but I am scared, I cannot hide it from you. It affects my abilities.

Tell me what is going on. I feel like I'm under sentence of death here.

A frisson of humour stole across her thoughts. *That makes two of us. I know what they are planning. They have already silenced Cleress with a spell to keep her sleeping. At least she will be spared this.*

You have to stop them. Erienne felt a rush of desperation.

I cannot. My energies are consumed with shielding your mind. At least Sha-Kaan has been wakened. That may delay them, I don't know . . . Erienne listen to me. If I should be killed, you must fight until Cleress can waken to your aid. The Xeteskians are planning to shield you but they don't understand the nature of the One. They will treat it like a college magic. It is not.

Oh, Myriell, I don't understand it either. Please help me.

Then hear what I say and pray that I have enough time left.

Another spell cracked against the ForceCone. Rinelle and Vinuun were holding but it was close. Beside Hirad, Sian'erei rested but had a SpellShield ready should the Cone fail. And in front of the barbarian, Auum, Duele and Evunn were poised to wreak mayhem amongst the Xeteskians waiting in the hub room beyond.

Hirad couldn't see them all but knew there were more than the seven mages and thirty-odd soldiers he could count. They had to be trying to get behind too and that bothered him. The six TaiGethen guarded the two possible access points. Thraun was with them, and his keen sense of smell should act as some sort of early warning but it would only give them a few moments. And he seemed distracted somehow. Next to him, Rebraal spoke words of encouragement for his mages. Darrick patrolled the corridor. Ever the general, ever the tactician, though there was little even he could add. They'd abandoned one desperate situation and put themselves in another.

In front of Hirad, the spell attack stopped. ForceCone was an excellent spell. A simple shape, easy to cast and mercifully also very easy to maintain. It was largely invulnerable to magic attack though a powerful enough mage, or several in concert, could crack it. The problem the Xeteskians had was that this Cone was covering a small area and was particularly focused. And while The Raven couldn't get at them through it because it barriered both ways, they didn't have the guile or the linked power to knock it aside.

Abruptly, the mages and soldiers moved left and right. From the stairs came more men, mages this time. They were six and five spread in a loose arc around one who stood forward. Ten Protectors followed them out and formed a three-quarter circle around them. A sense of awe and undeniable power caused Hirad's heart to skip a beat.

'This looks bad,' he muttered.

'It is,' said Darrick who had arrived at his right shoulder. 'That's Dystran and the Circle Seven minus Ranyl. It doesn't get more powerful than that.'

'Great.' Hirad turned his head. 'Unknown! I hope you're getting somewhere in there. We've got a little trouble out here!'

Dystran stepped close to the Cone. The temptation Hirad felt to order the Al-Arynaar mages to push it forward and crush him was almost overwhelming but Dystran, like his attack mages before him, would be very well protected.

'You are a master of understatement,' said the Lord of the Mount. 'Hirad Coldheart, isn't it? Delighted to make your acquaintance. You have quite a reputation.' Dystran's gaze travelled slowly over all that he faced. 'Remarkable. The Raven, or some of it at least. The extraordinary TaiGethen, or that is what I understand the elves to call themselves. And you, General Darrick. How is it, being an outlaw? I could offer you a senior position on my staff, you know. Now Lystern wants you dead, you are my ally, are you not?'

'Your logic is flawed,' said Darrick. 'I am no friend to you just as I am no enemy to Lystern. They, at least, are merely misguided.'

Dystran chuckled. 'Indeed. But they will execute you just the same. I don't want to have to mimic them.' His expression hardened. 'This is over. Very valiant and all that but you cannot hold out against us forever. Your mages will tire, your ForceCone will fail and we will take you.

'I repeat; you do not have to die. But you must surrender to me. I hold all the cards. I do not have to waste spells on you, I do not have to fight you. I simply have to wait.'

'Go ahead and wait,' said Hirad. 'We're in no rush.'

'Only The Raven could mount such arrogance in the face of such circumstances. I will kill you if I have to. There is no escape. Don't try my patience. It is already wearing very thin and the blood of too many of my men and mages is staining the stone of my college. I will not suffer more.'

'Patience is a virtue,' said Hirad. 'And you're going to have to learn to be more virtuous. We aren't going anywhere.'

Dystran nodded and Hirad could see the anger building in him. 'Yes. Ranyl has told me what you want from here. Very laudable. But we are not finished with the dragon and he stays here until we are.'

Hirad pointed a finger at Dystran. 'You do not control Sha-Kaan. Gods burning, but he is far stronger than you can possibly imagine. And you know something else, Xetesk-man? Given what I suspect is happening to your precious men on Herendeneth, you'll wish we'd already sent him home, believe me.'

'Really, Coldheart? Think you can threaten me with that? One dying dragon? One more chance. Drop the Cone. Drop the SpellShield. Drop your weapons. Do it all now.'

'Drop dead,' said Hirad.

'Fine. Seems I will have to take further steps. Can't risk you actually succeeding with my research now, can I?' He clicked his fingers and a Protector moved to his side. 'Time to take one of yours out of the game. Myx, you know the order.'

The Protector nodded.

*

Sol we can sense you. We know you hear us.

'Damn but you can't hear me,' whispered The Unknown. 'Can you?'

He was leaning on the dais with his hands, his forehead resting on the Soul Tank itself. The stone was warm and the temperature was increasing steadily. Beside him stood Kestys and Denser, both lost in the mana spectrum. Kestys was sweating profusely, his concentration held under duress and difficult to maintain. Denser was monitoring the construct Kestys was making, or rather, the unravelling of the spells maintaining the link between the Soul Tank and the demon dimension.

Information was sketchy and The Unknown hadn't had much time for explanations. But what he understood was that while each Protector's soul was linked to his body by a Demon-Chain, a fundamental linkage formed the basis of the deal with the demons, allowing them to draw life energy from the souls in return for keeping the elite fighting force thralled and effecting the soul communication that made them so devastatingly effective.

Parts of the knowledge had been lost in the intervening centuries concerning the inter-dimensional construction of the linkage. The Al-Drechar had filled in those gaps.

'How long, Denser?' asked The Unknown.

The dark mage held up a hand. 'Please, Unknown. The demons are resisting. Not long, I hope.'

'Please hear me,' whispered The Unknown, mouth all but kissing the Soul Tank, the clamour of voices in his head increasing as the souls within became more and more aware of the discord created by the warming of the tank. 'Fyr, Ahn, Kol, any of you my brothers, please.' He gripped the sides of the tank now, desperate to get through, hoping against all reason that his physical proximity would have an effect.

There is trouble.
We are one.
Sol is near.
Two across, catacomb right. Holding.
I am altered.
Change.
None are at rest.
The order is given. Ark, the Al-Drechar must die.

'No!' hissed The Unknown. 'No, Myx. Ark, for Gods' sake no. I am freeing you, don't do this.'

It is understood. My mage will be apprised.

We are one.

'No, damn you,' breathed The Unknown. 'No.'

He straightened and ran from the Soul Tank, running down towards the hub room where Hirad and Darrick stood.

'Myx!' he shouted. 'Tell him to stop! Tell Ark to stop. Xetesk doesn't understand.'

He saw Myx's head move. He took an unsteady pace. Next to him, Dystran raised an eyebrow.

'I . . . can't. Please, Sol.'

'Just tell him, for Gods' sake, tell Ark now. No one will hurt you. You can feel the heat in the Tank, can't you? Stop him!' The Unknown slid to a halt by Hirad. 'Call your man off, Dystran.'

'Fascinating,' said the Lord of the Mount. 'That you can still hear them. Why don't you rejoin them?'

'Because there won't be a them any more, you bastard. Now, instruct Ark off before it's too late for us all.'

'Drop dead,' said Dystran, smiling at Hirad.

Brace yourself, Erienne. Myriell's voice came to her clear and, for the first time, genuinely frightened.

What is happening?

They are coming for me.

No, Myriell. Run. RUN!

There is nowhere to run, child. Pray for me as I now pray for you.

Myriell. Protect yourself. A spell, use a spell. Leave me.

Too late. The Al-Drechar's voice sounded tired, beaten. *Be strong.*

Erienne ran. She had no idea what she was going to do. She tore out of the map room, saw The Unknown and Hirad and made for them.

'Hirad!' she screamed. 'Help me!' And then she caught sight of Dystran. 'Stop it now. You don't understand. You'll kill me. Please.'

'I rather think we can help,' said Dystran calmly.

Erienne backed away into Hirad's arms, shaking her head. 'You can't. You don't understand.' She was shaking violently. Her heart pounded so loud she could barely hear her own breathing rasping into her lungs in painful gasps. 'Please don't kill her.'

There was a heavy impact on the roof of the house. Sha-Kaan roared unfettered fury, his claws and mouth tearing at the slate and timber. Plaster dust fell in torrents, the noise was deafening. In moments he would be inside.

Ark strode towards the Al-Drechar, his axe raised, his orders clear but his mind a muddled fog. The Soul Tank was in uproar. He could hear his brothers but something alien was building. He felt uncomfortable, as if his body were generating heat it couldn't dispel and though Myx had been quite clear in his instruction from the Lord of the Mount, there was no doubting he was unhappy.

Sol had implored him not to but they had no choice. A demon's fingers were so close to squeezing his soul, his and all his brothers'. They were angry too. Everything he had known was unsettled.

What must I do?

Ark, you have the option you have always had. Sol wants us to be free but the demons are alerted. How can we refuse?

I have no choice.

We are one. We will grieve.

He was standing above the Al-Drechar now. She made no move to escape, merely looked up at him, resigned, accepting of her fate. It was not right. Surely they should be protected. But if the Lord of the Mount wanted her dead, who was he to question? A part of him felt ashamed such thoughts had arisen but ever since Sol had left them, there had been the germination of doubt.

Help me, my brothers.

We cannot refuse the Master.

Sol shouts that you should not.

The demons are close to us all.

May the Gods forgive me.

Ark raised his axe. 'I am sorry.'

The Al-Drechar nodded her head.

Ark tensed his muscles and powered in the swing and in the same instant all but fell. His mind was silent, loss deluged him and in the same instant, unrefined joy battled it, his soul crying out on return to its rightful place.

Panicked, he tried to drag the axe aside from its target, a cry ripping from his lips.

Erienne saw the Protectors in front of her sway. One buckled, others staggered, struggling for balance, clutching at anything around them. Shouts filled the air, shocked, disoriented, scared.

She turned to The Unknown Warrior. He clenched both fists.

'Yes! Yes, you bastard, yes!'

'We've done it!' she said, relief flooding her. 'Myriell, we've—'

Myriell's scream tore through Erienne's head like exploding glass, her death a cascade of pain, and a welling of power she couldn't hope to contain.

'No,' she whimpered. 'Denser.'

But the last thing she saw was the dismay in The Unknown's eyes as the One erupted into her mind and blew her consciousness to shreds.

Chapter 23

Denser had turned from the exhausted Kestys and reached the door of the Soul Tank chamber just in time to see Erienne scream his name and collapse to the floor. His triumphant words died on his lips and he had been about to move when a mana gale struck the catacombs.

Uncontrolled power surged from Erienne's mind, grabbing what it could from the elements and augmenting it with the keenly focused Xeteskian mana. Denser gripped the frame of the door but no one else he could see was so lucky.

While Erienne lay motionless, the Al-Arynaar mages operating the ForceCone were pitched into the hub room. Auum's Tai cell, reacting with typical speed, spread themselves linked across the passageway, sliding down it only gradually. But Hirad, Rebraal, Darrick and The Unknown tumbled in a heap, trying to grab each other to arrest their progress while Sian'erei was plucked from the ground and flung straight into Dystran.

And the Xeteskians fared no better. The gale hit them full force, scattering the Circle Seven and their confused Protectors like chaff in a breeze. He heard the clatter of metal striking stone and knew soldiers as well as other mages were suffering beyond his vision.

Dragging his head round, he could see Porrack and Jaruul clutching to corners much as he was while at the far end, Marack and Harroc were pressed hard against the wall, barely able to move.

Denser had no choice. He dropped to his hands and knees, braced himself against one wall and began to edge his way down to his wife and into the teeth of the gale in whose eye she lay helpless, her mind being ripped apart with every beat of her heart. Beyond her, chaos held sway. The Raven's warriors had been swept into the hub room to join the helpless mass at the mercy of the extraordinary wind. He could see them struggling to create distance between themselves and the enemy. Auum and his Tai still resisted and it might prove a crucial advantage.

Denser fought every inch against being thrown back up the corridor. He couldn't afford to fail. Not for The Raven and most particularly not for Erienne. The last few yards, he was flat on his front as the wind howled past him. Erienne was its epicentre and its focal point.

Reaching her body, everything stilled. He lay very close to her, feeling her ragged breathing, seeing the blood trickle from ears and nose, the drool from her mouth and her eyes twitching horribly beneath their lids. Her body quivered. Every muscle was taut to breaking and every nerve end fired. She was hot, too hot to live for too long, her face and hands sheened in sweat.

'Hold on, love,' he said, pushing aside his emotions for the moment. 'I'm here. Please hold on.'

He knew what he had to do. He could shield her from the Xeteskian mana, starve the One of its fuel. Of course, that was why the Circle Seven were present. In their typically arrogant way, they thought that by doing the same, they could keep her safe until they understood the power and brought her back to herself. It had led them to this ridiculous folly and risked her life.

Of course they had an advantage. They were six powerful mages and could keep up the casting indefinitely. He was one man and it was terribly draining. He looked up and caught Auum's eye. He mouthed 'be ready' and though not sure if the elf understood, bent to his task.

Partitioning his mind, he tuned to the mana spectrum and pulled in an oval construct, packed with pulsing mana energy. That was the simple part. Keeping the construct rotating and feeding on the mana about it, he sought the centre of the gale. What he saw all but made him lose his concentration. Into the darkened pit that was Erienne's mind, mana was being dragged like water thundering into a sinkhole.

And from the centre of that same hole, the power was being channelled out. Struck through with a deep brown, the Xeteskian-based energy was gouting from her, thrashing in every direction. But it shouldn't have been the Xeteskian colour.

Every fibre of his training told him that mana dragged into a Dordovan mind would be coloured the vibrant orange of that college because her manipulation of it, the lore she applied instinctively, made it that way.

He drew breath and moved the oval construct forwards, feeling it buffeted by the tumult around it. Dragging on every ounce of the learning he had gleaned from his time with Dawnthief, he forced his shielding spell in. He couldn't see Erienne's mind but he knew its position. He stopped the rotation of the spell, opened it along one side, shot it down the sinkhole and snapped it shut.

The effect all around him was instantaneous. Without the energy to get to his feet immediately, he opened his eyes and looked straight ahead. Quickest to react, Auum, Duele and Evunn stormed into the hub room. Swords in hand, they attacked the soldiers on the left-hand side. Only just regaining their feet and sense of direction, half of them were dead or about to die before they'd even formed a defence. Blood flowed across the floor.

Auum tore the throat from one man, backhanded his blade into the chest of a second and straight-punched a third in the windpipe. He couldn't see Duele but he saw the body that tumbled into view, Evunn leaping it smartly before crashing his left foot into the stomach of his first target.

In the centre of the room, Sian'erei wrestled free of Dystran and struck him on the nose, skittering back towards the corridor at an order from Hirad. She began to cast. The Raven warriors and Rebraal regained their feet quickly. The Unknown's blade flew from his scabbard, tapped once on the ground.

In front of them, the Circle Seven mages, ever quick when self-preservation was needed, had scrabbled to stand and were diving for cover behind the statuesque Protectors or running headlong for stairs or other passages. Denser saw Dystran take a single pace and disappear, a look of thunder on his face as he went. Another of the Circle Seven did likewise before all of them had taken themselves from the immediate vicinity.

Hirad snarled and lashed out at a mage too slow to rise. The blade caught him on the top of the skull, splitting it apart and spreading gore across the stone flags. Darrick fenced briefly with a soldier before dragging his blade hard across the enemy's stomach and stepping back smartly as entrails disgorged through his wrecked armour.

It was carnage, all watched with total detachment by the men in the masks, the former elite fighting force of Balaia. And it was all over in moments.

'Back off, back off,' said The Unknown. 'Auum, leave the Protectors. Sian, keep the shield going. Rebraal, make sure they understand.'

A shout went up behind Denser, urgent. Rebraal answered and the TaiGethen backed away into and down the corridor. Protectors watched them go, weapons slack in their hands.

'How is she, Denser?' asked The Unknown into the sudden uneasy calm.

'What are we going to do, Unknown?' Denser felt his world collapsing around him. 'What the fuck are we going to do?'

Sha-Kaan bellowed and tore a hole in the roof big enough for his head. He plunged it inside and snatched up a Protector, crushing his bones and spitting him aside. Somewhere a woman was screaming. He looked around again. A mage was backing away. Nyam.

He swivelled and took in the room. One Al-Drechar was dead. The other, apparently unaware, was asleep. Other Protectors stood in the room but none made a move. There was something altered about them. None made any attempt to cover the mage but three still stood in front of Diera who had run in, sensing something at the last moment. She was too late, though at least was safe. But it was she who was screaming. The babe in her arms was too traumatised even to cry.

He turned back to Nyam, arrowed in his head and stopped inches from the mage's face.

'Speak,' he ordered, knocking the man back against the wall with his breath. 'Explain now. Your life hangs by the merest thread.'

'We can't stay here,' said The Unknown. 'Denser, can you get up?'

Below him, Denser nodded and pulled himself up. 'Be careful with her. I'm shielding her but I won't be able to do it for long and it isn't protecting her, only us.'

'All right, Denser, all right. Let's get ourselves away from here,' said The Unknown, dragging the mage towards him. 'Keep your concentration. Thraun, carry Erienne. Be careful.'

Thraun nodded and padded over, smoothing Erienne's hair from her face before picking her up, resting her head in the crook of one arm, her knees across the other.

'She is fading,' he said.

'Just look after her,' said The Unknown. 'Ideas. Darrick?'

'Gods know how much time we've got,' said the erstwhile general. 'Not long. The Circle Seven mages all got out and they'll be back in strength. All we can do is lose ourselves from here, I guess. The TaiGethen are at the access points right now but whatever we're going to do, we need to do it now. What about them, Unknown?' He pointed at the Protectors.

There were fifteen of them standing in the centre of the hub room amongst the blood and bodies covering the floor. Weapons had been stowed and they stood in a loose circle, saying nothing.

'I think you're needed, Unknown,' said Denser, levering himself away, 'I'll be all right. Go on.'

'Right,' said The Unknown. 'Rebraal, Hirad, go with Denser into the research room. Take what he says we need. Everything else destroyed, all right? Oh, and make sure Kestys is dead. He knows far too much about all this.'

The Unknown walked into the hub room, his heart heavy when it should have been singing. He had released them, all of them. So simple in the end. And that made him angry. Dystran wouldn't ever have done it, however easy, and might even have increased the number. Behind him, Erienne was probably dying because of what that man had chosen to do, and in front of him were men he wasn't sure would thank him for returning them their souls despite the dream he knew they had harboured in the Soul Tank. It was different when you lost the brotherhood. He knew.

The circle opened when he approached, admitting him to its centre. It closed around him again. He turned slowly, taking them all in, still masked, unwilling to test their freedom. He understood that too.

'I know what I have taken from you,' he said. 'I know the loss you are all feeling. I know the quiet in your minds feels like the murder of your family. But I know the prayers of the Soul Tank too. The desire of every Protector. The legend of the free man. Me. I have survived. I have known the love of a woman and the joy of the birth of my son.

'There is life for you. It is different to anything you can remember from your pasts. But it is what you craved. And you will always have a bond as close as I enjoy with The Raven.' The Unknown allowed himself a pause. 'Tell me I have done the right thing by you. Tell me you can forgive me all that you have lost for all that you have gained.'

They said nothing. For a timeless moment the eye of every Protector bored into his head.

Hands moved to the backs of heads and buckles were snapped free. Slowly, nervously, masks were taken from faces and, one by one, dropped on the ground at The Unknown's feet.

He turned full circle again, saw youth, saw the strength of full manhood and the craggy knowledge of early middle age. Every face, pale and covered in red streaks and weals where the masks had rubbed, gazed back at him and on their first moments of a new life. Every eye held fear but it also held hope. It was enough.

'Good,' said The Unknown. 'Now if you'll take my advice, you'll put those back on for the last time and bluff your way out of the gates of the college. Find your other brothers. Get out of the city. Please. You owe nothing to anyone.'

'No,' said one, a voice The Unknown recognised as Myx's. 'We will not abandon you here.'

'You must. Ally yourselves with us and you'll be killed. Don't waste the opportunity. Please, I beg you.' There was no movement. 'If you respect me, you'll go. We will prevail. We're The Raven. Please, pick up your masks and go.'

'Do it,' said Myx but he kicked his own mask aside as his brothers stooped to retrieve theirs, watching it kick up a trail in the blood. 'I will come with you.'

'Why?' asked The Unknown.

'Because one with you means all are with you. We are brothers. We are one.'

The Unknown looked into his eyes, saw his conviction. His was a face that had seen so much beneath his mask. The first lines of age were on him and grey flecked his temples.

'I understand.'

'And,' said Myx, a glint in his eye, 'there is another way.'

Deep blue light flared in the corridor left.

'Move!' yelled Auum, flinging himself right.

The Protectors and Unknown scattered. Duele and Evunn turning to face the danger and dancing aside. The FlameOrb seared into the hub room, scorching blood into steam, baking dead flesh and splattering against the far wall, setting hangings on fire.

'Raven!' yelled The Unknown. 'We are leaving!'

'Brothers, obstruct,' said Myx ahead of him, running up the Soul Tank corridor, TaiGethen in his wake.

'Go, go!' shouted The Unknown. 'Follow Myx. Come on, Hirad. Anything you haven't got to hand, forget.'

'We haven't—'

'No time. Come on.'

The Raven, Al-Arynaar and TaiGethen charged away into the depths of the catacombs.

Dystran, dabbing his still bleeding nose, strode into the hub room behind a quartet of college guards, including Captain Suarav. He was met by the blank masked faces of over a dozen Protectors. One pace in, he slipped on the blood-slick floor, grabbing out at Suarav for balance and standing on a corpse while he regained it. He sighed.

'Look at this. Look at what they have done.' He shook his head. All his years as Lord of the Mount. All the years of near constant war and he hadn't seen this much death close up.

It stank. Entrails and their contents were strewn over the floor, still steaming gently. Bodies lay in the twisted attitudes of their deaths. Eyes stared at him, sightless and reproachful. The course of the FlameOrb was marked in blackened, smoking gore. But it was the blood that really shocked him. How many people were there lying here? Twenty perhaps but even so, how could they disgorge so much blood? It spattered the walls and the ceiling and across the floor it was a slick that splashed with every footfall.

'We didn't even kill one of them. And they've got away. Temporarily.' He turned on the nearest Protector. 'And what did you think you were doing, eh? Nothing. Standing like statues while real men were slaughtered by bandits. I don't know what they have done to you but I will find out. Anything to say?'

Silence.

'No, I thought not. Suarav, where are you?'

'Here, my Lord.'

'Extend the search. Split into six groups, it's your only choice. One Circle Seven mage with each group to direct you. Who knows what they think they're going to do? I also want every exit from here into the complex guarded. I—' He clapped his hands together. 'The vents.'

He walked towards the Soul Tank corridor. 'Of course, how can I have been so stupid. Suarav, let me show you something in the map room.' Protectors were standing in front of the corridor entrance. 'Out of my way.'

The three masks turned to look at him. 'Things have changed,' said one.

'Don't I bloody know it. But I still have the magical power to obliterate you. Now move. In fact, get out of the catacombs altogether.'

One of them shifted. 'Let us talk of respect.'

Dystran closed his eyes. He was going to have to be very careful.

'It's a good distance and they will find us,' said Myx.

He was keeping the pace high, trying to put a sensible gap between them and any immediate pursuit, but anything was going to be only a temporary breathing space. The Unknown and Hirad ran with him, Thraun and Denser behind with the unconscious Erienne. Darrick and the elves followed. Already, Denser had made them stop once to feed more energy into the spell around Erienne's mind and he looked a tired man.

'How big are the catacombs?' asked Hirad.

'Bigger than you know. It is mostly this.' Myx gestured around them. 'Interconnecting tunnels between each hub. We were in Dystran's hub. We'll slow at the next one. It has . . . history.'

The Unknown let the remark pass.

'And you know all this because . . . ?' asked Hirad.

'I am . . . was, the Lord of the Mount's Given. It was my job to know.'

'Fortunate.'

'I hope so.'

The Unknown had been a Protector such a short time but

still he understood the method behind the apparent madness of the catacomb construction as if it had been bred into him. Generations of paranoia bred by violently short tenure in the Circle Seven had led to the chaotic maze of finished and unfinished passages that encircled every hub.

It was a twisted morality that had driven it. While assassination by poison or blade had been a recognised method of advancement in years past, the use of destructive wards in the catacombs had always been considered unethical somehow. Naturally, entering a chamber uninvited was a different matter but in the myriad corridors which were considered almost neutral territory, such traps were beyond the pale.

The Unknown had no doubt they would have tripped many alarms and reminders for anyone working down here but that was a risk they had to take. To avoid every one would have been tantamount to suicide, so long would they have had to delay.

At the rear of the group, Auum jogged along easily. His limbs could stand the activity indefinitely but he was very unhappy. For the first time in his life, he considered that he was not in control of the situation. Deep below ground in the fetid tunnels of a Balaian city, he was out of anything he understood. He could, though, feel the patterns of space in the rock. It was the only crumb of comfort he had.

He had been confused by the turn of events, as had all his people. Rebraal's explanation did little to help. He understood that the woman, Erienne, carried an ancient elven magical power and that the enemy had murdered one of the Al-Drechar to claim her. It was typically human ignorance. The TaiGethen would attend to it another time.

He held up his hand and his Tai stopped with him, letting the echoing boots of the others recede. Marack turned but he waved her to continue. It would not be hard to find them again; the noise The Raven made would see to that.

'We will pray and we will listen,' he said. The Tai gathered on their knees. 'Yniss, hear us. Tual, hear us. Guide our senses in this place. Where the air is bad, where no birds fly or animals walk. Where no tree could survive or river creature swim. Yniss, we ask that you look down on us as we complete your work and return that which was stolen to your bosom. We remain, as ever, your servants.'

They remained kneeling, ears straining for any clue. Auum

could still hear the others moving away. He marked the direction which had not changed though their movement had slowed. He turned his head. Behind and to their left, the enemy were travelling. It appeared to be on a parallel path though it was difficult to be certain.

'Do you hear them?' he asked.

Duele and Evunn nodded.

'Ready your bows. Mine was broken while we fought the wind.' He stood up, motioning his Tai to follow him. 'I am tired of running. We will hunt now. Tai, we move.'

Chapter 24

Myx slowed, The Raven and TaiGethen closing up behind him. Ahead, Hirad could see that the nature of the passageway was changing, or at least its decoration. He looked behind him to check everyone once again.

'Where's Auum?' he asked, stopping.

'Helping,' said Rebraal. 'He'll find us again.'

'Helping in what way?'

'Hunting the hunters,' said Rebraal. 'It's better for him this way. And for us.'

'I hope you're right.'

The change in décor was abrupt. The pastel shades ended and in their place wooden panelling, dark stained, lined the walls. It affected the quality of the light, darkening the surroundings.

'What's this?'

'The next hub,' said Myx. 'Or rather, its borders. Not all of them are the same.' He smiled for the first time. 'Some former Masters had more style.'

He led them to the end of the passageway. Despite the magical augmentation, there was moss and mould in places on the wood. Hirad trailed a finger along it, feeling the slight dampness before replacing his glove. At a deep-blue painted door, Myx turned.

'We could face trouble in here,' he said.

'Whose is it?' asked The Unknown.

'Laryon's,' said Myx. 'Or it was. It is now an extension of Dystran's empire.'

'Well, it'll be a delight to clear it of all the detritus,' said The Unknown.

He drew his blade. Laryon. There was a name that would live

with The Raven forever. Laryon had been the master mage who sacrificed his life to free The Unknown from his mask. He had long championed the release of the Protectors and among Xeteskian mages had been rare in being truly respected by them. Dead these six years, his spirit lived on.

Myx reached out his hand to the handle.

'Whoa!' hissed Denser suddenly. 'Are you sure about that?'

'This door contains wards for explosion and lock. I am tuned out of them both. Once opened, the wards are disabled.' He turned to The Unknown. 'Be ready, brother.'

'Raven, let's concentrate,' said The Unknown. 'Nothing good in here, all right? Thraun, you stay outside 'til it's clear.'

Myx opened the door. Lantern light flooded the corridor. He cursed and slammed it quickly shut again. The roar of a spell shivered the timbers and the air outside chilled dramatically.

'Three targets,' he said. 'Go.'

This time he put a foot to the door and kicked it back. He ran in, plucking his weapons from his back, The Unknown and Hirad directly after him.

'Myx, no!' shouted The Unknown, seeing the former Protector falter on raising his axe to strike. 'Clear the path!'

In front of them were two mages and another man, neither mage nor soldier. Half skidding on the ice of the spell they'd cast, The Unknown closed in on the mages, who abandoned their attempts to cast again and turned to flee. He didn't have time for the niceties of combat and clattered his blade through the midriff of one mage before he'd taken a pace. On his shoulder, Hirad swiped at the trailing leg of the second, his blade carving into bone and sending the mage down screaming in pain. Before they could turn to attend to the non-mage, an elven arrow had punched him from his feet.

The Unknown finished off the crippled mage and looked about him.

'It's clear, Thraun, in you come. Last in, close the door.' He raised his eyebrows at what he saw. 'Where the hell did all this come from?'

To all intents and purposes, they were standing in the hallway of a house. It was wood-panelled like the passage outside, hung with tapestries. Tables along the walls were littered with ornaments, some now broken by the fall of the unfortunate mages. Three doors led off the hallway and at the end of the hall, a stairway led to an upper landing.

'Laryon always was a man apart,' commented Denser.

'Sol, I am sorry,' said Myx.

'Don't be. Your training is ingrained. You direct, we'll fight when we have to.'

'Through here, the whole way,' said Myx. 'Dystran keeps a big research team in here and a standing guard. Something important is going on.'

To emphasise his point, there was the sound of movement from up the stairs.

'Any other ways out of here?' asked The Unknown.

'Three,' said Myx. 'All up the stairs.'

'Up?' asked Hirad.

'Don't forget, we are underground. It may look like a house but there are no windows, no gardens.' He turned back to The Unknown. 'We should clear the rooms on this level.'

'Darrick, any thoughts?'

'House clearance was never in my training, Unknown,' said Darrick. 'But I'd be guarding door and stairs while we did it.'

'Agreed. Rebraal, can you do the honours. Thraun, Denser, stay with them. We need one mage with us to operate a shield. Let's move. They aren't hanging around upstairs.'

Myx indicated the single door left. 'Research room.'

The Unknown nodded and led Hirad and Darrick forward. Behind them came Sian'erei, already casting.

'Shield up.'

'Keep it that way,' said Hirad. 'And stay behind us. We can't risk you.'

'You need a bowman,' said Rebraal. 'No arguments.'

'None offered.'

The Unknown kicked the door at its handle, the timbers cracking, the catch bursting and the door shuddering inwards. He and Hirad crouched, Rebraal covering the area within. It was empty of life but dominated by a long table covered with papers and a complex wooden model.

'Turn,' ordered The Unknown. They backed and turned. 'Thraun, in there. Denser, cover them. Myx?'

'Drawing room, both doors.'

'Rebraal, left hand, take the angle, we'll draw any fire.'

The Unknown led them across the corridor, past the waiting

229

TaiGethen. Not a flicker crossed their expressions, their bows tensed and ready up the silent stairs. Defending mages had shields cast.

'Ready?'

Hirad nodded, choosing to unlatch the door and push it wide. A crossbow bolt buried itself in the wall opposite.

'Left edge, single target, red chair!' shouted Hirad, running into the room in front of his comrades.

The Raven warriors were presented with rugs, chairs, sofas, low tables and even a fire place. The crossbowman was crouched behind a chair, reloading. Mages stood by him, three of them. They cast but to no discernible effect, their arms quivering with effort, their faces betraying their anxiety.

'Oh dear,' said Hirad, hurdling a sofa, Darrick matching his move while The Unknown curved right.

Rebraal's bow sounded, taking the crossbowman in the hand, pinning it to the stock of his weapon. The elf followed into the room, reloading. Hirad landed, bringing his sword through from above his head and carving through the neck of the nearest mage. He went down in a welter of blood. Darrick, ever less dramatic, simply speared his target through the heart. The Unknown chose a similarly efficient path.

Three more dead, one soldier incapacitated. The Unknown hauled him up by his leather jerkin.

'Talk. How many in this complex?'

'I don't know. Ten?' Blood was pouring from his wound and he tried to support it, clutching the crossbow close and whimpering in pain. 'We were told to stay. You won't get out. They knew you'd come this way.'

'Who?' The Unknown shook him hard, drawing a gasp from him.

'All of them.' He managed a smile.

The Unknown dropped him, Hirad crashing his sword hilt into the side of his head, knocking him unconscious.

'Think he was telling the truth?'

'Every likelihood,' said Myx, looking into the room from a doorway.

'We'd better get out of here. We can't wait for—'

From the hallway, there was a shout of alarm. They heard the twang of bows and saw the glow of an Al-Arynaar FlameOrb. The volley was answered by shouts from above, the snap of crossbows and, lastly, a blinding bright blue light. Myx had taken half a pace into the room and turned just as the spell impacted. The detonation cracked the walls. The Protector was hurled across the room, thumping into the far wall and slumping down it. A gout of blue flame scorched the door frame.

Out in the corridor, they could hear the screams of the TaiGethen trapped outside. A burning elf staggered past and collapsed.

'What was that?' Hirad started towards the door but Sian'erei stopped him.

'We've lost the flow again,' she said, her eyes full of tears. 'They had no shield.'

Footsteps, a lot of footsteps, were clattering down the stairs.

Auum led his Tai deeper and deeper into the catacombs. Denser had been right. The place was a chaotic structure but although it was below ground, their prayers had given them strength and he was treating the confusion of passages and directions like the rainforest paths. No outward logic but animals left their marks on their best routes and humans were no different.

They had established the direction The Raven were taking and had chosen a path that ran above them and to their right. While there was no direct route, the Xeteskians had left plenty of signs. Less dust on the ground, grease marks from fingers on walls, shinier surfaces where clothes had brushed past. Easy to miss unless you knew what you were looking for.

Auum was five paces ahead of Duele, Evunn a further five behind him. His Tai had bows ready while he had unclasped his jaqrui pouch and had a short sword in his right hand. He was concerned that his Tai were running short of shafts and, even with those he had given them, a prolonged hunt would exhaust their supply.

There were men ahead of them, there were men behind. The Tai moved without sound and without speech, their signals and gestures all the communication they needed. Auum upped his pace. He wanted to pick off those ahead. They were moving with some urgency, twenty or more, making no attempt to hide their advance, assuming they were the hunters not the hunted.

He reached a junction of passageways. Left, he sensed the

catacombs opening up. The air was a little fresher, circulating more freely. It was probably another hub but the corridor floor had a thin film of undisturbed dust on its surface. Interesting that no one turned left to get there. He checked right. The enemy were clearly audible still. He padded around the corner and set off, gesturing his Tai to maintain distance.

Auum was running now. The corridor, like every other, was blue-lit, palely decorated. It inclined slightly and gently curved away right. He breathed it in. It was short. He powered around the curve, feeling an opening on his left before he saw it. The prey were close. Breasting the rise of the curve, he saw the last boot disappearing around a left turn not ten yards ahead of him.

He took the earlier left, pacing parallel to the hunted, feeling his senses focus to every sound. Nothing came from behind him, it was all to his right. He felt for what he needed and in the currents of the air, he found it, a crossway right, curving back towards the enemy. The Tai closed swiftly.

From their ultimate destination, Auum heard an explosion. Dulled by rock but fed through the tunnels on a wave of air it was not far off. The enemy responded, breaking into a run. To Auum, it was an advantage. He pushed on, seeing them cross his path right to left. They wouldn't see him, his angle left him in the periphery of their vision and they were intent on their way ahead. Not people who would last long in the rainforest.

The last pair of soldiers moved away with Auum four paces from the junction. He didn't break stride, reaching into his jaqrui pouch and sending a crescent whispering away. It struck the back of his target's head, slicing through skin and bone, before jamming to a stop in a spray of blood and sending him sprawling into those ahead.

Duele and Evunn compounded the instant confusion moments later. Arrows flew either side of Auum, cutting down two more. Auum's blade chopped into the lower back of a man who hadn't even responded to the damage inflicted on the one next to him. He fell to his knees, still moving forwards, arms flying backwards. Auum caught his head and cut his throat.

Only now did the soldiers respond. Shouts echoed through the corridor, panic and order mixed with the sound of swords being wrestled from scabbards and soldiers turning to face their enemy. Auum took what advantage remained. He unsheathed his second blade, and plunged it in to the neck of a soldier, pivoted on his right foot and kicked out down and straight with his left, cracking the knee of another and finally danced back a pace to free himself from the press coming at him.

Duele had dropped his bow and joined him, Evunn rattled in another arrow which skipped off a chain link and buried itself in the arm of a different target. At the rear of the pack, Auum could see a mage beginning to prepare. Happy that he couldn't cast any destructive area spell without killing his own men, Auum stepped into attack again.

The Xeteskians were still in shock and their defence was poor. They tried to fit three in a fighting line. It was too many and all they could do was fence. The TaiGethen had no such restrictions. Auum's blades blurred in front of him. He chopped aside a half-hearted prod and slashed a deep cut into one soldier's face, ducked inside another strike and buried both blades into the chest of another. Both men fell back. Duele sent another crashing to the ground, throat slit and blood fountaining into the corridor.

The Xeteskians faltered, those at the front of the line unwilling to suffer the fate so quickly handed out to their comrades. Auum followed them as they began to edge away. A blow came in low, he jumped the blade, pirouetting as he landed and smashing in a high kick that broke the soldier's nose.

He had them on the verge of breaking when the mage cast, his hands clutching hard at the air as if trying to crush a skull. Evunn cried out. He dropped his bow, his hands flying to the sides of his head. He crumpled, tortured choking the only sign he was still alive.

There were at least ten men between them and the mage. Too many.

'Duele, keep them busy.'

Auum took six quick paces back, watching Duele defend against two men, his body movements efficient, his swords working well against the heavier weapons of the enemy. At his feet Evunn stared at him, imploring the pain to stop. Ahead, the mage's hands tightened, the air between them diminishing.

Auum sprinted forwards. Two paces from the fight, he leaped forward into the air, swords before him. He passed like a spear over the soldiers and the mage, turning a roll in the air and landing flat on both feet. He spun round, crossed his arms over and out, his blades slicing into the mage's neck, almost severing his head.

There was no time to pause. Evunn was down. Anger flooded Auum. It was an emotion he shunned but now it fired his body, drove him to more speed, more precision. He moved in and with Tual guiding his every move, his Tai like a mirror opposite him, they brought death in the name of Yniss.

'Keep that bastard door shut!' Hirad shouted at Darrick as another heavy spell impact bent the timbers. It was smoking now but the general held the table against it, leaning in with everything he could muster. Rebraal was by him, waiting.

At the other opening nearer the stairs, Hirad kept the Xeteskians back. The hallway was full of soldiers, blood and charred flesh. Three bodies lay at the barbarian's feet. Blood from a cut to his forehead was dripping into his eyes.

The mages couldn't get an angle on him to cast offensive spells, nor on Thraun, who battered away at the enemy from the research room opposite him. But there seemed no end to the swordsmen. Behind him, The Unknown was tending to Myx but would soon be up to take the fight and Sian was searching the mana spectrum, hoping like them all that the Julatsan focus would form again.

Hirad kicked out straight, forcing his man back. He slithered on blood and fell but another took his place, sizing up Hirad before coming in two-handed, using the door frame to shield his open side. The barbarian beckoned him on.

'Like your friends,' he said. 'You're going down.'

The soldier didn't take the bait, preferring to defend the space. Hirad stepped in and slashed upwards. The soldier swayed backwards, fenced out with his blade, missing comfortably. Hirad stepped up on the downswing, his opponent off guard. His man stepped back further, blade cutting air again. Hirad smiled and rocked away himself.

'Nice try.'

Another spell crunched into Darrick's door timbers. The centre of the door splintered, shards of wood flew into the drawing room. The table heaved and Darrick was pushed well back.

'Next time!' he warned. 'They're winding up the Force-Cones.'

'We need an angle,' said Rebraal.

'Then let's make one,' said The Unknown, voice loud and close in Hirad's ears. 'If we're going to go down, it might as well be with their blood on our faces.'

Hirad grinned at his opponent, who beckoned him on.

'Soon enough, sonny. Soon enough.' He raised his voice. 'Hey Thraun, you all right?'

The scream of a Xeteskian soldier was all the information he really needed. Thraun spared him a glance, his feral eyes wild, his hair matted with sweat, and then another enemy took his fallen colleague's position and it began again.

Auum could hear the crash of another spell close by. He turned them all right and headed up a sharply inclined passage, sure of himself once more. Evunn's bow was over his shoulder, Evunn's arrows had been ripped from corpses and placed back in his quiver and Evunn himself hung between Auum and Duele. The elf was senseless. Not unconscious but talking nonsense, unaware of his surroundings. He was almost walking but lost his step so often it was easier to drag him. His eyes were unfocused and his arms twitched where Auum and Duele held them around their necks.

'Yniss tests us further,' said Auum.

'I am not sure that this isn't Ix demonstrating his power tonight,' replied Duele.

And it might have been so. The capricious God of the mana element was known for disrupting the works of Yniss, laughing in delight at the distress of his servants. Auum determined to have the last laugh. His anger had faded as the last Xeteskian fell in front of him, eyes wide with terror, drowning on his own blood. What had replaced it was perhaps more dangerous still.

He could hear the clamour of voices now. He heard a cry of pain, an order being given and the sound of running feet mixed with it. There was the echoing clash of steel; and on the air, he could smell fire and yet more death. He hurried them along a gloomy passageway where the light spells were weaker and the shadows a little more pronounced.

The construction of the corridors changed. They reached a junction where the walls were planked with wood. He edged

235

his head around to the right. Two guards stood at an open door, looking in. Fools. Beyond them, the sounds of fighting were unmistakable.

'Found them,' said Auum.

They laid Evunn down. He had no strength to resist but smiled faintly and closed his eyes.

'Two targets,' said Auum. 'I'll take the left.'

The TaiGethen elves stepped smartly around the corner, their bowstrings tensed. Sensing danger, the soldiers spun together. Their crossbows began coming to ready but death for them was already far too close for it to make any difference at all.

Chapter 25

'Let this one take the door, and be ready to act,' said The Unknown Warrior.

Darrick stood facing his own death. The Unknown trotted quickly back to where Hirad kept the same soldier occupied, ensuring the frame of the door was too full of the Xeteskian for anyone to risk a crossbow bolt. Rebraal was next to Darrick, his last arrow ready in his bow.

It was a desperate measure but they really had no choice. The one closed door was going to go and when it did, the way would be opened for them to be overwhelmed by spell attack. Their only chance now was to get at the mages and be in the thick of the enemy to stop any chance of more casting from up the stairs. That and crossbow fire. And that meant fighting with knives and daggers. It had been a long time since Darrick had practised. Time would tell whether he, or any of them for that matter, remembered the balance and moves to survive.

Myx was standing again and Sian had gathered herself even if she hadn't got her magic back. They had to break. Thraun was being slowly worn down and there was no way Hirad was going to let any of The Raven die without the others standing next to them, or at least fighting to get through.

He took a deep breath. There was a moment's calm out in the hallway, broken only by Hirad's taunting and the heavy blows of Thraun's sword. It really was now or never.

'Ready, Raven,' said The Unknown, his voice so reassuring that for a heartbeat, Darrick actually considered they'd survive this. Seeing the expression on his and Hirad's faces, he realised that was precisely what they believed.

They had faced death down so many times, thought Darrick,

and he hadn't. Not really. Not even at the Understone garrison or the fields at Septern Manse had he really thought he'd die.

In here it had been different from the moment the familiar had flown from Ranyl's window.

He saw the flash of the castings moments before the door disintegrated. Shielded either side of the doorway, Darrick and Rebraal suffered no injury, waiting a count of three for the Cone to disperse.

'Go!' shouted The Unknown.

Rebraal stepped around the door and fired his arrow, Darrick seeing it lodge high in the chest of the mage before he could scramble clear and let his soldiers cover him. Darrick breathed deep and rushed out of the door, sensing The Unknown and Hirad wading into the battle next to each other.

His heart lurched in his chest. Xeteskians were everywhere. The hallway could take three in a line with room to swing long swords but for now he faced only two. Behind him, the space to the door back into the catacombs was blocked by the hideous smouldering corpses of the TaiGethen and Al-Arynaar mages. Ahead, the enemy. Guardsmen lined the hallway, more were waiting on the stairs, many armed with crossbows which were swung to bear. Mages stood well back. He saw one on either side of the stairway and others on the stairs themselves.

He threw himself into the front rank of the Xeteskians. A bolt flashed past him, thudding into the door. Rebraal was by him, the elf's speed remarkable, his bow discarded and dagger and short sword now in hand.

'Keep close, watch the peripheries,' called Darrick as the shouts began to rattle around the enclosed space. He blocked two blows in quick succession and shoved his man back, looking for the angle to close. 'Don't give the mages line of sight.'

Darrick's man made his first mistake, attempting a round-arm strike. The general stepped inside, blocked the arm at the height of its arc and punched forward with his right-hand dagger, piercing the man's heart. He shuddered and the strength left him. Ready for it, Darrick leaned into the body shoving him back hard into those behind him.

With no time to admire his handiwork, Darrick leaped the body, hunching low to keep his frame out of sight. His new opponents were off balance but Rebraal hadn't been as quick dispensing with his first man and Darrick was exposed on his right. A blade flashed in. He blocked it, just, catching the blade on the hilt of his dagger and twisting down. Looking left, he jabbed half forwards, drawing a false stroke from his other direct opponent. A third man joined the line but couldn't strike from his far right position. For that he was grateful.

He planted a foot carefully behind and rocked backwards as a second strike came in from the right, feeling it swish past his face. His momentum brought him forwards again and he let it carry him, again getting inside his man but finding the way blocked by a chop to the top of his left arm. He whipped in his right arm, dagger blade planting into the man's side beneath his ribs, driving deep into flesh.

A heartbeat later, the second Xeteskian stabbed forwards. Darrick, not quite quick enough to adjust his body shape, felt the blade slice through his armour and cut across the top of his hip. The wound burned and the blood started to flow. He grunted in pain and dropped back.

'Rebraal, I need you.'

'Right here.' Rebraal's short sword took the right hand from Darrick's tormentor. The elf's dagger slashed across his face, removing an eye. Finally, he stepped up and kicked forwards, knocking the screaming man onto his back. 'Darrick?'

'I'll live,' said Darrick.

And with his right leg soaking in his blood, he drove forwards again.

Auum and Duele shouldered their bows and picked up Evunn again, their beloved Tai unresisting, drifting in and out of consciousness, his head slumped forwards. Auum feared for him but could not let that fear dominate him. He cleared his mind while they moved past the two guards. Duele paused to rip the arrows clear of the bodies and they ran on into what had to be a catacomb hub.

In front of them the noise level had increased. The spells no longer sounded but instead the sounds of close fighting filled the air, coming from an area ahead and below them. They were in what looked like the inside of a house. Wood-panelled and hung with pictures, the narrow corridor was lined with doors, all closed. Auum chose to ignore them, moving his Tai quickly towards the sounds ahead.

At an empty alcove, he motioned Duele to take Evunn while

he slipped forwards. The corridor ended in a blank wall and to the right, turned into a similar door-lined landing. He crouched low and peered around the corner. At its end were stairs and crowded on the landing were Xeteskians, he couldn't be bothered to count them. Doors on either side were open. The sounds of fighting and dying were loud in his ears and above it all he could hear the voices of those he knew, one louder than all the rest. Hirad Coldheart.

He was back with Duele moments later.

'We must leave him. We have work.'

'Here?'

Auum looked down at Evunn, his mind darkening anew. The Tai was unconscious now. 'He can come to little more harm than he has suffered already.'

He knelt down and kissed Evunn's lips, taking the stricken elf's head from Duele's lap and lowering it gently to the floor. Evunn's legs protruded into the corridor but that was a further risk he had to take.

'We will not leave you, brother. Stay with us. Yniss will protect you.' He stood, drew a short sword and unclasped his half-empty jaqrui pouch. 'I will not waste arrows on these men. They are less than animals and deserve no respect. We move.'

The two TaiGethen padded away, Evunn lying in their wake, their prayers with him but their thoughts ahead. Their only chance for him was to get a mage to examine him. Whatever spell the Xeteskian had used, it had attacked Evunn's brain.

Auum motioned Duele to run side by side with him. Without pause, he rounded the corner, jaqrui in his right hand, his sword held in defence as he passed doorways should he need it. After two set of closed doors, the next pair were open. Ten yards ahead, soldiers craned their necks to see the action below them.

Left-hand open door, a figure appeared. Auum didn't even break stride, reversing his blade in his hand and stabbing into the enemy's neck. He choked and fell back, a strangled cry emerging from his ruined throat. Above the clamour of fighting, the soldiers ahead heard it, turning to see their doom approaching at a speed they could never hope to counter.

Auum's jaqrui howled away. Now was not the time for quiet, now was the time to instil fear. The crescent blade scythed into his target's stomach at the waistband. Duele's found the arm of his man. Both yelled the alarm, demanding help, that would not arrive in time. The TaiGethen hit them like a whirlwind.

Duele dragged out his second blade and swept it into his enemy's face. Auum planted a foot, turned a high roundhouse kick and sent his man spinning backwards. Landing, he snapped in a punch to the back of the neck and stepped over the falling man. He jabbed his sword into the thigh of the next as the enemy fought to bring up a defence.

Auum let his limbs work without conscious thought, reaching that plane where he sat almost as an outsider, seeing everything, Tual directing his every move. They were so slow, the Xeteskians, their long blades cumbersome in these close quarters. They paid, every one that fell, for the crimes committed against the elven nation and, more immediately, Evunn and every TaiGethen who had fallen as a result of their masters' actions.

The calm settled on Auum. His blade worked inside the guard of another enemy, spearing into his eye. His free hand worked in double time, balled as a fist to smash nose or mouth, open and upright for the base of his palm to slam into forehead, nose and chest or straight-fingered to crush windpipe.

They couldn't get near him. His legs kept him dancing beyond their attempts to strike back, his feet swift, dealing out blows to knee and ankle if not balancing him to strike again or dodge blow after blow.

He could hear the whispering in his mind, his mantra to the Gods that he served, repeated again and again, over and over. I will serve beyond death, I will preserve all you have wrought.

Auum's blade blocked another attack, he sidestepped a second, ducked a crossbow bolt and killed another.

He moved forward again.

Thraun howled and thrashed his sword into the side of a Xeteskian head, where it lodged. He left it where it quivered, the man collapsing in front of him. The shapechanger plucked a dagger from his belt sheath and launched himself out of the doorway, enveloping another hapless guardsman.

It had to be this way. Ahead of him, in the fighting that had become a deadly brawl, The Unknown and Hirad were in danger of being overwhelmed. Blood ran from the cut in the barbarian's forehead, he had suffered wounds to both arms earlier and as Thraun watched, a quick slash opened up his chest leather. The material begin to darken further. But far from worrying him, the damage served to galvanise Hirad further and he surged forwards, both weapons burying in his victim's chest.

Behind Thraun, Denser stood sentinel over Erienne. His mana stamina was all but spent so he stood with his sword, waiting for Thraun to fail. He would not fail.

He bit down on to the nose of his victim, pushed his dagger hard into the flesh of his upper thighs and kept him close with an arm locked around his neck. Struggle as he might, the guard couldn't break free. Not until Thraun was ready and that was when he drove his dagger into the unprotected shoulder, driving down behind his ribcage.

Thraun growled again, dropped the corpse and sought another to kill. He could smell the blood and the death, he could taste it. In his mind the memories of the forest and the hunt crowded in again. The pain of what he had lost drove him on. He would not lose the pack he ran with now. Not while he still lived.

Those closest to him tried to back away but the press from the other side of the hallway kept them close enough. Thraun barked, saw the fear in their eyes, bared his bloodied teeth and waded in once more.

'Come on!' yelled Hirad. 'Any of you bastards think you can take me?'

Every inch of his body was covered in sweat and blood. His breath was acid in his lungs, his arms and legs burned and his head was thumping. Bodies littered the ground making footing difficult and he had slipped almost fatally when taking the slice across his chest. He could feel the wound every time he lashed out and he could see that despite the men he had downed, there were so many more.

He caught the eye of a frightened youth and snarled. The boy took a pace sideways and the next instant collapsed under The Unknown's massive punch to his temple. The more alert had discarded their swords now and fought for that modicum of space to allow two and more to attack each Raven target.

Just as hard, he and The Unknown battled to keep it tight, using their targets as shields against crossbows and mages, who stood ready but unable to cast or fire lest they strike their own. But he feared a senior mage or Circle Seven master joining the fray. They had the ability to deal with individual targets wherever they were.

But he couldn't let it worry him. He struck out, catching a guardsman on his arm, feeling the knife bite deep, ruining tendon and muscle. The man gasped and dropped his blade. Hirad pounced, balling one fist around a dagger hilt and punching into his enemy's mouth. Teeth broke and blood flew from split lip and torn gum. His left hand came round directly after, knife sliding deep into groin. He turned and twisted it before dragging it clear. The guard dropped to the floor, clutching himself and lost to the fight.

His vision clouded again and he wiped the blood from his face. A fist clattered into his cheek sending him staggering back a pace. He saw a sword arrowing towards him and no way to defend himself. But the blow never landed; instead its owner jerked violently and fell forwards, a curved metal blade jutting from the back of his head.

Hirad looked up the stairs. There was panic above and for good reason. Their limbs a blur, every strike finding its mark, the TaiGethen were back in the fight.

'Yes!' shouted Hirad. 'Yes!'

Energy flooded through him. He glanced right. The Unknown's fist connected with the chin of his opponent, knocking him from his feet to land on top of two men behind. He could hear Darrick encouraging Rebraal all the way and knew that the balance of the fight was shifting.

A mage was backing away beyond the stairs. Hirad snarled. He was next but there were enemies in front of him. He stepped inside the guard of another soldier, ducked a haymaking punch and stabbed upwards through his stomach. Still moving he pushed the dying man aside, lashed a fist into the face of a soldier targeting The Unknown and moved on again.

The Raven would be triumphant. It would soon be over.

Vuldaroq and Heryst had both been enjoying the news from Xetesk. Noting that their spies were both deeply embedded in the Dark College and highly skilled, they had settled back in their respective colleges to hear, through a cooperative

Communion, about the elven raid that had brought such chaos and apparent destruction.

While piqued that they had not been consulted, there was satisfaction in any mayhem and Vuladaroq found himself unwilling to appear disgruntled. Well, not completely. He wasn't enamoured with the Al-Arynaar mage who conducted the Communion. She was under duress from Lysternan and Dordovan mages, who felt the need for her to deal direct with their rulers. She, it appeared, didn't feel it was any of their business. It was not a way in which he was used to being spoken. Nor Heryst, though the Lysternan leader had other reasons not to make protestation. The shame of letting The Raven escape was hard to face down.

'And when exactly do you expect your raiding party to return?' Vuldaroq remained fascinated that anyone could breach the walls of the city so easily, let alone the college but it had most definitely happened.

'That is unknown,' said Dila'heth. 'Perhaps they will not return at all. We cannot be sure.'

'But you are sure they have completed their tasks inside,' pushed Vuldaroq.

'Your spies are more able to draw that conclusion. Clearly, the news that the library has been raided is very good. Auum will die before giving up the Aryn Hiil, should he have found it there.'

She sounded very tired. The pressure of the siege front, the second failure of the Julatsan mana focus and the stress of talking to the leaders of two colleges must be taking its toll.

'I am sorry that we press you,' said Heryst. His voice drifting across Vuldaroq's mind like balm on a wound. 'But there are other questions. Did not your raiding party seek to cause damage to the Dark College as part of their brief?'

'Your dispute is your business. We are, and have always been here in order to recover what was stolen from us,' said Dila'heth. 'When we have confirmation, we will move north to Julatsa as has always been understood.'

'Of course,' said Vuldaroq. 'And our heartfelt thanks for your aid, however given, will always be with the elven nation.'

'Do not patronise me, Dordovan,' said Dila'heth. 'Your conflicts have caused harm on Calaius. Xetesk may be in the dock but none of you are blameless.'

'Young lady I—' began Vuldaroq.

'I think what Vuldaroq is saying is that we are eternally grateful for your intervention. We have not deliberately sought to harm your country but we do seek to end any chance of that harm worsening by deposing the current Xeteskian regime.'

'I apologise,' said Dila. 'This war makes its mark on us all.'

'Indeed it does,' said Vuldaroq. 'Please do not take offence.'

'I do not.'

'Good,' said Vuldaroq. He drew a breath. 'One more thing. We understand there is trouble in the Xeteskian tower complex and catacombs, though we are unable to get too close for obvious reasons. I had no idea the elves were attacking there too.'

'They are not. The Ra—' Dila caught herself but it was too late.

'I beg your pardon?' Vuldaroq wasn't quite convinced of what he had just half heard.

'There are other targets in the college,' said Dila hurriedly. 'I was not privy to all the TaiGethen's discussions with their advisers.'

'Their advisers being The Raven, clearly,' said Vuldaroq casually.

'That is not what I said,' replied Dila'heth frostily. 'Now if there is nothing more, I have a war to fight tomorrow.'

'You understand that the allies seek The Raven,' said Heryst. 'They are criminals and must be arrested.'

'They are friends to the elves,' said Dila carefully.

'Meaning?' demanded Vuldaroq.

'Meaning, if I knew where they were, I would not place them in the hands of those who would harm them.'

'They are outlaws,' said Vuldaroq.

'They saved the elven nation almost single-handed amongst men. Their sacrifice is enough to absolve them of any crime in the eyes of elves.'

'Tell me,' said Vuldaroq. 'Are they in Xetesk or are they not?'

'I trust you heard my previous utterances,' said Dila. 'Would you like me to repeat them?'

'We will talk more when you are perhaps less tired,' said Vuldaroq.

'I think not.'

The connection broke, leaving Vuldaroq alone with Heryst.

'I trust your humiliation is now complete, my Lord Heryst.'

'Stop your tiresome jibes, Vuldaroq. We have serious matters to discuss.'

'Do we?' Vuldaroq smiled to himself. Not for long.

'The Raven are no longer just an irritation and a band of fugitives,' said Heryst. 'And before you snap back, I think you should consider not what happens when they escape Xetesk, but what happens if they do not. I will not treat you as a fool. You will be as aware as I am of the rumours surrounding Erienne. It appears she is locked in the Dark College. Dystran will know what we do. What if she should be captured?'

Vuldaroq considered. 'We will have to rescue her. For the good of Balaia.'

'Indeed,' said Heryst. 'And not just the good of one or other of us. If she is who we believe, she will not be silenced like her daughter.'

'But whose hands will she fall into, eh?'

Heryst sighed. 'That cannot be the issue, save that it should not be Xetesk's. Please, Vuldaroq, let us not compete over this. It is too important to us both.'

'She is Dordovan,' said Vuldaroq. 'She belongs with me.'

'If she is a woman of the One, she belongs to none of us, that is the problem.'

'If you capture her, you will surrender her to me,' said Vuldaroq.

'Don't be ridiculous. Any capture attempt has to be a joint venture. Any reward has to be shared,' replied Heryst.

'But what if they should escape and fall into your hands, eh?'

'Or yours?'

'Perhaps we must agree to differ on this issue,' said Vuldaroq.

'Vuldaroq!' shouted Heryst, his voice echoing painfully around the Dordovan Arch Mage's skull. 'This is not an argument about supply chains or battlefield communication. This affects the future of Balaia. A Balaia that you and I want to see returned to balance. Am I not right?'

Vuldaroq was silent.

Chapter 26

What had begun as a desperate breakout attempt became a slaughter. Panicked by the TaiGethen at their backs, the Xeteskian guardsmen had pushed forwards towards the Raven. The resultant jostling and lack of space meant no room to bring crossbows to bear and had brought first Thraun and then Hirad to the helpless mages.

The barbarian pulled his dagger blade from the chest of the last man standing and let the body fall, life fading. The silence was palpable, broken only by the sounds of hard breathing. His whole body ached. Blood ran from six separate cuts; the worst of them, on his chest, stung with his sweat.

'We should move,' said The Unknown, though the set of his body suggested he desired anything but.

Blood smeared his face and body, most of it not his own. He supported an angry wound below one ear and his arms were blood-slick and crisscrossed with cuts. Next to him, Darrick's face was ashen beneath the red spatters, one hand pressing hard on his hip. Rebraal looked to be in a state of shock, though it could have been purely surprise that they had survived.

Auum picked his way quickly through the covering of corpses and fatally wounded on the floor.

'Denser?'

Hirad pointed to the research room and followed the Tai-Gethen with his gaze. He strode up to Denser, grabbed his arm and pointed up the stairs.

'Evunn,' he said by way of explanation.

'What?' Denser looked up sharply from smoothing Erienne's hair, irritated at the interruption.

'Please?' Auum frowned and sighed. He called for Rebraal and snapped out a stream of elvish. Something in his voice pricked Hirad's attention, Rebraal was already heading for the stairs.

'It's Evunn,' he said for Denser's benefit. 'He's been hit by a spell.'

'He's not the only one,' said Hirad grimly.

'No, but he's alive. Auum says his mind is gone.'

'Oh no,' muttered Denser. He hurried out of the research room. 'Bastards, that's cruel.'

'What is it?' Hirad found it all bemusing. It was all he could do to remain standing. His legs were shaking. He leaned against a wall.

'MindMelt,' said Denser. 'Got to be.'

Auum followed him out, Hirad touched his arm and indicated the charred remains of the elves by the door. 'I'm sorry,' he said.

There was the faintest flicker in the elf's eyes and a tightening of the muscles in his face through his smeared paint. Auum glanced up the stairs to see Duele and Rebraal with Denser. He walked slowly towards the bodies, Hirad indicating that Darrick should give him room. For a few moments he stood looking down at them, hunched in the attitudes of their deaths. The FlameOrbs had consumed them, six TaiGethen and two Al-Arynaar mages. They were blackened beyond recognition, fused together, clothing and flesh burned away exposing bone and sinew.

Reverently, Auum knelt by each one, placing a hand on the head, speaking a few words and kissing the lipless mouth. When he turned and rose, Hirad caught the grief and fury in his eyes as he swept past and back up to Evunn.

'We aren't safe here,' said Myx, appearing at one of the drawing-room doors, leaning heavily on Sian'erei.

Hirad's sarcastic retort stopped at his lips. One half of Myx's face was burned and blistered, one eye swollen shut. His armour was shredded down the same side and blood oozed through the rents. He winced as he breathed and the air dragged over scorched lungs. The barbarian nodded and offered his support, freeing Sian.

'Thraun, you all right to carry Erienne?' he asked.

Thraun nodded, blood dripping from his nose, and limped back into the research room. There was a dark stain on his trousers just below the right knee. Hirad watched him pick up Erienne before turning himself and starting up the stairs.

'Tell me we're close to the way out,' he said.

'No,' said Myx. 'They knew we would come this way if I was with you and they will know where I am headed. But, if we hurry, we might get there before they catch up with us again.'

Hirad raised his eyebrows. 'We aren't in a fit state to go far.'

'There is nowhere else,' said Myx. 'This is your only chance.' He coughed, face screwing up, the air misting red in front of him.

'Hang in there, Myx.'

Approaching the end of the landing, voices were raised. Auum was remonstrating with Denser, Rebraal trying to translate as best he could.

'Tell him I can't just fix him. It's not that simple,' said Denser.

'He says your mages made him this way and you can put it right,' responded Rebraal.

'Maybe. But not here and not now.' Denser's face was reddening, his temper at breaking point.

Auum reacted angrily to his statement, jabbing a finger back towards the hallway. The Unknown increased his pace.

'Hey!' he said. 'Enough. All of you.' Whatever it was in his tone, it transcended language barriers. 'Thank you. Now, Denser, is he dying?'

'He's not in immediate danger, no.'

'Is he deteriorating?'

'Slowly.'

'Are a few hours going to make any difference?'

'Not really.'

'Right.' The Unknown looked squarely at Auum. 'Rebraal, translate this, it's the final word. We can't help Evunn now but he isn't going to die. We will carry him out like we will carry Erienne. But if we don't move right away, none of us will get out. So we are going. Now. Myx, which way?'

'Follow me.' Myx and Hirad, moving quickly together now, walked ahead and turned right at the end of the landing and down to the blank wall. Myx reached into what transpired to be an illusion and slid back a panel. 'New building going on. If Dystran doesn't come through this way, it'll save us some time.'

The light was poor but was enough to walk by. Every surface was rugged and unfinished, the curve of the tunnels often not far above their heads. Myx had to stoop. In places, chambers had been completed, but elsewhere all that could be seen were marks on the bare walls.

The lattice was uncomplicated thus far with little more than the major corridors fashioned. Myx took them in more or less a straight line, angling down then back up. It was a walk that had no discernible end and Hirad's nervousness grew with his awareness of their vulnerability.

One arm around Myx's waist to support the struggling Protector, Hirad carried his blade in the other. He tried to ignore the pain firing across his chest while concentrating on listening hard for sounds ahead and treating every turn and crossing as a potential ambush.

But it was difficult to maintain, this made more so by their pace which slowed remorselessly. Myx's breathing was truly tortured, his legs more badly burned than he wanted to let show. Thraun, with Erienne in his arms and refusing to pass her to The Unknown, limped badly. Darrick was forced to lean on Rebraal, his hip bleeding steadily. And the surviving TaiGethen carried their sick brother between them. Only Denser and Sian were uninjured though Hirad could only guess at what was going through their minds.

The corridors became progressively darker and somewhere ahead, water was dripping, both factors evidence of spells decaying. Apparently, work was suspended now the war was on. Abruptly, Myx stumbled and fell to his knees, gasping, his armour pulling across his burns.

'Come on, big fella,' said Hirad, ignoring the fresh blood from his chest while he half dragged the Protector upright.

'Just a moment,' said Myx, his voice hoarse.

Hirad feared for him. It wasn't his legs that had caused him to stumble. His breath was short and agonised, his face covered in sweat and his body carried a tremble. Behind them, Auum spoke and Rebraal translated.

'We are pursued.'

'Shit,' managed Myx. 'It's Dystran. It has to be.' He pushed himself on, breaking into a half-trot. 'Not far. Come on.'

He was ahead of Hirad, using the wall to propel himself along. The Raven ran blind behind him, knowing that if he fell, they were lost. Hirad didn't know how many turns they made, he couldn't gauge the slopes they travelled, he lost count of the side passages they crossed. Head down, every pace pulling at his wounds, he ran, looking behind him to check his friends were all with him when he trusted himself not to fall. He couldn't hear the pursuit but the haunted look on Rebraal's face told him it wasn't far enough behind.

Ahead, the failing blue light was replaced by a misty grey luminescence.

'Tunnelling spell. It's decaying like the light,' said Denser as they ran. 'It should be as bright as the sun.'

The sound of water was louder, a steady trickle into puddles. The going was slippery and muddy underfoot, the walls even more ragged, sharp edges of rock protruding from dense wet clay.

'Where are we now?' asked The Unknown.

'Outside . . . the . . . city.' Myx struggled to frame the words. 'Not far.'

And it wasn't. At the edge of the grey light, Myx turned down a narrow unfinished side passage ending in a blank wall. Again he felt inside the illusion and pushed a panel aside, waiting for them all to come through before closing it.

'Can you lock that, Denser?' he asked.

Denser shook his head. 'Barely. I'll try but it won't add up to much. After that I'll be spent.'

He stepped up and began casting.

'What about Erienne?' asked Hirad.

'Whatever I do here, we need another mage to help me. Soon.'

'I've got an idea. Don't worry, Denser. I'll see to it,' said Hirad. 'So, where now?'

Myx pointed down the passage they found themselves in. It was finished and well lit, apparently in regular use. A chamber lay to their right, empty and chill. Ten yards ahead, a large leather bound basket sat on the floor. It was attached to a rope that disappeared through a sizeable hole in the roof.

'Oh, great,' muttered Hirad.

'Izack said he assumed they were getting in supplies,' said The Unknown. 'Looks like he was right.'

Myx nodded, his breath a little more even now but still pained. 'The top is hidden by illusion. There's a grille to stop animals falling as well. It comes out in a bank of gorse and bracken to the west of the city. It has proved useful.'

'What is it usually, a ventilation shaft?' asked Darrick.

'Yes. There are six altogether. Four have been sealed. The other is not far from here.'

Denser turned from the door. 'I've done what I can. It won't keep them for long. Certainly not if Dystran is with them.'

'Right, let's get moving.' The Unknown made quick assessment of the rope and basket, staring up into the dark above. 'Right. Thraun, me and you will go up, Sian between us. We'll haul up Evunn and Erienne in the basket. Denser, you with Erienne, Auum or Duele with Evunn. We'll have to pray it'll hold but it looks strong enough to me. Then, climb one by one, fast as you can. The remainder have to hold off any attack. If it gets bad, shout, I'll be back down. Go.'

He pointed at Thraun. The shapechanger passed Erienne to Denser, who stood her into the basket. It would be just big enough for them both standing upright. Thraun stood on the edge of the basket, grabbed the rope and disappeared up the shaft, which was something in the order of five feet wide. They could hear him bracing himself against the sides, dust and grit showering down. Soon after he disappeared, Sian'erei went after him.

'How high?' asked The Unknown.

'I don't know,' said Myx. 'We aren't at the lowest level. Over fifty feet. You'll find a pulley wheel and brace stowed at the top of the shaft that you can lock into position.'

The Unknown raised his eyebrows. 'The fact that that is the best news I've heard since we got in here says everything.'

It seemed an eternity before they heard Thraun moving the grille. The Unknown started to climb.

'Be ready, Denser. As soon as we're set, we'll pull.'

'Understood.'

Hirad turned to face the illusion, imagining a Xeteskian horde tramping towards them.

'How far away are they?' he asked Rebraal.

'By now, all but on us.'

'Right,' said Darrick. 'Let's organise. Myx, move away and sit down. It's a long climb for you later.'

Myx was about to raise an objection but a thud on the panel stopped him.

'Move, Myx!' hissed Hirad. 'Darrick, I'll stand up.'

'No Hirad, you're hurt.'

'And you're not?' Hirad growled. 'I'm not shifting. Rebraal will stand by me.'

The Al-Arynaar leader nodded and moved forward but he was pushed aside by Auum.

'Right,' said Darrick tersely. There was another experimental thud on the portal. 'Rebraal, stand with me the other side of the basket, we can't afford to be backdoored here.'

The group rearranged. Hirad looked across at Auum and nodded his gratitude. The TaiGethen spoke a few words he took to be a prayer for their safety and drew a single short sword, the fire undimmed in his eyes.

'Don't you die down here, Coldheart,' said Denser.

'I'll do what I can,' said Hirad.

There was another impact. Heavier this time.

'That was a spell,' said Denser.

'How long before they get through?'

'Not long enough to get us all out, I fear.'

Hirad waited, his thrill at the prospect of the fight absent. He stood here because of those he protected, nothing more. But even that knowledge couldn't hide the ache in his limbs, the biting pain from his wounds or the exhaustion in his mind. Unbidden came the thought that if the Xeteskians broke through, all of them would have to be downed for the rest of The Raven to escape. Alternatively, someone would have to make the ultimate sacrifice.

He gripped his sword tighter and smiled grimly. At least he would be able to reacquaint himself with Ilkar. Sooner than he expected but a prospect he welcomed, not feared.

A warmth filled Hirad's mind, Sha-Kaan entering his consciousness gently.

These are not thoughts I am happy to feel, said the Great Kaan.

I had not realised you could sense me, said Hirad.

He was dimly aware of a concerted attack on the panel. Swordsmen were trying to weaken the timber so making Dystran's job breaking the WardLock easier. Even in his weakened state, it was clear that Denser's skill was considerable.

But they are the thoughts I would expect of such a man as you, Hirad Coldheart, continued the dragon.

Accepting death has always been my way of avoiding it, said Hirad.

I— Sha-Kaan stopped. *That is by way of a joke, is it not?*

Sort of. Sha-Kaan, this contact is fortunate, given where I stand now. I need to ask you to help us.

Ask.

We know one of the Al-Drechar was murdered.

Myriell, confirmed Sha-Kaan.

Erienne's mind was damaged by it. She is unconscious now and Denser has been holding back the storms. But he's spent and he can't help her where she needs it most. We need Cleress to be with her, in her mind. She's in trouble.

I will do what I can. Cleress is asleep under a spell now but she is also free of the Xeteskians. When she wakes, I will be there.

Thank you. And for you, we have the information we need. When we get out, we can make it happen.

Renewed warmth and sudden joy flooded Hirad's mind. *Then, frail human, you had better ensure you survive. I will have need of my Dragonene when I return home.*

I'll do what I can.

I am sure you will.

Sha-Kaan's contact ceased. Hirad came fully to himself, with the battering on the door constant and the pressure beginning to tell. Behind him, the basket carrying Denser and Erienne lifted out of sight, creaking and protesting, the movements deliberately smooth. He focused back on the door from which Auum had never taken his eyes.

Another impact, and the illusion collapsed.

'Can that happen?' asked Hirad.

'Apparently,' said Darrick from the other side of the shaft.

Hirad was looking at a plain panel of oak, dark and heavy. There was a recess to the left into which it would slide. Not that Dystran planned anything so gentle. When the WardLock failed, the door would go with it. Already, the wood was stressed and warped, only Denser's spell keeping it in place now. Hirad backed up three paces, Auum following suit, understanding they were too close for comfort.

The hammering of weapons continued while Dystran presumably gathered himself. At Hirad's back, the basket rattled down, slapping onto the floor. It was wet, the rope above it dripping and dirty. Duele and Evunn were in the basket in moments. Duele tugged the rope hard to indicate he was ready and up they went, quicker this time with Denser clearly on the rope too.

'Come on, come on,' muttered Hirad. The hammering on the door ceased. 'Here we go.'

Auum clutched his sword tighter and looked half away, braced against the expected blast. The spell hit the door, driving into the mana lattice of the WardLock. Blue light sparked across its surface, a rush of air hit them and the door began to topple forwards.

For a heartbeat, Hirad stopped to wonder why the wood hadn't splintered and Myx was past him, hurling himself against it and ramming it back into place.

'Help me,' he said.

Hirad and Auum leaned their weights against the panel. It was warm. On the opposite side, the enemy pushed hard, handicapped by the narrow passage width on their side.

'Rebraal,' called Hirad. 'When the basket comes down, you're next.'

'No—'

'Yes,' snapped Hirad, arms shaking under an impact. 'You're the quicker climber. Darrick, you're after him, the rope will take you both.'

'I hear you.'

Hirad could hear the reluctance in his voice but unlike Rebraal, he understood who led down here.

The pressure on the door grew more sustained. They could hear shouts ordering more men to the press. Inexorably, the panel was moving. Myx turned and braced his legs against the stone floor, his broad shoulders flattened across the panel. Either side of him, Auum and Hirad, leaned side-on. Hirad looked up into the face of the Protector, saw the sweat on his brow and knew they didn't have long before his strength deserted him.

The basket crashed to the floor, cracking on impact.

'Rebraal, go!' shouted Hirad.

He saw the elf leap to the rope and start climbing. Darrick watched him too. The barbarian could see the pallid colour of the general's face. He had lost too much blood.

'Don't faint before you get to the top,' he said.

Darrick was stone-faced. 'I'll make it,' he said.

'Three to go,' said Hirad. 'This should be interesting.'

Suddenly, the pressure against the panel vanished and it thudded back into place. Hirad would have preferred had it not. Dystran's voice sounded in the sudden quiet.

'Let me through, idiots. I'll do it, myself.'

'Not good,' muttered Hirad.

'We're out of time,' said Myx.

'Right,' said Hirad. 'Auum, go.' The TaiGethen looked at him. 'Spell coming. Go.'

Auum nodded, understanding and respect in his gesture. He sheathed his sword and jumped onto the rope.

'Go, Hirad,' said Myx.

'The rope won't take four.'

'You have no choice.'

'You're coming with me. I'm not leaving you here.'

Myx met his stare. 'I will not yield. Go. Sol understands. We are one.'

'You'll be killed.'

'We are one!'

Hirad hesitated but Myx had turned away. It felt wrong. This wasn't necessary. He eyed the rope which flexed and jumped, under the strain of those climbing it. He stepped onto the rim of the basket.

'The Raven will help you,' he said. 'You should come.'

'No.'

Hirad sliced the rope below him, sheathed his knife and began climbing hard.

'Pull!' he yelled. 'Darrick, make them pull. Myx, come on, you can make it.'

Below Hirad, the world turned blue, a force of air whipping up the shaft bouncing him from side to side. Myx tumbled beneath him like a doll cast carelessly aside, shards of the oak panel a storm about him. Urgent shouts were followed by soldiers clustering under the vent bringing crossbows to bear.

'Oh shit,' said Hirad. 'Pull up, pull up!'

Bolts clattered and bounced in the shaft, one thumping side-on into his boot. He climbed faster, hand over hand, legs driving him upwards. The wound in his chest, pulled and twisted, fresh blood dripping down his body.

At the base of the shaft, the reload was complete but the shots never came. From nowhere, Myx barrelled across his vision, head down, arms wide, sweeping into the bowmen, pushing them away. The sounds of the fight followed but Hirad couldn't see it because at last, the rope began to rise and he was pulled quickly from sight. He could hear though, and all too soon, the sounds ceased.

Hirad closed his eyes for a moment before turning his head upwards. Fresh air reached his lungs and drops of rain hit his face. He could hear the wind howling across the top of the shaft. It had been calm when they had entered Xetesk and now a storm had begun. It was somehow entirely appropriate.

Chapter 27

Dystran stared up the ventilation shaft, dodging backwards when, predictably, the rope dropped down. They had escaped him for now and the thought made him as angry as he had ever felt. But he couldn't shake the grudging respect he also felt. They'd escaped from two colleges in the past four days, and he recalled they'd done something similar in Dordover when recovering a Dawnthief catalyst from the crypts there a few years back.

'Extraordinary,' he said quietly. 'Quite extraordinary.'

He wanted to shout, lash out, anything to ease his frustration. Uncharacteristically, he chose not to. Turning and looking at the men around him he saw fear, shock and relief. He saw trepidation too. He knew they were anxious about his reaction. They expected him to blame them. He found he could not.

Down at his feet, Myx lay dead. He'd known the Protector for a decade and had never seen his face until now. A man. How easy it had been to ignore that fact. He looked peaceful in death, his face relaxed, his eyes closed and the red marks fading from his face.

Part of Dystran feared the passing of the Protectors. Something of Xetesk's invincibility went with them into history. He knew the political will to reinstitute the order wouldn't exist and that he was weakened because of it.

He shook his head and took a last look up the shaft. How often had he heard that you should never underestimate The Raven? He should have listened. He blinked away the dust that was falling, dislodged by foot and rope. They were outside the city but not outside his control. Not completely, and not if he acted quickly and decisively enough.

There was so much to organise, so much to do. The war had taken a turn against Xetesk. His hand was about to be forced. Fortunately, it was a strong one. He turned back to his men.

'Let's get out of here. Any of you who feel able to help clean up this mess our friends have created gather in the dome when you've had a stiff drink. Suarav will organise you. Any who don't, stand yourselves down until dawn.'

'My Lord,' came the response.

'My Lord?'

Dystran faced the soldier, he didn't know his name.

'Speak.'

'We will get them, won't we? We've lost so many friends tonight.'

Dystran smiled sadly. 'I know,' he said. 'I'll do everything in my power to catch them. They've hurt us and I'm sorry for those of you who have lost friends. Tonight, we assumed no one could get in and get out and we were wrong. It's a hard lesson, isn't it? We can stand here and say we had no luck in catching them but The Raven would consider there was no luck involved. We have to accept that they may be right. Come on, I'll show you the way out.'

Ark stood in the warm air of the early morning. He couldn't sleep. He thought perhaps he never would again. Herendeneth was quiet once more but everything had changed.

He felt the air playing over his face and couldn't resist the temptation to touch his skin. It itched where the mask had rubbed and the soothing balms worked to stop infection. He traced the contours of his features, fascinated. The freedom to stand in the open and let the night see him was so alien and he couldn't shake the thought that he would be struck down for experiencing it.

He wished the sensation was something he could enjoy. But the only enjoyment he had ever derived had been in sharing his consciousness with his brothers in the Soul Tank. That had gone forever. His soul was within him now. It had been the prayer answered but the price was a loss that dragged at the heart and left loneliness untamed in the mind.

Freedom to be as other men. He wondered what he would do with it and, for the thousandth time, sought contact with his brothers, only to find silence. He turned. Four stood behind him, hair blowing in the warm breeze, dark clothes and armour at odds with their unmasked faces. Faces that mirrored his confusion.

'We have work, my brothers,' he said.

They nodded. 'We are one,' they said.

They followed him back to the house. It stood stark against the deep of the night. The dragon, Sha-Kaan still sat on the torn roof, his great body still, his head inside, close to the surviving Al-Drechar. None came near her bar her elven servants.

They walked the corridors to the private rooms where blood had so recently been spilt. The dragon's eyes bade them approach. He knew their minds and their desires.

'I will accept only peace,' said Sha-Kaan. 'There will be no more threat to Cleress or the family of Sol.'

The voice from the cavernous mouth brooked no dissension. He had killed to protect them already. He would not hesitate to do so again.

'We will stand with you,' said Ark. 'We are one.'

'I know your loss,' said Sha-Kaan. 'But your gain is greater. Your brothers in my land enjoyed their freedom.'

'Cil,' breathed Ark, invoking the name of another who, like Sol, lived beyond the Soul Tank but was thought lost.

'Yes,' said Sha-Kaan. 'He is one of three.' He was silent for a moment though his breath like a roaring fire filled the space. 'There remain on this island those that would threaten me,' he said. 'Together, they are powerful.'

Axes snapped from back clasps.

'We understand,' said Ark. 'They are no longer our masters.'

Removal of threat. It was what Protectors did best.

The storm across Xetesk had brought strong winds and driving rain but the air smelled fresh and vibrant after the confines of the catacombs. For long glorious moments, Hirad hadn't cared where they were. He had lain flat on the muddy ground, heaving in air untainted with the stench of death while rain washed over his aching body, pattering on his face and sluicing blood from his armour.

Eventually, he'd pushed himself up on to his elbows, his body a little calmer, the pain throbbing down to a dull ache. Reality had intruded harshly. They were hidden in a bank of thick gorse, scattered with bracken as Myx had described. The thorny bushes offered a solid barrier around the small clearing in which the vent was situated and provided some break from the wind. Low tunnels ran away through the bank in three directions.

In the small space, Thraun cradled Erienne in his arms while Denser, Auum and Duele crowded round the prone Evunn. Paint was smeared and running over their faces, anguish plain beneath the spoiled camouflage.

Darrick was standing close by, his feet edging into the illusion that so comprehensively hid the vent grille that even close inspection might reveal nothing to the eye. Sian'erei sat under the gorse, trying in vain to keep herself dry. Of Rebraal and The Unknown, there was no sign though he could hear one or both of them approaching through the gorse.

'How far does it extend?' asked Hirad when The Unknown appeared.

'Well, this vent certainly wasn't positioned here by accident,' said The Unknown. 'Fifty or so yards east towards the city, there's a short crag. Twenty feet down, no more but no one's going to ride this way. South it extends probably a mile along a shallow slope, north probably the same and given that Rebraal isn't back yet, I'd say west, the way the Xeteskians bring in their supplies, the gorse will extend a couple of hundred yards. It's neat, I'll give them that.'

'Sounds like an ideal place to rest up,' said Hirad. Darrick didn't see his knowing smile.

'I think that would be an extraordinarily bad idea,' said the general. 'Dystran knows our exit points. He wants to stop us. I can see us suffering familiar attacks any time. Just as soon as he gets organised.'

'So you think we should throw ourselves on the mercy of the Lysternans or Dordovans instead?' asked Hirad.

'No,' began Darrick.

'Or perhaps whatever's left of the Black Wings' army of the righteous.'

'Hirad you aren't helping,' said Darrick.

Hirad winked at The Unknown. 'Actually, we're probably strong enough to take them on. Couple of spent mages, several injured warriors and the seriously ill. No problem.'

'Hirad, stop now,' said The Unknown. He held up a hand to

Darrick. 'What our barbarian is trying to say in his bludgeon-ing, tactless way is that we need a place to hole up, at least for a few hours. We're too sick to travel to the Al-Arynaar camp right now. But we can't afford to be behind the Xeteskians when they break the siege.'

'I know all that,' said Darrick rather testily.

'Yes,' said Hirad. 'And you're carrying a wound more serious than you are admitting.'

'I'll live,' said the general.

'That's not good enough,' said Hirad.

'Meaning?'

'Meaning you're no good to us crippled. You could help yourself by sitting down for a start. Then turn that mind of yours to where we *can* rest relatively safely.'

Darrick glared at Hirad but sat next to him anyway. 'A lot depends on Denser,' he said.

'Doesn't it always?' replied Hirad.

'And on Sian,' added Darrick. The elven mage looked up. 'Are you able to cast?'

'It is difficult,' she said, feeling for the words. 'The mana is dark. Weak.'

'That does not sound encouraging,' said The Unknown. 'Denser, what's your situation?'

Denser pushed himself to his feet, giving Auum's shoulder a consoling squeeze as he did so.

'I have nothing left,' he said, walking across to stand by The Unknown. 'Evunn is not as bad as I feared but he needs a mage soon who understands MindMelt to undo the damage. It's a senior spell. And my spell around Erienne's mind is bleeding away. I have to rest and I have to seek the demon gateway to get my stamina back quickly. But there doesn't seem much prospect of that. There's more. I did have some time to look at a few of the theories back there in the in the Laryon hub. It's dimensional connectivity and power they're looking at and I didn't like the look of the way the research was headed.

'We should warn the allies, because if you remember the DimensionConnect spell Xetesk used at Understone a few years back, they'll need to be prepared. So, all in all, I'd say the situation is somewhere between dismal and desperate. The only bright spot is that the familiars won't be able to fly in this. There's too much power in this storm, it'll upset their senses.'

'So where do we go right now?' asked Hirad. 'None of us is fit to fight, we don't have a mage that can cast and we're carrying Erienne.'

'Like I said . . .' Denser glanced across at Erienne. Thraun was hunched over her, keeping the rain from her face. 'Erienne is the real worry. She's battling the One on her own until Cleress wakes. This storm will seem like nothing if Cleress can't help her and I dread to think what damage is being caused to her mind.'

'She is strong,' said Thraun, looking up for a moment. 'She fights.'

'I know Thraun but I can't be there with her. It's not . . .' Denser trailed off and the desperation he'd been trying to hide burst on to his face. He stood helplessly, the rain pounding down harder now, and gestured uselessly. 'She's alone in there. What if I've lost her?'

Hirad scrambled to his feet and stood in front of Denser, grabbing his shoulders.

'No one's losing anyone,' he said. 'Not this time. We can beat this, all of it. We're—'

'I know,' said Denser, his smile weak but genuine. 'The Raven.'

'And don't you forget it. She's not alone and neither are you.'

Rebraal had returned during the exchange and was checking on Evunn.

'Here's what we do,' said The Unknown. 'The elves go back to their lines. Evunn needs help and maybe he'll get it there. We have to get ourselves away from here and hidden. Darrick, how far can you walk? Hirad, Thraun, you too. No exaggeration.'

'It's a question of where, not how far,' said Darrick. 'We're the opposite side of the city to where we need to be. And we're too close to the walls. I'd say the walk back for us under normal conditions would be about three hours. It's four 'til dawn. There's nothing I'd call good cover without taking a massive detour. We either head for the Al-Arynaar, or burrow in here. Getting halfway and being captured in the daylight won't help us.'

He was right and they all knew it. Hirad felt his chest. The bleeding had stopped but he'd lost a fair bit of blood. He couldn't fight again until the cut was at least partially healed. Darrick's limp was pronounced and Thraun's trouser leg was stained dark with blood. Four hours wouldn't be enough.

'Then we have to stay here.'

'No,' said Rebraal, joining them. 'It's too dangerous here. Supplies come here every night.'

'So what do you suggest?'

'We will run back with Evunn. Sian will stay with you and you walk as far as you can. The ClawBound will find you. We will send help. Elven help.'

'We can't afford to be caught in the open,' said The Unknown.

'The ClawBound will find you first.'

Hirad shrugged. 'What choice do we have?'

Dystran had changed his blood-soaked shoes and washed the sweat and grime from his face and hands before joining the survivors of his top team. None of them looked any better than Ranyl who had also made the early-hours meeting in the minor banqueting hall.

He surveyed the tired, drawn pale faces in front of him. The Circle Seven was broken. Two had died, one in the corridors under attack from the TaiGethen, one by The Raven. Kestys was dead too, so was Gylac, removing his most senior dimensional and elven archive expertise. The mages who had been researching the connectivity spells were gone too, slaughtered in Laryon's hub. The Gods knew how many others had fallen. Suarav and Chandyr had yet to confirm the number of dead college guard and reservists but it had to run close to three figures.

The shock around the table was understandable. All this damage, and caused by so few. Dystran took them all in one by one. Suarav and Chandyr sat together, backs to the door, which was flanked outside by guards. The oval table was only half full. Ranyl, with his cat in his lap, was the only one exhibiting calm. For the remainder of the Circle, Dessyn, Prexys and Hyloch, the night in the catacombs had shattered their belief in their own security. Each of them knew that they were alive only because they had not run into The Raven or the TaiGethen.

'Gentlemen,' began Dystran, once a servant had poured him

a mug of sweet herb tea and withdrawn. 'I am aware of how you must all be feeling. I am aware that it is tempting to cast about for blame. We will not fall to that temptation. The purpose of this gathering is to assess the damage to our operation quickly, agree what actions will follow and so allow us, those that can, a few hours' rest before dawn.'

'We must examine the failings of our security,' said Dessyn, the Soul Tank Master. He was a middle-aged man of massive magical ability but no real strength of will.

'I think I have already made myself clear,' said Dystran. 'The time for such an assessment is in the future. May I remind you that outside our city, there are a considerable number of enemies determined to win the war. It is our duty to stop them and examining our security lapses will not do that. Besides, we know how they got in and where they got out.'

Dessyn opened his mouth and had half-raised a finger to point at Suarav when Dystran cut him off.

'Enough. Dessyn, if any of us had foreseen that Denser and The Raven were not only at Xetesk but with the elves in the raid, we would not be having this meeting. Do not point at others except in so much as to blame yourself. After all, Suarav knew nothing of the passage from the warehouse. No non-mage did until tonight. Instead, tell me this. Where are the Protectors?'

'Not all are accounted for,' replied Dessyn, his face reddening from the rebuke. 'Some have disappeared into the city, others tried to leave Xetesk altogether. Thirty-seven are currently inside the college. We are holding them in the barracks.'

'Leaving how many loose?'

Dessyn looked at Chandyr. 'Commander?'

'Given I don't know if any, other than Myx, were killed in the catacombs, though I doubt it, that would leave sixty-eight at large. I am assuming they are not necessarily loyal but not necessarily a threat, either.'

'Very well,' said Dystran. 'Chandyr, you need to assess those we hold. I suspect like you that they will not fight with us. Make sure they are treated well. They are a problem of our own making and they will be respected. None will be hurt or forced to do anything against their wills. Ensure they understand that and see that word gets out into the city. Don't waste resources searching for the lost; let's hope they choose to come to us.

'Next, research.'

Faces around the table became, if anything, longer than before. Dystran tried to ignore them.

'Elven translations?'

'Unfinished,' said Ranyl. 'And with Gylac and his assistant dead, we would struggle to confirm any theory, or indeed complete our researches even if the Aryn Hiil and associated writings hadn't been taken.'

'Right, so that's a disaster,' said Dystran. 'Let's scrub it for now, there's nothing we can do about it in the short term. Dimensional connectivity and inter-dimensional focus?'

'Well, Kestys demonstrated the Soul Tank linkage was divisible without risk,' said Prexys, dryly. 'At least it suggests our calculations of dimensional alignment are correct.'

Dystran rather liked Prexys. He was ancient, older than Ranyl, and trustworthy because he had no desire to rule. Not any more. His age had refined his acerbic wit, though this time, Dystran was the only one who smiled.

'That's something, I suppose. Did anyone check the research rooms in Laryon's hub?'

'Nothing has been damaged there, my Lord,' said Prexys. 'Unlike your own base. Much of the information there has been destroyed or taken.'

'And what has gone?'

'Oh, nothing much,' said Prexys, eyebrows rising. 'The latest map, the seeker-spell routines and the gateway structure research.'

'Nothing much,' muttered Hyloch. 'The damage they have done.'

'It is not terminal,' said Dystran. 'It is a setback, nothing more. It changes nothing except the speed of our actions.'

'They have taken the basis for everything,' said Hyloch.

'But not the method for that which we need most urgently.' Dystran could see that they didn't understand. He leaned back. 'Let's go back a little way. The vents. Suarav, tell me your plan.'

Suarav looked surprised. 'Well—'

'For the benefit of us all,' added Dystran.

'Oh, of course, my Lord.' He composed himself. 'They are being blocked as we speak. We must assume the supply chain is compromised and the vents do, or did, represent a potential point of enemy entry.'

'So, you see the extent of our problems. However, we can strike back but it must be sure. I believe we have one option only. Stop me if you disagree.' He spread his hands. 'You're tired so I'll try and be brief. To swing the war back in our favour and ensure our plans for the rulership of Balaia and Calaius are not irreparably damaged, we must reclaim the elven writings. We must also, given the likely and immediate destination of both The Raven and the remaining elven mages, break the siege quickly.

'I would remind you all that though Julatsan magic is weak it is far from dead. To irrevocably shift the balance our way, it must be suffocated. That means thwarting any attempt to raise the Heart. Am I clear so far?'

He saw nods, lips moving and the gesture of a hand.

'Good. My friends, it has come to this. Our adapted magics are not fully tested, nor fully theorised. But we do not have the time to wait. We have to confess to being outthought by the elves and outfought by The Raven. This means that occupying the siege forces for a moment longer while we research is rendered pointless. We will also begin to suffer quickly with vital supplies now being denied us.

'So, Commander Chandyr, you will put into operation the advance plans we have been working on so diligently. Please report to me as soon as you can about the state of the familiars, mage-defenders and assassins. When this blasted storm dies down, we can send the familiars out; I feel they may be a potent weapon. Captain Suarav, you will assist, in addition to activating the backward college defence plans. You know how long you might have to defend us. The numbers against you will only become clear when the siege is broken. Commander, you haven't as long as I wanted to give you. One day and one night, to be precise.

'I will personally oversee the final hours of work on the dimensional spells and will make a decision which spell to employ nearer the time. You, my Lord mages, will rest. Gather your wills and your strengths. Advise those trained of what is to come and relieve them of their duties in order to rest. I will not look kindly on failure.

'At dawn the day after tomorrow, we will show those bastards what a big fucking mess is really all about. Any questions?'

Chapter 28

In the end, the One-inspired storm did more than keep familiars from the air. It kept the sky dark until well after dawn. The Raven, exhausted, wounded and carrying Erienne, who showed no signs of regaining consciousness, had made tortuously slow progress through the gorse and then across open land, first west, then south and finally east and back towards the Al-Arynaar camp.

Though they kept to deep shadow, shallow valley and tree or scrub where they could find it, they ran a constant risk of encountering Lysternan or Dordovan patrols. It made the walk mentally as well as physically draining, the wild weather conditions merely compounding the problems they faced.

The first ClawBound found them after perhaps an hour. It might have been more, Hirad couldn't be certain. The rain was driving head-on into them, the wind forcing their movement back to little more than a shuffle. He was leading, the blood loss from his chest making him light-headed, with pain spearing his lungs every time he breathed. The Unknown was at his side, one arm around Darrick's waist. The general was in trouble, his hip having stiffened, sending an ache up the entire side of his body and into his neck and face, his blood loss from beneath makeshift bandages a cause for real concern.

Behind them, Thraun's huge arms enveloped Erienne, keeping the worst from her, while beside her, Denser shivered with the cold and mental fatigue, his cloak wrapped around his wife. Sian'erei walked with them too, cutting a lone hunched figure, lost in dread thoughts about the death of Julatsan magic.

The panther had approached from downwind, appearing from the dark and wiping a wet flank along Thraun's undamaged leg. Another had immediately run out of low cover to their right and not long after, came their unmistakable elven partners. Tall, long-fingered, impossibly graceful, their white-and-black painted faces unspoiled by the rain.

Hirad had felt a relief that surprised him, while The Raven were happy to have their direction changed, edging them south-east. One of the pairs walked with them, the other well ahead, scouting the terrain for cover and any sign of allied patrols. The pair with them didn't stray from Erienne. The panther walked easily by Thraun, the elf on his other side. Normally impassive, the elf's face wore a frown and he rarely took his eyes from her. As if he could sense the turmoil within her.

Hirad relaxed. Not just because the ClawBound would give early warning of any attack, but because he had to. He couldn't fight his weariness any longer. His chest was freezing and a riot of pain, his whole upper body felt like he'd taken a beating with iron bars and his legs were leaden and sluggish. The only way to keep himself going was to retreat inside himself and concentrate on just putting one foot in front of the other.

Even so, by the time they had walked for over two hours, he was forcing himself to continue by sheer effort of will. He could sense The Unknown struggling too, though he had the considerable burden of Darrick to weigh him down. The general could hardly walk at all, but they would not stop, and nothing would stop them. Not the wind throwing dirt and leaves in their faces, nor the rain tearing at their clothes and chilling their skin.

'Can you ride a horse?' asked The Unknown suddenly, his words just carrying over the gale.

'I would kiss anyone who presented me with one, kiss the horse and leap on its back in a single bound,' said Hirad.

'I look forward to it.'

Hirad raised his head. Incredibly, The Unknown was smiling. The big man nodded forward, Hirad followed the gesture. There in the path ahead, hidden from plain view by a bank of trees on the downslope of a shallow valley, was a group of elves. Each one had a horse by its reins, the animals grazing quietly or looking about them vacantly. Actually, they weren't all elves. One was bigger and broader; he was standing next to Rebraal.

'Blackthorne,' said Hirad.

'I've heard that beards rub the skin of the face,' said The Unknown. 'Pucker up.'

Hirad laughed. It was brief, the pain flared across his chest. The elves and Blackthorne were walking the horses towards them. The barbarian stopped and looked behind him. He felt like sagging to the ground but knew he'd never get up again. Relief was stamped across Thraun's face and Denser's had softened just a little.

'You boys need a ride?' asked Blackthorne as he reached them.

'Now you mention it,' said Hirad.

Blackthorne's dark eyes sparkled but his expression was grim when he took them all in.

'Come on,' he said. 'Let's not waste time. You need help, all of you.'

Hirad nodded. 'I'll kiss you later.'

'Pardon?'

'Never mind,' said The Unknown. He clasped Blackthorne's arm. 'We won't forget this.'

It was a long time before Erienne even recognised that the world she knew was gone. It was a long time before she recognised anything at all. Awareness was not something she could take for granted, she thought. Or did she? This could be a dream, in which case, she was not necessarily aware. She had no sensation of breathing, movement or life. None of her external senses revealed anything to her. She might well even be dead.

In fact, the more she thought about it, the more likely that outcome became. Her memories were fragmented. Not those of her past; they were as clear as they had always been. But there had been a transition. And somewhere between Myriell's shattering cry and the restart of her thought processes, the memories had been broken, scattered.

Parts of it were still there. Dimly-heard shouts. A pain like she had never experienced before, splintering through her mind. Voices in the darkness. A curious odour like paint burning. An enveloping of her consciousness in a strangling mesh. Contracting, contracting.

It was this she had woken to, with the thought that she must fight. With no idea of the passage of time, she was unaware how long her mind had been under attack. And it was an attack, she was sure. Like it had been waiting for a slip, the One entity inside her had reacted instantly to Myriell's death and the removal of the suppression of its potential.

Now she could recall it burgeoning within her with a power far too strong to control or even deflect. It had used her mind as a focus and gorged itself on the elements around it. But it had not been allowed to give unfettered vent to itself. Something had blocked it from the outside. Denser. It had to be. Only he understood. Only he among those she had been standing with was capable.

For the first time in what felt like an age, she experienced warmth in her mind. She reached out and probed gently for Cleress but the Al-Drechar was not there. She might be dead too. Probably was. That meant that she, Erienne, was alone to fight the One. Not to defeat it, but to bend it to her will. She imagined it like a spider, the great mound of its body resting on her conscious mind, its eight legs gripping her and squeezing. She couldn't hope to push the body away, not with her limited experience. But she had to stop the constriction. So, in her mind's eye, she had to keep on prising away one of the legs, or maybe two. Keep it occupied, keep it off balance.

The question, of course, was how.

What had Myriell and Cleress told her? She struggled to remember. Her mind was clouded, the One all around her, trying to feed off her, drag her mind's energy, leach it away and use it. It came to her. The One was not sentient and it was dangerous to think of it as such. That was what they had said. In fact, it was little more than a channeller for elemental forces as much as her mind was a focus for those same forces.

This was where she had had difficulty understanding them. It was not sentient but in one sense it had to be an entity or how had they managed to transfer it from her dying daughter to her? The point was, she had been told, that it was an unguarded channeller. Her mind had to be both guardian and focus. And it was the guardianship that was hardest learned, the suppression of the ability of the One to suck in energy and use it destructively.

That was what the Al-Drechar had been doing. Closing off its access to the elements. And this was what made it different from any magical power. Mana was naturally chaotic and unfocused, harmless in its natural state. So were earth, air, fire and water harmless. The One entity, though, gave them direction. And the mind of the mage in which it rested gave them focus, gave them outlet.

In order to prise one of the legs away, then, she had to force her mind to focus in the way she wanted it to. Wrest back control. Imagination was the key as it was to most magic. The ability to see the shapes the power formed and imbue them with the necessary motive force.

Actually, she thought as she swam towards some form of active conscious thought, that was a very simplistic view. Her Dordovan masters would have chastised her for it. The Al-Drechar would have praised her.

She kept the idea of the spider and its legs uppermost in her mind. The first thing she had to do was stop the dragging in of elemental chaos. That was like a gale inside her head. Once she had done that, perhaps she could begin to bend the One her way. Perhaps not. She looked deep inside herself and saw the yawning chasm the One had opened up to the flow of the elements. It was terrifying, like standing at the mouth of a volcano as the lava boiled up and knowing she had to close the crater.

She quailed from the task, immediately feeling the legs begin to tighten.

No, she said to herself and for the benefit of her unwelcome parasite. *I will not yield to you. You will not have me.*

And it will not, said a voice. *Not with your strength. And not while I have mine.*

Cleress? Delight flooded her. Another voice. A hand in the dark.

I am weak but I am here. Come on child, let us get you back to those who love you. The One blocks you. It is a case of knowing where to push and then how to hold open the door.

Can I do it?

Only you can ever know that.

Tessaya, Lord of the Paleon tribes, and leader by consent of the Wesmen nation, had been pleasantly surprised by the response of the lords and tribal heads gathered before him as dawn broke over the encampment.

His palatial tent was full of leather and fur-clad senior tribesmen, all of whom he knew by name. The air was thick with pipe smoke, sweat and opportunity. The eyes that stared back at him from beneath hard brows were concentrated with energy and desire.

Representatives of forty tribes had answered his call, spurred to action by the mode of communication, passed by the tribal Shamen through the Spirits rather than by bird or rider. War council was invoked, his message had said. Muster your men. Be ready for victory over our oldest enemy. Come and hear my words.

And they had come and Tessaya was pleased. Now they waited for those words.

'The storms have passed and we have emerged strong and united. That you are all here and in such obvious health is proof enough. Through the harsh times, we did not fight. We shared, we survived. We are fit, our crops grow once more and our children laugh while they play, their bellies full.

'It is not so in the east.'

Murmurs ran around the tent. He saw Riasu nod and smile. He knew more than most but less than Tessaya. It would forever be the way while he lived. Information was the key to power, not strength of arms.

'My Lords,' said Tessaya, holding up his hands. 'The warring colleges are tearing the east apart. The colleges blame each other and a single small child for the forces that raged against them. I prefer to think the Spirits have exacted their vengeance. Now it is our turn.

'It has set college against college, mage against mage. It has set man against his brother. But more, it has weakened them and the fabric of the society of which they are so proud. They sneer at us across the Blackthorne Mountains, terming us savages. Yet who is it whose children die in the streets in front of their fine-built houses? Who is it who determines to war until the last man lies dying in his own blood?

'We may not have the minds of mages. We may not have the great cities and ports. But we have something far more import-ant.' He thumped his chest. 'We have heart.'

The Lords in front of him roared their approval. He waited for the noise to die down, draining his goblet and refilling it, enjoying the atmosphere. It would not be so easy from here.

'The true test of a people is that they can thrive in adversity. We have done so. We have emerged stronger but I also like to think we have emerged wiser.'

The assembled tribesmen quietened further, sensing they were not to hear exactly what they expected.

'The wars of six years ago have taken their toll. We are no longer a numerous people, able to mass tens of thousands of willing warriors for the fight. Indeed, had we taken Balaia in the last invasion, we would have lost it again when our enemies regathered. The Wytch Lords sought dominion by destruction. My vision is of a place where the Wesmen tribes can prosper, becoming stronger every day. A place where our children can run free and where each of us here present is spoken of as our Gods are today.'

He paused and smiled, noting their reactions. Some were confused, others disappointed, most angry.

'So, are we to fight the colleges?' asked Riasu.

Tessaya nodded. 'No Wesman will ever offer them the hand of peace. For us nothing but their elimination will make our children truly safe and let us build our world. The colleges are a curse on this land. In that, if in nothing else, we agree with the Black Wings. But they would have been our masters in an unequal alliance. The reason their bodies smoulder still is that the Wesmen will be mastered by no one. No one.'

Faces were relaxing, expressions softening.

'I will invite your thoughts in a moment,' said Tessaya. 'And I will invite your support also. In this fight, we must stand together and not stray from our singleminded path.

'Julatsa is still ruined and only hanging on to its status by the merest thread. Every piece of intelligence I have points to Xetesk being on the verge of collapse under the onslaught of Lystern and Dordover, who are in uneasy alliance and supported by elves who will return south when their work is complete.

'I propose that we strike now at Xetesk. We take the city as we did Julatsa. We destroy the college as we did Julatsa. When Xetesk is gone, the balance of power will shift. Dordover will fight Lystern for dominion. All we have to do is wait for them to weaken each other while we reinforce and plan. When the time is right, we will move north and take them, one by one.

'But we will not repeat the mistakes of our past, when our lust for victory drove us on and on, ever thinner in strength. We will not fragment and we will not overstretch. So when the colleges are gone, we will stop, build our lives and share our new lands. And we will trade with the Barons and Lords of Eastern Balaia, letting their greed help us grow to dominace. What say you?'

'We are a warrior race,' said a voice from the back. It was Quatanai, a man with plenty of popular support. 'It is not our way to farm ourselves into decadence.'

'Neither is it our way to live in cities,' said Tessaya. 'Why should we tear them down when they can work for us? The colleges must be destroyed because magic must die. But beyond that, it is surely better to parley from a position of strength, make the Eastern Balaians trade with us on our terms.' He smiled. 'How many of us do not enjoy Black-thorne's wines?'

He heard chuckles and affirmatives and shrugged his shoulders, his palms up.

'Who here knows they can ferment the grapes better than the Baron's men? It is simple, my Lords. We keep what we need, destroy what we do not. Anything else is a waste of our blood and I will not have my people die needlessly. Not now, not ever again.

'Now, are you with me?'

The massed cry of 'Aye!', the clashed goblets and the cheers told him he had them, for now at least. But he didn't fool himself that they bought all that he had said. For them, the chance to strike the killing blow against magic was enough. The test of his leadership would come should that battle be won.

Tessaya caught the gaze of Quatanai, saw his thoughts as plain as if he had spoken them aloud.

He would have to be careful.

Chapter 29

'Denser!' Thraun's voice was low and urgent.

It was mid morning. The sounds of fighting at the east gates of Xetesk rolled up the gentle slope, filling the air with discordance. From where he had been lying, Denser had guessed that the combat was mainly magic-based, the two opposing armed forces having all but fought themselves to a standstill.

But this morning, both sides would have renewed hope of a breakthrough. With no Protectors in the Xeteskian lines and no elves in the allied lines, both were weakened in muscle and in spirit. Mere men opposed each other now. And those with the greater will, who had remained the stronger through the days of battle, would prevail.

Denser scrambled to his feet. Above him, the trees were calm and a warm sun dried the sodden ground. While he had been resting on leather under his elven-made bivouac, the mana had coursed into him through the dark gateway Xeteskians had used for centuries, and the mana storm had blown itself out.

Thraun was sitting by the embers of the night's fire, one leg stretched in front of him. The trouser had been cut away and he wore clean bandages through which a hint of blood had soaked. Next to him lay Erienne, beautiful but so pale in the broken sunlight. He stroked hair from her face and looked up at Denser.

'She is strong,' he said. 'I told you.'

Hope gripped Denser. He dropped to his knees at her side and stared at her face. Beneath their lids, her eyes were moving.

'Erienne,' he said, leaning in close, his lips brushing hers, feeling their warmth. 'Can you hear me, love?'

'She fights,' said Thraun.

'How long has she been like this?'

Thraun frowned, struggling to frame the words. Denser prompted him.

'An hour ago? Just now?'

Thraun nodded. 'Now,' he affirmed. 'The sun helps her.'

Denser understood. Thraun had refused to leave her side when Denser had been forced to rest to regain mana stamina. She had slept in his arms under a leather and leaf shelter, his warmth about her. They went back a long way. Thraun had been a good friend of Alun, her first husband, and now the troubled shapechanger was uniquely positioned to understand her pain. Like him, she was possessed of a force she hated and craved in equal measure.

'You think Cleress is there?' he asked.

Thraun nodded again. 'Her spirit is calm.'

'Thank you, Thraun,' said Denser. 'What would I do without you?'

Thraun shrugged. 'Raven,' he said by way of explanation. 'You must rest more.'

Denser couldn't refuse. He looked into Thraun's eyes and saw the frustration boiling there. He didn't think Thraun would ever quite recover himself. The worst thing was that Thraun knew it too.

'I know it's hard,' he said, climbing slowly to his feet and putting a hand on his chest. 'But in here, you are everything you always were, and we'll never forget that.'

He walked back towards his bivouac. Placed at the heart of the elven camp, they were shielded from the prying eyes of the Lysternans near them. It was probable that the allies suspected they were here, or at least very close. The mana storm would have seen to that. But the camp was sealed by TaiGethen and ClawBound. None would dare cross the line. The elves would not hesitate to fight back.

He paused by the sleeping forms of Hirad, Darrick and The Unknown. Men pushed right to their limits and now paying the price. On their arrival back in the elven camp it had been immediately apparent that all needed spell treatment in addition to their bandaging and wound cleansing. Their plan to leave at next dusk was simply not practical.

Darrick was the worst. He'd collapsed from his horse the moment they'd stopped. His blood loss was serious, the wound across his hip deep and open through his forced action. The spell had knitted the damage, bandages held the wound closed but only time would replace the blood. He would be weak for days.

Hirad's armour was being repaired elsewhere. What was left behind was a shirt barely recognisable as such. Both arms were ragged, his chest was bandaged from throat to gut and his forehead too was hidden beneath clean coverings.

The Unknown had fared better in the fights but had followed that exertion by all but carrying Darrick for over two hours into the teeth of a gale. His was a muscle weariness only rest would relieve.

Strange. Before meeting the elves of the Al-Arynaar and TaiGethen, there was no way The Raven would have slept without one of their number on guard. How necessity bred reliance and trust, how the world moved on. Denser dragged the leather from his bivouac and lay down in the warm open air. He began to relax into himself, seeking the demon gateway from where the mana flowed to feed Xeteskian mages at rest. The demons would close it if they could but until that day, it was the best source of stamina replenishment a dark mage had.

Dimly, he heard the soft padding of a panther, no doubt come to check on Thraun and Erienne. That was why The Raven could rest. Denser closed his eyes.

'She is so close,' muttered Vuldaroq. 'And we are powerless.'

He pushed a forkful of food into his mouth and chewed slowly, looking up and across the table at Heryst only when he'd swallowed. He reached for his wine glass and sipped.

Lystern's Lord Elder Mage had arrived in Dordover the previous evening to discuss the next moves in the war. So far, the allies had been less than convincing in their efforts to overcome the defence of Xetesk. They had been surprised by the tenacity of the enemy and had been forced to commit too many men to the watcher ring around the city. Rightly they feared the excursions of familiars and assassins but had failed to stop the attacks by both demons and Cloaked mages. They had also failed to stop supplies entering the college, and The Raven were still free.

The strained relations with the elves hadn't helped. They couldn't deny their intervention was valuable, even critical, to the effort. But it wasn't as a partner in belief. The elves had their agenda. And now they'd taken what they wanted and were moving on. That changed the battle plan, as did the worsening of the Julatsan mana focus.

Vuldaroq found himself wondering about the benefits of Julatsa failing terminally. Heryst, he was sure, was not.

'We will bide our time and wait for our opportunity,' said Heryst. 'She and The Raven have the protection of every elf on the battlefield. We cannot act now. She's going nowhere except, presumably, Julatsa. We can wait.'

'Tempting, though, isn't it?' said Vuldaroq.

Heryst smiled briefly. 'You and I can sit here and say that. My commanders on the east gate front would say otherwise. I suspect we do not have the warrior or mage strength there to take them on though we outnumber them almost three to one. And even if we did, we would have to leave the east gate unguarded to do it. Like I say, we wait. She will fall to us eventually.'

'And when she does, we must be agreed on how she is handled,' said Vuldaroq.

'She must be treated as a joint asset, Vuldaroq. We have been through this already. Please don't claim fealty over a woman who does not see herself as belonging to any of us.'

Vuldaroq held up his hands. 'Another time, my Lord Heryst. Other matters are more pressing.'

'We agree there.'

'Now, clearly your forces at the east gate will be most affected by the departure of the elves to Julatsa. And, with Izack's very astute decision to reinforce the north front with Lysternan forces, you are further weakened there. I have some reserve still in Dordover that I can offer to you. What do you need from me? Men? Mages?'

Vuldaroq smiled inwardly at Heryst's reaction. How easy it was to disarm a man who expected nothing from you.

'That is a most kind offer. I thank you for it.'

'Surprising too?' Vuldaroq couldn't help himself.

Heryst raised his eyebrows. 'It is not your most common stance,' he said. 'We are, I believe, faced with a critical decision. My commanders, who have briefed me extensively, are in no doubt that the war will turn upon it. It has doubtless been on the minds of you and yours.'

Vuldaroq inclined his head, sure of Heryst's direction. He was not disappointed.

'Xetesk wants Julatsa gone and the elves threaten that. Their move north will not go unchallenged and that has an effect directly on us, which is why Izack has reinforced the most likely place for an attempt to break the siege.

'But, in my opinion, we have to take wider factors into account. I am not sure that providing extra strength at the east gate is the best use of our forces, not least because they may be too late. After all, the breakout is liable to be staged very soon, and there is no doubt that we will struggle to contain them, given the information we have about their reserve strength.

'As you'll be aware, Baron Blackthorne has joined the struggle on our side and has brought with him seventy swordsmen and eight mages. This represents almost all of his trained guard and he has taken the gamble of leaving his lands guarded by Baron Gresse whose small militia is already stretched over almost the whole of the south. Why are they doing it? Because while this war goes on, the economics of the entire country are destroyed more each day.

'And they are not alone in their anxiety. Havern is sending men, so is Orytte, so is Rache. Many other Barons aren't capable of sending anyone, of course. But again, reinforcing the east gate might be pointless. It may be that riding north to Julatsa is the better decision.'

'Sorry,' said Vuldaroq, raising a finger. 'You sound as if you don't necessarily agree with the turn of events.'

Heryst refreshed his water glass. 'It adds a layer of complexity. Blackthorne has agreed to put his men under the command of Izack and indeed is not planning on staying too long on the field himself. That's because he feels he needs to exercise his diplomatic skills in the heart of the country. He, as you know, along with Gresse, is an exception. Both are Barons working for the common good, not purely self interest. Many of those deciding to join the battlefield have more personal agendas to complete.'

'But you can't deny that more forces committed to bringing down Xetesk has to be a good thing from our point of view.'

'Are you really convinced of that, Vuldaroq? I suggest you familiarise yourself with the histories of some of the relationships between those ostensibly coming to help us. We may be here to restore the magical balance by first deposing the current Circle

Seven but there are landed Barons out there who would like to see all the power of the colleges subservient to them. We must be careful that we remain the directors of this war.'

Vuldaroq smiled indulgently. Heryst sometimes thought too hard. On the other hand, it wouldn't do to unnecessarily raise his suspicions.

'I have been open with my talks with any Barons or Lords,' he said. 'Any forces I am hiring are signing themselves to serve under my battlefield commanders. You do not have to worry about their conduct. We are all after the same thing.'

'Are we?' Heryst's smile was thin.

'Who among us does not want peace for Balaia?'

'Vuldaroq, that is not in doubt. It is the nature of that peace which taxes me.'

'Then we must strive to ensure it is a peace which suits us all,' said Vuldaroq, feeling a growing irritation. 'But we are diverted from our task for today. You were talking about the east gate before outlining our options as you see them?'

'I was,' said Heryst. 'If I don't have enough men to preserve the balance now, there will not be time to reinforce. However, I have hope. I may have lost the elves but I have gained Blackthorne's men and magic, and Xetesk has lost the Protectors. We have no choice but to fight there and occupy as many Xeteskians as we can.

'We have no more men to commit in time. Indeed I suggest that we never really had enough to force a significant breach in Xetesk's defences though we have all fought hard.

'You mention Baronial forces joining you. Like I have said, I have others joining me and their management is very important. But the decisions to be made are tactical. The most critical is this. Do we assume the Xeteskians will break through whatever our strategy and therefore let them out and take them on open ground? We still have the time to organise that. Plans are in place.

'But can we prosecute such a fight successfully? Can we contain them on the open field? And if we can, where do we draw our line? Who should be in overall command? There is more, Vuldaroq, but this will do as a beginning.'

Vuldaroq was impressed and annoyed in equal measure. His commanders had not brought up all these questions, some of which were blindingly obvious issues.

'Are you sure none of your people have been in contact with Darrick?' he asked.

'I think not,' said Heryst. 'And I resent the suggestion that he is the only man capable of assessing our tactics. Many of my commanders have served under Darrick in the past. His knowledge has been passed on. I won't deny we could do with him but he made his decision and will live or die by it.'

'And what is the considered opinion of your command team as to our next moves?'

'Our first priority is to give the elves as much time as possible to get away to Julatsa. They are preparing to leave now and will begin travel at dawn tomorrow. We have to hope we can hold the Xeteskians inside the city. We cannot risk Xetesk beating us in the open. If they do, we have nothing left.'

Vuldaroq considered. It was the most sensible solution but also the one Xetesk would expect.

'It has little surprise in it to upset Xeteskian plans.'

'And little room for them to surprise us. Even if they did break out east, for example, we would have considerable forces blocking their path.'

'Have you thought about the remnants of the Black Wing army?' asked Vuldaroq. 'I understand them still to be encamped in significant numbers.'

'They are a leaderless rabble,' said Heryst. 'Selik is dead, my spies report Devun is missing, and every day, more of them are returning to their homes. We should encourage that. Significant numbers, no. There are only a couple of hundred still there and they are the ones with literally nowhere else to go. They are an irrelevance to us.'

Heryst pushed a leather satchel across the table. 'Our full recommendations and current strengths at each front are here. Consult your advisers; mine are on hand to answer questions and I have a Communion link to Izack on standby should you need it. But we need answers fast.'

Vuldaroq nodded. 'I will be back within the hour. Why don't you rest by the fire there? I have a particularly fine spirit you might like to try.'

'Thank you, Vuldaroq.'

The overweight Arch Mage pushed himself from his chair. There were many matters to consider here. Heryst had outlined a solid plan for the benefit of the whole country. Vuldaroq just wasn't sure he wanted to go back to being a mere part of the balance. There was opportunity here, the question was, could he unlock it fast enough?

Sha-Kaan had returned to his favoured place on the upper slopes of Herendeneth, with its views of the terraces and the house below. Calm had returned to the island. The Protectors were back working to repair the damage caused by fight and flood; Cleress was awake and helping Erienne until her energy was gone, and Diera and Jonas were safe once more. No mage bar the Al-Drechar remained alive.

He watched as Diera approached, her boy in her arms though struggling to get out. He could just catch his noises of frustration on the hot breeze and worry filled his mind. How easy for humans to reproduce. Not so for dragons. Back on Beshara, the Kaan birthings were imminent. He should be there, protecting his Brood at their most vulnerable time.

He knew what he had to do. So did Diera; it was why she was coming to see him now. He waited for her to come close, setting her son down. Typically, he gazed at Sha-Kaan until he'd convinced himself he'd seen it before and returned to the more interesting experiments he was conducting with walking.

'He is a remarkable child,' said the Great Kaan.

'I think he understands you are friend not threat. And you have been so good to us,' said Diera.

'We have helped each other,' he replied. 'Your child has been a source of light during these last days, lifting my spirits as I wait for the news I am so desperate to hear.'

'And you have heard it,' said Diera.

'I have,' he said. 'I can almost feel the currents of air over my Broodlands. I can smell the scents of my world.'

'And now you're going, aren't you?'

'I must,' Sha-Kaan said, feeling a pang of guilt. It surprised him but it shouldn't have. He had learned so much about human emotion recently. Why should he not start to feel for them? It was difficult, he conceded, to remember exactly how he had thought before his exile. He determined not to forget how he felt now after he returned.

'Jonas will miss you,' she said. 'So will I.'

'And I likewise,' said Sha-Kaan. 'But I am dying here. I will begin the flight back to Balaia at dusk. I must help The Raven. I cannot afford for them to fail.'

'And that's why I want you to go, more than anything.' Diera smiled. 'Knowing you will be watching over my husband will be a great comfort.'

'But your contact with him will be lost,' said Sha-Kaan.

'I know. But it's a price I'm happy to pay if it means he lives to see us again.'

'I will be speaking to Hirad again before I go. There are things he must know about Xetesk's meddling with inter-dimensional space. Be here with me and you can pass messages to Sol.'

'Thank you, Sha-Kaan,' she said. She reached out a hand and touched his muzzle. He could barely feel it through his thick hide but the gesture was enough.

Jonas had sensed a change in the emotional atmosphere. He crawled quickly to his mother and pulled himself up her leg, looking him in the eye.

'Kaan!' he said suddenly, pointing and smiling.

Diera laughed. 'That's right, darling. And soon it will be time to say goodbye.'

'Bye,' said Jonas.

Deep in the plains of Teras, Sha-Kaan's Brood mothers were calling to him. He could feel it.

Chapter 30

The first signs of light were beginning to edge over the horizon and the allied camp outside the east gate was ablaze with activity. Lysternan and Blackthorne guards were being readied to take the field, the night watch was withdrawing and the Al-Arynaar were close to departure. Izack had already taken much of his cavalry to the north gate front, leaving one detachment to defend the foot soldiers. It would have to be enough.

The Raven were eating a quick breakfast. The horses given to them by Blackthorne were being saddled and prepared. Sore, stiff and tired, there was nevertheless an energy about The Raven that came with imminent action.

Denser, having seen to Erienne, cleaning her after the night and checking that Cleress was still hanging on, had joined them, sitting by Hirad who was inspecting his repaired armour.

'Will it hold?' asked Denser.

'It's a fantastic job,' said Hirad. 'Can't say they don't know needlework, these elves.'

Across the fire, The Unknown sat gazing at his boots, one hand massaging his neck.

'She'll be fine,' said Denser, guessing his trouble.

'Of that I have no doubt,' said The Unknown. 'I just can't help feeling it's going to be a long time before I see them again.'

'Just as long as you do one day,' said Denser. He turned his attention back to Hirad. 'Now listen, I know you were right not to wake me when you spoke to Sha-Kaan last night but I need to know exactly what he said.'

'I told it all to Rebraal. He's spoken to the Lysternans and the message has gone round all the fronts. They are as prepared as they can be which is not at all since we don't know what, if anything, Xetesk are going to do. But they'll have the shield lattice up and concentrated. That's it.'

'So tell me,' said Denser. 'What did he say?'

Hirad sighed. 'All right. He said he'd been sensing something for a while. Ever since the Xeteskians got home with the information from the Al-Drechar. Initially he was happy because he supposed that they were investigating inter-dimensional space to send him home. Now he knows that wasn't the case and the feelings he gets are as if they're channelling the energy out there. He doesn't know why but it doesn't feel right. He likened it to someone diverting rivers to form a waterfall. Right now, the level isn't high enough but he can sense it growing.'

'Right,' said Denser. 'And did he say anything else?'

'Yes,' said Hirad. 'And this made him happy and angry. Happy because he can sense the dimensions again, meaning the Xeteskians have been successful in realignment and mapping, something like that. Angry, because he says the meddling, which got much worse yesterday apparently, has aroused the attentions of the demons. He said they would be waiting and that Xetesk doesn't understand what it is doing. He said we should stop them.'

'That's going to be difficult,' said Denser.

'That's what I said.'

'And is that all he said?'

'Isn't it enough?'

'Actually, it probably is,' said Denser, feeling his heart sink. As if it could get any lower. 'What I saw in the Laryon hub were papers and maps outlining cooperative spells drawing on the raw power in inter-dimensional space. I couldn't tell how close they were to being ready to cast. But I think the allies need to be prepared for more than the offensive power they've been used to, that's all.

'It's a shame we can't get Sha-Kaan up there. He could probably disrupt it.'

'Why can't we?' asked Hirad.

'Well, because he needs a gateway opening here. He can sense the flows but he can't access them without it. When we do that, he'll be able to travel home, his dimension will be there for him if he's right and the mapping has been success-ful.'

The Unknown cleared his throat. 'I don't understand. How does Xetesk's knowledge of where the dimensions are currently located translate to Sha-Kaan flying home?'

'Right,' said Denser. 'Good question and forgive my incomplete knowledge. Effectively, what Xetesk's researchers will have done is take the information from the Al-Drechar and use it to read the pathways in inter-dimensional space. Don't ask me how but there are some and its forces are like mana that flow along them, seeking the route of least resistance in a way. But to get a complete and ongoing picture, they'll have sent focused streams of mana into space and bounced them off dimensional shells, along pathways and all that sort of thing. Those streams will always be there and the signature of the bounce will give Sha-Kaan his direction because he knows what his dimension feels like.

'It only works from this direction and he'd find other signatures of other dimensions confuse his senses. So his path will be clear because it'll be the only one he can make sense of. That's what I understand from talking to him and my scant knowledge of dimensional research. Sorry if it's vague.'

'Good enough,' said The Unknown.

'For you, maybe,' said Hirad. 'Once again, I thank the Gods I am not a mage.'

He pushed himself to his feet and began to stretch, pushing his arms back and chest out very slowly and deliberately. Denser saw him wince a couple of times but the expression on his face told of pleasant surprise at how he felt.

'Feel all right?' asked Denser.

'Stiff but not bad,' said Hirad. 'I may even be able to fight again sooner than I thought. Can't say the same for the young general, here.'

Darrick was spooning broth into his mouth as if he wouldn't be allowed to eat ever again. Torn bread sat by him on the ground and a mug of the elves' enriching herbal tea steamed away by his left boot. His face was pale still, dark rings around eyes that sat deep. He had a slight shiver.

'Can you ride, Darrick?' asked The Unknown.

Darrick nodded. 'Let's just not go at a tan gallop all the way, eh?'

'We'll do our best. Perhaps we can persuade Sha-Kaan to give you a lift,' said Denser. 'When will he arrive?'

Hirad shrugged. 'He can't fly too fast, you know his condition. If we go as well as we want to, we should all arrive at Julatsa at about the same time.'

'That's handy, because I might need help opening this gateway. Assuming the mana focus is strong enough, that's where I'll get it.'

'So,' said Hirad. 'Are we all ready?'

He wandered away a few yards in the direction of Xetesk. They'd found a point where they could see through the trees to the battle front. No doubt he was having a look at the set-up for the day of battle which would begin in earnest any time. Already, a few desultory spells were probing at shield lattices while the lines drew up and closed.

A sudden gust of wind blew through the trees, rattling branches and dislodging leaves and blossom. Denser looked across at Erienne where she lay under the sentinel-like guard of Thraun. A frown crossed her forehead, gone in a heartbeat.

'Thraun?' he asked.

He shook his head. 'Not her. She feels it.'

'Denser, what the hell is that?'

Thraun trotted over to Hirad, and The Unknown and Darrick likewise. No one had to ask what Hirad was looking at.

Up in the partly cloudy sky, two slashes had appeared, moving gently, like seaweed resting on the surface of the sea. But there was nothing restful about the intent behind them. One sat above the east gate, the other to the north. It was impossible to guess exactly how big they were at this distance but the measurement would run into hundreds of feet.

Each slash was edged in the deep blue of Xeteskian magic and inside darkness roiled, occasional flashes of a dull red spitting outwards. Another breeze rolled across them, and there was a rumbling like thunder as the air of Balaia came into contact with the raw energy of inter-dimensional space. With a crack that echoed across the battlefields, the blue edging brightened to a dazzling level and began to pull apart, the blackness growing.

Down on the field, the fighting had stopped almost before it had begun and wary Lysternans were beginning to back away, fearful of what they were seeing. It wasn't going to be anywhere near enough to save them.

'Dear Gods, they won't stand a chance,' said Denser.

He turned and began running towards his horse, Hirad and The Unknown calling after him. He yelled over his shoulder as he went.

'Come on! We've got to make them clear the battlefield. Raven let's go! Mount up, come on!'

'Denser no!' shouted Hirad. 'You can't expose yourself. They'll catch you.'

Denser spun on his heel and ran back, grabbing Hirad's collar and pointing over the barbarian's shoulder. 'See those people. They are going to die. Very soon. Maybe we can save some of them. Hide here if you want.'

Hirad growled but his face cleared. 'That's why I like you,' he said. 'Unknown, we're going. Thraun, Darrick, get the elves moving. Let's go.'

All around them there was noise. Mages shouting for more lattice-strength, soldiers demanding orders. Out on the battle-field, the Xeteskians were falling back fast, the allies, unsure, began a push forwards only for it to peter out with the rent in the sky above them yawning wider, the thunder louder, the blue edges fizzing and jumping.

Denser ran into the makeshift paddock in the elven camp, grabbed the reins of his horse from the hitch pole and mounted up.

'Come on!' He kicked the animal's flanks and it shot for-wards, jumping the rail. Elves scattered out of his way. 'Get moving. North now!'

He didn't know if they could understand him, he didn't really care. He galloped down the muddy path that led to the battlefield, yelling for anyone who could hear him to clear the battlefield. He cleared the camp and the wooded area, flying down the slope, angling across to the Lysternan command position. He felt The Unknown and Hirad come up on his shoulders, driving their horses hard.

To his left and above, the rent was enormous. The edges flailed; Denser imagined the mages struggling to maintain cohesion. He prayed for one, just one, to fail. The Lysternan command was in turmoil, everyone shouting at once. A huge soldier sat on horseback bellowing for his men to advance, to drive home the advantage. A mage next to him was passing messages out via runners. None of it was going to help.

Denser dragged his horse to a halt in front of them.

'Clear the battlefield,' he shouted into their faces. 'Clear it now, it's your only chance. Signal the north gate. Make them do it too. Now, damn you!'

The soldier pointed at him, at them. 'You're wanted, Raven.'

'Do you think I care, you bloody fool? Your men are going to die,' he said feeling the blood run into his face. 'Listen to me!'

'Arrest these men,' said the soldier. 'Hold them.'

'Fuck's sake,' spat Denser.

He hauled on the reins and set off towards the front, hearing Hirad shout some abuse and The Unknown order him away.

'Denser!' called The Unknown. 'Keep clear.'

'Clear the field!' Denser had never shouted so loud in his life and, even so, he knew they couldn't hear him. The thunder was deafening, the air flattening against his face, the pressure growing beneath the rent. He carried on, an eye on the spell as it grew, determined not to be caught in whatever it was that was cast.

He rode directly behind the fragmented line, bellowing for people to run, to scatter, to make for the camps, anything. They were beginning to pay heed but were caught in two minds. The field lieutenants were watching the flags from the command post and were loath to disobey orders. The cloaked man riding along their rear exhorting them to flee was surely either mad or a spirit sent to save them. They didn't know which it was, he could see it in their faces.

There was another crack, the sound whiplashing over his head, spearing pain in his ears. 'We're out of time!' he shouted.

There was nothing more he could do. Knowing Hirad and the Unknown would follow him, he turned his scared horse and rode directly away from the battlefield, hunching over its neck, praying he wasn't too late. A few hundred yards later, the spell was released.

A blast of air caught Denser on the back. His horse, terrified, bucked and threw him, too confused to know where to bolt. He rolled over on the ground, came up and watched as his worst fears were realised right in front of him.

From the dark mass of inter-dimensional space, sheets of deep red-tinged blue light flared out. They were shot through with forks of pure energy, the whole striking the ground with incredible force. Sheet after sheet slammed downwards, exploding on impact, sending out fingers of light which lashed away.

Great mounds of earth blew into the air, men were picked up like leaves and flung aside. Others caught the forks and fingers of energy directly. Some simply disintegrated where they stood, others burst into flames, saw limbs or torsos instantly burned or had their bodies torn apart. At least the screams didn't last for long.

The shield lattices were not designed for such pressure. Denser saw them flare green, deflect the first wave but crumble under the second. And still the spell came down. Sheet after sheet, deluging the area in front of the gates where the Lysternans had stood. He could see survivors running, saw the dead collapse, saw men with their faces burned off walking blind, and others who became so much ash on the wind that howled down after the lightning.

BlueStorm. Those were the words he had read in the Laryon hub. That was what he was witnessing. And Dystran would be behind it all. All Denser could think of was that the same would be happening over the north gate. Xetesk had struck the most enormous blow. Hirad's shout told him it was only getting worse.

The spell finished with a splitting slap of sound, the rents whipping shut, the BlueStorm cutting off, leaving an afterglow in the dawn sky, smoke and dust like a fog around Xetesk and the smell of smoke and carnage in the air.

But the fog wasn't so thick he couldn't see what was happening now. The gates had opened. Xeteskians were running out to join their forces, swelling their numbers and charging ahead east and north in an arc that would take in the camp. Above the walls, mages flew, safe from spells now, like the familiars that accompanied them. Dozens of them breaking away in as many directions, their chittering laughter on the breeze, their sense of delight at destruction clear in their cavorting.

'Denser, let's move.'

The Unknown and Hirad both had men across their saddles, snatched from the lines as they turned to run. The lucky two were pushed away, The Unknown trotted up and handed Denser his reins and the mage remounted.

'We've got to join up with the elves,' said The Unknown. 'There's nothing more we can do here.'

The Lysternan force at the east gate had been all but destroyed. The Raven trio rode hard through milling survivors and those who tried to come to their aid from the camp. The Lysternans were in rout, fleeing back into the trees and beyond. Denser prayed they would regroup.

The Unknown led them along the base of the slope that marked the edge of the panicked Lysternan camp. The command post was deserted as they galloped by, only a couple of hundred yards ahead of the Xeteskians who were advancing on foot, any horsemen riding behind the lines.

But above and ahead, the familiars circled, diving on any enemies they found, crushing skulls with their inhumanly strong hands, biting deep into flesh and goring cuts with their tails.

The Unknown turned them just east of north before they reached the corner of Xetesk's walls. The roar of battle echoed from the direction of the north gates, smoke and dust hung and blew above the gatehouse and Denser could clearly hear the thunder of a cavalry charge.

Breasting the corner, the situation became distressingly clear. The joint Dordovan and Lysternan force there was scattered, destroyed or in full retreat. No order existed and the Xeteskian forces were driving north fast, chasing down the injured, slow and shocked. More familiars flew, more mages in the air directed the battle but at least here they met some resistance.

Izack and his cavalry, their shield and offensive mages in their centre, were performing heroics in the face of the rout. In charge after charge, Izack broke the Xeteskian advance, targeting weaker areas of the slightly disorganised lines, getting out before the enemy could close around him. As he watched, a concentrated Orb shot out from one of the cavalry mages, catching a familiar full in the chest. It screamed and fell, its master by its side tumbling from the sky, his hands gripped around his head.

Denser should have felt sympathy for the mage. He'd experienced the pain of losing a familiar himself. But all he felt was the lift of a tiny victory over the college that he had loved for so much of his life.

Even Izack couldn't hold back the tide. Behind the soldiers and horsemen came wagons and carriages and mages on horseback. This breakout had been well-planned and executed with typical Xeteskian ruthlessness. It threw all the allied plans into chaos and, more urgently, made Julatsa incredibly vulnerable. The elves would have to travel fast to arrive with enough time to raise the Heart. But even if they did, would it matter? The Xeteskians wouldn't stop. Somehow they had to bring enough defence to the college to keep them at bay and then drive them back. He wasn't sure that was possible.

Denser switched his attention ahead of him. They were riding well ahead of the remnants of the Lysternan forces whom he could still see scattering east and north. The way before them was clear, across open fields and away towards the first cover on their run to Julatsa.

Before long, they had left the slaughter outside Xetesk behind them. The Xeteskian charge had slowed a little, as it had to if it was ever to become organised. Having won such a devastating victory and having dispersed their enemies beyond any immediate chance of renewed cohesion, they could afford to take time.

Half a mile beyond the battlefields, he saw what he'd been waiting for. Quick, disciplined and organised, the elves were moving north. Riders in the midst of the advance meant Darrick, and Thraun. He spotted him, carrying Erienne in front of him, holding her head against his chest.

They had scouts forward, ClawBound pairs ran the flanks and at the rear, TaiGethen marauded. They moved with purpose and represented Balaia's best hope of holding the Xeteskians at bay. It was difficult to guess how many there were; their movement was fluid, they dropped in and out of sight against changing backgrounds and into trees and tall grass.

Whether the estimated requirement of two hundred mages were with them he doubted. His best guess was that he was looking at a total of less than four hundred warriors and mages. But that hardly mattered now. All that had to be done was to preserve the mages they had. Every one that fell on the run north was a blow against the survival of Julatsa.

But like Hirad and The Unknown, who rode ahead of him, Denser would not let Ilkar's dreams die.

Chapter 31

Vuldaroq strode through the cloister corridor of Dordover, seeking out Heryst, whom he had been told was in the Chamber of Reflection, a room of polished granite slabs, fountains, small waterfalls and wicker furniture. The perfect place to relax. Or to contemplate disaster.

Heryst was sitting with his head in his hands. It had been a shattering blow, leaving Xetesk firmly in command of the battle. Unless fortune favoured the allies, the war was now Xetesk's to lose.

Reports from outside the city were still sketchy but it was clear that both the eastern and northern siege fronts had collapsed completely. South and east, the allied lines had fallen back, fearful of a similar fate, leaving Xetesk unmolested. Xeteskian forces had also withdrawn inside the walls of the city, comfortable now that not enough force could be mustered to mount a serious threat, at least for the time being. They were right, too.

Heryst looked up when Vuldaroq's sandalled feet slapped across the marble floor. The Dordovan lowered himself onto a two-seater bench, the wickerwork protesting at his weight.

'Anything new?' he asked, keeping his voice respectful and quiet. Though they had both lost men, Lystern had been the harder hit overall and Heryst, he knew, would take every death personally.

'We had committed so much. Why did we have no clue what they were preparing?'

'A message was relayed but none of us could have guessed the magnitude of what was cast at us. The Raven knew something. The word is, they tried to help.'

'I heard!' snapped Heryst. 'Sorry. I heard. And when the

spell was forming they tried to clear the battlefield and even saved two men. Damn but it's hard to hunt them.'

'We cannot stop now.'

'I know.' Heryst was silent for a while. 'I have no real idea how many men and mages I have left in the field,' he said eventually. 'I've been in three Communions since dawn. Two of them with terrified individuals barely able to keep their concentration and talking about scattered bands of my people being hunted down by familiars, mage defender trios and come nightfall, no doubt, assassins too.

'Neither could put a figure on the casualties but, conservatively, let's say the reinforced line this morning lost eighty per cent. Say it's the same north. It leaves us with a force of less than three hundred facing nearly a thousand Xeteskians just north of the city. And that's assuming we include the walking wounded and can regroup to form a sensible defence. We're finished, aren't we?'

Vuldaroq surprised himself by reaching out a hand and laying it gently on Heryst's arm.

'Not until the last of our soldiers lies dead. Not until Dystran himself stands before me in my own Heart. Don't lose hope. Not now.'

Heryst nodded. 'I know, I'm sorry. Bad moment.'

'Forget about it. Instead, tell me what you're planning for those you still have camped south of Xetesk.'

'You know, I haven't planned at all. We've been trying to pull the pieces together.'

'Join with me, then,' said Vuldaroq. 'Our belief is that Xetesk has only enough men inside the city to defend it, not strike out at any other targets. Move your men with mine north to Julatsa because the battle for Balaia will be fought there. If you have enough strength left in Lystern you must do it.'

'I will direct them to your command,' said Heryst.

'Good. That's a wise decision. And now, I'll leave you. I think you have people to contact, fears to quell as best you can.' He stood to go. 'One thing. Your man, Izack. He saved a lot of Dordovans this morning. I won't forget that.'

Heryst smiled. 'Thank you.'

Vuldaroq nodded and left, the door to opportunity pushed a little wider open.

*

She understood her name but she could not recall it beyond her Loved speaking it to her. But she knew why she was here and who was friend and who was prey. She could sense that which instinct told her she should not. And she understood that which mere men did not. She was ClawBound and no one could break a bond forged since birth. No one.

She padded swiftly through the unfamiliar lands. Every scent was foreign, every pawfall unlike any other she had experienced before the journey. A brief shudder ran down her flanks. The ocean had been broad and the land had moved upon it. Small and stinking of men, though the Keepers were in charge. And her Loved had always been by her side.

The memory was distant and it passed quickly through her mind. Now, she protected. The Keepers were running. Threat was everywhere. It could not be allowed the freedom to strike.

So she moved beyond them, her Loved nearby, directing and calming her, stroking her mind. She sampled the scents that assailed her, distant and close. The plants, the flowers and the trees, healthy and growing. The small prey animals, quivering and scared when she passed them, ignoring them for now.

Upwind, there was threat. It was not far. She let free with her emotions, her Loved understanding the change within her, the tightening of her focus ahead, the increase in her pace. He matched her.

A small animal appeared in the path. Fur black like hers, the size of a cub but sleeker. She would have termed it a relative but the scent told her it was not of her family. It radiated danger. Her Loved closed in to guard her while she investigated.

The animal stopped in front of her, waited for her to approach, didn't flinch as she pushed her muzzle in very close. In every mannerism, it was a distant cousin, small and fragile. But it radiated a strength and a strangeness that she had never encountered before. It scared her. She withdrew a pace and growled low in her throat.

The animal mewled, darted in and pushed a paw into her face. It should have been playful but the claws bit deep. She bared her teeth and cuffed the animal hard. It tumbled over and over into damp leaf mulch beneath a tree. But as it fell, it became another. Bigger, with limbs like a monkey. The fur vanished and a head full of fangs and spitting anger looked at her, a long leathery tail whipping behind it.

She yowled in shock, leaping away unsure, her Loved coming to her side. The creature rushed at her, making a chittering sound. Confused and fearful though she was, instinct took over. She crouched low, waited her moment, and sprang.

The creature was fast but she was faster. It had looked to bite her but instead found her front paws, claws exposed thumping into its chest and bearing it to the ground backwards. It screeched and spat, tried to work its arms and tail free, its legs scrabbling just beneath her belly but far enough away. She clamped her jaws around its skull, looking for the crushing grip. She flexed the muscles in her face, pressing and pressing but there was something wrong. Although it was helpless under her weight it was not trying to struggle and her teeth were making no impression. She released and bit again, striking hard. Again, no impression.

She pulled back her head, knowing above all that she must not let this creature gain purchase. She looked down at it, snarling, saliva dripping from her mouth. It looked back, cocking its head on one side. It spoke. She could not understand. But then the sky burst with blue and there was noise everywhere.

They hadn't tried to hide their progress and their intent was clear. Hirad watched them fly clear over the elves running hard north, well out of range of any spell. He counted four familiars, ugly shapes against the afternoon sky, and four mages, their masters, grouped behind them. Somewhere, he was sure there would be riders, swordsmen to add defence to the strike that was certain to come in against the forward runners.

'Who's ahead?' asked Hirad of Rebraal who ran easily by the side of his half-cantering horse.

'ClawBound. Three pairs. TaiGethen sweeping behind them.'

'That won't do it. The familiars can only be damaged by spells.' He looked round. 'Sian, get up behind me. Darrick, Thraun, you're staying here. Raven with me!'

Sian'erei swung up behind Hirad, clutching him around the waist. He dug his heels into his horse, The Unknown and Denser behind him, elves scattering from their path.

'Come on!' Hirad felt an exhilaration flow through him as he urged his horse to greater effort.

They were riding through the wreckage of a small wood, trunks broken and bent, dead wood scattered thick and wide. Branches hung low and obstructions were everywhere. His horse picked a clear path, forcing him and Sian to duck and sway in the saddle. The air blew about his head, his braids flying out behind him. It was a wonderful feeling in the midst of such desperation.

They were closing fast on the forward positions of the TaiGethen when the first spells began to strike about a quarter of a mile ahead.

'Concentrate on the familiars!' he shouted to her. 'One at a time. We'll protect you. Take the mages and swords out for you.'

'I understand.' Her voice was unsure.

'You have to trust the magic, Sian. Believe it won't fail you.'

In front of them, TaiGethen sprinted from cover, bows strung and taut, arrows ready or swords and jaqrui in hand.

'Hirad, circle!' yelled The Unknown. 'Let's backdoor them.'

Hirad pressed his thigh in left and dragged the reins around, turning his galloping horse. Above, a familiar dived from tree-top level, lost among the odd living bough that studded the wreckage. The damp smell of smouldering vegetation and the first tendrils of smoke reached them. To the right, he saw TaiGethen pause, release arrows and run on again.

'Twenty yards,' he warned Sian. 'Hang on.'

He hauled the reins in, horse protesting at the treatment, snorting and stamping.

'Off, off!' he ordered, swinging his leg over the horse's neck and jumping down, dragging his sword from his scabbard. 'Behind me. Stay behind me.'

He ran back in towards the centre of the woodland, The Unknown joining him on his left, Denser with him, forming the shape for a spell as he ran. Hirad wasn't sure if Sian had that sort of skill.

The way ahead was cluttered. He could see shapes moving in and against the trees and broken trunks and branches, vanishing into shadow or behind drifts of brush. The clash of swords rang across the space, men were shouting. There was a low thud, dirt kicked into the air.

Hirad charged in. Checking left, he thought he could see riderless horses, confirming that Xeteskian swordsmen were in the fight. The scene became clear. Familiars were attacking ClawBound and TaiGethen at the edge of a small clearing, mages behind them in cover, swordsmen almost certainly with them. He couldn't tell how many.

He hunched as he ran, signalling with The Unknown that they should keep close. Without a shield, they were vulnerable but it was a chance they had to take. Familiars were probably the greater risk.

In the few yards before they were seen, Hirad could see that the fight remained in the balance. He watched a TaiGethen cell split with dizzying speed as a focused Orb flashed their way, two tumbling gracefully to the sides, the third dropping and rolling beneath the spell. All three were up and running before the Orb struck a rotten trunk behind them, exploding in a shower of mana fire and flaming splinters.

The cell closed on the mages but a pair of familiars blocked their path. Jaqrui whispered out, striking harmlessly. The TaiGethen had no answer to the demons, just hoping to hang on until mage support arrived. And though they were wary of the familiars, they displayed no fear. Hirad smiled. It was time to even up the odds a little.

Hirad ducked under a branch and felt something pass just over his head. Looking up, he saw the familiar flit away. It called a warning and swordsmen came running.

'Two your left, Unknown. I've got centre. Sian, target overhead. Denser, you know it all already.'

Hirad heard The Unknown's blade thump the ground ahead of him. The familiar dived, cracking through dead wood.

'No sho ,' said Denser. 'Hirad, he's on you.'

The barbarian sized up. The first swordsman was only a few paces away. The familiar cackled. Hirad stepped back smartly, his sword flashing above his head. The wound across his chest pulled painfully. He felt the blade bounce from skin. The familiar yelped and, knocked off balance, tumbled hard into a tree, dropping to the ground dazed.

Hirad didn't have time to look further and faced front. The soldier, wearing thick chain armour, swung a heavy two-handed blade at him. He heard a whistle as his keen axe sliced the air and barely blocked the stroke, his defence battered by the other man's power. He felt his wrist spring at the impact and he stumbled backwards.

Encouraged, the Xeteskian advanced. Hirad had no strength in his right wrist. Quickly, he switched the sword to his left. Behind him, sudden heat and blue light, The familiar screeched and burned. Somewhere ahead, a man screamed. Hirad managed a smile.

'And you've had your chance too,' he said.

The soldier spat and struck, another huge carving swing. Hirad dodged this one with more comfort, catching enough of the blade on his to off-balance his man just a little. He readjusted quickly and thrust straight, his sword grating off the shining chain, gouging up sparks and bruising his enemy's ribs, forcing him backwards. Hirad moved after him, cutting downwards this time, hoping to get inside his enemy's guard. But the man was quick, rebalancing after a single pace and bringing his axe back up in front of his body.

But he used fractionally too much force and caught Hirad's sword only a glancing blow. The momentum of his swing took his axe too high. He began to fall. Hirad had seen it before. He jumped in, shoulder first, and put the man on the ground. He snatched out a dagger with his weaker hand and punched it through the Xeteskian's throat.

No one else directly threatened him. The Unknown was advancing again, sword dripping blood. Behind, Denser stood with Sian, watching for familiars. They were all engaged ahead. One TaiGethen lay wounded, perhaps dying, another wrestled with one of the demon creatures briefly until a panther tore the thing from his chest and bowled it away, fizzing with frustration.

A ForceCone knocked two elves flat. It had come from the left. Hirad looked, saw the mage. They locked eyes, the Xeteskian going pale. Hirad roared and charged, the mage losing concentration on his spell, turning and running, calling help to him. The familiars disengaged, other soldiers moved in, a pair of mages appeared from shadow to join them.

'Break off!' came the shout.

The attack folded. With TaiGethen and ClawBound sprinting past the slower Raven warriors, the enemy mages cast as they ran, ShadowWings powering them skywards, familiars shadowing them into the relative safety of the air. Hirad flung his dagger, watching it just miss the trailing foot of the last mage to take off.

He cursed but it wasn't quite over. From his right, Denser and Sian both cast. Focused Orbs flared away into the after-noon sky. The blue missed their target, the yellow did not, ploughing into a mage and setting clothes and hair on fire.

Helpless and in agony, he plummeted from the sky, his familiar circling him, desperate, its keening wails soul-piercing. A ClawBound pair watched them fall, running to intercept. The mage hit the ground dead, bouncing sickeningly. The familiar trailed after him, strength going quickly, hovering just too close. The panther leapt, snatched it from the air and bore it to the ground, savaging the dying creature, its protection fading, its skin vulnerable to raw power.

Hirad winced when the creature's neck broke and it flopped still.

'What a way to go.'

'Almost as bad as that.'

Denser was pointing away into the trees. A TaiGethen cell had trapped two soldiers. They stood back to back, swords ready. They didn't even see the blows that killed them. Two of the cell drew their attention, the third launched into the air, drop-kicking one flush on the left hand side of his chin. His head cracked round and back, slamming into his comrade's. There was a sickening crunch as bones fractured.

The elves had turned to go before either man had stopped moving, trotting back towards their wounded and dead. Around the woodland, a low growl sounded, taken up by the ClawBound, elf and beast mourning their fallen.

Hirad and The Unknown Warrior walked over to the bodies of the two soldiers attacked by the TaiGethen. One was still breathing. Hirad stared down at them dispassionately. Both men wore similar chain mail and carried two-handed blades.

'What do you make of this, Unknown?'

The Unknown shrugged. 'They're mage defender guards, no doubt about it. But I've not seen them in such heavy armour before. I wonder who it was we were attacking?'

'Circle Seven?'

'Not a chance,' said Denser, joining them. 'But without the Protectors, the trios are weakened. I'm guessing these are elite college guards.'

'Yeah?' Hirad raised his eyebrows. 'Perhaps we shouldn't be running after all.'

'You turn and face them all, I'll be right behind you,' said Denser. 'Several hours behind you, to be precise and heading in the other direction.'

Hirad chuckled and slapped him on the arm.

'C'mon, Xetesk-man, let's collect these spare horses and get you back to your wife. I need someone to look at my chest again, too.'

'Good idea,' said The Unknown, looking at the advancing shadows of the lengthening afternoon. 'This isn't a mistake they'll repeat. It'll be dusk in a couple of hours and we need a plan. The assassins will be next.'

Chapter 32

Commander Chandyr knew his destiny was upon him. It was inextricably linked with the fate of the college and city of Xetesk but he preferred to consider just himself and his men. Facing the responsibility for the futures of so many mainly innocent people was more than he wanted to cope with right now.

The Xeteskian force were making steady progress through the mage lands, taking the quickest route to Julatsa. They would skirt Triverne Lake, leaving the sacred lands unsullied, taking nothing, not even water. He had time to see the irony of that. Despite all the horror that had been visited on Balaia by the colleges, that was still seen as a step too far.

Riding sedately in the middle of his tightly organised twenty-wide column of men, he considered his current tactical challenges. For a student of the military, which he considered himself to be, they were very interesting. As he always did, he tried to put himself in the mind of General Darrick. Or was it ex-General Darrick? Idiots, the Lysternans. Only the pretentiously pious would seek to destroy their greatest asset because of a moral misdemeanour. Had they engaged him rather than trying to kill him, Chandyr suspected the war would have followed a very different path. More pressure on the walls of Xetesk, no panic in the face of the dimensional spell's power. Still, it was no concern of his.

At his disposal, Chandyr had approximately thirteen hundred men, a hundred of whom were horsemen, the rest divided into six equal companies under field captaincy. Most of his men were relatively rested, having been cycled carefully at the fronts. Some were raw but all had undergone at least basic training. He had seventy mages, most with little battle exposure beyond the recent siege, and experience only of basic offensive and defensive castings. And all of them were young, graduates of the last five years. This worried him. Linked shields, cooperative offence and long-distance Communion could be beyond them.

More pleasing was the well-organised supply train. Food would be basic, and they were expected to forage and hunt to supplement themselves, but they would not starve. They had blacksmiths, stable masters, field medics and a talented quartermaster to run their camps. Chandyr was not expecting a long battle but they were well served should it prove to be so.

In front of him was a fragmented, but in places very dangerous, guerrilla force. He had already decided not to attempt to slow up the elves. His testing of the forward scouts had cost him too much and setting a large enough force in front of that enemy wasn't feasible in the time available. They were over two hours ahead of him and moving fast, still catchable by horse but his cavalry were by no means numerous enough to risk. He would take them on in Julatsa instead. In the meantime, his assassins and familiar-backed strike groups were tasked to kill identified leaders, The Raven if they could, and to steal back the elven texts if they got very lucky.

Elsewhere, his scout mages were slowly building him a map of the enemy close to him. Fragmented groups of Lysternan and Dordovan soldiers were scattered over a wide area. Many small groups of soldiers, often injured and clearly without direction, were heading back towards their home cities. These he would ignore.

Others, those with mages in their midst, were clearly receiving orders and either heading directly north in front of Chandyr or moving to intercept other groups and swell their numbers. These he wanted to keep fragmented, his outriders attempting to harry them, mage defenders attacking them and the threat of assassins exhausting them through the coming night. He fully intended to stop them, his scouts telling him of any meaningful moves being made. With the enemy already sapped in energy and morale, he didn't expect anything.

Not even from the two groups of horsemen who were his greatest concern. One, the remnants of Blackthorne's men and including the Baron himself, was making a nuisance of itself connecting the split enemy forces. The other, Izack's excellent cavalry, perhaps seventy or eighty, had broken off its initial attack but was patrolling the space ahead of Chandyr, denying his ground scouts and outriders the freedom they needed.

He was sure that Izack wouldn't attack him head-on and neither would Blackthorne or the elves. But he was equally sure that Izack would be able to slow his movements by judicious charge and withdrawal. His mages were experienced rider-casters and would be able to protect themselves against spell and familiar attack.

And everything Chandyr had learned of the elven warriors through his long days of observation on the city walls told him that these were natural-born hunters and frighteningly skilled with bow, sword and those deadly curved throwing blades. More, they were equally at home fighting night or day and he couldn't believe they wouldn't try to disrupt the Xeteskian march.

Interesting. He could send his cavalry out to tackle Izack but he wasn't convinced they would prevail despite their superior numbers. Izack was a star pupil of Darrick's. And succeed or fail, having no horse guard left his own flanks exposed for a greater or lesser time to attack from elves.

He could push on, marching into the night and resting only sporadically but his men would tire and they had a fight ahead of them, whatever his strike groups' successes against the disparate pockets of resistance. And moving at night, without the capacity for a fixed perimeter guard and internal fire ring, the elves would rip them to pieces at will.

Chandyr could detach more of his core fighting force to sweep north and push back Izack but again, the Lysternan commander was too clever to be sucked into a combat that would leave him open to attack from horse, mage or familiar.

What would Darrick do? Actually, it was obvious. He was doing most of it already and that pleased him. He would keep harrying the enemies he found, keep them and their comrades on their toes, with their nerves jangling and their bellies empty for want of the hunt. He could destroy much of what was left because he had them running scared. He would let the elves go. He couldn't stop them getting to Julatsa ahead of him and they were better off the field in any case.

But the critical thing Chandyr considered was this. He knew a good deal about what he chased but nothing about what lay in Julatsa. They had mages, they had soldiers, they had militia. Not many, he knew that, but some nonetheless. It was not going to be an easy fight and he would need every man and mage at his disposal to quell the populace and reach the college with enough strength to tear it down.

Yet even as he nodded to himself and let the finer points of his march strategy coalesce, Chandyr was sure he had missed something. Left out a factor that might turn the tide against him. It nagged at him but he couldn't pin it down. Was it as simple as he thought? Darrick had always lectured that the straightforward tactic should always be the first considered because it was less likely to fail in the face of the enemy.

And he'd picked the straightforward, hadn't he?

He remembered something else that the general had said to him personally after a lecture at Triverne Lake a few years back. It made him laugh suddenly and heads turned towards him. He waved that he was fine and the heads turned away.

What history has told us, Darrick had said that time, is that battle theory is best left on the table in the castle, three hundred miles from the fight. Because what you need most is a nose for that thing you forgot. And when you smell it, you'd better pray to the Gods you can communicate it before whatever it is comes at you from downwind and slits your throat.

Chandyr sniffed the air. Dusk was coming and it was going to rain again.

And now Pheone had lost contact with her deputation to the elven lines outside Xetesk. Just at the time she had thought them on the verge of being saved and feeling joy despite her grief and another mana-flow failure. The elves had recovered what they wanted from Xetesk and were preparing to come north.

Everything had finally seemed to be coming together. She had been giving the good news to every mage in the college when another Communion had come through. She had recognised the signature and accepted it immediately. In less than two hours, the whole situation had changed. Xetesk was coming, the elves were running ahead of them, the allied defence was smashed and no one knew who would get to Julatsa first.

The Communion had ended abruptly and she had not been

able to raise it again though every mage had lent their strength to the signal. They were lost, they had to be.

So now she stood, as she had so often in the past days, gazing down into the pit containing the Heart, her thoughts chasing around her head, settling nowhere.

'You know why it's fading, don't you?' said a voice near her.

She turned. It was Geren, a mage she had distrusted when he had appeared, a dishevelled, stinking wreck, from the Balan Mountains something like a year ago but who now represented much of the will to survive that they still retained. He was a young and energetic man. Not a great mage but willing.

'No I don't, why?' she asked, biting back on her frustration.

Geren scraped some lank black hair from his face, pushed it back behind his ears and scratched his nose.

'It's because we are so few.'

'What?'

'Think about it,' said Geren. 'This shadow appeared and deepened at the same time the Elfsorrow was killing the elves. Think how many mages died, lapsed or not, during the plague. It weakened the whole order. And every day since they arrived here, the survivors have been whittled away. More and more Julatsan mages dying. Remember how it deepened more after the first mana-flow failure? I reckon that's because of the elven mages who died in the Xeteskian barrage that followed it.'

'I don't understand what you're saying,' said Pheone.

'I'm saying it isn't a one-way flow. I'm saying I think that every Julatsan mage alive feeds power back into the Heart, keeps the flow a circle, if you see what I mean. Doesn't matter how far they are away, they still do it. And now we're so few in number, we can't feed in enough power and so the Heart is fading. Don't forget, now the Heart is buried the normal cycle of mana beneath it is gone so it can't self-sustain.'

Pheone frowned. She looked hard at Geren, trying to see doubt in his eyes but there was none at all. Could he be right?

'It makes sense, doesn't it?' he asked. 'Have you checked the shadow on the Heart today? I bet, if you do, it'll be deeper. Not much but you'll see it. More mages died today. Julatsans. Why don't you check?'

Pheone shook her head. It didn't seem worth it. She could sense the sickness without tuning in to the spectrum to see the dull yellow, like thick dust on paint, that covered the mana flow.

'Have you told this to anyone else?'

'No,' said Geren. He smiled but it was a regretful gesture. 'It hardly makes any difference does it?'

'Why not? I mean, if this is the answer . . .'

'Then all we know is that with every mage that dies, we get weaker, only it's worse because the Heart weakens with us. We knew most of that already and the conclusion is still the same. The fewer of us that attempt the raise, the less likely it is to succeed. Let's hope your elves make it without losing anyone else or we'll be left with nothing but a shadow Heart in a few days, won't we?'

Pheone gazed at him and he returned her stare apologetically.

'Was there anything else you came to tell me?'

'Yes. The city council is here, like you asked. What are you going to tell them?'

Pheone began to walk to the new lecture theatre. It stood in the ruins of the six the Wesmen had pulled down and was a less impressive structure than any of its predecessors. 'Hear for yourself, why don't you?'

He shrugged and followed her in.

The audience in the lecture theatre was sparse. Thirty rows of stepped benches climbed up to the back of the medium-sized auditorium, all looking down on a brightly-lit stage containing a single long table, a huge raised blackboard and a podium. The lantern light was augmented by LightGlobes and the last of the afternoon sun, which shone through huge angled windows set in the roof.

Pheone walked straight to the podium, nodding at the five temporary college elders at the table supporting her. Geren walked across to sit with what looked like every other mage in the college, ranged along a few benches to the left. She counted about fifty. Pathetic, really. Perhaps one per cent of the number the college should have and could comfortably support. Geren's theory was looking solid.

To the right sat the city council of Julatsa. All decent people, she had to admit. Businessmen, the commander of the city guard, such as it was, local nobility and the city mayor.

'Thank you all for coming,' she said, her voice carrying easily to the empty benches at the back of the theatre, augmented by engineered acoustics and amplification spells. 'I just wish I was here to bring you good news.'

A ripple went round the sparse auditorium.

'The siege of Xetesk has collapsed. At dawn this morning Xeteskian forces using a powerful magic we are still trying to understand, swept through the Lystern and Dordovan defences north and east. Our information is incomplete at best but we have to assume that at present, there is nothing standing in their way. We know that the elves, who were not taking part in the siege this morning, have escaped almost unscathed and will arrive before the enemy, but not long before.'

She paused, listening to the depths of the silence, every eye upon her.

'Ladies and gentlemen, we know why the Xeteskians are coming here. They are coming to destroy this college and its Heart before we have a chance to raise it. Indeed, they may be too strong even if we do. As Julatsan mages, we have to stay here, we literally have nowhere to go and nothing to gain by standing aside. Everything we have striven for is here. As is our future as mages.

'But you, mister Mayor, honoured council members, are not under any direct threat and neither are the people of the city.' She paused again. This wasn't coming out quite right. 'What I am saying is this. You are innocents in this conflict. Xetesk doesn't desire destruction of the city like the Wesmen did. The people of Julatsa have a choice and they must make it quickly.

'Those who are tired of war and suffering should leave now. Join those who already find the city claustrophobic and those who do not want to face hunger in the name of a future here any more. No blame could possibly be attached to any that leave after the sacrifices all have made in the name of the college and city of Julatsa since the end of the Wesmen occupation.

'Those that choose to stay, and I pray it is the mass of the able bodied and willing, I urge to lend their strength to us because if Xetesk beats us and throws down our college, the freedom you have enjoyed so long will be gone. That is all. I welcome questions.'

The silence hung like a thick cloying fog before a hand was raised among the twenty council members.

'Master Tesack, please speak.'

'If we pledge our strength to you, can we win?'

Pheone spread her arms wide. 'I do not know. I believe so, as I must, but there is no certainty that any strength of arms we can muster will be enough. We do not know how many men Xetesk is bringing, nor the strength or state of the remaining allied force that might or might not arrive before them.

'We might laugh or we might be swept away. But I could not live with myself if I did not tell you the risks we are facing as a city and college. There will be a battle fought in our streets, in our parks and squares. Xetesk will struggle to the last man to reach the college and people who get in their way will be killed.

'What you must ask yourselves and the people of this city is, after everything else that has befallen us, can you stand with us again or must you try to find another place to build your lives? The choice is that simple.'

Another hand was raised. It was Geren. Pheone nodded for him to speak.

'I have not always been the perfect loyal mage,' he said. 'So you might choose to ignore my words. I have not always lived here to lend my support to the cause. But I could not leave now, whether I was a mage or not. The Heart of the college is also the heart of the city. If it dies, the city dies with it. And the wider implications of the loss of a college for the whole of the country do not bear thinking about. Any able to defend are honour-bound to do so.'

'For me the choice is simple,' said the city guard commander, standing. 'I am the appointed defender of this city, part of which is the college. I have forty full-time officers and experienced soldiers and I have perhaps a hundred volunteer constables. We will not leave. We will stand and fight side by side with our mages to defend our city.'

'Thank you, Commander Vale,' said Pheone, smiling. A smattering of applause ran around the gathered mages.

The Mayor rose to his feet. He was a tall man, his gaze imposing and his shining bald pate instantly recognisable.

'Pheone, you speak openly and, I assume, honestly. As have all who have spoken thus far. Yet I do not know how I should react. With gratitude that you have forewarned us and given us a chance to save ourselves? With anger that you might think we would consider deserting a college that has sustained us so long? Or with cynicism because you have left us with no real choice but to bear arms in defence of our city – and that, because living with a magic college in our midst invites trouble?'

Pheone's jaw dropped. There was a rumbling of voices from the table and the assembled mages. She waved them to quiet. 'Should you not just be glad that we have given you maximum warning and genuine choice? We have been ready to speak to you since this morning. I just don't want to see innocents die. Would you have preferred your first knowledge of Xetesk's arrival to have been as soldiers marched past your house?'

The Mayor raised his hands. 'Pheone, please, don't over-react. I am merely expressing the range of emotion that the people will express. The history of Julatsa is well-known to all here. And I concede that much of what we have here is credit to the college.'

'Good of you to say so,' muttered Lempaar, the old elven elder.

'Indeed,' said the Mayor, smiling. 'The glory and the destruction. It is the way of cities. Korina grew because of its docks, those required to service them and those using them for profit. But wheels turn full circle. Surely the pattern of trade is such that the docks now serve the people, should they ever be rebuilt. And perhaps it is so with the college of Julatsa. The world moves on. And my city is saying to me, how long can we support this college? This elite gathering that in the last decade has brought us so little but cost us so much?'

Pheone could not quite believe what she was hearing. The Mayor had begun with a confused message. Now his opinion was becoming unfortunately clear.

'Mister Mayor, we don't have the time to debate theories and attitudes. We need to know what it is the people of Julatsa intend and what you will recommend. We have to make plans quickly.'

The Mayor's expression hardened. 'Then I will not delay you. Clearly the complex feelings of the city are of no real concern to you.'

'That is not—'

'I understand,' he said. 'The college comes above all considerations.'

'I am talking reality, not theory. Xetesk is coming.'

But the Mayor was enjoying himself. He looked to his

council who, Commander Vale excepted, nodded their support.

'This city is so much more than its college. This city is its people. And those people are tired of being targets in conflict, tired of suffering for the good of the college, and tired of being hated for things beyond their control.

'All across our country, people are starting to put their lives back together. After the magic-inspired storms we all suffered, crops are growing again. In the baronial lands, towns and villages are being rebuilt, farms are working. Perhaps you have been disconnected from life outside of the college lands but I have not. No one wants this war. In fact there is no war outside the mage lands, barring what we might call normal baronial disputes. Even Arlen, practically destroyed by Xeteskian forces, has been ceded back to its few survivors.

'Why should we Julatsans suffer one more day of conflict? Why should innocent people in any college city do so? I understand who is coming here. I understand what they want. I also understand that I cannot stop them. But I will not stand by while they destroy what little we have left. Our esteemed city guard's commander is out on a limb, siding with you.' He didn't look across as he spoke, focusing solely on Pheone. 'I will not have fighting in the streets of this city. If he wants to stand with you, he can do it on your walls. If Xetesk has come to tear down the college, I will not ask my people to stand in its way.'

Pheone nodded. 'Am I to understand,' she said into the void, 'that you are going to chaperone an invasion force to its target? Is that right?'

The Mayor shrugged. 'I won't stand in its way. Indeed, I will be trying to organise matters such that it makes its way through my city peaceably. There will be no battle on these streets, in the parks or squares. The message I will send to the people of Julatsa is simple. They will have nothing to fear from the Xeteskians. If they wish to leave for the time being, they can. If they wish to fight with you, they must join you here.'

'Gutless coward,' snarled Geren.

'Geren, stop,' snapped Pheone. 'Insults get us nowhere.'

'You had better hope Xetesk prevails, hadn't you?' Geren said ignoring her.

'Are you threatening me, boy?'

'I am theorising,' said Geren nastily. 'About what might happen to the balance of power in this city if my college repels the invasion. And repel it, we will.'

'I hope you do,' said the Mayor, though his voice was cold. 'I hope still to count you as friends. But I must look after my people. They are not to be sacrificed on the altar of magic.'

'Friends?' said Geren. 'Friends stand together. You are no friend of this college.'

'I do not like your tone,' said the Mayor.

'You aren't supposed to.'

Pheone just watched and listened as the clamour grew, unwilling and unable to stop it. Commander Vale stood and walked out, brushing aside the council members who sought to stop him. He shook hands with her and the elders before striding purposefully from the lecture theatre.

But what could he really do? The Mayor was popular and his views shared widely. If he had his way, ordinary Julatsans would not lift a finger to help them and her thoughts of the enemy being hounded on every street corner went up in smoke. Dammit but this man would practically escort Dystran to the gates of the college. Pheone bit back the tears of anger and frustration but felt, as a physical pain, another nail being hammered into the coffin of Julatsan magic.

Chapter 33

Night was falling over the mage lands north of Xetesk. Auum had found the run a release after the cramped passageways of Xetesk's catacombs, and they had made good progress. He and Rebraal had organised their forces into scouts, flank and rear defence, and hunter-gatherer parties, while the mages were defended by Al-Arynaar swordsmen supported by TaiGethen.

ClawBound did as they always did. They took no orders but knew instinctively where to be, what to watch and when to report. The loss of two of the dozen pairs, along with three TaiGethen in the earlier attack, had hurt them deeply; and the ClawBound calls that echoed across the miles of charmless damaged countryside were laced with mourning. The information they carried, though, was important and welcome. The Xeteskian forces had stopped and set up camp. Fires were lit, tents were pitched and horses picketed. This was not a brief halt.

But there was an undercurrent of anxiety in the communication. Not every enemy was in the camp and some were sensed and not seen. There was danger everywhere, some of which would melt out of the night to strike. They could not lower their guard for a moment.

Auum had continued the run for another hour before his forward scouts reported a perfect site for a camp. Flat ground along the banks of a river was bordered on the other side by steep crags and with narrowed access front and rear. While he was only too aware that Xetesk could attack from the sky, the assassins, he had been told, would be on foot. They would find their task harder tonight; he would see to that.

Offering a prayer of thanks to Yniss for their fortune, he led his people in. One by one, his hunting parties returned and, though the meat was not plentiful, an abandoned farm had yielded some root vegetables among the weeds and they would have broth before the fires were doused.

Auum and Rebraal saw to the structure of the camp defence, positioning elves on riverbank and crag heights as well as front and rear. The mages were scattered through the camp in groups against the risk of spell attack and the ClawBound rested or scouted as they pleased.

Satisfied, the pair walked to the centre of the camp where The Raven sat, their horses picketed nearby. Their fire, like all the others, was soon to be doused but while they could, they enjoyed its light and warmth under the cool, cloudless sky.

Auum still wasn't sure about them. For humans perhaps they were exceptional and it was true that their actions during the days of the Elfsorrow made them friends to all elves. But he couldn't help but blame them for the problems they encountered in Xetesk. They were too driven by their emotions, and in combat, Auum did not believe that was the way to win. Even so, he was forced to concede the truth of history. They still fought, and won, sixteen years after they had started.

Auum accepted the mug of tea Hirad handed him and walked over to where Sian'erei tended Evunn. The elf lay next to Erienne, who still had not regained consciousness. Once more, Denser was protecting them from the power of her mind while Cleress slept to rest and regain her strength.

'Tual has smiled on him,' said Auum. Evunn looked so much better. His face was relaxed and the colour back in his lips and cheeks.

Sian looked up. 'He has,' she said. 'The Lysternan mage has healed his mind. There is no damage that I can sense now. The mana aura is complete around him. When he wakes, he should be recovered, though we were warned that his memory of recent events might be incomplete.'

'He will be happy Tual has blessed him with another day,' said Auum. 'And the One mage?'

They both looked down at Erienne. Thraun sat beside her, Denser nearby, already looking tired from his spell casting.

'I do not know,' said Sian. 'Her mind is a confusion to me. They say she improves but I cannot see any signs. But she is warm and breathing. Her body is strong and her friends are always with her. All we have for her is hope.'

Auum nodded. 'Thank you, Sian'erei. The Tai are in your debt.'

She flushed and smiled.

Auum turned and took a seat next to Rebraal. The Raven had banked their saddles on top of leather wraps, creating something passably comfortable to lean on.

'Let's talk,' said Auum to Rebraal. 'I want to understand these assassins and the winged creatures more. We must also consider our route for tomorrow. Translate for me.'

'Of course,' said Rebraal. 'Hirad, Unknown, may I interrupt?'

'Why not?' said Hirad. 'How are we doing?'

'Well, the camp is as secure as we can make it. The Xeteskians have stopped for the night. We have hunters out in the field. They will strike if the risk is warranted. ClawBound too may wish to exact retribution. Auum, and I for that matter, need to know more about what we might face tonight.'

'Denser, you know about this stuff,' said Hirad.

'It's not complex,' said Denser. Auum looked hard at him. The strain of the last few days was not being kind to him. There were deep shadows under his eyes and there was a cut in his voice. He needed Erienne to awaken. 'I doubt we will come under familiar attack. They are vulnerable to spell attack and we have a hundred and thirty-odd mages here. But if they do attack, remember that you can't hurt them with swords. And if their mages are with them, killing one will damage the other. It gives you options. But if I were Xetesk, I'd be sending familiars over shorter distances and attacking Lysternans or Dordovans without mage cover. Stands to reason.'

'They are not natural creatures,' said Auum.

'No, they're demons. Be careful of them. They are strong and to be feared.'

'Not by the elves,' said Auum. 'However ugly or strong, they are not a match for us. Tual protects us.'

Denser half smiled. 'I noticed. Now, assassins are altogether different. They will travel Cloaked, silent and in pairs. Always in pairs. We need to worry about these men. They are powerful casters, ruthless knife- and poison-killers and they leave no trail.' He nodded at Auum. 'They are the closest thing we have to the TaiGethen. They won't kill indiscriminately, it isn't their way. Indeed, they may not attack at all tonight, preferring to watch. If I know Dystran, they will be tasked to recover the Aryn Hiil, kill The Raven, barring Erienne, and also kill any elf they identify as key. That means you two for a start.'

Auum nodded. 'The ClawBound must be informed,' he said through Rebraal. 'And then every elf in the camp. The breeze on your cheek could be the passing of an enemy. This won't wait.'

He rose and, having spoken quickly to Rebraal, he trotted out of the firelight.

Hirad watched him go then raised his eyebrows in Rebraal's direction.

'He wants to get the message out. They are also going to mark the camp accessways with leaves and brush. It might help but the wind works against us. We will have to be vigilant.'

'We've got another idea,' said Hirad. 'We think that the assassins' first target will be us. Judging by the pace of the main Xeteskian force, they think they can take you on at the College so they'll let you go. If we aren't with you, you'll be free to move faster and in darkness if it suits you. We can outrun the assassins, the familiars and the mage defenders. We'll take the spare horses as well. We'll be leaving before dawn. Hopefully, we'll be seen, if you see what I mean.'

'Is that . . . ?' Rebraal paused and frowned. 'That's a risk. A big one. You are much safer with us.'

'But we're putting you at greater risk,' said The Unknown. 'Think about it. It makes sense. We can act as decoys, we can look after ourselves. We aren't helping you here and we don't like that. We'd be happier on our own.'

'Doing things The Raven's way, is that it?' asked Rebraal.

Hirad smiled. 'Now you're getting it.'

'What about Erienne?' he asked.

'She comes with us,' said Denser.

'She's one of their main targets,' added Darrick. The pale general was lying against his saddle already half asleep, the day's ride having worn him down.

'I don't know,' said Rebraal. 'Splitting our forces, isn't it? And you aren't just hunted by Xetesk.'

'Oh, I think Lystern and Dordover have other things on their minds,' said The Unknown.

'I'll speak to Auum,' said Rebraal. 'I don't think he'll like it.'

'It isn't like you have a choice,' said Hirad. 'We're going

to sleep on it and if we like the idea when we wake, we're going.'

Rebraal sucked his lip, his cheeks reddening slightly. 'Right,' he said and pushed himself to his feet. 'Right. Well listen, don't leave without saying something.'

The Al-Arynaar looked crushed. Hirad couldn't let him leave like that.

'Hey, Rebraal, we'd love you to come with us. Gods know, we could do with your skills. But your place is here, with your people. Ours isn't. Anyway, it's for two days. We'll see you in Julatsa.'

'You'd better. The ClawBound will shadow you.' The elf left their fire.

Out in the camp, flames were being dampened. Hirad and The Unknown followed the lead, kicking dirt over their already guttering fire.

'Denser, get some rest,' said The Unknown. 'I'll wake you when I wake Hirad for watch. Darrick, you're sleeping and no argument, you look terrible.'

'Who's arguing?'

'Good answer,' said The Unknown. 'Listen, we know what could be out there. We know how good the elves are but we've encountered assassins before. Let's not lapse, all right?'

He stood tall, sampling the night air, his thoughts clouded by the wrong. Her emotions of anger and loss were in his mind too, and thrashing through his veins. He yearned for the canopy above him, the heat of the day, the cacophony of night. The comfort of the rain.

But he was here doing Tual's work. The TaiGethen had asked many of the ClawBound to stay and so they had. He looked to the right and locked eyes with his Claw. She was standing stock still, feeling his emotional tide as he was hers. Around them, the scents of the alien land came to them on a soft breeze, dry and cool.

He took in the landscape, its hues standing out in stark tones of grey. The tall grassed plains that ran away to the south-west and the bulk of the enemy, the hills rising north and the undulating land close to the elven camp. The sounds of the river, though it was quite distant now, were as clear as the rustling of the low brush and damaged trees in front of him.

They moved on south, sorting the scents. Cooked meat, a fresh kill, wood smoke and ash, horses, grass. But overlaying it all was the stench of man. His hand was everywhere, tainting all that he had. Humans knew so little about their land, how to keep it, how to work in harmony with the riches their Gods had given them. There was no comfort in the land, it felt aggressive somehow to the ClawBound. Ill at ease.

Ahead of him, a broken fence led on to the overgrown fields of an abandoned farm. He hurdled the timbers easily, seeing also through his Claw's eyes the tangled vegetation at ground level and understanding the scents that she encountered there. A wisp of leather, the strong smells of damp earth and rotting vegetables.

Nothing moved in the ruins of the farmhouse. It had no roof and all of its wooden walls were holed and splintered, one collapsed entirely. Beyond it, and quite suddenly, a new scent was on the air, coming to them on the prevailing breeze. They halted again, she flat against the earth, he crouching by a broken wall. It was an unusual taste, masked such that although it was undeniably human, it was frayed somehow, hard to pinpoint.

His Claw echoed his slight confusion, even her highly developed receptors having difficulty deciphering what she was scenting on the breeze. Ultimately, her mind cleared and she set off, angling south and west, paws making no sound, head up, constantly checking her direction. He strode behind her, watching the land and the sky, determined that they would not be surprised from the air, or by hidden creatures as their unfortunate kin had been.

They travelled on, leaving the farmhouse far behind, his Claw turning first west and then north-west. He could see the route turning inexorably towards the elven camp. A threat approached the resting elves. They would hunt it down.

The panther increased her pace and he ran too, the scent strong, its masking failing as they closed. Ahead of them, open land rose gently towards the camp. It was empty but they had been told to trust their noses and disbelieve their eyes.

They ran on, the knowledge of the threat all around them but nothing bar the scent to confirm its presence. They had no clear target and the breeze picked up immediately they hit the open ground. He slowed and stopped in the rise, his Claw circling, growling deep in her throat. They were close, he could feel it. He ignored the emptiness, turning a slow circle himself, the smell all around him but stronger in two areas. They had been told this too. These men did not travel alone.

Beneath his feet, the grass was wet and footfalls quiet upon it. He studied it, looking for the darker trails that would signify the passage of man over the ankle-high grass. And there were trails but they were so many. Animals passed this way and these men were clever, walking in the tracks of the fox or the horse.

His Claw's ears pricked and she stopped in mid stride, paw raised, her whiskers twitching. Her head swivelled round until she was staring at the space right in front of him. Her eyes could discern something his could not. He used them, seeing in the few yards between them, a ghosting over the landscape, a caressing of the grass in the tracks of an animal. Like a mist that moved so slowly it barely blew at all. But move it did.

He flexed his long strong fingers and felt each of his sharpened nails in turn against his thumb. The outline, broken by its spell and reflecting nothing but the night scene around it, was moving away from his Claw and towards him but so slowly.

Perhaps in the brightness and noise of the day, the outline would have been truly invisible but in the stark monochrome of ClawBound night sight, any blemish stood out eventually.

He waited, appearing to look away, his Claw's eyes giving him his information. The man, for it was a man, tall like him, stealthy and patient, came closer, closer.

He straightened the fingers of both hands and whipped his left shoulder round, his nails spearing flesh. His right hand followed, fingers gouging deep, nails of both hands clicking as they met within his victim. In front of him, the man flicked into vision, eyes wide with shock, mouth moving only to deliver a choking sound and a spray of blood.

He dragged his fingers from either side of the man's neck and watched him fall, gasping for air, suffocating in the open, his windpipe wrecked. The assassin's partner attacked, a noise betraying him before he too became visible. From nowhere, the Claw swatted his lower back with a taloned paw, brought him down face first and bit down on his neck, breaking it easily.

She licked her whiskers, he sensing the warmth of the blood and the unpleasant sharpness of the taste. Not like the blood of true prey. Their eyes met again. There would be more.

They ran away south and west, searching.

He soared high and his mood was higher. His master was asleep and safe within the confines of the camp. No enemies were close enough to strike and so he was free to fly and to kill, though he was minded to be careful. The enemy might be weakened but enough mages remained to threaten him if he should attack the wrong targets.

So he searched for those who carried swords and who huddled in little groups, fearful of the night and what might come from it. He chuckled to himself, his thoughts full of the taste of blood and the feel of human offal on his hands. And he dreamed that one day all his kind would be free to plunder this land as they wished, to kill whom they wished and drink the fire of the souls of any human. Barring his master, barring all such masters. These were warm and he loved them all for their gift to his strain. None more so than his own master, who looked over him and protected him always.

He swam in the air, turning a circle, spinning his body and letting himself fall fast, only to spread his wings and curve away. He laughed again, this time aloud, hoping some of those hiding below would hear him and be afraid. And there was movement below. Just a little but his eyes were so keen in the darkness.

A shape stood against a tree in amongst a small sheltered wood. He quieted himself and dropped lower to investigate. Through the branches and leaves, the man couldn't see him. He landed lightly on a bough and stared about him. On the ground by the standing man, another lay. Both were soldiers. Neither was obviously injured and that made them fortunate. But not for long. No one else was near.

He took off, flew high and away, banking gently around to find his target. He meant to come in from the side. The man was looking ahead still, back to the tree. The demon licked his lips and dived. The wind across his body was chill but invigorating, his arms were stretched in front of him, ready to grip the skull. Entering the wood, he slowed a little, needing control for the quick kill. He could smell the man now, the anxiety bled from his pores, his sweat stinking, his clothes damp and reeking.

Too easy. He was silent, his target had no notion of his

approach. He wanted to see the terror. At the last, he chattered his delight and the man began to turn.

Sudden green light erupted to his left and heat, terrible heat, seared into his flank and the side of his head. He screeched and tumbled away, unable to stop himself striking the ground, one wing ruined, his whole body burning with the mana fire.

'No, no, no,' he wailed as he rolled in the mulch on the ground, the spell eating into his flesh, unquenchable, draining his life from him.

His thoughts flew to his master. He could feel his pain across the miles, the crushing in his mind, the howling agony and the loss that was to come. He rolled over and two men stood above him, watching him die. One had a greying beard, his expression stern and cruel. The other, younger man he recognised too. He led the cavalrymen of Lystern.

'I'm sorry, master,' he muttered, knowing it would make no difference to his pain.

He could feel himself slipping away and a tear squeezed from his eye. The bearded man spat on to his scorched body and he was too weak even to threaten revenge.

'Very good, Izack,' said the bearded man. 'Let's get to the next sector.'

The cavalryman nodded and the two turned away. The demon's vision faded and greyed. He felt the pull and was gone.

Denser couldn't sleep. He knew he needed the rest, the spell cocooning Erienne's mind was so draining with the One fighting to break it every moment. He poured mana into the structure to keep it strong and saw that mana picked apart by the enemy in his wife's mind.

It was a battle he was helpless to aid. He lay down beside her, stroked her face.

'Please wake, my love,' he whispered. 'Give me something to tell me you're fighting.'

He tuned in to the mana spectrum and tasted the turmoil surrounding Erienne. He could sense the power of the One through his shield and the Dordovan mana that resisted it. The force surrounding her was immense. He could see the raw fuel of magic being dragged into her mind, into the One entity. The damage it had to be doing . . . he could hardly bear to watch.

There was no way to cap the well. Erienne and Cleress had to do that. And so they did when Cleress was awake and with her. But the ageing Al-Drechar was alone and when she was forced to rest, all her work was undone. He snapped out of the spectrum and swallowed hard.

'You can do it, Erienne. You have to. We can't lose you,' he said. 'I can't lose you.'

Helpless. Weaponless. Impotent.

'Please,' he said, hearing his voice strain with the desperation and feeling the tears begin to come. 'Please.'

He felt strong hands lift him and arms crush him close.

'Let it go, Denser,' said The Unknown. 'Or you will never rest and she needs you rested.'

'But it won't help her,' he managed, choking back a sob. 'I can't help her.'

'You are helping her. If the power could escape untamed, you know the One would draw in yet more to feed it. You help her, you help us all.'

Denser nodded. Perhaps it made sense but it was so difficult to see. He drew in a shuddering breath and pushed away from The Unknown, wiping his eyes.

'I'm sorry,' he said. 'Sorry.'

'Why be sorry?' said The Unknown. 'We all yearn to help the ones we love and when we can't, what's left but tears?'

Chapter 34

However many times he had told them, in live exercise, in training rooms and now, in the reality of action, both in the early hours when he had toured the guard positions and the evening before when they had stopped for the night, they hadn't taken heed. Not when it really mattered. And men would die in their sleep because of it.

Chandyr had no time to don his armour, merely grabbed his sword and ran from his tent. He'd been awake, just composing himself to get out and organise the cook fires. He'd wanted to be away at dawn. The first impact had been enough and he'd left his tent before the second and third had hit. There had been no prior warning and that was what made him seethe.

'Get out to the margins!' he yelled, hurdling a fire pit and racing out to where the green Lysternan mana fires were burning tents and helpless soldiers. 'Get the cavalry mounted. What did I bloody tell you!'

So quick, so incisive, exactly as he had warned. While his mages were preparing shield defence and attack, he heard the thundering of hooves.

'To arms!' he hollered. 'Where was my fucking perimeter!'

He was joined by some of the quicker minds and limbs. Ahead of him, all was in disarray. He could see six tents on fire, men running in every direction, too many straight towards him.

'Get back. Think it's over?'

And in they came, forty-plus horses and riders in close form, undoubtedly under a defensive shield. It would be a single thrust, just like he'd said. Izack wasn't amongst them, he saw that immediately, but they didn't need him. They rode thirty strides into his camp, chopping down any one that got in their way, those mages not involved in the shield dropping HotRain and scattering men and precious equipment with ForceCones. Torches in the hands of half the riders flipped away, setting more tents and wagons on fire.

They had turned and begun to ride out before the first spell lit up their shield and the first arrows flew in. That brought down one man. One. His own cavalry galloped around to his right, setting off in pursuit. They wouldn't catch them. They had a hundred and fifty yards and it was more than they needed. At least it would keep them from another attack. Not that Chandyr thought they planned one.

He stopped running and slammed his sword flat on to the ground.

'Shit!'

He rubbed his hands across his face and set them on his hips, his face burning with an anger he had scarcely felt in his life before. All around him, the bedlam was in full flow. Injured men were being helped away, orders were being called to get the fires out and the cries of the dying echoed into a dark sky just edging with first light.

A lieutenant, smeared with soot and with a livid wound across his cheek ran up, saluting smartly, his expression betraying his apprehension. Chandyr glared at him.

'Don't try and make it sound good,' he said. 'This is a calamity that could have been avoided had any of you idiots listened to a damn word I said. Just report.'

'We didn't see them,' he replied, voice shaking. 'The perimeter was set but they were on us from the dark.'

'Which way were they looking, eh?' snapped Chandyr. 'There is no way those spells could have reached our tents without the mages being inside the perimeter. That is why I set it where I did. You're telling me you didn't see them? None of you? Where was the alarm, tell me that?' He stepped in very close. 'Men have died because you were not watching. You let your guard slip and the men under your command were either slacking or sleeping.

'You will consider yourself relieved of your duties. Join your column when we march. I'll be promoting your sergeant. Dismissed.'

'Sir.'

Chandyr turned to face the rest of his command team, who had sensibly assembled behind him.

'This will not happen again. I cannot afford to lose men to incompetence and dereliction of duty. This is not some jaunt. We are facing desperate men and some very skilful leadership. We can still lose this fight if we are not at our best for every hour of every day.

'Right, I want a full report on the casualties and hardware we lost, and I want the perimeter guards who managed to avoid seeing forty cavalrymen in front of me by the time I reach my tent, assuming they are still alive. Move.'

Chandyr watched them go, spun on his heel and took a slow walk back through his camp.

The moment Thraun confirmed that Cleress had joined Erienne once more, The Raven had ridden from the elven camp. They were at little more than a canter, the shapechanger still carrying the stricken One mage and holding her head against his chest. To balance her against him, he leaned back in his saddle. It was uncomfortable but it would serve.

They put quick miles between themselves and the elves, heading due north. ClawBound had run with them for a time but soon peeled away to continue their scouting. It was another two days' long ride to Julatsa. Two days in which they had to survive the best Xetesk could throw at them while distracting those same enemies from attacking the Al-Arynaar mages on whom so much hope had come to rest.

They were still so much below strength. Darrick was pale and weak but recovering, Hirad had problems with his right wrist and they were all tired from so little rest. Thraun himself was feeling strong but his heart was weary. He tried to be strong for Denser, to believe that Erienne could live through this but in truth, he was unsure. Not because he didn't believe that she was strong but that he wasn't sure anyone would have the sheer will.

It was curious. He didn't know why he should think this way or why he should know so much. He was not schooled in any of the art behind the One magic, nor any magic. But something was giving him feelings that helped him to understand. Perhaps it was the elemental nature of the One magic. He too was close to nature in the raw, could smell its moods. But the actual link between that and his innate sense of the trouble in Erienne's mind was one that eluded him.

She had not moved since she had fallen back in the catacombs and he had sworn on seeing her that he would not leave her side until she awoke. The Raven had seemed to understand. And for Denser, it had relieved him to do what he had to do, though the strain was telling on him quickly, both mentally and physically.

Thraun had managed to feed Erienne, stroking her throat to trigger the automatic swallow response, and had cleaned her too. He would not stand by while she lay helpless. He and Denser had maintained her dignity, desperate in their own ways to do anything they could to help her.

He wondered whether she could sense him through her unconsciousness. He hoped so and that in some fashion it gave her comfort and left her free to fight the One. He rode with Denser next to him. The Unknown and Hirad were at the front, both with other horses tethered to their saddles. Darrick was behind them, a spare mount with him too.

No one challenged them the entire morning. The sky had been clear and bright since dawn and mercifully free of the erratically moving dark shapes of familiars. But they were under no illusion that they would be followed. They might get clear of foot-bound assassins but Chandyr wasn't stupid, and if he could get riders through, particularly mage defenders and familiared masters, he would do so, trailing them until dusk, when they would be at their most vulnerable.

It was a great risk they were taking but one they felt they had to take. The elves would move better without them and had mapped a separate path to bring them to Julatsa. Given that they would run late into the night, it was touch and go which of them would arrive first. Thraun wondered whether The Raven would arrive at all.

The shudder that ran through Erienne's body had been so sudden that he had nearly let her fall. She had spasmed twice and murmured something unintelligible.

'Denser! Raven stop!'

He pulled up sharply and climbed from his horse with her in his arms, laying her on dry grass under a warm mid-afternoon sun. The Raven came running, gathering round him, staring down at her.

'What is it?' said Denser, dropping to his knees.

'She moved,' he said.

But she was still again. Denser's face creased.

'Are you sure?'

Thraun nodded. 'She fights. Cleress fights.'

'What does it mean?' asked Hirad.

'Let's not lose focus, Raven,' said The Unknown. 'We'll break and eat, it seems a good time. Hirad, Darrick, let's check out the immediate vicinity. If we aren't defensible we'll move until we are.'

Thraun didn't look up while his friends ran away to their tasks. He just gazed down at Erienne, praying for her to open her eyes.

Erienne didn't understand what Cleress was asking her to do. Like falling on the fire to snuff it out, or plugging the hole by wedging your own body in. It didn't make any sense.

I will be giving myself up to it. This is surrender, Cleress.

It might be that, child, but I don't think we have any other choice.

Why not?

I am failing, Erienne. I cannot get enough rest and the power in you is burgeoning so strongly. I know what your husband is doing and it must be exhausting him too. But he is young and I am old and so tired, Erienne. And what I do to hold back the One is so much more draining than the shield he casts. He does all he can and it is not enough. I do all I can and I am merely holding back the inevitable too.

Erienne thought she had heard Cleress beaten before. But the sheer enervation in the Al-Drechar's voice sent shivers through her subconscious mind where she had retreated to battle the enemy within her.

You can't leave me alone.

I will be with you for as long as I have the breath.

Erienne considered for a moment. The wheel had turned full circle. For so long she had shunned the Al-Drechar, refused to let them enter her mind to help her, believing that she could hold back the One on her own, stifle it until it withered and died. But the pain had become too much and she had been forced to grudgingly let them in. But they had helped her so much. Only time had been too short. Even with Myriell, it had been a struggle and she had feared being alone. Now there was just Cleress and she already knew why she feared solitude inside her mind. The spider's legs clamped ever tighter when she was on her own.

She craved Cleress's mind-touch and soothing caress. Was not sure if the knowledge that it had gone would be too much for her. To fight the spider alone, that bulk pressing down, the legs clamped over her will, crushing, trying to break it. She shivered violently.

That's good, said Cleress. *Your friends will know you are still alive in here.*

That isn't funny, Cleress. This isn't a game.

I know that, child! But you must retain yourself if you are to succeed. And for that you have to remember you are flesh and blood. Always remember that.

What difference will that make?

If you forget who you are, the One will take you.

You know I can't do this.

I know that you must, child, or we are lost anyway. I will protect you for as long as I can but you must understand that the power you are about to let flow through your entire body will quickly overwhelm me. You must be ready to snap out. You will only get one chance. Will you do it?

But you have so much to teach me.

You will have to learn it for yourself. And that is the hardest road of all.

Cleress, does it have to be now? Don't you think you have longer?

Child, every time I go to sleep I am surprised to see the dawn. It has to be now, while I have the will left in me.

Erienne let the thoughts run wild in her mind for a while, feeling the One shifting, trying to tighten its grip but she and Cleress combined to keep prising up the legs. Yet she had known deep down that it was always a temporary measure. That Cleress would announce a solution sometime or other. And the time was now. It was just that the solution seemed pure madness.

Let's try it, then.

Remember, Erienne, what you are using your body to do. You have to be aware of every part of it. Feel it with your mind. Force the One to distribute through you.

I don't like being a plug.

If this works, Erienne, believe me, you will be a great deal more than that.

329

And if it doesn't?

I hope The Raven can run fast enough.

I wish you could hold my hand through this.

Ah, Erienne, to hold you close through your torment is all I desire but I'm afraid that chance is gone now. Keep this in mind. Do what I ask successfully and physical contact will be returned to you.

So, this is goodbye, is it?

We'll see, child, we'll see.

Thank you.

No, you are the one who we all should thank. You are the one who can save everything we hold dear.

Why?

You will survive this and you will see. One day soon, I think.

You can't tantalise me like that! Erienne felt indignation growing in her.

It's all I can clearly see. But use it to help your determination. Erienne, this will hurt you. The One will fight you and those dearest to you will have to understand. It is a power you cannot fight with your mind alone, not yet, and that is why you need the substance of your whole body. It is a skill we have all learned. For you it will be difficult as you will be alone. Remember, you are a One mage with everything that is you.

I think I understand.

Good. Then let us begin.

Erienne felt Cleress leave direct contact. She withdrew into her subconscious, and looked within herself, seeing the One entity there, menacing, determined to break her will. And she saw it buckle suddenly and withdraw, become smaller somehow, as Cleress drove it back with everything that she had left.

It was now or never. Dragging every iota of her belief to her, she broke from her subconscious, feeling the pain through her body as she reached out once again to the body she had abandoned. She felt herself judder, saw the One react and fight back, trying to expand itself to crush her back into the small space she had occupied and where it could bring maximum force. So hard to believe it wasn't sentient but a power reacting automatically to her mind and body. Better she kept the thought of its sentience alive; it gave her more to focus on.

With the One still shrouded in Cleress's essence, she fought her way back to her conscious state. It was like swimming up from a great depth, her breath locked into her lungs and bursting to get out. She could not fail, had to reach the surface. Sensation returned to her fingers and toes. She could feel the air on her face and hear, indistinctly, the sounds of voices. Still locked inside herself, she battered at the One, pushing it further back, feeling Cleress with her for one fleeting moment.

And then she was gone and the One spread to envelop her once again. This time, though, she was ready, and though it wrenched at her muscle and thought, she swam upwards still, defying the power that sought to drag her back down. She saw the body of the spider flatten and spread, the legs try to grip her consciousness as it expanded to every extremity.

It was too slow. She felt herself judder again, felt a tingling across her skin and the feel of her clothes. The surface of her mind was so near. The noise of life assaulted her ears, she could smell horse and grass and . . . and Denser.

Gasping in a lungful of air, she opened her eyes.

The joy that flooded through Denser weakened him and he almost fell on top of her, just managing to lock his elbows again. She reached up, wrapped her arms around his neck and kissed him hard, her tongue seeking his. Almost at once, she let go and lay back down, looking at him.

'You're back, love, you've beaten it.' She did not reflect his smile.

'No, Denser,' she said and she sighed as if in pain. 'Remember I love you. Remember I love all of you. Whatever happens now.'

'I don't understand? You're awake, you've won.'

'It is in me now,' she replied. 'It touches everywhere. Please don't think badly of me.'

'Why would I ever—?'

He saw something pass across her eyes, like a black cloud across moonlight. And when she looked at him again, those eyes were so cold.

Chapter 35

Dystran had thought to ride with his small army to Julatsa but Ranyl had dissuaded him, despite the lure of glory. Another wise decision, given what he had heard from Chandyr via Communion report this morning. What would he do without him?

He had sat in Ranyl's rooms for much of the day, talking to his dying friend, acutely aware of the brevity of the time they had left together. The old master had reacted badly to the attack on Xetesk and the intrusion into his chambers, shock settling on him, weighing him down.

'I could not have fought back,' he said for the tenth time that day. 'I was powerless.'

Ranyl was sitting in his favourite chair by the fire which roared out heat despite the warmth of the day beyond his open balcony doors. His hands wrung together, his face was damp with sweat, and the agony of his cancer was evident in every breath he drew. His skin had taken on a yellow pallor and his body had a distinct tremor to it. He had refused food all day.

'They meant you no harm,' said Dystran gently. 'It was me who failed you. I am sorry.'

'I was in my own chambers and they just walked in,' he said.

Dystran could see the fear in those bright, wise eyes and was reminded that great mage though he was, Ranyl was first and foremost an old, tired man facing death and scared at the prospect.

'I have news for you,' said Dystran, determining to take his mind off it.

It was news he had known since before dawn but had not revealed while Ranyl struggled with his pain as he always did for half of the day. At such times, it was best to talk memories but today, his mind had been preoccupied.

'Oh yes?' Ranyl perked up and Dystran wondered if he had made a mistake in delaying.

'As you know, we put scouts into the field last night,' he said. 'It seems the damage we inflicted was worse than we hoped. The southern and western camps have been abandoned. They are moving north but of course almost a day behind us.'

'It was an obvious move in some respects,' said Ranyl, straightening in his chair. 'They have guessed rightly that we cannot afford to send men from here to harry them, we would leave ourselves too exposed. And they of course, can no longer attack us here. Are we assuming they are headed for Julatsa or are they actually going to return to Dordover and Lystern?'

'That's difficult to answer,' replied Dystran. 'They have over a hundred wounded with them, and I suspect they will be returned home. But the bulk of the force, something in the order of four hundred could well continue north.'

'Interesting.'

'What do you suggest we do to counter them?'

Ranyl was silent for a while, rubbing the top of his nose with an index finger. 'I am no military tactician,' he said eventually. 'Chandyr is best placed to assess the threat. Surely if we keep scouts trailing them and him informed, that is our best option. Unless . . . When will we be able to cast dimensional magics of the same magnitude again?'

Dystran raised his eyebrows. 'In two days, I am told. And this time the window is much longer, perhaps a whole day before alignment becomes unhelpful again.'

Ranyl nodded. 'Well, it's an option. Chandyr may have other ideas but should we not consider getting a team of mages into the field and behind the enemy now? Not let the distance get too great. They can rest on the trail enough to be able to cast. I must say, it worries me that the elves will reach Julatsa before Chandyr has taken the college. Three hundred is a significant number in this game.'

'My thoughts exactly.' Dystran smiled. 'Thank you.'

'It is always a pleasure,' said Ranyl.

He coughed, the pain wracking his body. On his lap, his familiar raised its head weakly and settled down again, looking nothing more than a sick cat.

'You need to rest,' said Dystran.

Ranyl chuckled. 'I will have an eternity to do that, young pup. An eternity that is very soon to begin.'

North and west, the people poured out of Julatsa. The meetings across the city had been brief and harsh. The mayor had played his cards well, barring mages from the gatherings, determined to ensure that the people heard the unexpurgated truth, as he put it. Anyone who Pheone had managed to speak to following the meetings, which had gone on well into the night, reported nothing short of rabble-rousing.

The result had been angry but directionless demonstrations outside the college, a few threats levelled at the mages within for the trouble they had brought to the city and now this exodus. Early guesswork and a close watch on those leaving suggested that the charge, for such it appeared when it gathered momentum in the early afternoon, had been led by those who had only come to Julatsa for shelter.

The ranks had been swelled by women and children chaperoned by a sizeable number of armed men, often on horseback. It was a somewhat different story among businessmen, who could see their already precarious livelihoods collapsing around their ears if they left. But while many of these people determined to stay in the city, keeping open areas like markets, bakers and blacksmiths, they were not openly declaring their support for the college.

Julatsa, they had said, is my home and I will protect it and my business. If I help the college as a by-product, so be it. Hardly the vote of confidence Pheone had been hoping for. To be fair, friends had come to the college to pledge their support but they were so few that Pheone had considered sending them away for their own safety. Instead, she had welcomed them in and put them to work.

Despite the ever-present risk of mana failure, Pheone watched the ordered column of Julatsans leaving the northern border of the city from under ShadowWings. The effort of structuring and maintaining the simple casting told her all she needed to know about the depths of trouble in which Julatsan mana found itself but she was determined that she would not be scared out of using it. Indeed, if Geren was completely right, using magic helped maintain the Heart.

A determined movement from below caught her eye. Someone was waving up at her. She dipped lower and smiled sadly. Another friend deserting the city. The woman was beckoning her down and she obliged, pulling up to land just outside the last house before the empty north route guard tower. She heard muttering behind her at her arrival but no one spoke up.

'Hello Maran,' she said. 'Sorry to see you're leaving.'

'I'm sorry too,' said Maran. Her daughter, Maranie was walking along hand-in-hand beside her, the five-year-old sensing only the excitement, not the uncertainty. 'But I can't let her see what might come.'

'I do understand,' said Pheone. 'You are why I spoke to the council. You should be assured of your safety. It's what everyone in the college wants.'

'The Mayor didn't speak too kindly of you. None of you but you in particular,' said Maran.

'I'm sure he didn't.'

'You know, most of us don't believe much of what he said.'

'And what did he say?'

Maran paused before speaking. 'That you courted war and expected us to defend you. That you felt above every other citizen, assuming yourselves rulers of the city. He was quite forceful about who was really in charge.'

'It's not something I've ever disputed,' said Pheone. 'We only ever wanted to work together to make the city great again.'

'He said you had become a cancer that should be excised.'

That stopped Pheone in her tracks for a moment. 'This is our city too,' she said. 'Why are you turning against us?'

'We're not. Well, I'm not. I just have to think of Maranie. I can't take the chance.'

Pheone had heard enough. The Mayor had turned full face against them, that was clear. His words of passivity had turned to active hostility and she wondered what exactly he would say to the Xeteskians if he managed to talk to them.

'I have to get back,' she said. 'Good luck.'

The two women kissed cheeks. 'I'll see you when I get back.'

Pheone felt a sudden rush as of cold water across her body. She stumbled suddenly and gasped a breath, ShadowWings disappearing, leaving a pain in her back.

'We're dying and you're running,' she said, the shock of the mana failure forcing unbidden anger into her voice.

'I'm not—'

'I wonder what city it is you will come back to, Maran. Perhaps you shouldn't come back at all.'

She turned and walked back into the city, the void where her connection with the mana should have been tearing at her soul.

The desperation of the day before had made way for an extraordinary sense of optimism. It had no foundation. The allied forces were largely destroyed and the survivors only now banding together, with a force probably six times their complete size only a couple of hours behind them and closing, but still hopes were raised.

The only factor Blackthorne could attribute it to was the fact that, the more bands of twos, threes and fours he brought together, the more men who had thought all was lost saw that it was not quite as bad as they had believed. All animosity between Lystern and Dordover had disappeared. Strangers were greeted like long-lost brothers.

But in the face of this lightening of mood, Blackthorne was reminded of their situation all too often. His had been a simple yet challenging brief from Izack, one that he had been happy to accept from the Lysternan commander, who had demonstrated himself an exceptionally brave man.

Riding with the eight members of his guard who had survived the BlueStorm, he had undertaken to be the link between the fleeing groups of allied soldiers and mages, using the pace of his horses to cover the ground and his powers of persuasion to make those he found change direction in order to unite.

But for every three groups he found, from two terrified men clinging together, to one of a dozen and more with guard mages, he found another which had not escaped familiar, assassin or mage defender. He'd seen bodies scattered across a clearing; men who had died back to back, their desperate defence not enough; and the eyes of the dead open to the sky. What terrors they must have seen. The situation had worried him enough that he had ridden alone the previous night to speak to Izack. As a direct result, the familiar traps been laid, catching some and scaring off many more.

Now though, Blackthorne was tired. He hadn't slept since before the siege had been shattered. He'd changed horses twice and the one beneath him was showing reluctance. Making instant decision, he dismounted and led the horse by the reins, its expression pathetically grateful.

He was walking with the united shards of the allied force. He had found forty-seven soldiers and six mages. Paltry. Yet it was something. His men had heard of another four groups west or slightly ahead and were trying to round them up now. To keep up the spirits of these men and the pace of the walk, which pushed many beyond their normal limits, he dropped his baronial air.

He moved among them, cajoling and joking, asking after their health and promising plenty he could never deliver. And though it kept them going, it made his heart heavy. Mentally and physically, these men were finished. It was three days' walk to Julatsa. And even if he got them there, what good would they be to the defence?

It was a question with a simple answer and that meant he had to change his plan. He had considered his options for an hour while they marched, mercifully without incident as they had been doing the entire day, when he heard a rider approaching. Natural consternation quickly gave way to relief when the men recognised the man in the saddle.

He cantered up to Blackthorne, dismounted and walked beside the Baron.

'My Lord,' he said.

'Hello, Luke,' he said. 'So, what news do you bring me from Izack?'

'Good news,' said Luke, the orphaned farmer's son who had become one of Blackthorne's most valuable men after their chance meeting during the Wesmen wars that seemed an age ago. 'Izack raided the Xeteskian camp at dawn as planned. Fired tents, killed some, broke wagons and got out losing one man and two injured.'

'Did you hear that lads?' called Blackthorne. 'Izack has struck another blow at the Xeteskians. A successful one!' There was a cheer. 'He's minding our backs, let's pray he comes through.' He dropped his voice. 'How far away are the enemy?'

He glanced back over his shoulder. The terrain was the same from here to Julatsa. Undulating and studded with low peaks, sharp valleys and woodland, much of it broken down. A clever enemy could get very close without being seen. Blackthorne hadn't got rear guards. No one wanted to be alone out there just yet.

Luke shrugged. 'Marching, probably three hours, but he's pushed his cavalry ahead this morning to keep Izack away. If they pushed hard and beat Izack in the gallop, they could be on us in less than an hour.'

'Hmm,' said Blackthorne. 'Still, it leaves their flanks exposed. Someone ought to get word to the elves about that.'

'Someone already has.' Luke smiled. 'He is smart, isn't he?'

'Izack? Yes, very. Schooled by the best of course.'

'You, my Lord?' There was a twinkle in Luke's eyes.

Blackthorne laughed. 'You'll go far, young man,' he said. 'Keep that wit, you'll need it.'

'Yes, my Lord.'

'Now, then, I have something more to ask of you,' said Blackthorne. 'I need you to go back to Izack. Ask him his opinion of the pace of the enemy march and its direction. Will it deviate? So far, I suspect they will walk in our footprints.'

'Might I ask why, Baron?'

'These men need rest. If they march into Julatsa three hours ahead of Xetesk, they will get none and be slaughtered because of it. Chandyr's men are sleeping at night. Mine are not. I want a place to hide away from the route. Somewhere secure enough we can hold out against familiars and assassins if it comes to it. I don't think Chandyr will change course to confront us, we are not enough of a threat for that.

'I'd rather lead these men on a rear assault when the battle is already joined than see them pointlessly cut to pieces because they are too tired to cast or hold their blades steady. Take that to Izack, find out his views. He gives the orders and I will follow them but be firm in expressing my recommendation. Do you understand? Strike that, I know you do. Are you fit to ride?'

'Yes, my Lord.'

'Good. Then go when you're ready. The sooner the better. I'd like an answer before sundown.'

Lord Tessaya stood with Lord Riasu near the entrance to Understone Pass. It was a place in which he had stood once before. That time, he had been directing the Wesmen armies and his Shamen, backed by Wytch Lord magic, as they attacked and destroyed the four-college force that had taken the western end of the Pass. It had been a day of death and respect, his enemies never turning and running to the safety of the dark but standing to fight and die to a man. He did not have such respect today for the rulers of the four colleges who let themselves be divided by a hunger for power.

Today, he stood and watched the Wesmen assemble once more. Riasu, his lands encompassing the Pass entrance, had his tribesmen already assembled by the time Tessaya and the Paleon arrived. Tents were pitched in traditional order, standards and banners hung and tribal distance respected. Almost two thousand were camped, representing over half the force he expected though he hoped to be surprised.

He had the best men from a further twenty tribes coming, those that could muster above fifty men. The others, tribes who had suffered hard at the hands of the east and the mana-driven storms, would not march. Never again would he allow any tribe to risk disappearing altogether. Enough had to remain to ensure survival.

Tessaya looked forward to seeing the banners of his people arrive. The Heystron, the Liandon, Revion and Taranon, great names in the warrior history of the Wesmen. All had lost their commanders in the last wars, all sought vengeance.

He breathed in the spring air, felt its warmth in his chest and nodded his head.

'Can you feel it, Riasu?' he asked.

'I believe I can, my Lord Tessaya. I believe I can.'

'There is a change in the very air. The shadows lengthen over the rule of the colleges. Never before have we genuinely had such an opportunity. Never. Think, Riasu, how we trusted in overwhelming numbers and assumed it would be enough. We took Julatsa but the cost was so high. Now, mage numbers are low and the colleges take more from the game every day, strengthening our hand if they but knew it.' He nodded again. 'We must not fail.'

'We won't, my Lord,' said Riasu. 'Every man down there can feel it too.'

He gestured at the sprawl of tents. Smoke rose from a hundred fires and the noise of tribal life was punctuated by the menacing barks and snarls of Destrana wardogs. The plain would soon be full. And then it would be time.

'How long before the Taranon arrive?'

Every Lord who had responded to his summons had also responded to the call to arms and waited for the word to march east. The Shamen had passed on the message through the Spirits who watched over them, and had bade them be victorious.

'I am told it will be two days,' said Riasu.

'Then on the dawn following their arrival, we shall go,' said Tessaya.

There was a surge of men towards the southern edge of the camp. Cheering and songs broke out. Away in the distance, he could pick out standards fluttering on their long poles. The Liandon were come and would be sung in all the way. The sound raised Tessaya's heart and he felt his blood rushing through his veins, invigorating him. He was old to be leading men to battle but he felt like he had just crossed the threshold from childhood.

He led Riasu from the rise and began to run towards the camp. If they were fast enough, they would be in time to join the songs and greet their brothers to the gathering.

Chapter 36

Dusk was beginning to take hold on the second day of the run north to Julatsa but Auum had a different target, and his Tai was complete once again. He ran with an extra spring, Duele and Evunn flanking him, the shadows that gave him every confidence that he needed. Tual had smiled on them, Yniss had too and Evunn had awoken as Sian had said, none the worse physically but with hazy memories. When time was once again with them, they would tell him the story he had missed.

They had parted from the main elven group at midday, leaving Rebraal in sole charge, and heading on a long curved route that took them well away from any enemy scouts. They had not rested until they had reached the rear of the Xeteskian column. ClawBound had been with them all the way, keeping them from harm and completing the picture of what they faced. Now, they walked with two pairs a mile adrift of the nearest rear guard or scout, safe in the knowledge that those familiars and assassins that remained were concentrated ahead. Some of the latter had tried to get into the elven camp the night before and their remains had been left just beyond the forward perimeter of the Xeteskian camp before dawn.

Auum had no feelings for these people. He knew the Claw-Bound wanted revenge for the deaths among their number and while he understood the reaction, it was not the way of the TaiGethen. Nor of the Al-Arynaar. But the ClawBound were a breed apart and one who channelled their anger without compromising themselves. It was the bond the pairs shared that kept them clear and decisive. For Auum, it was merely necessary to reduce Xeteskian numbers as far as possible to aid the Al-Arynaar.

Ahead and to their left and right, the pairs walked, their

quick pace forcing the Tai cell to trot to keep up. None of them needed a tracker to follow the Xeteskians. Even a blind human could follow the trail left by cartwheel, foot and hoof. Debris littered the path too, just one more example of their casual disregard for the land, their misunderstanding of what their Gods had given them. A broken buckle, a square of cloth, a chipped and rusting dagger. He'd seen so much that it failed to surprise him any more.

They closed steadily and stealthily on the rear guards, ten men in pairs, spread across an arc a half mile wide. ClawBound had reported that this circle existed all around the marching column now the cavalry were marauding ahead. It was a reasonable strategy, Auum supposed, but he was no expert on military movement. He didn't need to be. All he knew was that those detached from the main group without the skills to sense the threat were vulnerable.

Like the lame deer in the herd. Unprotected. Easy meat.

He brought the cell to a halt. Ahead of them, a river the enemy column should just have crossed, wove through low-lying marshy land between a series of gentle rises scattered with heavy brush, bracken and woodland. They had waited for the sun to decline and now the terrain was perfect.

Auum led them in a prayer to Yniss to watch over them, and to Tual, the God the ClawBound most revered, to guide them.

'There can be no sound,' he said. 'Our jaqrui pouches remain closed, the Claws must restrain their voices. We are few. We can inflict damage to help our brother Al-Arynaar and repay the debt owed to the ClawBound but we must not be heard. There is nowhere for us to run from their mages and their familiars.

'We have our targets. We move.'

The ClawBound pairs made no gesture to suggest that they had heard or agreed. They were still for a moment, and then ran away, one pair directly ahead, the other to the right, leaving the Tai cell to take the left flank.

'Care with your bows,' said Auum. 'Only if you are certain of a clean kill.'

He drew his twin short swords and sped away through thigh-high grass towards a bracken-covered mound, while Duele and Evunn, bows prepared, moved five yards left and right and ten behind.

Auum sensed every footstep he made, minimising the pressure, feet finding sure hold. The drying ground still held treachery for the unwary but the elf, born to the rainforest, would rely on it as he would solid rock. He breasted the bracken, easy movements at one with the direction of growth, stems eased aside rather than crushed underfoot. Beyond the mound, the land fell away sharply to a muddy tributary. He sized it up as he approached, the fast failing light no barrier, finding the solid ground, footfalls not sounding.

Climbing up from the tributary he slowed momentarily, assessing the land ahead, seeing a knot of trees left, another fall in the land and clear tracks through tall grass. At the base of the dip, a figure disappeared into another small wooded area. He raised a hand, pointed to the relevant tracks and curved away, sprinting hard down the slope, eyes to his right.

He could see them both now, walking calmly through the trees that sprouted new life after the storms that had all but destroyed them. The men were close together, eyes ahead, looking forward to their rest. With the sky near full dark, it would not be long. But they were not destined for rest among their friends.

Auum checked his run and curved back towards the right, closing in. He held out an arm, three fingers straight, his order taken up by Duele and Evunn who made up the ground for the cell to advance in line. Duele was running with his bowstring taut, an enemy in range but no definite kill shot available. Evunn still searched, his mind perhaps not as keenly resolute as those of his Tai fellows.

Auum did not think he would need either of them. The ground plateaued in front of him and he crossed it with barely a whisper. He could hear them talking, their quiet tones carrying to him above the sounds of breeze and tree, rodent and predator. At the base of a tree, its bulging trunk stripped bare by deer, he stopped, watching. They were oblivious. They were looking around themselves again, checking back and watching the route they had travelled now their eyes were adjusted to the dark.

The Tai had needed no such wait.

Auum let them move ahead ten yards, nodded to Duele at his right and moved in. Beneath the trees, the ground was soft and damp. No twig lay underfoot, tinder dry, to snap. He was within four paces when one felt the skin crawl on the back of his neck and began to turn.

Auum took off, body spinning and right leg stretched, catching the man in the cheek, his cry muffled by Auum's boot smearing across his mouth. The TaiGethen landed next to the other man and jammed a short sword up under his jaw, spearing his brain through the roof of his mouth. He dragged the blade away, made to finish off the other but he already had two arrows in his chest.

Duele and Evunn trotted in and cut the shafts free, cleaning and dropping them back in their quivers. Auum nodded their direction and the cell set off again.

Not a bird had been put to flight though the blood of fresh death stained the earth.

Thraun missed the closeness of Erienne, her hair and the feel of her skin. He missed that he couldn't help her any more and that she had no use for him. For any of them. He treasured the touch she had given him, cupping his cheek, her lips just brushing his and then she was gone again as she had been from Denser. He had felt hurt but now he just felt deeply sorry for her because, to him, the torment she was going through was obvious.

Not just that every move she made was jerky and uncertain somehow. And not because she said very little but to make demands to stop, to ride, to eat or drink. But because he had seen into her eyes and not even Denser had seen the raging within. Every cell of her was fighting to restrain the One and it took her almost completely from them.

But he knew that she was better for the fact that she could sense them again. The times she had been close to him, the briefest touch or a lifting of the corner of her mouth told him she was still there with them.

Thraun's was the watch now that they had eaten and the fire was doused. It was dark but his lupine eyes could separate the shades and his nose was keen, the strong smell of wood smoke hanging in the air just one of the myriad scents he could discern. The Raven were sleeping and that was compliment enough. He sat with them, right in their midst, silent.

From where would the threat come, he wondered. They had camped as they must, hidden from plain view land- or airborne but there was no geographic feature nearby to guard any point of the compass. So threat could come from anywhere and strike at anyone. Not Erienne. She would not be killed though she could conceivably be taken. But any member of The Raven was as critical as any other.

The question was, who would they target? If, indeed, any of the Lord of the Mount's assassins were even in the vicinity.

Thraun pushed himself to his feet and padded carefully across the small camp site to where the horses were tethered. He stood with them, watching as they did, the eddies of the night around them. Horses were always nervous with him on first contact. This group had calmed now but they sensed something other than the human in him. It was just something he had to accept.

Like so much that was frustrating. Like his lack of language and the gap between thought and articulation. Like the love that remained for his wolven side but that he denied because he feared the prison of the animal form. So much he didn't fully understand.

He stood with the horses for some time, their warmth and innocence comforting. They demanded so little. But they missed almost nothing of what was around them. There was a moment when all their attention was in the same direction. Thraun moved away from them then, walking smoothly back towards his friends. Denser was stirring but in his anxiety he might have done that at any time. Might have.

Thraun paced evenly and very quietly towards Denser, seeing the mage flap his arms as if pushing away an unseen enemy. Indeed. Thraun saw the shimmer against the heat signature of the dead embers. He walked past Denser's feet, bent down and dropped his hand on the Cloaked figure, catching him a little high but adjusting his grip. Thraun pushed, the assassin becoming visible as he stopped moving, his face driven into the ground, a knee on his back. The shape-changer growled.

'Knife,' he said.

The assassin held out his right arm. The dagger in his right hand was coated. Thraun punched his wrist and the weapon dropped from his grasp.

'You will not move,' said Thraun. He tightened his grip on the assassin's neck, dragging him backwards and up, the other arm wrapping around his front grabbing his groin. 'Raven!' Thraun's voice boomed across the campsite.

Around him, they awoke, rolling and standing, shaking sleep from their minds and dragging swords from scabbards lying on the ground.

'Form up!' shouted The Unknown.

Quickly, the four Raven men ran to positions around the still sleeping but stirring Erienne. Thraun pulled his man inside the ring.

'Where's your friend?' asked Hirad.

The assassin said nothing. Thraun pulled him closer, both hands gripping a little tighter.

'Talk.' Where there was one, there would be another. He would be watching them, probably from close by. 'Talk.'

The assassin let go a small groan of pain. Denser turned at the sound. Thraun saw the disappointment in his face.

'Takyn?' he said. *'You?'*

'I am sorry, Denser,' replied the assassin. 'I am so ordered.'

'That's just bloody great,' said Denser, he swung back round. 'Now they're sending my friends to kill me.'

'You should have chosen better friends,' said Hirad.

'I did.'

'Yes, Denser, you did,' said Takyn.

'Call the other one out,' said The Unknown. 'Either that or have him watch you die.'

'I'll do it,' said Denser. 'Gythen, I know you're there. Come in and join the party. Let's work this out and all walk away with our lives tonight.'

'Don't be naïve, Denser,' said a voice from the dark. Thraun struggled to pinpoint his direction. 'How can you possibly let us go? Takyn knows it. I know it.'

'Come out and take us on, then,' said Hirad.

They heard a dry chuckle. 'Getting myself killed on duty has never been in my plans.'

Denser turned to Takyn. 'In a moment, it looks like you'll never be able to father children. Call him out, we won't kill you.' He paused. 'How could you accept this job? Don't our years of training together mean a thing to you?'

'They were a long time ago,' said Takyn between measured, difficult breaths. Thraun did not slacken his grip anywhere. 'You chose your route, I chose mine.'

346

'But *this?*'

'I'll admit I never expected to be assigned to The Raven but you have to be prepared. You know how it works. You'd have made a good assassin.'

'I'm so flattered.'

'Denser,' said The Unknown sharply. 'This is not helping our problem. Gythen, this is your chance to walk away with your friend, not alone. Show yourself.'

Hirad spoke to Takyn over his shoulder, loud enough for the other to hear.

'Denser may have trouble killing you but I won't. Anyone who does Dystran's bidding shares the blame for the death of my friend. All your lives are forfeit.'

'Hirad, please.' said Denser.

'I'm just telling it how it is.'

Erienne stirred again and awoke, finding herself in a ring of men, tension in the air. Thraun watched her puzzlement turn to irritation, the light that was in her eyes diminishing quickly.

'Assassins,' he said.

'So kill him and let me rest,' she said, her voice rough and dry. 'I must have rest.'

'We're dealing with it, love,' said Denser. 'But there's another one. You could pinpoint him. You know you have the talent.'

She was on her feet now. Thraun could see her expression clearly when she looked at her husband. It held contempt and impatience but she forced those alien thoughts away, leaving Thraun to see the struggle she was enduring and the fear when her face relaxed.

'I don't know if I can stop it if I start it,' she said, her voice now small and desperate.

'What are we debating this for?' asked Hirad. 'I'm with Erienne. Denser, light up the site, I'll slit this bastard and we ride out. The coward in the shadows can get us back if he can keep up with a galloping horse. How about it?'

'Ever the diplomat, Hirad,' said Denser.

'We have a Code,' added The Unknown.

Hirad scoffed. 'Assassins have no honour. I will show them none in return.'

He spun round, his movement quick enough to surprise even Thraun and Takyn started violently. The barbarian's sword point prodded Takyn's chest above his heart. 'Any of you think you're quick enough to stop me?'

Erienne's voice in the void was enough. 'If it's any help making up your mind, whoever you are out there, you are moving very slowly to my right. You have just ducked under an overhanging branch. In your next pace, you will pass a small drift of leaves. Denser's FlameOrbs will be ready in moments. You can't get away from the splash zone. Your call.'

Thraun watched Erienne's head fall to her chest and her arms clutch at her ribs as if she was feeling an acute pain. Outside the circle, Gythen blinked into view.

'Sorry, Takyn,' he said.

Takyn shrugged. 'It's why we want her.'

'Not another word,' said Hirad.

'Gythen, drop your weapon,' said The Unknown as Darrick moved purposefully towards him. 'Right now. Hirad, lower your sword.'

'Un—'

'Now!'

Thraun watched the conflict on Hirad's face. His respect for the big man prevailed over his desire for more revenge. His swordpoint dropped and he pushed his face into Takyn's.

'Consider yourself one lucky bastard.'

Next to Thraun, Erienne swayed. He thrust Takyn at Hirad and caught her before she fell. The Unknown spoke into the moment's uncertainty.

'Darrick, bring him over here. Denser, you can forget the Orbs now, I think deep sleep is more what they need. And us, for that matter. Man on watch guards them too.' He nodded in some satisfaction. 'Reckon that makes us safe tonight, don't you?'

Erienne sank into brief and broken, haunted dreams, feeling more alone than at any time in her life. Since forcing herself back to consciousness to do battle with the One entity throughout her body, she had sought Cleress but the old elf did not or could not answer her. There had been occasions when she thought she had heard a voice but it was vague, like a whisper in a gale. Perhaps the One had shut her out. Perhaps she really was dead.

The effort of adopting the structure allowing her to see

Gythen had taken such energy. The technicalities of the casting were simple, enough. Stopping the One from using it as a route to vent power was not.

The Al-Drechar had taught her so much in the short time they had been with her. The possibilities and the dangers, so closely connected, the partitioning of her mind that was demanded to keep castings under control while capping the well of One power. But she hadn't understood the most basic lesson they had been trying to teach her since that first day she had let them into her mind. She understood it now.

Every moment of her training in Dordover had taught her that magic was an element controlled purely by the mind, formed into shapes by the mind and using physical movements merely to focus the mind to perfect the desired construct. Physical tiredness was the result of the mental effort. She had brought this doctrine to her dealings with the One.

But the One was so different. The One demanded, if you were to control it for any length of time, the use of the whole body. Muscles were flexed, tendons tightened and arteries swollen, with the blood driven through them in pulses. Mana was just one element of the larger magic. Everything else was open to her too and the One entity attracted the raw fuel like moths to light. From metal deposits, to water and the air around her, to verdant foliage and the living earth. Anything with a vitality that could be stripped.

The problem was, it was an unbalanced magic. Where mana would dissipate on casting, returning to its natural chaotic state, the One magic did not, making it potentially so much more destructive. It could not simply be formed into structures and let go. The structures of the One, through which power was vented in a controlled fashion, had to be disassembled to make it safe. Otherwise a structure could drag elemental energy from around itself, becoming almost self-perpetuating while it slowly unravelled. How easy now to understand why the storms and disasters Lyanna created had been so vicious, so long-lived.

Her poor daughter's body had simply been too small to exert the physical control and her mind alone was helpless to contain the power it held. That was what the Al-Drechar had been trying to explain since the beginning but her grief at Lyanna's death had stopped her listening.

Erienne's body was strong enough, though barely. She had wondered why the Al-Drechar hadn't asked her to accept the entity as part of her entire being rather than just her mind but even that made sense now. The mind had to be trained first. The mind had to be the cork in the bottle as well as the casting focus. The body could only be trained once the stopper could be put in place.

What her body did was channel the One in an endless circuit. It had no outlet and could drag no more power in unless she chose to open the bottle to cast a spell. Every urge in her body told her to yank out that mental cork because doing so would relieve the surging she felt inside her. Every thought in her mind drove her to keep the stopper in tight. What a paradox. The very time when in theory she should be in maximum control of the One magic was the time it was at its most dangerous to her and everything around her.

Now she understood, truly understood, the challenge that faced her. She would never fully control or cap the energy the One contained. All she could do was suppress it. And whenever she cast she had to use just exactly the right amount of power to achieve her end. That right amount being dependent on the strength of her body and the freshness of her mind combined. Too much at the wrong moment and she was lost. Not enough and the casting would fail.

Erienne's mind began to relax just slightly as her path became clearer. She was aware that she would hate what she had been forced to become. The spider would always be there, looking for a way to break her. And yet she could never fight it, never beat it. Just cage it and let it run to her design.

A more peaceful sleep overcame her now. Her last thought before the shouting woke her at dawn the next morning was that she was going to have to get to know herself all over again. She hoped her husband would understand.

Chapter 37

Hirad had been left with the last watch of the night and The Unknown cursed himself for his stupidity and complete mis-reading of Hirad's emotional state. The big man himself was the first awake that morning, Hirad shaking his shoulder. He'd looked and known what Hirad had done. Now he and the barbarian stood over the scene, his eyes adjusting to the early light of dawn.

At least he had been clinical. Both necks were broken. There was not a mark on either of them but the stillness of the dead had a quality about it that forewent any thought that they might still be sleeping.

'Oh, Hirad, what have you done?'

'I thought about slitting their throats or cutting out their hearts but in the end that would have been messy.'

The Unknown looked across at Hirad. He was assessing them like he might assess a selection of cuts of meat for his table. There was no remorse or regret in his stance or expression. In his mind they had deserved death and so they had died. It made the moral conversation he was about to have completely redundant.

'This isn't what we agreed,' said The Unknown, changing tack.

'We agreed we'd guard them,' said Hirad. 'If it makes you feel better, imagine they both broke their spells and tried to run or something. Do you think we should move them before Erienne wakes?'

'Or Denser.'

'Denser is already awake,' said Denser.

'Oh dear,' said The Unknown to himself, hearing the dark mage get up and walk towards them.

'What's the—'

'Denser, I think you'll need to consider the larger picture,' said The Unknown.

Denser was standing to Hirad's right, his face darkening with fury.

'What the fuck has happened here?' He gestured at the bodies, plainly unable quite to convince himself about what he was looking at. Hirad filled it in for him.

'I killed them, Denser. What does it look like?'

Denser took a pace back, his mouth falling open in almost comical reaction. He stared at Hirad, naked disbelief in his face slowly dissolving into incredulity. Hirad wasn't looking in his direction. The Unknown knew what was coming. All he could do was be ready to step in if it got out of hand.

'They were my friends,' began Denser.

'Not for a long time,' said Hirad. 'They didn't come here to ask after your health.'

Denser gestured down. 'But how could you? They were no threat.'

Finally, Hirad turned to meet his gaze. 'No threat? Are you taking the piss? These two came here to kill us. They walked in invisible and if they could have stuck a knife in all of us, they would. And then taken Erienne. Well, now they can't.'

'It wasn't your decision to make,' said Denser. 'We're a team, as you're so very fond of telling me.' He was about to say more but bit his tongue.

'And one that I will not see torn up by assassins. I can't believe you would consider any other option for these bastards.'

'But it wasn't what we had agreed. There was a decision to be made and it might not have been this one.' Denser knelt by Takyn, reached out a hand but didn't touch him.

'And what was your idea, Xetesk-man?' Hirad's voice was getting louder. 'Ask them not to do it again and send them on their way?'

Denser surged back upright and went nose to nose with Hirad. 'We could have disarmed them, turned them loose with no chance of finding us again. Made them safe as far as we were concerned.'

'Well they're safe now, aren't they?' Hirad didn't flinch. 'Don't see them giving us too many problems now, do you?'

'You've murdered them, you bastard!' shouted Denser, shoving Hirad hard in the chest, sending him stumbling back. 'In cold blood. Where's your precious Code now? You're just a murderer.'

Hirad tensed and advanced on Denser menacingly.

'Hirad,' warned The Unknown.

The barbarian ignored him. 'You think they'd go and not come after us? Do you? You can't be that stupid. They are assassins. They have a target and that target is us. Xetesk is only a few hours behind us and Julatsa does not have walls. Why should we risk it, Denser? We cannot afford to be picked off and I will not risk any of us dying because you knew someone a few years back. Ilkar's memory is what matters, and you'd better start seeing it.' He let his voice drop to a harsh whisper before continuing. 'And don't you ever quote the Code at me again, Denser. This war is ongoing. It is only murder outside the rules of war.'

'They were our prisoners,' said Denser.

'They were trying to kill us. I have just removed that threat. What does it matter how it was done? If we'd killed them on sight last night would that have made it better for you, Denser?'

'It mattered to me,' said Denser. 'This is a step down a path we should not be treading. Back off it.'

'Don't come over all moral on me, Denser. I did what had to be done.' He gestured around at the camp. Darrick, Thraun and Erienne were all awake now. 'And though they might not admit it to you openly, they all know this had to happen. You should be thanking me for keeping your conscience clear.'

Denser gagged on his reply and The Unknown saw his self-control snap. He bunched a fist, ready to strike but found his arm caught by Thraun. The shapechanger looked at him for a moment.

'His knife was above you, Denser,' he said.

Hirad smiled. 'Right. You'd have been and would still be the first. Some friend, eh, Denser?' He turned away. 'I'm going to saddle the horses. And if you don't like the path I'm going down, feel free to ride in a different direction.'

The calm over Julatsa was unsettling everyone in the college. Pheone had been restless on the college walls most of the day, and much of the night before. The latest failure in the mana focus had been prolonged and deeply disturbing. And when mana did return, they had stood around the Heart pit, tuned in to the mana focus and felt chill at what they had seen. The shadow across the Heart had deepened. Fingers of dark grey spread from it and the vibrant yellow they sought was dull and tired, suffocating beneath the cloying blanket.

But now, more than ever, they couldn't afford to be fearful. They had to invest as much as they could in strengthening walls and gates. The spells that bound the stone and wood had to be strong or they would be torn apart by the Xeteskian mages who would not just outnumber them but would be operating without risk once any attempt to raise the Heart got under way.

They had found, though, those few Julatsan mages inside the College, that their mana stamina levels were low; that forcing spell structures and lattices to coalesce was terribly difficult; and that for castings of any complexity, two of them now had to do the job of one. Progress had been slow and demoralising.

Having orchestrated wall bindings throughout the morning, Pheone had been spent not long after taking lunch. The expressions of those around her reflected her own inescapable feelings that whatever they did, it simply would not be enough. That no matter how many elven mages came through their gates, they would fall short of the number needed to raise the Heart.

Before saying anything she might regret, she had returned to the walls. Despite her weariness she had walked their circumference again and again, trying to gain some hope or comfort from the warmth of the day and the irrepressible goodwill of birds whose songs gloried in the vitality of spring.

It hadn't worked. Outside in the streets, the quiet was ominous. So many had left Julatsa, for the Gods alone knew where, leaving behind a void where the babble of life should have been. She could hear the odd cart rattling over the streets and smelled bread baking and forges working. But the sense of community was gone. The mayor might have been right to urge his citizens not to fight but in effectively driving so many from their homes in fear, he had ripped the soul from the city.

And now, all Pheone and her pitiful band could do was wait to see who arrived first. If it wasn't the elves, everything was lost anyway and, frankly, she wasn't sure if she'd have the energy to fight in that case. If she was true to herself, she wasn't sure she had fight in her in any case. The thought that they might walk away had crossed her mind but every time it did, she was reminded of the appalling emptiness of life without the ability to touch mana. It gave her the reason to carry on.

Below her in the college, the work went on. Commander Vale had brought his guard into the college and the militia had joined them once their families were gone and their houses boarded over. He had been vocal in his condemnation of the Mayor and felt that this betrayal of Julatsa left him, Vale, with no alternative but to pledge his allegiance to the college alone.

It was a grand gesture and one that had brought back some much-needed but temporary belief. The truth of the matter, however, was in the numbers. Not many more than a hundred armed men had come to stand in defence and less than half had any experience of battle at all. Xetesk was bringing hardened soldiers.

She heard someone call her name and looked around. Ahead of her on the west side of the parapet, he was waving at her. She waved back and set off towards them, seeing a couple of others gather and look away out. Closer to, she could see it was Geren. He seemed to be everywhere and his belief had never wavered. He had redeemed himself completely; transformed from the shambling ingrate who had walked through the gates a year before, and he was a lesson for them all.

'I hope this is good news,' she said as she joined them.

'That remains to be seen,' said Geren. 'Look.'

He pointed out into the cloudless sky. Beyond his finger, Pheone could see the dark mass of the Blackthorne Mountains and the dazzle of sunlight reflecting off the Triverne Inlet way distant and sending up a glittering haze.

'What?' She spread her hands. 'It's a beautiful scene, I'll grant you but—'

'Look higher, above the mountains.'

She looked. A V formation of geese or ducks was high in the sky. She tracked them for a while and saw them scatter and dive quite suddenly. A black dot was left in the space where they had been, growing larger very quickly.

'What is it?' she asked.

'It's quite simple,' said Lempaar. The old elf had joined them unannounced. 'It's a dragon.'

Pheone had no idea how to react to that statement. Out of everything she might have expected to hear, it was the least likely. But it made a kind of bizarre sense nonetheless and the connections were not long forming in her mind. She supposed also, that there were few other things of such apparent size that it could possibly have been. At least it wasn't a completely ridiculous suggestion. There were dragons somewhere south, she'd heard. And The Raven were friends to them. Ilkar had spoken of it before and had clearly been moved by his encounter with them.

She felt fear and anticipation at once and felt her pulse quicken and her throat go dry.

Before long they could all make it out and Pheone sensed panic spread from them and whistle through the college. People were shouting, some making for buildings they thought might be safe. She heard the frightened whinnies of horses and then the question to which she had no answer.

'What will we do?'

'There's nothing we can do. It could be friendly and if it is, we should . . . I don't know, welcome it? If not, I fear we aren't enough to stop it killing us all. If I were you, I'd be praying to whatever God you think might help you best.'

She knew that was pathetic but the faces of those by her told her they had no better solution. So they watched as the extraordinary beast flew closer. Seeing its shadow cross the city, Pheone got an early impression of the sheer size of it. Its great wings stroked the air, propelling its huge but graceful body through the air. Its head, on the end of a long, ridged neck held a mouth that could swallow a horse whole. Its rear legs, carrying powerful taloned feet, were swept back under its bulk.

Those feet swung forwards as it closed. Pheone saw its startling blue eyes searching for a landing place. The wings beat back. She felt the breeze through her hair and across her face, breathed foul air and heard the whump of the sails as they applied a braking force. The sight almost blinded her to her duty but in the last moments, she turned her attention to those below and yelled out.

'Do nothing! Don't attack, keep your distance.'

She should have laughed. As if anyone would do anything else. Instead she felt a nervousness clamp around her body and realised she was shaking. She watched the dragon sweep once around the college and land with a shuddering impact in the centre of the courtyard and knew she was the one who had to approach it.

'Stay here,' she told them unnecessarily.

She made her way to the nearest stairs, seeing the dragon fold its wings back and wobble slightly as it gathered itself to settle down. Descending the stairs, it was lost from sight and she hurried the last flight and trotted through the buildings surrounding the courtyard, waving people to adopt a calm she did not feel herself.

Emerging from between a lecture theatre and the infirmary, she paused for a few moments, trying to take in what she saw. Ilkar had told her they were awesome but he hadn't prepared her for this. She was looking at its flank, the sunlight glinting off the few golden scales that sat within a duller mass. Its back arched high, three or four times her height, and its tail curled back along almost the entire length of its body.

She started moving again, open-mouthed, letting her eyes track down the long neck that had a girth wider than most trees she had seen. Temporarily, the head was lost to sight. The dragon was looking into the Heart pit. She approached in a wide circle, not wanting to get too close, aiming for the edge of the pit. It seemed to sense her and the neck withdrew for what seemed like an age, the head appearing above the lip of the pit, one eye fixing on her. She stopped moving immediately.

It did not. The head came towards her, the breath firing from its nostrils, blowing sour air into her face. She swallowed hard, helpless as it came on. The mouth opened to reveal its fangs, stretching wide, saliva dripping to the ground. It stopped maybe three feet from her, its eye level with her head, its snout pointing past her. It considered her for a moment.

'I feel the echoes of friendship here,' it said. Its voice boomed across the corridor and every other noise stilled instantly. 'This is Julatsa.'

Pheone didn't know how to respond. The sheer scale of the animal she faced was completely overwhelming. So long thought to be mythical but always there had been rumours that Masters in her college knew more than they would say. That some were friends or servants to dragons. Presumably that was what this one meant.

'Yes,' she said, her voice so small next to the dragon's. 'I . . .'

'You have trouble believing I exist, or at least that we are talking,' said the dragon. 'I am, after all, just an animal.'

'No,' she said quickly. 'Not at all. I just feel. You know.'

She assumed it was laughing, or whatever passed for laughter for a dragon. Gouts of air blew into her and a gravelly noise emanated from its throat.

'Do not worry, frail human, it has all been explained to me by my Dragonene who is not as shy of speaking. At least, not now.'

Pheone gripped herself mentally. She knew every eye was on her and that full panic was just a heartbeat away should the conversation go astray. She asked what she had to ask.

'Why have you come here?' she asked.

'Let us begin by exchanging our names,' said the dragon. 'I understand humans do that vocally. I am Sha-Kaan, Great Kaan of my Brood.'

'Pheone,' she replied and found herself proffering her hand. She snatched it back, feeling very stupid but the dragon didn't seem to have noticed.

'I am pleased to make your acquaintance, Pheone of Julatsa,' said Sha-Kaan. 'You are a troubled people but the fact you remain here says a great deal about your courage. The Brood Kaan has profited from it over the years.'

'There is war coming here,' said Pheone, experiencing a modicum of relaxation. 'Will you . . . I mean, have you come to help?'

'Ahhh.' Sha-Kaan's exhale was full of regret. 'I wish it were so. I have friends that travel here and I would prefer to help them and you. But I am weak. So I await them because they have the knowledge to send me home.'

Pheone hadn't expected such an admission from a creature so obviously powerful. But there was something in the eye that had not left hers that told her of troubles at which she could only guess.

'I am sorry to hear that,' she said, heartfelt. 'Is there anything we can get to make you comfortable? Food or drink perhaps?'

'No, Pheone, thank you for your concern. I will rest until dark and then hunt my food. The lands near your mountain range, the Blackthornes, are quite plentiful.'

'Did you not fly over the college lands?' she asked.

'I was told there are enemies who should not see me in case it sped their progress. I saw none of them, nor was I seen. I flew very high.' He shifted his hind legs, Pheone feeling the ground vibrating beneath her feet. 'Now, tell me. Why is it that deep under the earth your essence is failing you?'

Pheone sighed and explained as well as she was able, the shadow over the Heart of Julatsa.

It was well after dark but the elves had not stopped running. The lights of Julatsa glowed brighter as they neared and the memories of the Al-Arynaar mages were fresh enough to keep their route sure. There had been attacks the previous night. Four mages were dead and only the intervention of a Claw-Bound panther had stopped further damage.

The camp had woken angry and vulnerable and the consensus was for a long run all the way to the relative safety of the college. Auum had returned from his attacks along the rear of the enemy line and had forced the Xeteskians to slow still further, their lookouts now scant yards from their wagons and their caution maximised. It would buy the allies a few more hours but nothing would prevent them from reaching the city.

Rebraal ran at the head of the elven column, ClawBound spread in an arc ahead, the active TaiGethen cells sweeping rear and along the flanks. He was sure they had outpaced any enemy and the familiars had kept their distance since that first skirmish but they had to be certain. He was relieved the demons had not been aware of the loss of magic in his ranks or they could have found themselves in serious trouble.

A few miles from the city, with the night full and dark, he had seen a shape climbing away from the ground and flying west. He presumed it to be the Kaan dragon of which Hirad often spoke. He quelled any anxieties by assuring his people it was friendly, his words helping him in equal measure.

He began to worry less than a mile from Julatsa. The Claw-Bound had reported seeing no one. No perimeter guard, no scouts looking for the enemy advance, no routine patrols on horseback. It was as if the city was at peace. The scents in the air, he was told, were of mass movement to the north and west but the ClawBound had not been free to investigate.

'Where are the defenders?' asked Auum, jogging easily beside him, Duele and Evunn ever his shadows.

'I don't know,' said Rebraal. 'We must be prepared that the situation here is more grave than we thought.'

'Or perhaps they expect us to help them though they are unwilling to help themselves.'

'We will see.'

'Pray to Yniss it is not so,' said Auum. 'We are not numerous enough alone and the will must be there or they will crumble under attack.'

The streets were deserted too. Houses were locked and empty. Street lanterns were lit but they illuminated empty cobbles and darkened windows. The atmosphere might have been fitting for a city sleeping in the hours before dawn but this one should have been crawling with those desperate to see that Xetesk did not invade without a struggle.

Rebraal knew little about city defence but surely every main junction should have been defended. Guards should have been walking or riding every lane, thoroughfare and back alley. The people of Julatsa should have been too fearful of invasion to sleep. Auum expressed the fear that he held.

'They have gone,' he said.

And it seemed, to a large extent, that they had. The only concentration of lights in the city was at the college and there they burned bright. During their run from the first abandoned perimeter post to the closed college gates they saw fewer than ten people. And all of them just stood and watched the elves pass. No one challenged them, no one raised a hand in welcome or a fist in threat. It was as if they didn't care.

Rebraal could feel Auum's contempt while they waited to be admitted to the college.

'If you believe, you fight,' he said.

'It isn't the college,' said Rebraal. 'It is the city around it.'

'They are part of the same,' he said. 'Yet their history means nothing to them, it seems. That is what makes them trivial, and takes them away from their Gods, whoever those nameless ones are. And you ask why it is I dislike humans?' He checked himself. 'Most humans.'

The gates opened and the elves ran in, gathering in the courtyard. Coming towards them were mages from the college accompanied by Hirad and The Unknown Warrior. The barbarian looked angry, The Unknown weary.

'Glad you made it,' said Hirad.

'You don't appear so,' said Rebraal, smiling.

'This place is a complete bloody shambles,' he said. 'Sorry, Pheone, this is Rebraal and Auum. People who might save your lives. Pheone runs the college.'

The woman was so relieved to see them she was on the verge of tears.

'I cannot tell you how much it means to us that you're here,' she said. 'Please, let my people show you all to accommodations. We need to speak to your lead mages as soon as we can. There is much to be done both to the defence of the college and in preparation to raise the Heart. I don't think we have much time.'

Rebraal translated to Auum who turned away and began issuing instructions, his voice full of the irritation he was feeling.

'Our lead mages will wait here to talk to you,' said Rebraal. 'And you are right, we don't have much time.' He turned to The Unknown. 'When did you get here?'

'Late this afternoon, replied The Unknown. 'How far behind are they?'

'They'll be here well before dusk tomorrow. What is going on in the city? Why is there no guard?'

'Because all that are left are inside here already,' growled Hirad. 'It is the most pitiful expression of loyalty I have ever seen. I'm almost glad Ilkar isn't here to see it.'

'It's worse than that,' said The Unknown. 'Until we got here, the gates had been left open. If Xetesk sent assassins here when the siege broke, they could already be here in hiding.'

'Shambles,' muttered Hirad.

Rebraal nodded. 'The TaiGethen and ClawBound will sweep the college.'

Hirad turned to Pheone. 'And make sure everyone keeps out of their way and treats them with the respect they deserve. Someone's here trying to rescue your college, even if your city folk aren't.'

'I know, Hirad,' said Pheone. 'I share your frustration, believe me.'

'He does,' said The Unknown. 'But your council have struck

the biggest blow yet against their own way of life. Forgive us for feeling as we do when we come to help.' He turned to Rebraal, wincing and putting a hand to his hip. 'As soon as you can, bring Auum to the refectory. It's the building over there.' He nodded to a low structure whose doors were open to spill light on to the courtyard. 'We have the guard commander in there. He seems bright enough. We all need to talk and then we need to rest. Too many wounds from the catacombs are not healed enough.' He paused and chewed his lip and for the first time since he'd known him, Rebraal saw doubt in The Unknown's eyes.

'Let's just hope your Gods are behind us, eh? I think ours have run north with the Julatsans.'

Chapter 38

Pheone was up with the dawn the next morning feeling torn and unsure but strangely confident. For most of the college, optimism was the dominant feeling.

The arrival of the elves had galvanised the college effort. The extraordinary warriors, the painted TaiGethen, had moved like ghosts through the rooms and corridors in a sweep that left no hiding place. They, together with the mysterious and disturbing ClawBound, had established that there were no Xeteskian assassins in the college but it was more likely as the hours went by that these killers would be present in the city. So the gates remained closed and they scanned the skies ceaselessly.

The Raven, though, their effect had been amazing yet entirely predictable. Among the hundred and seventy or so mages, guards and militia, there was the undeniable feeling that they could no longer lose because The Raven never lost. And here they were, fighting for the college. Pheone couldn't help but feel the same. Something about their air of confidence when they rode into the place, their bearing and their authority. When The Unknown Warrior spoke, you listened. When Hirad looked at you, you tried harder. When Darrick explained a better way to work in defensive teams, it seemed obvious.

But she had seen them later on that night, talking with Commander Vale, and it left her wondering whether this might not end up being their graveyard. There were three of the six over whom she had serious concerns that she dare not voice. Darrick, who had been weakened by a deep wound on his hip and who had plainly suffered through their three days of hard riding. Hirad, who, though he would never admit it, was barely free enough to fight, having sustained a sprained wrist and a damaged chest that restricted the movement of his upper body. Both clearly pained him. And, of course, Erienne. She had heard so much about Erienne and now she knew what the poor woman carried. There had been so much grief in her life, so much pressure and now she was alone with a magical force she could have no real idea how to properly control. That she was at the table at all was impressive enough. But her temper was short and she was isolated, as if continually biting back something that wasn't her. Something that might escape if she invoked its name.

Pheone wasn't sure whether the rest of them could see the trouble she was in and the energy she consumed in just trying to remain herself. Pheone could but, like them, could offer no assistance. Even so, she couldn't shift the irrational thought that, once the fighting started, they would prevail. And if that belief was shared throughout the college, then The Raven would already have had the desired effect and for that she was eternally grateful.

After breakfast, with the elves still resting for the attempt on the Heart that would take place after midday, she climbed up to the walls as was her habit, finding Hirad standing there, looking south. He wasn't the only one up there. It was another fine day and away past the boundaries of the city, anyone who cared to look could see the cloud of dust that signified the approaching Xeteskians. All of them had their fingers crossed that more allies, particularly Izack and Blackthorne, arrived before their enemies.

'How far do you think they are away?' Pheone asked, coming to his shoulder.

He turned and smiled at her. 'Hard to say. Half a day, perhaps a little more. Like Rebraal said, they'll be here before nightfall. I reckon they'll posture for the rest of the day, try and get us to surrender and then attack at dawn. But they'll send in assassins and familiars if they can before then.'

'It's not a happy picture.'

'No,' he agreed. 'But we have to know what we face. No sense in hiding, is there?'

'I guess not.'

There was a long silence. Although the college walls were taller than most buildings in Julatsa, their vision of the open spaces beyond the city was still obscured by rises in the ground. When and if Izack did appear, they'd have little warning.

'Pheone, I'm sorry about last night. It had been a long day.'
It was an apology she hadn't expected and struggled to accept easily.

'It's fine,' she said. 'We were making mistakes.'

Hirad shook his head. 'It's not that, really it isn't.' He paused. 'I miss him. Every day when I don't hear his voice it adds to my anger and I can't let it go. You understand. It's funny. When I didn't see him for years, it hardly mattered because I knew he was fine. Now he's gone and that time seems such a waste.'

Pheone couldn't find the words to say anything meaningful, just nodded her head, feeling vaguely embarrassed that this man, who looked so uncompromisingly tough and had seen so much death, would speak to her like this.

'He's why I'm here you know,' Hirad continued. 'Ilkar wanted us to come and help raise the Heart but it's gone beyond that now. I can't help with that. But I can strike back at every one of those bastards coming here. They are all to blame.'

The warmth and sadness in his voice had vanished, to be replaced by something entirely cold. Pheone leaned away a little, desperate to change the subject.

'But we will do it. Raise the Heart, I mean. Even if it's only a temporary victory it'll be for the memory of Ilkar, won't it?'

'It won't be temporary,' said Hirad and he turned and stared at her, his eyes burning into hers, not allowing her to look away. 'Because we aren't going to lose.'

'I know,' Pheone said, hoping she sounded as convincing as he did.

'I hope you do because belief is everything.'

Hirad had none of the charisma of The Unknown Warrior but he had a heart so proud and full. No wonder Ilkar always spoke of him as the man who made The Raven live. At least now she could see exactly what he had meant.

'Where's Sha-Kaan?'

Hirad chuckled, his eyes losing their penetration and his expression softening. 'Yes, he told me he'd made your acquaintance yesterday. Don't be scared of him. He actually quite likes humans these days, I think.'

'That's a relief.'

'He'll be in the Blackthorne Mountains, resting. Some cool

cave or other that reminds him of his homeland, I expect. When we're ready to send him home, I'll call him. He's excited about it. Can't say I blame him. Sometimes I wish I was going with him.'

'Why don't you?'

'Because I won't betray Ilkar's memory,' he said.

'Do they live in caves, then, dragons?' Could it really be like all the stories she'd read?

'No. They have places called Chouls where they go to rest with their Brood brothers sometimes. They're a bit like caves. Mostly though, Sha-Kaan's land is hot and humid and they live in buildings built by their servant race. I'll explain it all to you one day. Maybe take you there.'

Pheone couldn't fathom Hirad at all. That was an offer no one could turn down and so casually made like you might buy a round of drinks. From anyone else, it would surely have sounded boastful, flaunting of influence. From Hirad, not so. And he clearly meant it.

'Could you do that?'

'Why not?'

'I'd love to.'

'Good. Another reason why you need to believe we can win, isn't it?' Hirad stretched his arms and a flicker of pain passed across his face. 'Right, I've got to go and have some balm put on this damn chest.' He paused at the top of the stairs, massaging his strapped wrist. 'Thanks for being with him the time you were,' he said. 'You meant a lot to him, made him very happy. I won't forget that.'

She watched him go and the tears began to fall.

'Neither will I,' she whispered.

All things considered, it couldn't have gone much better for Dystran. He had to put aside the debacle in his catacombs because, as Ranyl had pointed out, something always goes wrong, but everything else was working out perfectly.

With few real alarms, his forces were closing in on Julatsa, where they would crush the college, the remnants of the allied forces and the elves. They would take The Raven apart, capture Erienne and the elven texts, and be effectively unopposed as rulers of Balaia.

There was no way Lystern or Dordover could threaten

him now and it really just came down to how long he left them alone before crushing them too. How both cities must have wished they had built walls. How both must have wished for a less ethical approach to magic. Vuldaroq alone saw the mistake his college had been making but he wouldn't have time to put it right. They would all pay for it now. At Dystran's leisure.

He should have been concerned that the mages and guards he had dispatched after the few hundred allied men left him a little exposed to a concerted attack but frankly, there was none coming. His scouts had had the run of the mage lands for three days and nothing was heading his way.

The pathetic few tents that represented the army of the righteous, as that fool Selik had dubbed it, became fewer every day as more and more realised the Black Wings weren't coming back. He'd even recalled his spies from the encampment. It was a waste of resource.

He had spent a great deal of his time in the Laryon hub, now that the place had been cleaned. He and his newly assembled research team checked and rechecked their calculations. In a day, a spell would be available to them and for a prolonged period. He had ordered his dimensional casters not to strike until the allies were within sight of Julatsa. He wanted the enemy to see their comrades destroyed if he could.

It was just a shame that the BlueStorm could not be cast. That particular conjunction would not happen again for some time. Still, the alternative would be just as devastating, if less visually impressive.

Dystran foresaw the end of the war in a maximum of three days from now. Standing on his balcony before flying across to see Ranyl, he reminded himself to give some thought to the order of the country once he had assessed his own home strength. It was going to be a big task, ruling Balaia, but, as the only magical force left, he would be uniquely positioned to be its first ever sole leader.

It was a frightening thought, he had to admit. He cast ShadowWings and drifted slowly across the space to Ranyl's tower. One day soon, he would land and find the old man dead. The one man he needed more than any of them.

He hoped today was not that day.

*

The refectory was empty barring one table in its centre. Across it were spread maps of the city and hastily drawn sketches of the surrounding mage lands. Though they had all begun sitting down, all but Erienne were standing now, intent on the plans. Izack had arrived shortly before midday and the meeting had taken place immediately, with Xetesk's forces just a few hours behind and marching with great confidence. Izack stood with The Raven, Commander Vale, Pheone, Rebraal and Auum.

'So you're saying that Blackthorne won't be here before Xetesk?' asked The Unknown.

'Yes,' said Izack. 'Right now, he's holed up here.' He tapped the map of the land between Xetesk and Julatsa. 'He's made the right decision. He's got about fifty with him but they are in no condition to fight. Better he rests a day and attacks the rear when he can. We'll be in contact so I can direct him.'

'I'll trust your judgement,' said The Unknown.

'On a brighter note, we know that the allies have moved from their siege positions south and west of Xetesk and are coming to reinforce. They'll be here a day after the Xeteskians, all things being equal. Now Xetesk will know they are coming so they'll be pushing very hard when they attack which, I think, we all believe will be tomorrow. But it could be late this afternoon, so we have to be prepared. Agreed?'

There were nods around the table.

'Right, General.' The Unknown winked at Darrick. 'Since you're a wanted man but Izack doesn't seem too keen on taking you into custody and his men have searched high and low but can't find you, perhaps you'd like to repeat what you suggested to us last night.'

'Be glad to,' said Darrick. 'All right by you, Commander Izack?'

'I'll only arrest you if I don't like the plan.'

Darrick almost smiled. 'All right. Well, it doesn't take much to see that the numbers don't add up. This college is too big for us to hope to defend the walls from the inside. We simply don't have the forces. Not only that, not all of our skills suit defence of this nature so I'm advocating a split approach.

'You, Izack, need to hide the cavalry outside of the college. There are good stabling facilities to the north of the central market and there's little reason to believe you'll be found. Even so, we are going to do a general sweep of some areas with

ClawBound, should they agree, before the Xeteskians arrive in force.

'Second, the TaiGethen are masters of the hit-and-run, and of close-quarters hand-to-hand. So, I'd like most of them outside these walls. Same goes for the ClawBound. This leaves us with all the mage strength, the Al-Arynaar archers and old warriors like Hirad to keep the walls and gates clear. We're presuming they'll try and breach the walls with spells, because they won't have siege ladders or the time to build them, and roping up is suicide. What we have to do is stop those spells and I'll go into how to do that in a moment. Remember, they have to get in fast or risk us not just raising the Heart but being rested as well.'

He stopped and poured himself a goblet of water.

'Are you all right with this, Izack, or do I consider myself under arrest?'

Izack shrugged. 'No General, you remain a free man. It's the plan I would have suggested. My only comment so far is that we must be mindful of Chandyr's cavalry. He has kept it out of sight during the march so he may be anticipating this sort of move.'

'It's a fair point. Now, I'm assuming, Pheone, that the investiture of spells in the walls and doors is healthy?'

'It's solid. We've been lucky. The problem we could face at any time, mind you, is the inability to reinforce should the mana focus fail. We just can't rely on it.'

'Also, if there has been an attempt to raise the Heart, we'll have a lot of tired mages and little spell capability,' said Denser. 'Don't forget that.'

Darrick paused and clacked his tongue. 'When are you attempting the rising?'

'Any time,' said Pheone. 'We've been ready since mid-morning now that everyone has been reminded of the casting.'

'So why has Chandyr not pushed on faster, I wonder,' said Darrick. 'If he knew you could act almost immediately.'

'I very much doubt he did,' said Pheone. 'Look, all colleges have castings for this eventuality but only in Julatsa is it woven into the basic lore and structural teachings from a student's first day. In Xetesk, they'd have to study from scratch, isn't that right, Denser?'

Denser nodded.

'But here it's different. It's a question of history. When

Julatsa was founded, we were under threat for years. So the ability to bury and raise the Heart had to be at the middle of everything, just in case. And now it's our way of getting a student started. The construct is very basic. The energy we have to pour in is not.'

'Good,' said Darrick. 'And how long does it take?'

'Under normal circumstances, no time at all. Today? I'd hate to guess.'

'Then if you don't mind taking an order from an ex-general, go and start now. Maximum time, maximum rest.'

'You don't need me?'

'Not that much,' said Hirad. 'Get on and good luck.'

Pheone nodded and left to calls for good fortune from around the table.

'Right,' said Darrick. 'Let's wrap this up and go and watch. It fascinates me.'

'Hold on,' said Hirad. 'We're forgetting one thing on the magic front, before you go on.'

'Which is?' asked The Unknown.

'Sha-Kaan,' said Hirad. 'There's a casting to get him home. That has to happen before the battle. Denser?'

Denser turned a carefully neutral face to him. 'Why must it be done before the battle?'

'Because we can't take the risk of dying and leaving him stranded here. Not now we have the knowledge.'

'Old friends dying is a risk of war, as you so ably pointed out yesterday morning,' said Denser. 'I need my stamina to protect this college. He'll have to wait.'

Hirad stood quietly for a moment, Izack watching his face. It betrayed no anger though his body had tensed.

'That isn't acceptable,' said Hirad.

'Rough justice,' said Denser. 'If he can wait six years, he can wait another few days.'

Hirad thumped the table. 'No!' he shouted. 'He has to go now, today. I spoke to him last night. The flight nearly killed him. He has so little left that a few Xeteskian mages could take him down. Think, Denser. And do the right thing.'

'Hark at you, Coldheart.' Denser shook his head. 'The right thing is what you think at the time, isn't it? Well, no dice. This time, I'm in the chair and I decide. And there's nothing you can do about it.'

Hirad breathed in deeply. His shoulder muscles bunched then relaxed and he held up a hand. 'Denser, please. If there is one innocent in all this it is Sha-Kaan. Gods, he was trapped here saving us and now he has to go home. He's not a part of this war. If you want to take out your anger about what I did, then do it on me. Don't use him as a pawn. He deserves better than that from all of us. He deserves to live and if you don't send him back now, you might be condemning him to death. Please, Denser.'

Denser looked at Hirad askance and then turned fully to face him. 'You know, Hirad, I'm genuinely impressed by that. And I'll not often say that after hearing you talk. Look, let's get this meeting over with and I'll go and check the texts I took from the catacombs. If I'm right, it shouldn't take too long. All he needs from me is a line to follow, after all.'

Hirad beamed but then remembered himself and nodded solemnly.

'Thank you, Denser.'

Denser shrugged.

'And I'm sorry, all right?'

'Later, Hirad. Let's discuss it later.'

Hirad slapped the table. 'So, General, what's the big idea?'

Chapter 39

Erienne listened to them for as long as she could. Men standing round maps discussing the futures of other men. Who lived and who died being tossed around like an orange stolen by children in a market. She wondered if they ever actually stopped to think about what they were doing. That positioning that man there and that man there actually condemned one man and saved the other.

Probably, they didn't. And a part of her didn't blame them because they made the same decisions about themselves and lived or died by them. But the larger part thought of them as playing gods because they mentioned her name and assumed her compliance without knowing any longer what she was capable of doing. They remembered her Dordovan magical skills. She didn't think she could use them any more.

She tried to tell them but they wouldn't listen. All they could find to say was that they would help her, that they would be there and that they were The Raven. So instead she walked out into the sunlight to watch the attempt to raise the Heart. She didn't feel much of the warmth of the sun and everything seemed a little detached. She knew why. The One was probing her senses, keeping her away from the people she needed in any way it could. It was trying to deprive her of her humanity. Her hearing, her sight and her touch all seemed to be under attack.

Erienne watched the elven and Julatsan mages gather around the Heart. Almost two hundred of them in two concentric rings coming no nearer than forty feet. Though she might not be able to feel the warmth of the sun, she could certainly sense the atmosphere. She had never known one so tense around a casting. They should all have been confident. Instead, they feared a dropout of the mana focus, a darkening of the shadow. It would be catastrophic.

Pheone stood next to Dila'heth, the elf relaying the human's instructions. A thought clear as spring water came to Erienne's mind. She probed the Heart of Julatsa. The sight jerked her back to herself. She should not have been able to view the mana with such clarity, almost as if she were Julatsan herself. Another thought. Of course, she was every mage now. Magic was just one element. For her it was no longer split along the lines of college and lore.

Feeling an almost voyeuristic excitement, Erienne tuned back into the Julatsan mana spectrum and watched, expanding her viewpoint to take in the mages congregated around the Heart pit.

The Heart itself exhibited all the signs of a mortally sick organ. It pulsed rather than flowed at its deepest level, sending vibrations into the flow around it. Its energy was low, constricted by the shadow that sought to crush the life from it altogether.

What should have been a brilliant yellow oval, imbuing every Julatsan mage, was in reality a stuttering tarnished teardrop. The desperation to raise the Heart was all too easy to understand. It had to be returned to its exact previous position to stop it deteriorating further. Like a sundial partially hidden in shadow, it had to be moved to where its effect could be maximised. And then enough Julatsan mages had to be trained to build its strength. Pheone had asked her opinion on Geren's theory. She had thought him almost certainly right. That meant raising the Heart was only one step on a long trail back to strength.

Erienne noted with great interest, the effect of the mana flow on the elemental power streams about it. The pure magical force dragged them into similar shapes, upsetting their own rhythm. The free energy of the air and earth around the Heart were weak in its presence and she could feel the solidity of the buildings surrounding the courtyard.

The combination of the elements was so potent. Beguiling almost. She knew she could draw on any of it, all of it. That the failure of all the colleges would not stop her practising magic. She could be the only mage, giving true title to the name of her magic. One.

Erienne clamped down on the thought and felt the pressure of the One entity ease. She fought her breathing back to near normal and refocused, seeing the structure for the raise begin to form.

Like so many core castings, the structure was inherently simple. To Erienne, it looked like nothing more than an eight-sided splint. Each panel of the splint was linked to those adjacent by cords of pulsating mana and inside it, there were as many links into the Heart itself as there were mages to cast the spell.

All of these links were mirrored by poles of mana on the outside of the splint, one representing each mind. The formation was quick and without error, each mage feeding in as much energy as the next to keep the balance perfect.

When it was done, they paused. Erienne heard Pheone issue a series of quick commands, tidying up a slightly tattered edge here, filling in a striation in one of the splint panels there. When Pheone was finished teasing at the few imperfections, they waited again, all watching the dull-coloured but powerful shape, making sure it was settled.

Now it got tricky. Slowly, on a single command, all the mages tensed their minds in unison, clenching their fists for emphasis and raising their arms gradually as their minds gripped, dragging the Heart upwards, agonisingly slowly. But move it did. Inching upwards, the mages taking the strain.

Erienne sampled their minds, felt the draining effects of the expense of such levels of energy. So much poured in to keep the shape true through the shadow that covered everything they did. She could see the delicacy of their operation. Every mage had to push at precisely the same rate, the balance had to remain perfect. Each was responsible for making sure their rate of input placed no lateral strain on the structure. And where they did, Pheone linked in, cajoling or smoothing, evening the flow. She was a natural.

Erienne felt a twinge in the elemental forces surrounding the Heart and focused in. There, buried deep within the stone of the building that housed the Heart, and that they raised along with this most vital of mana structures, was a mote of darkness.

She could see the mass of the energy from the earth, air and stone spiralling in support, dragged upwards by the intensity of the mana and mimicking the shape of the sheath. But there was a blemish and it was fast infecting the point at the base of the Heart.

She couldn't tell whether it was a coincidence or a direct result of the casting but it was happening all the same. The swallowhole in the elemental energy expanded quickly, soaking up into the Heart, distending its shape fractionally at first but then faster and faster. It was enough to begin a chain reaction, the Heart darkening, deep shadow consuming its already dull colour. And all the time around Erienne, the mages continued to inch the Heart and its surrounds towards the surface.

They seemed oblivious, they were oblivious. The focus was failing and none of them had noticed. For a heartbeat, panic gripped Erienne and she considered trying to absorb the black hole in the elemental energies, cover the vortex that was destroying the focus. But a beat later, she knew she could not. Dark lines pulled and shadows thickened over the surface of Julatsa's Heart.

And still they lifted it, their minds so concentrated on the splint and its coherence, and on the stamina they were having to feed in that the drain on them was escaping their attention. Their minds were linked as one to the construct, their combined force stopping them sensing what any one individual would see instantly.

There was nothing Erienne could do to slow the rate of the shadow's advance. At the base of the Heart, yellow was gone, replaced by grey and darkening every moment.

'Pheone,' she said, her voice loud, pitched to penetrate. 'Release the structure now. The focus is failing.'

'So close,' moaned the mage. 'We can do it.'

The spell had her, like it had them all.

'No,' barked Erienne. 'Trust me, listen to me. Abort the attempt now.'

'Nearly there, we have momentum.'

'Dammit!' spat Erienne. Without thinking, she reached out, harnessing the elemental energies surrounding the splint. They coalesced immediately into a hard edge. In the centre of the splint, darkness was flying along the length of the Heart. When it eclipsed it entirely, the splint would collapse violently, reversing its energy through every Julatsan mage mind. It would mean the end of the college.

Erienne had no time to think of the short-term pain she was

about to cause. She forced her mind to firm the edge still more, feeling the One entity surge painfully within her. Trying so hard to keep the stopper in its power, she whipped the edge through the poles of mana spiking the outside of the splint, releasing mage after mage as she sheered through them.

It was so easy, Julatsan magic so weak and unable to resist. The One edge flashed bright, sucking in the raw mana it freed, Erienne fighting to keep it sharp, imagining with increasing desperation a knife carving through water, up and down.

Quickly, with fewer and fewer mages feeding power into the splint, it began to sag, the Heart falling back down. From its apex, the raising construct unravelled, Erienne scything through the poles while the blackness gorged on the Heart. Abruptly, the spell collapsed and Erienne shut off the edge with the last of her energy. She opened her eyes and tried to pick out Pheone who was standing close by. The mage was blurred to her sight as she swayed on her feet.

Somewhere she could here people running. Elsewhere, shouts of anger and gasps of pain.

'What did you do?' demanded a voice. Pheone, she thought. Yes, definitely Pheone. 'I felt you. It had to be you. We were so close. What have you done?'

'Done?' she repeated, feeling her strength give way. 'Not much. Saved your college and the lot of you. That's all.'

She tottered and crumpled.

'How is she?' asked The Unknown.

Denser turned from Erienne's bed in the infirmary and shrugged.

'Hard to tell,' he said. 'She's not as bad as before. I think it's just the exertion but there's no sense from her yet.'

Denser stood and looked towards the doors. They were open, letting the mid-afternoon light and breeze into the spotlessly clean building. The warmth touched the four occupied beds of the fifty in the infirmary. Three elven mages had been injured when Erienne disrupted the Heart-raise attempt. Their damage was, like hers, difficult to assess, though for different reasons. Mind-damage from the backwash of a spell was always so.

'Come on,' he said, beginning to walk. 'I don't want to stay in here right now.'

'Stay with her, Denser,' said The Unknown. 'We can prepare without you.'

'It's all right,' he said. 'This place is just too full of memories. I'm having her moved to our rooms.'

The Unknown nodded. He felt it too. In fact he felt it all over the college. A battle site revisited. So much had been rebuilt since the Wesmen invasion and not a speck of blood remained. But the memories were still fresh. The infirmary had seen the results of the suffering on the walls and gates. And it was where Will Begman of The Raven had lost his fight for life. Thraun wouldn't go near the place. Not even for Erienne.

'She did save them, didn't she?' asked The Unknown.

'All of them,' said Denser. 'The mana-focus failure followed the same path as all the others, according to Pheone. They were lucky Erienne was watching.'

'And is the focus still gone?'

'Apparently not but it makes little difference. Every Julatsan and elven mage has gone to rest. None will cast again before tomorrow.'

'That could prove costly. We're liable to face familiars.'

Outside, the waiting was beginning to tell. The TaiGethen, ClawBound and Izack were all hidden around the city and the Mayor and entire city council were being watched. Darrick wasn't risking what he'd heard of their actions becoming out-right betrayal. The gates of the college were closed and the dust cloud signifying the approaching Xeteskian army was almost at the city borders.

Lookouts were spread around the college walls, with a heavy presence at the gatehouse where Darrick, Hirad and Thraun stood with the impressively determined Commander Vale. The Unknown and Denser headed in their direction, feeling the mood. The optimism of the morning was gone, replaced by a sombre introspection. Their best chance was already gone and the enemy was not even at their gates. The Heart remained buried and without spell protection they faced a force they could not stop with swords and arrows alone for long. A force that would be on them within the hour. And it wasn't the men that worried them the most. Enough familiars could make the difference if they were employed in the right way.

And as he walked up the steps of the gatehouse tower, a thought struck The Unknown hard.

'Are you feeling strong, Denser?'

Denser managed a smile. 'That thought has occurred to you too, has it?'

'Only just now.'

'Do you think Darrick overlooked it?'

'You'd think no, but even great generals are fallible.'

Not this one, though, Denser thought a short while later. At least, not this time.

'It isn't the plan I would have chosen,' Darrick said, 'but we have no choice. We do have some protection here. We can keep them on their toes for as long as we have arrows but that's as far as it goes. After all, there will be magical shielding though soldiers might not enjoy the same protection as the mages. It depends how many mages they have and how many the Xeteskian commander thinks he needs to knock over the walls. Everyone here is briefed to watch and move in the case of spell attack. Izack and Auum both have their targets. I had to leave the cavalry mages with Izack. He represents our best chance of winning this so long as he can deal with the Xeteskian horsemen.'

'And meanwhile, we just stand here as targets?' said Hirad.

'No, Hirad, you stand here and don't turn away. Strength for us, anxiety for those attacking us. That is why all The Raven are here. To be seen. Anyway, the more spells they waste on the walls, the better I like it for the time being. Assuming Pheone's assessment of the shielding is not too generous.'

'What about the ClawBound?' asked The Unknown.

'Well they're out there,' said Darrick. 'But since they don't really even like to speak to the TaiGethen, you can imagine how far I got. Anything they do is a bonus.'

'You know what the Xeteskians will do once they realise we have no spells, don't you?' said Denser.

Darrick nodded. 'It had not escaped my attention. I have grouped the Al-Arynaar archers and they are fast around the walls. Plus, Izack knows what to look for. Any conventionally shielded concentration of mages is a prime target.'

'And what if they make, say, four groups?' asked Hirad.

'They'll need twenty at least in any group-casting to do breaching damage,' said Darrick. 'I don't think they have enough strength to make four such groups.'

'Or you hope they don't.'

'Hirad, if there is only one variable in this battle, I will be very happy.'

'Whatever you say.'

'We're standing above the weak point now. We're where we need to be. This is where they will come.'

And they did, within the hour as predicted. Marching through the streets, cavalry outriders keeping them ordered. The noise of their approach wasn't triumphal. None of the few citizens who looked on from upper windows waved, cheered or quailed. There were no songs, no taunts, no jeers. Every side had lost too much to make any assumptions. But there was purpose and there was belief. The Unknown worried about that. The moments to come would be critical.

The college of Julatsa was an island surrounded by a sea of cobbles. Heading off the square were roads to the central market, the grain store, the merchant quarter and the north tenements. Without a fuss, the Xeteskians surrounded their goal under the watchful eyes of The Raven, Commander Vale and his small but loyal guard, a handful of volunteers. The Al-Arynaar looked on with blank contempt.

The Unknown saw Darrick stiffen as the enemy general rode up to the gate house, flanked by two riders carrying flags of parley in white and deep blue quarters. A shield mage rode behind him. He led a disciplined force. There was no talking in the ranks, they just stared, their confidence in their numbers obvious.

'I believe I should be addressing Commander Vale or a mage named Pheone,' said the Xeteskian. 'Though, and I mean no disrespect, I am before perhaps more illustrious company. General Darrick, it is an honour to remake your acquaintance.'

'I remember you well, Commander Chandyr,' said Darrick. 'However, I do not speak for the college of Julatsa. Commander Vale stands to my right.'

'I am Vale,' he said. 'What is it you wish to discuss?'

'Commander Vale, my request is simple. Open your gates. Lead those inside from the college grounds. You will not be harmed, merely disarmed. We have come to take control of Julatsa.' Chandyr's voice echoed for all to hear this side of the college. Vale's was similarly resounding.

'You understand that what you ask is impossible,' said Vale.

The Unknown watched him, confident he would not flinch.

379

Talking with him had been to hear a man possessed of a keen understanding of what was at stake here. Not just for Julatsa, but for Balaia. A shame his erstwhile council colleagues had not been so well informed.

'Any student of magical history is aware of the critical importance of maintaining a balance between the colleges,' continued Vale. 'Each strand of the art as supporter and moderator of the others. Leaving our college would lead to irrevocable destruction of that balance.

'Our counter request is also simple. We call for an end to this conflict and aid in placing our college back on an even footing. We ask that for ourselves, yes, and also for the whole of our country, which we can all agree has surely suffered enough. If we do not work together as we did until so recently, magic across our land will ultimately die.

'Finally, I would remind every Xeteskian mage of the personal consequences every Julatsan mage faces should you destroy this college's Heart. I cannot speak from knowledge but I have seen the haunted expressions of those contemplating a life without magic. Ask your mages what they fear the most. For all of them it is the same. Can they willingly submit their fellows to that appalling fate?'

Chandyr did not reply immediately. He was a man confident in command and aware enough to test the atmosphere among his own men. He turned in his saddle to see what, if anything, his mages betrayed. When he looked back, his face was bleak. He shrugged.

'The reality of war is harsh, Commander. The victors gain what they desire and the vanquished suffer. Sometimes this is death, at other times imprisonment or servitude. And for mages in this conflict, it will be the loss of their life purpose and worse.

'I cannot be sentimental. War is fought by at least two sides. Neither are blameless, neither desires the pain they inflict but they see there is no alternative. War comes when every other option is exhausted. Commander, I will repeat my offer. Surrender the college. No one else has to die. The conflict will end and Julatsa will remain self-governing.'

'We will not surrender,' said Vale. 'We cannot.'

'I know you can't, Commander. But I am not an honourable man if I do not offer you terms. I also offer you this. One hour to talk and think. If the gates are not open in that time, you will be attacked.'

Vale nodded. 'Go sharpen your swords, Commander Chandyr. You will need them. Should we relinquish this college, it will be at the severest cost to yourselves that we can inflict. And we have allies. Are you so sure you can defend against them after that cost is borne?'

'One hour,' said Chandyr.

He turned his horse and rode away with his men back to his lines. The Unknown watched him go before following Vale and The Raven back down into the courtyard inside the gates.

'I think a cool drink is in order,' said Vale, leading them to the refectory.

'It was a fine performance,' said The Unknown. 'It will give him cause for thought.'

'It'll do more than that,' said Darrick. 'Your last comment about his strength even should he win was very well judged. It will make him cautious.'

'It only occurred to me at the last moment,' admitted Vale.

'Such things turn battles,' said Darrick.

'So, General,' said Hirad. 'How well did you train him, then?'

'He was a good student,' said Darrick. 'But Lysternan soldiers always had extra lectures and training. Wouldn't do to tell them absolutely everything, would it?'

'Bloody hell,' said Hirad. 'Even thinking about fighting them as you taught them.'

'Yes Hirad,' said Darrick, ushering him into the refectory. 'And learning about all of their weaknesses too. And Chandyr is about to show us one of his.'

'Which is?'

'Impatience.'

Chapter 40

Darrick had a last look around him as Chandyr's patience ran out. His forces were stretched so thin. All it would take was the Xeteskian to see the opportunity and the college could fall before nightfall. He had played his cards and now he had to trust those outside to save them when the time came, if it came.

Around the walls, the waiting was all but over. He had committed all of his bowmen to the walls, forty in the arc around the gatehouse, the one entrance into the college. Around the walls, they were collected in five groups of fifteen, each connected by hastily trained flagmen of the Julatsan guardsmen and knots of Al-Arynaar warriors.

The solitary fit mage, Denser, stood with him, as did all The Raven. They were powerless right now but should a breach be forced in gate or wall, The Raven would be all that stood between Xetesk and a rout. They would never turn their backs and run.

Buildings obstructed his view across the college, as they did at points all around the walls. Communication, he had insisted, would be critical if they were to react to Xetesk's moves. This would not be a conventional siege. Xetesk had to get in before the Heart could be raised or risk facing enough Julatsan magical power to hold them off.

Darrick wasn't surprised Chandyr had chosen to attack tonight but he thought it was a mistake. His men had marched for three and a half days, covering the ground quickly. Their horses would be tired too. He had familiars and mages high in the sky, looking at what they could see from beyond spell range but they should have been looking further out into the city. Out there, their enemies were far more deadly.

Chandyr might be aware that the cavalry weren't saddled and

ready in the compound, but Darrick doubted he'd thought about the possibility of the small allied forces being split inside and outside the college walls. He was soon to get one of those lessons Darrick kept for Lysternans only.

'Let's be ready,' said Darrick. 'Signalman, flag the stand-by.'

'Yes sir,' the young guardsman, excited by the chance to stand with not just General Darrick but The Raven too, turned and held his flag horizontally above his head, hands either side of the bright yellow material. The signal was passed quickly around the walls.

Chandyr had massed his cavalry, a hundred of them, behind his lines facing the gate. It was all the evidence Darrick needed that the Xeteskian had no idea where Izack was and it was the move he and his former second-in-command had been counting on. But Chandyr wasn't showing his entire hand. He still had his foot soldiers scattered in a loose ring around the college, and of the mage group there was no clear sign.

Chandyr rode up and down in front of his men, watching the walls of the college, waiting and hoping. He would have waited until the day he died for the gates to be opened for him.

'Here it comes,' said Darrick. 'Signalman, when it starts, listen to my commands. We will need our response to be instant.'

'Yes sir.'

Chandyr stopped, dragged his horse to face his enemies, nodded once towards them and held up his sword in salute. He kicked into the flanks of his horse and dragged back on the reins. The animal reared, his sword swept down and the battle commenced.

Orders rang out around the courtyard and Chandyr's soldiers formed up. Shield bearers moved to the head of two large groups in front of the gates, crossbowmen and archers behind them. In the centre of each group, unarmed men who had to be mages, came together. Darrick counted twenty at least in each group. Swordsmen stood at the flanks but as they approached, he could see the rear of each group not defended.

'Archers, pick your targets!' he shouted. 'I don't want to see a single shaft strike a shield. Signalman, flag the attack. I want your response as soon as you have it. Don't be polite.'

'Sir.'

'Waiting,' said Darrick. 'Waiting. When those spells come over, remember what we practised.'

The message passed along the lines immediately left and right. Al-Arynaar archers stood ready, Julatsan guardsmen creating the illusion of numbers though Darrick was keen to ensure no concentrations of men. Scattering was still an option. Above the gatehouse, the carved stone roof gave significant protection. Elsewhere on the walls, no such protection existed. Gods, they never thought they'd need it again and even above Darrick, the stone was more ornament than armour.

Forty yards from the gates, more orders and the groups stopped. To Darrick's left, a bowstring twanged, the shaft skipping off the cobbles well ahead of the enemy. The General glared at the guardsman.

'Take your lead from the elves,' he hissed. 'Elevation, timing, everything. We do not have the arrows to waste.'

Two ranks of men held shields, the first at ground level, the second at head height. It was a decent wall but there weren't enough to go around. A good archer would find the gaps. Another shouted order from the courtyard and arrows and crossbow bolts began to fly, smacking into walls and flying high over the parapet. It was a poor first salvo but that wouldn't last.

'Return fire!' ordered Darrick. 'Do not flinch, they will be casting now.'

His order was translated and forty elven bows were brought to bear. The air filled with metal-tipped shafts carving their way into the enemy, slamming into armour, shields and exposed flesh, forcing Chandyr's bowmen to duck their heads. Another volley from the elves took out more along the flanks but the mages were well-protected. A third volley bounced off Hard-Shields, none getting through.

'Come on, Auum, where are you?' whispered Darrick.

'Sir, single group attack to the rear. No others,' reported the signalman.

'Thank you. Move two groups of archers rear.'

'Sir.'

The deep blue glow was visible a split second before the spell was cast. It was a single FlameOrb, the size of a covered wagon. It appeared above the heads of the left hand group, a second mimicking it above the right hand group. They hung for a heartbeat before flying straight and fast towards the gatehouse, one for the defenders, one for the wood.

'Watching!' roared Darrick. 'Watching!'

The lower Orb ploughed in fast, shaking the walls around it, blue fire splattering wide.

'Go!'

The gatehouse defenders ran left and right as instructed, clearing the area in moments, scattering around the walls, crouching below the ornamental battlements and watching the spell crash in. It burst like a waterskin, fire raining over the roofing, blasting through the open spaces where they had just been standing and shooting high into the sky. The wall bindings crackled but held comfortably, the mana blaze dying away quickly with nothing to feast upon.

'Form up!' said Darrick. 'Let's stand tall!'

He led the defenders back into the gatehouse, Hirad and The Unknown next to him.

'This is fun, isn't it?' growled Hirad.

'They can't cast forever,' said Darrick.

'They won't have to,' said The Unknown. 'Not like that. As soon as they know we're not shielded, they'll change their attack.'

'I know,' said Darrick. 'I know. Where are—'

A shuddering impact behind them sent smoke and blue flame soaring into the sky from the rear of the college. Into the relative quiet that followed, Darrick heard the sound of hooves on cobbles and, nearer to him, the roar of a panther.

'Our turn.'

Izack had walked his horses as close as he'd dared while the Xeteskians arranged themselves for battle. Chandyr had shown his naivety as Darrick had hoped, assuming everyone would be inside the college. And the fact that the city had capitulated had worked to their advantage, allowing Chandyr to feel relatively secure he was not about to feel an arrow in his back from every window.

But he had set a perimeter guard nonetheless and before reaching them, Izack had taken the muffles from every hoof and had mounted his men. He had precisely sixty. Fifty swordsmen and ten mages. He knew his route to the rear of the college, aware that a central street would give the attackers thirty yards of warning when he rounded the last right hand turn. But he would be at a gallop, and their minds would be elsewhere.

Stopping for a moment, he turned in his saddle and nodded at his men. Spell and HardShields were up, his swordsmen were in disciplined order and would spread to fill the street as they entered it. They had their attack orders. He would call the fight after first contact. He faced forwards once more, raised his sword arm and swept it down, simultaneously kicking into the flanks of his horse. The animal sprang away and the Lysternan cavalry pounded through Julatsa, the voices of his men loud and confident.

Izack rounded the last corner, his cavalry fanning out to left and right, straightening and powering in for the college. He saw spells striking the walls, arcing out to scatter defenders. HotRain was falling like a torrent in one quarter, the rocks of an EarthHammer were standing jagged from the cobbles in front of the walls which were displaying the first crack. The Al-Arynaar answered as best they could, picking targets but seeing most of their arrows bouncing from solid magical shields.

They were seen at the full thirty yards' distance by the perimeter guard whom Izack could see shouting the alarm. The Lysternan cavalry ate up the space between them, closing fast on the thin line of perimeter guard to whom help was coming but too late. Izack, his horse bred for this and not flinching, watched the odd crossbow bolt bounce from the shield surrounding them, held his sword down and to his right. He set himself low in his saddle and whipped his blade up into the defence of the first perimeter guardsman, battering it aside and knocking the man from his feet.

He didn't look round, knowing the enemy had no chance under the hooves of his cavalry, and drove on. In front of him, Xeteskians were running in from both sides and the tight-formed group attacking the walls was breaking as bowmen turned, swordsmen tried to form up to take on the cavalry and defend their mages who still pounded the walls.

Izack yelled for the charge to increase pace and kicked again, feeling his horse surge beneath him. 'Single charge and break!' Although if they could hear him, he'd be surprised. What they would do was follow his lead.

He felt a thrill course through him, the air thick with noise and fear and the strong smells of horse, leather and the acrid taint of spell fire. He set himself again and drove into the half-made rank of Xeteskians, his horse kicking up and out, landing hard. Izack drove his blade straight through the chest guard of his first target, dragging it clear, his momentum carrying him forwards. Next blow took the arm from a bowman and he slowed dramatically, his men widening their attack behind him and sweeping up the flanks of the group.

'Care your open flank!' roared Izack, hearing the shout relayed.

He blocked a blow to his right, saw his left-flank man smash his sword into the helmet of another enemy before a third Xeteskian reached up a hand and pulled the man from his saddle. Izack kicked his horse again, and stepped in two more paces, thumping his blade down on the shoulder of an enemy, sending him sprawling. Directly ahead, the mages had broken, some were running right, others casting again.

'Push!' shouted Izack. 'Push!'

He saw a thrust blocked aside but leaned out in his saddle to change his angle and whipped his sword back, right to left, and scored a deep gash in the enemy's upper arm. Another pace and he was through the defence and into the mages. Knowing it was a brief chance he laid about him with all the energy he could muster, his sword carving into chest, head, arm and back.

All around him, the press of cavalry had broken the Xeteskian group. A handful of riderless horses cantered in confusion but the attack had been a great success. He knew more than to outstay his welcome. Xeteskians were closing in good numbers left and right and he could see, emerging from around the right hand wall of the college, the Xeteskian cavalry.

'Break!' he yelled.

Heaving his sword one more time and feeling it connect with unprotected flesh, he dragged on the reins and began to force his way out.

'Keep form, mages let's go.'

The Lysternan cavalry clattered their way from the carnage they had made and began to make their escape. In front of Izack, a lone Xeteskian swordsman stabbed straight through the leg of a cavalryman, the blade carrying on into his mount. Both cried out, the horse rearing and galloping away, the rider flung back and left, his leg rotating around the sword as he fell screaming. He was dragged a short way before the blade tore free, the horse, pumping blood, running terrified after its kin.

Izack at a fast canter himself, despatched the swordsman before he had time to turn or grab another weapon and headed off back the way they had come. Shouting encouragement, he drove his remaining cavalry hard, seeing over his shoulder the Xeteskians continuing their chase. Cheers from the walls reached his ears and he could already imagine the arrows starting to fly from elven bows now the Xeteskian shields were down.

Sensibly, the enemy cavalry carried on the pursuit, never closing too much but not letting them out of their sight. Izack, moving through his men to lead once again, galloped through the empty streets across a beautiful blossom-strewn park, through an area of high-walled tenements and out into open land. Behind, the Xeteskian cavalry stopped at the city boundaries.

Izack reined in gently, holding up his sword hand. They slowed to a halt, spread to a line and turned. He had a quick count. Eight of his men were gone but four of their horses were with him.

'Well done!' he shouted. 'That is a blow we can never repeat but you are all exactly the men I thought you to be. Xetesk will not be caught like that again so we must make contact with the TaiGethen before we attack again. Now, we must rest, remember those we have lost, and bind our wounds. We have friends trapped in that college, including General Darrick, so though we may have made small victory today, we have much more to do. Gentlemen, I salute you!'

The answering call warmed his heart and he led his cavalry away.

Auum responded to the call of the ClawBound panther and led his small band of TaiGethen towards the rear of the enemy. Of all those cells that had travelled to Balaia, only five now remained and he led the only one with all of its original members. The toll had been terribly high and would leave them vulnerable to their enemies on Calaius if they did not defeat them here.

On every first street junction beyond the college square, the enemy had posted guards. For him, that presented the immediate threat of only six men but even these he would not strike down yet. They knew how the Xeteskian commander would react to the cavalry attack on the other side of the college and so they waited.

Reminiscent of their concealment in Xetesk, the TaiGethen hid in narrow alleys that let directly onto streets which connected with the main thoroughfare to the college gates. With them, the ClawBound stood quiet. They had called when the cavalry began their charge. Other pairs watched over the enemy lines though Auum was sure he would hear for himself, the moment the inevitable response was made.

He was not disappointed. Simultaneously with the roars of four ClawBound panther throats, the sound of multiple hooves rattled and echoed into the air.

'Let Yniss watch over you and Tual guide you,' he said to them all. 'Tais, we move.'

They sprinted into the street, heading left to the guarded junction. Duele and Evunn as they always were, at his shoulders, the other four Tais in their formations left and right of him. ClawBound padded behind.

Bows were flexed and fired on the run. Two shafts found their targets, another four did not. Auum unclasped his jaqrui pouch and felt inside for a throwing crescent, counting the diminishing number. He gripped one, dragged it out and flicked it away in one movement, hearing its keening wail. The target couldn't see it against the dark of the buildings and it struck him high on the forehead. The enemy shrieked, clutched at his head and fell, the blood pouring down his face.

The TaiGethen hit the three remaining guards like a wave breaking over sand. The cell to Auum's right arrived first. Swords flashed, men fell. Only one withstood the first strikes, backing away, fear marking his face. He fended away one more blow but the Tai leader landed a kick in his chest, knocking him back and off balance, leaving him open to the flanking Tais to drag blades through throat and gut respectively.

Auum didn't break stride, racing down the centre of the street, seeing the gates ahead of him. Up in the gatehouse stood The Raven and Al-Arynaar elves. In front of them, what had to be at least three hundred men in two tight groups. Spells were pounding against the gates, which smoked but held firm. No one looked in their direction but it would not be long. Auum cared little. These enemy deserved the fate that Shorth had in store for them and, face him or not, they would still die.

The street was wide and the TaiGethen spread into a single line. ClawBound joined them, three pairs striding easily alongside. They were no more than ten yards away when the first enemy sensed the silent peril behind him and turned, only to catch an arrow in his throat as he opened his mouth to shout the alarm. Too few Xeteskians were strung across the entrance to the square to mount real resistance. All swung about as their comrade fell choking to the ground in their midst and the mood of the battle changed instantly from confidence to panic.

Auum threw another crescent ahead of him, seeing it gouge into the arm of his target. He took another two paces and leapt, one leg outstretched, the other gathered beneath him, two short swords now in hand. His foot connected with his enemy's face and he felt the man's nose crumple and his teeth break beneath the blow.

He landed softly, turned and plunged his sword into the chest of the same man, finishing him. He darted right to dodge a blow from the left, spinning on a heel and reversing his sword into the ear of the nearest opponent. Duele had swept the legs from under a third and dropped his knee into the prone man's throat, bouncing to his feet and running on.

Ahead of them, the mage groups remained well defended, their guard turning now, bows and sword coming to bear. Around Auum's right, a ClawBound panther growled and pounced, her partner two steps behind her, jabbing his fingers into the neck of a bowman, ducking under a careless swing and biting into the face of another, bearing the screaming man down, bloodied hands free to rake flesh from his victim's cheeks.

Auum called Evunn and Duele to him, saw his other cells closing and drove into the Xeteskian rear flank, waiting for the ClawBound call to pull back.

Denser watched the awesome speed of the TaiGethen attack. They were so fluid and quickly so deep into the heart of one of the Xeteskian attack groups that the enemy had no real idea how to defend against them. The elves were too close in for bows, the mages were helpless and swordsmen were being chopped apart, not knowing where the next strike was coming from.

The other attack group had faltered in its mission. Spells had stopped striking at doors and walls and nervous glances were being cast left. Field captains were exhorting them to concentrate but the storm of the few TaiGethen and ClawBound was simply mesmerising.

Denser, like all of The Raven surely, was watching Auum. He was so graceful and so accurate and, with Duele and Evunn next to him, the whole cell appeared quite simply unstoppable. He knew they would be fearful of the MindMelt that had damaged Evunn but it hadn't stopped them attacking and Denser knew that spell would not be cast. Only the mages they attacked were close enough and none of them would have the peace to construct it.

He tried to follow Auum's movements, occasionally finding it hard to do so, counting to himself. The TaiGethen leader ducked and struck, leaped high to dodge a blow and was alert enough to lash a leg out as he dropped to shatter an enemy jaw. He whirled on his standing leg to drag his blades through the chest of another, jabbed an elbow into the throat of a third in almost the same movement and head-butted a fourth before taking another pace and trying again.

Denser had counted to six.

But not everything was going right. Behind, the Lysternan cavalry was being driven off, their hoofbeats fading fast. He heard cheers but they were short-lived, the tenor changing. He swung from the spectacular demonstration of fighting below him and could see immediately why. Above, the familiars had stopped circling and watching. They were diving and neither the elves who stood and waited or the guardsmen who scattered, could harm them.

'Raven!' he shouted. 'Trouble!'

He didn't wait to see if they would follow but began to race around the walls to the opposite side of the college. The problem had been seen by others within and without the college. Elves were chasing ahead of him, guardsmen backing off. Behind Denser, The Unknown barked at them to stand their ground but from below, arrows, crossbow bolts and spells were flying in at suddenly undefended walls.

Denser tried to cover his head with a hand as he ran, hearing arrows biting into the stone around him, feeling the air whip as a shaft passed by just in front of him. HotRain began to fall but it was behind them. Another FlameOrb sailed out.

'Down!' roared Hirad.

Denser flattened himself on the walkway, the heat of the Orb singeing hairs on the back of his hands as it passed to fall into the courtyard below. He was up on his feet immediately, looked ahead and saw the first familiar strike down. It collided hard with an Al-Arynaar archer, knocking him off balance. The elf raised his hands to try and grab the demon from his face but it was too strong, its momentum too much and both fell from the walls. Only one struck the ground, the familiar climbing back into the sky, chittering and laughing.

'We've got to catch them and hold them,' Denser shouted back over his shoulder, now only twenty yards from the fight. 'I'll be ready with the spells.'

There were four familiars in the attack, flitting around elven heads. The Al-Arynaar, Rebraal amongst them, had almost all dropped their bows and held short swords or knives. The remaining archers were being forced to look out to counter the returning threat from below while trusting in their kin to keep the familiars from pitching them over the walls.

Thraun, Hirad and the limping Unknown, all with daggers in their hands, overtook him and joined the Al-Arynaar. He heard Hirad shout instructions to Rebraal, who was weaving a complex pattern above his head with his short blade while the familiars wheeled just above them. As he approached, Denser constructed a FlamePalm.

'One at a time!' shouted The Unknown to The Raven. 'See the one with the red flash on its forehead. He'll do.'

Denser paced into the centre of The Raven's loose circle. Hirad was dangerously close to the unrailed edge to the court-yard below but in typical fashion, was more worried about the threat to his friends than his own position. He stabbed up, catching a familiar on an outstretched claw and sending it spiralling and yelping. They couldn't damage the familiars but that didn't mean they felt no pain.

'Keep it tight,' said The Unknown.

He reached up a hand and grabbed at a foot but missed. Next to him, Thraun jumped to do the same. The familiar's tail whipped and cut the back of his hand.

'Careful, Thraun,' warned Denser, fighting to keep his concentration.

Thraun growled, his knife carved at the air again and his hand whipped out a second time, this time catching that flailing tail and dragging the familiar down, kicking, raking and squealing.

'Hold him, hold him!' shouted The Unknown.

The Raven warriors dropped on the monkey-sized beast, trying desperately to get a hand on any of the flailing limbs, the head that held those snapping jaws or even the heaving chest or wings that beat against the ground. All Denser could do was watch or he would lose his concentration as the demon, with a strength far beyond its size, fought for its very life and the sanity of its master.

Hirad took a claw right down the inside of one arm but came back and punched the familiar square in the face, slapping the back of its skull off the thick wooden parapet. The Unknown had knelt on the demon's legs and was trying to grab at a wing while Thraun, the tail still in one clamped fist, was attempting to get a grip on its right arm.

'Don't let go of anything,' said Hirad. He punched again, his chest wound protesting, drawing a snarl of fury from the indefatigable beast.

Above them the other three familiars flew to their captured one's aid, the elves, finding themselves no longer the targets, organising quickly to drive them back or take another one down. Denser felt his hair parted by a claw and clung on grimly to his concentration. The Raven almost had the familiar subdued but still it spat its vitriol, promising them all death.

Hirad snared an arm, The Unknown had his wing and Thraun got a hand on the top of its skull, stilling the head.

'Keep it there,' breathed Denser. He knelt down quickly, trying to keep away from the free limbs which etched at the air.

'Denser,' drawled the familiar. 'Your death is mine one day. Let me go. Your Raven's soul will fill me with energy and you will suffer—'

'Quiet,' said Denser and clamped a hand on the familiar's mouth, sending his FlamePalm shooting into its skull, holding steady while the mana fire extinguished its life. 'One down, one mage too. Let's go again.'

'Denser!'

It was Rebraal. Yards away, they were holding a familiar by its wings. It could find no angle to get at its captors but it was slowly dragging itself free. Denser began casting again, knowing he wouldn't make it to use another FlamePalm before the demon broke away.

'Against the wall.' He pointed. 'There.'

The Al-Arynaar threw the demon face first into the battlements. It hit them hard, fell to the ground and turned immediately, shaking its head to clear its vision. Denser caught its eye, smiled and cast, his focused FlameOrb engulfing the small body. The familiar screamed, tried to fly but succeeded only in flopping out over the walls to crash in front of the Xeteskians. Above Denser, the fight was done. The other two had fled. Horns sounded from below and the Xeteskians began to pull back.

Denser sat down to gather himself. Hirad crouched in front of him. He could hear shouts from below and the sound of running feet.

'Good work, Xetesk-man,' said the barbarian. 'Got anything left for my dragon?'

Denser nodded. 'Should have,' he said. 'But I'd rather wait until morning. I never did do that reading. Things rather overtook us this afternoon, didn't they?'

Hirad nodded, stood up and held out a hand. Denser grabbed it and dragged himself to his feet.

'I can wait. Xetesk have finished for the day.'

'What about the TaiGethen?'

'Well, I suspect that they did rather well, given the haste of the retreat tonight.'

Denser smiled and walked with Hirad back around the college walls to the gatehouse. The Xeteskians were indeed leaving the college square, taking their wounded with them. The Al-Arynaar, bows ready, let them leave, as did Darrick who was nodding to himself as the rest of The Raven came back to him.

Down on the cobbles, blood slicked the ground. Denser counted two dead elves among the dozens and dozens of Xeteskian bodies. One panther too lay dead, its partner lying next to it, preferring to die in defence of the fallen Claw than leave with the rest. He watched the Xeteskians clearing themselves away and wondered where they had placed themselves.

'Today was good,' said Darrick. 'Tomorrow will be far more

difficult. I wonder if we can delay the Heart raise. We need those mages. We can swing it with them, I think.'

'Tomorrow, we'll know,' said Denser. 'Erienne should be awake and she can tell what she saw. Otherwise it's more of the same. Reckon we can see it out in a full day?'

'Well, there is no surprise element now,' said Darrick. 'The cavalry will be watched for like the TaiGethen. Getting close to here to distract them will be a challenge. Chandyr is not a stupid man.'

'But can we hold out?'

Darrick considered a moment. 'Without help from the south? No. But we'll take as many of them with us as we can.'

'Come on, Raven,' said Hirad. 'Let's eat.'

Chapter 41

Erienne awoke in the middle of the night and sat up, biting back a scream. Her dreams had been full of tortured magic and the cries of mages shivered from the mana forever. They had been full of a crawling blackness that consumed everything it touched, that dulled the brightest tones and choked the songs of the young. She had seen herself at the gates of the college, presiding over the demise of all magic, laughing down at the upturned faces.

And around her feet had been her children, brought back to her from death. Returned to where they would be forever safe. At her side, being as she was. One.

'Shh, love, it's all right.' Denser's voice from next to her in the bed did nothing to calm her heart.

'It cannot promise that,' she said. 'Nothing can promise that.'

'Promise what?'

'You wouldn't understand,' she said, tasting the bitterness in her own voice. 'Leave me. I can beat it.'

'Don't shut yourself away from me,' urged Denser. 'Let me share the burden, please.'

'What can you share?' she snapped. 'It's all inside me. I cannot give it away, I cannot let others carry it. It is in me. It is trying to beat *me*.' She forced herself to stop, to lower her voice. She had turned to face him, still lying there, hurt in his eyes and concern in his face. 'It taunts me, Denser. But how can it? It is not sentient. How can I beat something that is not there at all?'

'Whatever your mind sees as the fight is what must be beaten. It is a fight for control of your own body too. I know I cannot really help you but don't shut me out. Please don't do that.'

She stroked his face. 'I'll try,' she said. 'But it's so hard. I feel like I am the only thing stopping a flood from drowning us all. It's so hard to find room for anything else.'

'Then do not.' Denser smiled but his eyes retained their pain. 'I will understand.'

'Tell me that in a year,' she said. 'Or in a season.'

'Assuming we live that long,' said Denser. 'We might not see out another day.'

He shifted his position, sat up, his hands behind him, taking his weight.

'Tell me what you saw today,' he said. 'What made you break the spell?'

'Their casting caused the problem,' she said immediately. 'I'm sure of that now. The very mana they forced into focus triggered something in the stone around the Heart, like a black stain spreading upwards. It was like it was being forced to close, to shut down. It'll happen again the next time they try.'

'Darrick doesn't want them to. Not tomorrow,' said Denser. 'He doesn't think we can hold out another day without the Julatsans casting to stop Xetesk.'

'Well they can't,' she said, frustrated at his lack of understanding. 'It's obvious, isn't it?'

'No,' said Denser. She sighed impatiently, caught herself at it and stopped herself retorting.

'Sorry.' She calmed herself. 'It's mass use of magic that causes the problems. If they are all out there casting shields tomorrow, the focus will fail. There's no doubt about that in my mind. Geren was only half right. The only chance is to raise the Heart, get it back into the place where it can generate the flow again, and hope the shadow can be suppressed while they raise it.'

'How?'

She shrugged. 'Well, I'll have to think of something, won't I?'

'Like what?'

'How the hell do I know! Gods Denser, I'm not the bloody oracle.'

'Yes, but you are the only one who can do something to help. No one else can even see the problem, let alone do anything to stop it.'

She pushed away and stood up, feet chilling on the cold

stone. 'Great. Erienne, the saviour of Julatsa. Erienne, the saviour of the whole bloody world.' She turned on him. 'Pity is, I have no idea how to do it.'

'Well, can I—'

'No!' she shouted. 'No one can.' She put her head in her hands. 'Sorry, Denser. Please go back to sleep. You need rest for tomorrow.'

'Come back to bed,' he said, voice gentle, the one she had fallen in love with.

'I can't sleep any more. I need to think.'

'When will the Al-Arynaar be able to cast again?' asked Denser after a pause.

She shrugged. 'They were drained, you know. I couldn't help that. Maybe in the afternoon. Maybe later.'

'I see,' he said. 'Erienne, will you do something for me?'

'If I can,' she said.

'Tell everything you've told me to Darrick. I don't think he was going to sleep much tonight and he should know. He'll be in the refectory or the gatehouse.'

'It's as good a place to walk as any.' She searched around for her shoes and a shawl to put around her shoulders.

'I love you, Erienne.'

'Don't you forget it.'

The news for Blackthorne was as good as it could possibly be. Communion between Dordovan mages had informed him that a force of around two hundred and fifty was closing in on Julatsa. With those he had with him, they would make three hundred and they could yet strike the decisive blow.

A Lysternan cavalry mage had brought further news in the early hours of the morning that the college still stood and that Izack was planning another assault on the Xeteskians at the earliest opportunity. Though their cavalry was stronger, the Xeteskians had lost the day and were camped just outside the city to the south. He had been advised to enter from the north or west.

It was not quite dawn when Blackthorne roused his band of tired but willing Dordovan and Lysternan fighting men and mages. With them rode his own few men and their spirit had grown by the hour as their wounds had healed and their aches and pains eased. There would not be a better time to move and attack, and he was not going to miss the rendezvous point a mile west of the city.

They marched quietly as they approached the silent college city. Away to their right, the sun was beginning to climb over the horizon and the enemy had to be close. But friends were closer still and would soon be in sight.

'This could turn out to be a great day, Luke,' said Blackthorne. 'If The Raven can mastermind holding onto the college for another morning, we could be on them. The war is not yet lost.'

'I have prayed that we wouldn't be too late, my Lord,' said Luke. He was smiling, his young face bright and alive.

'Some day, everyone's prayers are answered. Perhaps today it is your turn.'

Blackthorne was leading his ragtag bunch up a gentle wooded incline. At the crest, they would be able to see all the way down to Julatsa. He was hoping too that they would be able to see where the allies were waiting. He was looking forward to seeing a friendly army for a change.

The further they walked, the more Blackthorne demanded quiet. He had dismounted and was leading his horse as were all of his own men. One hand was on the bridle, the other flattening his sword against his waist to stop it from jangling. It would not do at this time to blunder into an enemy they had not foreseen. His scouts, however, few though he could spare, had reported nothing for a mile all around them ever since they had left their rest stop.

Those scouts had returned now and were only a hundred yards or so ahead, the furthest still in sight, just cresting the rise. Blackthorne saw the scout crouch suddenly and slither off out of sight. Immediately, he stopped the march, the men already knowing better than to question the Baron. He waited and it was not long before the scout reappeared, haring down the incline and sliding to a stop.

'My Lord,' he said.

'Calm yourself,' said Blackthorne. 'Tell me what you see.'

'The allies are not far ahead, they are along the banks of the River Taalat no more than a mile distant. The city is close. But there are others closing in on them. I cannot be sure but I would say they are Xeteskian. Mages. There are few but they move with great purpose. My Lord, I would stake my life that they aim to attack.'

'And do the allies outnumber them?'

'Ten to one, my Lord.'

'Then . . .' Blackthorne trailed off. Everything became awfully clear. He turned to his men. 'The allies are going to come under spell attack. For ease, split down college lines. Dordover, run to them, warn them off but don't get too close, Luke go with them, take four of our people. Ride hard. They may not see you early, that's why I need Dordovans behind you making a racket. Lystern, come with me. We have some mages to kill.' He swung into his saddle. 'Oh, and we'll be running and we'll be shouting too. The time for quiet is at an end. Come on!'

The band ran up the slope, Blackthorne at a half-canter at their side. Luke and the other riders had ploughed off and were already over the slope and heading hard towards the Dordovans. Blackthorne breasted the rise and saw it all laid out before him. The allies, oblivious to the threat that approached them from the south-east, the Xeteskians, and he was certain his scout was right, riding quickly towards their goal, directed by familiars, flying above them.

'Let's go!' shouted Blackthorne, and set off down the long slope after the Xeteskian riders.

He was well in advance of the foot soldiers but he had three of his own about him. It didn't matter if he was killed, so long as he disrupted for long enough the casting he was sure was coming. He closed the gap steadily but the Xeteskians were well ahead, their familiars now high in the sky, hovering over the allies who were, he could see, beginning to shift, unease rippling through them.

Way to his left now, Luke was flying along, hair streaming out behind him, one arm waving wildly. Blackthorne fancied he could hear the boy's shouts.

'Just don't get too close,' he said to himself.

Ahead, the Xeteskians dismounted and formed a tight group, swordsmen remaining mounted, cantering around in a protective ring. Behind him, the Lysternans were making a game attempt to keep up but he was already fifty yards ahead and pulling further clear.

A pressure beat down on his ears and his horse slowed dramatically, its head rocking from side to side, its flanks shuddering. A black line appeared in the sky, quickly resolving into half a dozen such lines, crossing to make a star that dragged cloud to it in great swirls that thickened and darkened.

'No, no!' Blackthorne shouted and urged his horse on but it was reluctant to move.

Ignoring the growing pain deep in his ears, Blackthorne dismounted and began to run on towards the waiting horsemen whose own mounts had suffered the same discomfort as his; the loose mage horses had bolted, heading away to sanctuary wherever they could find it.

Blackthorne could still see down the slope to the allied camp, where men were now running in all directions. Unwilling horses were being mounted and people starting to scatter. A half mile from them, Luke had been forced to stop.

Above them all, the star opened like the petals of some malevolent flower. For a heartbeat, Blackthorne thought the spell must have failed. No lightning was disgorged, no interdimensional power bit the ground. But this was not BlueStorm and in the next instant, he was forced to his knees by a high-pitched whine in his head that flattened his strength and threatened to blur his sight.

He clamped his hands over his ears but it made no difference, yet looking up, he saw that he was one of the lucky ones. The allied camp had been the target and there, the spell struck with appalling force. The river rippled and bounced in its bed, flowers and bushes were pressed down, their leaves and petals driving away as if propelled by some unseen hand.

And the men and horses. Oh dear Gods, the men and horses. Like the trees near which they stood, they sagged, helpless and writhing. Those that could, shouted and screamed. It was impossible but it seemed that they grew in size, inflated against their clothes and their skin. Men wailed and gasped, horses kicked at the air, trees ripped along their trunks, their leaves falling like autumn. And when the pressure became too much, they burst.

Like being detonated from the inside, they exploded outwards and upwards, just lumps of flesh, bone, shivered wood and skin. The debris filled the air like a cloud tinged pink and still the spell was not done as it ripped up the ground too, catapulting rock and earth high into the sky then shutting off.

Instantly, the pain eased and a fury gripped Blackthorne. He drove himself to his feet and called his men to him. And when they were all standing and ready, he charged. They bellowed their rage and their disbelief at what the Xeteskians had done, their swords whirling around in their hands, catching the sunlight.

Ahead of them, the mounted soldiers forced their horses into order and rode at them. Blackthorne felt possessed of the energy of a teenager. He rolled under the blow of a horseman, came up on to his knees and savaged his sword through the legs of the next beast past him. Not waiting to see what he had done, he rose and ran on, slashing out at another rider, feeling his blade connect he knew not where. He had one target in mind and one only.

The mages were in no condition to cast or to defend themselves but it would hardly have mattered otherwise. Blackthorne and his men fell on them like wild animals, carving through hands that tried to protect heads, splitting skulls, slicing stomachs and puncturing chests, groins and backs. And above, the familiars who had directed it all, screamed and fell as their masters died. No one was spared, no one escaped and the blood soaked into the green grass, staining it as black as the robes of the men they had slaughtered.

But that was as nothing to what the Xeteskians had wrought. When he was done and the exertion and shock fell on him like a cloak too heavy to wear, Blackthorne walked to the scene of the spell and looked on it. He felt detached from the horror and that was surely the only way he could have stayed standing and not fall to his knees, vomiting his guts into the river.

Scraps of flesh lay everywhere. It was impossible to distinguish man from beast. Blackthorne had visited an abattoir once. The waste buckets would have been full of pieces of meat this size. Chunks of gristle and bone that were no use for anything but grinding down for dog food. He could barely believe that this had ever been men.

He turned to see his men gathering behind him. Many had succumbed and were sick, others had let swords drop from nerveless fingers while they stared in complete incomprehension. It only took a moment to see that none of them could go on. Not right now and perhaps not ever. So he gave them an alternative.

'We must take news of this to Dordover and Lystern,' he said, his voice thick and shaking. 'Xetesk must be stopped. Not at Julatsa but at its very heart, in the college itself. This power can never be used again.

'Look at what they have done. Hundreds of men with no chance. Remember what you have seen here, remember why you will want to fight at the gates of the Dark College again.'

He turned and led them away.

'Contact cannot be made,' said Dystran, sitting by the bedside of his old friend Ranyl.

The master was fading fast now and perhaps would not even see out the battle. His voice was brittle, every cough brought up fresh blood and his face was grey and terribly thin. He had not eaten in two days and even a sip of water was taken with the knowledge of certain pain. But still he clung on and those eyes reflected the pin-sharp mind inside his failing body.

'But they cast the PressureBell?' he asked, Dystran having to lean in close to hear the grinding whisper.

'Yes, it was cast. We monitored it from here,' said Dystran. 'But we do not know its effectiveness. It is apparent that not enough survived with energy enough to link a Communion with me.'

Ranyl nodded. 'Best assume they are all dead, young pup.'

'And we'd better pray the allies were destroyed. We suffered heavy losses yesterday. But the walls and gates are weak and the Julatsans cannot cast, or so it would seem. We can break through today. We must.'

Dystran looked out through Ranyl's balcony doors. Another fine day was dawning, the wispy clouds already burning off. A good day for triumph.

'We are so close,' said Ranyl, a tear of pain squeezing from his eye, the cough spraying blood on to the cloth he held to his mouth. 'I may yet live to see it.'

'You will, old dog, you will,' said Dystran, starting to believe it himself if the battle could be won today.

There was a tentative knock on the door.

'This had better be important,' muttered Dystran. He stood and strode to the door, snatching it open to reveal Suarav standing there. The guard captain looked anxious. 'Yes?'

'I am sorry my Lord but you must come to the walls of the city.'

'Any particular reason?' asked Dystran. 'An odd cloud

formation perhaps or may be a herd of deer galloping across the battlefields of yesterday.' He dropped his voice to a clipped whisper. 'Can't you see I'm with a dying man?'

Suarav dropped his voice too, and spoke so low that Dystran had difficulty in hearing. He caught one word though, or thought he did and prayed he was mistaken.

'I beg your pardon?' he said.

The Wesmen songs had reached a new crescendo when they had reached the eastern side of Understone Pass. Their pace had increased, as had their belief in victory. Understone itself lay in ruins, the stench of death reaching them hundreds of yards distant, as did the calls of the flocks of carrion birds, fighting over putrefied flesh.

There really had been no one left to fight them, just as his scouts had reported. So the four thousand warriors, led at a rhythmic trot by Tessaya, Lord of the Paleon Tribes and ruler of the Wesmen, picked up their voices and drove themselves north to glory.

Tessaya felt the energy through every muscle as he ran. He sang too, his bass voice adding to the throng of sound that delighted his ears and would terrify all who heard it. The Wesmen were back on eastern Balaian soil and this time, they were here to stay, he could feel it.

They had camped for a glorious, dancing- and fire-filled night only six miles from the walls of Xetesk, their Destranas howling and hunting, the Shamen conferring the strength of the Spirits on everyone there assembled. No one fought, no tribe sought to gain advantage. Here was unification, here was an army that would be unstoppable.

Before dawn they had risen, their few hours' sleep enough, their vigour undiminished. They had heard Tessaya's words and then they had run again, faster than before, desperate that the head of every rise should show them a view of their goal.

And now it was in sight. They could see a few houses dotted below them, farmsteads that would no doubt serve them as they had served Xetesk before. They would not be damaged, their people would be unharmed because this now was the Wesmen way. Their effort had to be singleminded, nothing wasted.

The army gathered about two miles from the imposing walls

and towers of the college city. They could see smoke rising through the haze of the morning, the sun shining down to pick out the seven spires that represented the college's power base. It was an awesome sight and one that had filled Wesmen with dread and thoughts of the centuries of defeat.

Not this time. This time the fields outside the city were already soaked in Xeteskian blood and the ground was trampled and dead like the spirit within the walls. Tessaya climbed a nearby dead tree and stood out on a naked bough, one hand resting on the trunk. The expectant face of every Wesman turned to him.

'My brothers of the tribes, we are come.' The shouts were deafening. Tessaya held up his hands for quiet. 'You see before you the mountain we must climb. You see high walls and solid gates. On those walls will be mages and archers and swordsmen. But they are few and we have archers of our own. No longer can they destroy us with their magic.

'We will not try to storm the walls only to die. We will wait and we will kill and when the walls are clear, we will send our grapples onto the battlements and gateposts and we will climb. Harvest the trees you see here. The wood is still strong. We can use them as ladders, we can use them to batter the gates. Nature provides and the Spirits watch us and give us their blessing.

'My brothers, the next few days will see the fruition of all that we have planned. It will see the deaths of our people avenged and it will see the Wesmen attain their rightful place as rulers of Balaia!'

Dystran watched from the south walls of the college. Half a mile away, the last handfuls of the Black Wings' failed army were scattering. Dystran understood how they felt. He saw tree after tree come down. One hundred-foot oaks, thick-trunked pines, anything that had withstood the gales, it seemed, was being felled. And when they were done, the Wesmen ran towards Xetesk.

There were thousands of them.

'You have got to be fucking joking,' Dystran breathed.

Chapter 42

Chandyr had been badly stung by the defeat of yesterday. Nothing had gone according to his plan. Darrick had out-thought him, and Izack's cavalry and the quite extraordinary elven warriors had comfortably outfought him. He had ridden back from chasing away the cavalry to find carnage by the gates. He had a hundred men dead or wounded, fifteen of them mages, while his charges had taken down three elves and one panther.

He knew they were good, but frankly he hadn't thought them that good. However, the ten man patrols he had sent through the city to search for them had been lost and now he faced the gates again with his men demoralised, reduced in number, while the same faces stared down at him.

But today would be different. Today, his cavalry was ready and split around the college. He didn't care how quick an elf was, a galloping horse was faster, more powerful and would trample them without mercy. So he had told his men that they should not fear. That setbacks were a part of war. He told them that their efforts had not been in vain and that the enemy could not cast and the gates were weakened. And he had told them that the allied forces chasing them had been destroyed.

He hoped fervently that last statement was true. The fact was, no one knew for certain. The spell had been cast but there were no reports of its effects. Still, if lie it turned out to be, at least it kept his men facing the right way. And Chandyr wanted to be inside the gates by midday.

He ordered the attack. Same two fronts as yesterday, same weight of mages but this time, there was little backup. Around the walls, his loose mages sent HotRain into the air to fall on the unshielded defenders, driving bowmen from the walls and allowing his mages more comfort to link, to concentrate and to cast. FlameOrbs battered the gates, ForceCones heaved against the timbers and EarthHammers undermined the foundations.

Again and again, the spells struck and the defenders seemed to have no answers. Few arrows came and, critically, no spells at all. He watched from his horse, knowing the tide was turning. He ordered DeathHail to strike the battlements and saw men and elves die. He demanded another EarthHammer from every mage in the link and at last the gates shifted.

He knew his mages were tiring but surely they could make the breach. Another FlameOrb, the size of his house in Xetesk crashed into the timbers and this time he could see the flame take hold. His soldiers roared in approval.

'Come on!' he shouted. 'One more, the bindings are failing.'

And he knew it was true. Already men were running from the walls, no doubt to take up defence in the courtyard beyond. Only The Raven still stood in the gatehouse, smoke billowing across their faces. They were the factor that concerned him most. While they still stood, the Julatsans would not break, and so far his attacks on them had come to nothing. Worse, they had even found time to kill familiars, leading him to keep the rest back. He couldn't afford the cost in mages.

The ForceCone swept towards the gates. He could hear the flaming timbers protesting, the weaker of them cracking. He saw the gates buckle and one of the great iron hinge braces snap. But still they stood.

'Again,' he ordered. 'Again. Stand ready. Captains, have your men stand ready!'

Across the courtyard his companies formed up. Moments away. He was just moments away.

A shout to his right caught his attention through all the noise, flame and smoke. Men were pointing into the sky. He followed their arms. He saw it too, watched it grow larger and larger, great wings scooping back the air, powering it towards them. He had believed them all dead but it was not so. A chill gripped him. Dragons were friends of The Raven.

'Change target!' he yelled to the mages. 'Right and up. Quickly!'

He saw it in their faces when they turned. Their concentration was gone. The dragon stormed in, its bark eclipsing all other sound. It was huge. Dear Gods, it could take them all.

He fought down his panic and tried to calm his horse, which bucked beneath him. Men were beginning to break from their formation. Arrows had started coming again from walls suddenly full of elven archers. Men were dying. His men.

'Hold!' he screamed. 'Hold! Mages FlameOrb. Hold!'

His horse reared and he was flung backwards from the saddle, crashing heavily into the ground. He fought himself groggily to his knees and saw, through the smoke from the gates, his mages bending their heads to cast.

Sha-Kaan had rested in the cool of a cave high up in the Blackthorne Mountains, far from the prying eyes of man. He had hunted well and the chill over his body in the cave had been a welcome counterpoint to the warmth of the sun. It had eased some of the aches of the long flight and worked the stiffness from his wings. Now he was ready to go home.

Hirad Coldheart's mind, however, was not calm. The battle at the college had been sudden and brutal and he had begged one more night for Denser to be fit and able to cast. Sha-Kaan had grumblingly consented. After so many years, one more night would make little difference.

However, the folly of that decision was as clear as the dawn light that had flooded his resting place. The enemy had attacked ferociously the next morning and the outside defenders, the elves and cavalrymen, had not struck back. He did not know why, nor did he care. All he knew from his most brief of contacts was that Hirad and therefore Denser, were in great danger and he would not die because they were killed while he waited uselessly.

And so he flew, Hirad's protestations loud in his mind. He flew low and fast feeling the wind rushing past him, his wings strong and his talons flexing. He had no fire and he would not need it. If he could drive them back it would give him the time he needed for Denser to cast for him. And much though he wanted to stay and help The Raven, he had to return home. The birthings were imminent but, more than that, he had to assess what damage the Xeteskian dimensional spell-casting had done to the space between. He had felt another casting this morning and their lack of awareness was rupturing the boundaries.

Sha-Kaan kept the thoughts of home fresh in his mind. The

scents of the Broodlands, the calls of his Brood and the Vestare who supported them so selflessly. The feel of the warm, damp air over his scales, the taste of the flame grass and the embrace of the clouds. Today he would return to experience it all or he would die on Balaia.

He saw the spells pounding the gates on one side and a section of wall on the other. He saw scattered elves trying to pick off targets and others lying where they had been hit by spell or bow-fire. He saw the first enemy look around and the mass of faces that followed the inevitable shout. He saw them lose their discipline and some start to run. He barked loud, the sound splitting the air, and he dived.

Driving in, wings swept back and away to present the smallest target, he could make out mages in a group, sitting quite still. He knew their plan. Arrows flicked past him, any that struck bouncing harmlessly from his scales. Those men could not hurt him. He barked again, his jaws wide, sucking in the air. He closed them with a snap that could be heard a mile away and plunged in, seeing the spell released.

It was a ball of blue flame, bigger than his head and streaming smoke behind it as it rushed towards him. He let it close then unfurled his wings, the sudden bite on the air slowing him and giving him dramatic lift, sending him soaring above its trajectory.

He arced gracefully in the air and came in again. Below him, most men were running for cover but the mages, now split into several groups and defended by the most courageous, were steadfast. Barrelling in just above the rooftops, he swooped into the college square, his huge bulk seeming to fill one side of it completely.

He landed deliberately hard, crushing men beneath talon and body, sliding forwards and ripping up the cobbles, and using his wings to brake him and send him back into the air before he collided with the buildings the opposite side. He banked sharply and came in again, his bark echoing from every wall. He beat down, slowing, hind feet stamping down on more men, his neck jabbing forwards to snatch and crush mage after mage.

Sha-Kaan flung them at the ground, bit them in two and spat out the remains. He moved heavily across the ground, feeling the pinpricks of swords. His fore-claws lashed out, ripping heads from shoulders and gouging great rents in chests and stomachs. Bodies were flung away and there was nothing they could do. He ran forwards and took off again, climbing hard, banking and turning for another pass.

Below him, men crawled or ran from the square. He had broken them. He trumpeted and dove again, swooping low and snatching another man from the ground. Hirad's warning came too late and he hadn't seen it. From around the corner of the college, came a torrent of hail, driven by a mana wind. He dropped the body and tried to climb but the hail raked down the underside of his body, tore into his wings and peppered his great tail.

Sha-Kaan howled in anguish, the pain biting into him, deeper and deeper. The mages from the other side of the college had been quick. Too quick for him and he had been blinded by his success. He had to climb away, to reach safety where he could see to his wounds. But the hail had damaged the wing membrane and it was weak. Too weak to withstand this atmosphere for long. The muscles at the roots were cut deeply and blood poured from him like rain.

He looked down. Only one place to go, only one hope remained. He angled sharply again and half flew, half fell into the college.

'No!' roared Hirad. He pushed past The Raven and began to run down the gatehouse stairs.

He knew where Sha-Kaan intended to land. He had felt the pain of the DeathHail strike as if it was his own. But he was unharmed while the Great Kaan was seriously, if not mortally, wounded. Weakened from his long years of exile, he was so vulnerable. Why had he not listened?

Hirad burst into the gateyard and ran up the wide pathway that crossed the entire college and that had as its centre point the Heart pit. The Al-Arynaar and Julatsan mages were gathering there for the second, and what would be final, attempt at the Heart raise. Denser and Erienne were with them, all of them looking into the sky at the stricken dragon trying to control his fall.

'Get out of the way!' he yelled as he ran. 'Clear the area. Move, move!'

He was waving his arms frantically and it took an age for

410

them to see him. When they did, they began to run, heading for cover in the refectory, the infirmary, the lecture theatre or any long room that was close enough. He saw Denser shepherding Erienne to safety and breathed again, not slowing his pace.

Sha-Kaan took the roof off the lecture theatre, his hind legs ripping through stone, wood and slate, bringing half the building tumbling down. The impact drove him up a few feet before his wings folded and he crashed to the ground, legs giving way, sending him rolling and bouncing over the Heart pit. His tail bit through the frontages of both refectory and infirmary, striking stone, his neck was coiled in to protect his head as he rolled and eventually he slid to a stop, his back hitting a long room with a shuddering force that bowed the stone.

Behind him, dust billowed into the air and Hirad ran with a hand over his mouth and the other trying to keep the grit from his eyes. He was half blinded but he could see the heaving mass of Sha-Kaan and the neck still moving, dragging his head around to fix on his Dragonene.

Hirad slithered to a halt by his head and looked into a slowly blinking eye. He didn't have to ask after the dragon's condition, he could feel everything. Sha-Kaan couldn't shield the agony from him. The spell had blistered him where it struck, the cold hail prising up scales that had torn free when he crashed. He seemed to be bleeding from every part of his body.

Hirad placed a hand on the dragon's head, fighting back panic. Around him, he could hear running feet and cries from those who had sheltered in the wrong places. He sent a short prayer that few had been badly hurt and turned his full attention to the ailing beast.

'It was not my best landing,' said Sha-Kaan, his voice choked and pained. 'It was the landing of a newly weaned birthling.'

'This is not the time for jokes,' said Hirad. 'You've got to hang on.'

'You have told me that there was always time for jokes,' responded Sha-Kaan.

'Not now, not now,' said Hirad. 'What can I do. Gods but you are a mess.'

The startling blue eye blinked very slowly, the lid seeming to struggle on its way back up. 'There is little you can do,' he said. 'I have overstayed my welcome in your dimension.'

411

'So we'll send you home. Now,' said Hirad, turning. 'Denser! Denser get over here!'

'Hirad, I don't think I have the strength to get up on my feet, let alone fly inter-dimensional space back to Beshara. Keep your mage's strength, you need it more than I.'

'No way,' said Hirad. 'No way. Hold on.'

He felt the surge of pain that ran up and down Sha-Kaan's body. Ribs were cracked, wing membranes torn, neck sprained and tail broken. He turned and opened his mouth to shout throught the dust cloud that still swirled around the Heart pit.

'D—'

'I'm here,' said Denser, running up, Erienne with him. 'Oh dear Gods, is he all right?'

'Of course he's not bloody well all right! He's dying.' Hirad swallowed. 'Please Denser, it has to be now. We won't get another chance. Before the Xeteskians get themselves reorganised. Please.'

But the Xeteskians were already reforming. Darrick was issuing orders and a quick glance told him that the next spell against the gates was only moments away. The General himself was clearing the gatehouse and a defensive line was in position beyond any backwash when the gates gave way.

'Don't do it, Denser,' said Sha-Kaan. 'Finish what I started. Keep them away. Raise the Heart. I will wait.'

The eyes were closing.

'Don't listen to him, Denser, please.' Hirad grabbed· his shoulders, shook him while he spoke. 'We could all die here. It looks like we will. But if there's one we can save, we can't miss the chance. Sha-Kaan is that one. For everything he has done. Please.'

Denser nodded. Hirad dragged him forwards and kissed his cheek.

'Don't—' began Sha-Kaan.

'Now you listen to me, Sha-Kaan,' said Hirad, rounding on him. 'You are not going to die here. I promised that you wouldn't and I keep my promises. You cannot let it end like this. You have work, we have work and yours is on Beshara, leading the Brood Kaan.

'You've had your rest and now is the time to roll back on to your feet, test your wings and be ready. Got that?'

Sha-Kaan's nostrils flared. 'Frail human, I am not so weak I cannot snuff out your life.'

Hirad grinned. 'That is what I like to hear. But you'd better be standing up first or I'll outrun you. Denser, make sure whatever it is you open, it is right in front of his face.'

'No problem,' Denser's voice was faint with concentration.

'Hirad!' Darrick's voice carried to him. He could see the General running over.

'Right with you,'

'Now, Hirad,' said Darrick. 'They're coming through any moment.'

'Right with you,' repeated Hirad. 'Erienne, that Heart has to come up.'

'I know,' snapped Erienne. 'It was happening until he dropped in.'

'No time for argument, get it done,' said Hirad. He caught her expression. 'Shout all you want but we're on borrowed time here.'

'Can it work?' asked Darrick. 'The Heart raise?'

'Of course it can.' Erienne led their gaze to the pit to which elves and Julatsans were already returning, some being supported by their friends.

'But will they have anything left when they've done it?' he pressed. 'Anything at all?'

Erienne smiled at last. 'Enough,' she said. 'Perhaps.'

Hirad barely concentrated on the exchange. Darrick was already running back to his defensive postion. He felt an impact through the ground and heard timbers giving way.

'Hurry, Denser,' he said quietly.

He placed a hand on Sha-Kaan's head again. The eye opened and fixed him with an unblinking stare.

'Move aside.'

Hirad moved and so did Sha-Kaan. Slowly, painfully, he rolled, pushing with a twisted hind leg and feebly flapping a free wing. But he moved upright, his neck still dragging on the floor, he without the strength to lift it or his head. But with his legs finally beneath him, he pushed and relieved the pressure on his chest and torn underbelly. Blood ran from the hundreds of puncture wounds and he sighed.

'Next time you touch down, it'll be in your own Broodlands,' said Hirad. 'Think on that and keep yourself strong.'

Sha-Kaan said nothing, merely concentrated on breathing that was getting more and more ragged.

Denser was lost within himself, picking at the air with deliberate movements. Once again, Hirad found himself wishing he could see what a mage took as read, the mana flow, the structures it made and the wonder of it all. Next to him, Sha-Kaan twitched violently and his snout picked up off the ground.

Hirad jumped, made to ask what was wrong but instead felt the warmth of rediscovery flood through him. Around Denser's head, a tiny slit had appeared and emanating from it was a line of blue light, hair-thin and rippling in one direction.

'Follow your path, Sha-Kaan,' Denser said, his voice hushed. 'It will take you all the way home.'

Hirad felt the Great Kaan move and that head nudge him gently, almost knocking him from his feet. He twisted his neck and looked one more time into the deep blue pupil.

'Don't you dare die,' said Hirad. 'Not now.'

'Thank you,' said Sha-Kaan, the simple words burning into Hirad like the gratitude of thousands.

The Great Kaan shifted out of Balaia.

Behind Hirad, the gates of Julatsa were sundered.

Chapter 43

Izack moved his cavalry forward but he was not going to enter the city from anywhere but the south this morning. He had half of his shield mages in the air, spotting ahead, one having reported back on the attack by Sha-Kaan. For a few glorious moments it had seemed that the dragon had singlehandedly broken the enemy but the mages from the rear of the college had gathered, having driven him away, and now they assaulted the gates once more.

He led his men in at a gentle canter, watching for the signs in the sky. Darrick had instilled in him the importance of not making a hasty move and he had been proved right already today. His spotters had been chased by familiars and harried by Xeteskians but they had seen enough to stop him sacrificing himself in front of the walls at dawn. Nor had the TaiGethen been drawn to attack, but now the situation would change.

Izack waited his moment. They were very much alone. No support was coming. The Xeteskians had destroyed the relief force completely and all that was left was Blackthorne and he had gone his own way. High up the three spotters circled, diving and climbing to avoid the menacing familiars. The demons were the only immediate threat now that every available Xeteskian mage was presumably at the college gates.

While Izack watched, the flight pattern changed. The slow circling and diving switched to the figure of eight, each mage describing his own. Simultaneously, new smoke rose above the city. The spotters, their job done, dropped into the college to provide support.

'Lystern, let's move!' shouted Izack. He snapped his reins and the cavalry accelerated. He had two miles to travel and the

415

gates of Julatsa were down. The next stage of the fight relied on The Raven.

The heavy gates had rocked back against their hinges and the left-hand had sagged and fallen. Splinters filled the air and with a roar, the Xeteskian soldiers stormed in through the breach to be met head-on by Al-Arynaar warriors, Julatsan guardsmen and, at their centre, The Raven.

Hirad had run the moment Sha-Kaan had vanished into inter-dimensional space, dragging his sword from its scabbard and howling some barbarian cry that Denser never had understood. For himself, he took just a moment to collect himself, readying a HardShield and sprinting in Hirad's wake to the back of the defensive line.

Up on the walls, Al-Arynaar archers were firing the last of their arrows into the backs of the attackers who, temporarily unshielded, were taking significant losses. But while he watched, FlameOrbs exploded in three places in the parapet. Elves were catapulted screaming into the air amongst clouds of stone chips, wood slivers and dust, to fall burning to the ground behind the defensive lines.

On the ground, the Xeteskians had run into solid defence as they knew they must but were still moving forward, trying to clear a path for a cavalry charge. Denser could see Chandyr lining up his horsemen. Crossbow bolts traced out over the forward line to strike at the line of elven archers responding in kind and he had to take his life in his hands, running across the space to where he could cast and direct.

'Shield up,' he said.

Hirad nodded but didn't take his eyes from the enemy in front.

'Pushing Raven!' he roared.

Hirad's blade, quick as ever, licked into the face of an enemy, reversed and chopped down through his chest guard, dragged out and turned away another blow. Next to him, The Unknown was deep in the heart of the enemy line, the dagger in his left hand blurring as he struck out, the long sword in his right carving gracefully, blocking, twisting and thrusting.

His power was immense, every blow from either weapon knocking opponents back, giving him all the time he needed for the killing thrust. One man died with the dagger clean into his eye when he had thought a heartbeat earlier he had scored a hit on the big man. Another took a cleaving blow into his side which opened up his gut and he fell, spilling entrails over the blood-slick ground.

To The Unknown's left, Darrick and Thraun fought in a partnership that was beginning to work very well indeed. Darrick, the consummate swordsman, played defender while Thraun, raw power in every blow, thrashed his blade two-handed into enemy faces.

But it was the flanks that worried Denser. He could see the Xeteskians pressing there. For all their speed, the elves were very lightly armoured and their short blades didn't have the reach. Too often, they were being dragged a pace forwards, too often the result was a cut, a body blow or a killing thrust.

'Flanks weakening,' warned Denser. 'Cavalry waiting.'

'Archers!' shouted Darrick, pushing away a man. The Unknown clubbed him down with a huge blow to the top of the skull. 'Flank support! Fire at will.'

Rebraal stood in the left flank, sporting a cut to his face and holding his left arm gingerly, his sleeve soaked red. He called out in elven and Denser heard the bows stretched behind him. Another shout and every elf to the left of Thraun dropped to his haunches and turned a backward roll, arrows flying over them into the enemy beyond. They stood back up to run in but a volley of crossbow bolts from behind cut hard into them, felling four at least.

'We need more shields!' called Darrick. 'Someone get me a Julatsan from the pit.'

But there was no one free to do it and, Denser suspected, not a single mage able to detach by now. The enemy pressed on both flanks while making no progress against the centre. He heard a shout from behind and the thundering of hooves. At the rear of the Xeteskians, the press of hundreds parted and the cavalry, two abreast galloped in.

With no respect for the few of his own caught beneath hooves, Chandyr drove his horses through the weakened left, scattering Al-Arynaar and knocking Thraun from his feet.

'Break!' shouted The Unknown. 'Reform at the pit. Go, go!'

Denser dropped concentration, turned and ran. The Raven were all in a group, Al-Arynaar behind them keeping the cavalry from forming a charge. Spells detonated behind them, arrows filled the air and the sounds of hoof beats rang loud in the courtyard.

Racing for the path to the Heart pit which ran between the library and the long room Sha-Kaan had fetched up against, Denser dragged in concentration for a new casting. No time for defence now. He had to disrupt the charge.

'Turning, Denser!' warned Hirad.

Denser stopped and turned. A dozen cavalrymen were charging them. Behind them, the gateyard was chaos. Al-Arynaar fought in packs, Xeteskian soldiers and mages formed up into a cohesive line again, and more of Chandyr's cavalry piled through the shattered gates. In front of him, The Unknown tapped his blade. This time, though, Denser was faster. He brought his arms together across his chest, his fists clenched, held at his shoulders. He focused on the centre of the charge now ten yards distant and widened his mana vison. His voice was calm and certain.

'HellFire.'

Multiple columns of superheated blue mana fire scorched down from the clear sky, seeking the souls of the cavalry. The centre of the charge was deluged in an instant, the lead man disintegrating under the force of the spell, his horse driven into the ground, legs ripped to either side. On either flank, the columns gorged on flesh, their targets screaming briefly before dying. Fire splattered everywhere, riders veered away and circled, the burning horses plodding painfully to a halt, collapsing in agony. A wave of heat washed over The Raven and to a man, they staggered backwards.

'Too close,' breathed Denser, feeling the exertion of the powerful spell drag at his reserves.

'Good work,' said The Unknown, his sword still tapping its rhythm.

Al-Arynaar were running in their direction, aiming to strengthen their line. Out in the gateyard, the Xeteskians were slowly winning, their superior numbers telling. But The Raven couldn't break. Here they had to make a stand. Behind them, the last chance for Julatsa was being played out.

But to Denser's ear came the unmistakable manic laughter of familiars and following that, the calls of the ClawBound.

Erienne had seen the mages fly in and heard them call out their college allegiance as they came. A quick dip into the mana spectrum had revealed the truth and she had bade Pheone carry on the preparations. Mercifully, Sha-Kaan's untimely crash into the grounds of the college had injured several but killed none and the wounded had all come out to cast.

'You can hold off the shadow, Erienne?'

'We'll soon find out, won't we?' she said. 'One way or another, this is it. Get casting.' She had turned to the first Lysternan mage. 'Guard us,' she ordered. 'Never mind what's going on out there, The Raven will handle it. Familiars are my biggest concern. We can't afford to have any distractions, and you can't afford to show them any fear. They can be downed with magic. Believe in yourselves.'

'I understand.'

'Now leave me be.'

Erienne immersed herself in the elemental spectrum and saw its colours. She could see the deep blue of Xeteskian magic mixed with the dull yellow that signified Julatsa and, surrounding both, the multiple hues of brown and dark, dark green that made up the base of the elemental flow. The power churned from the stone of buildings, from the earth at her feet, and from every living creature. She could pick out every mage standing around the Heart and, further afield, every man and mage who fought at the gates.

She narrowed her focus and found the Heart. So much darker than yesterday before the failure. The tendrils of shadow had thickened to corded strands and were twining about each other, adding to the solid grey already covering the core structure. And there, right at its base, she found the pulsing fracture that flared up whenever Julatsan magic was cast. That was where she would fight her own personal battle while the Julatsan adepts fought theirs against the shadow.

She waited, watching again the construction of the splint and its connections, saw the poles form and attach, saw them puncture the shadow to grab at the Heart itself. She felt a moment's pure panic. They all had no choice but to trust her completely. Should she fail, and should the darkness take the Heart once more, there would be no coming back. Julatsan magic would have been destroyed.

Around her, the mages took the strain and the Heart began to lift. She ignored its delicate progress and instead edged the stopper from the well of One power and began to try and meld it to a form she could use to suppress the darkness. Almost immediately, she saw it begin, the trickle of black into the base of the Heart.

Erienne reached out with her mind to touch it, felt its intense cold, like the power of the dead earth flow through her. She jolted and drew back. It grew and grew, spreading up. She had no choice. Letting her mind free, she dragged in the live flows of all the elements around her and plunged into the dark, screaming as the cold force channelled through her.

Auum led the TaiGethen to the fight one more time. Claw-Bound moved ahead. The gates were crowded with men trying to get in. He could hear the desperate fight inside the college and knew there was no way he could wait.

'Right-hand side,' he said. 'Single point of attack.'

The Tais cruised in, jaqrui and arrows punching into the men just to the right of the shattered gateposts. The survivors reacted, turning and backing off as the elves tore at them, no man wanting to face them alone.

Auum hurled his last jaqrui into the neck of an enemy, grabbed his second short sword from its scabbard and let his mind stand above his body. A blade was thrown towards him, flicking end over end; he swayed left and it passed him. From the right a spell was cast, flaming blue in his peripheral vision. He hit the ground and rolled, coming up to his feet in one movement, momentum maintained.

He was on them in the next stride, a ClawBound pair savaging into the men to his left, Duele and Evunn his shadows. He held both swords horizontal, one slightly above the other. The upper he backhanded into the face of his first target, the second stabbing low, foot coming through in the next beat to kick the man away.

Swords were thrust at him, he ducked one, blocked a second away and killed the third man before he could finish his strike. He moved on, sensing the panic among the men, who outnumbered the elves by twenty to one. Tual guided him, let him free. He reversed one blade in his hand, battered the hilt into the jaw of his enemy and stabbed through his shoulder blade on the downstroke. He dropped to the ground to sweep the legs from the man to his right, slicing his hamstrings as he rolled to escape.

A panther leaped clear over his head, driving back the attackers. One more man and they had the space they needed. Duele, cut on the cheek, took him down with a straight-fingered blow to the windpipe and the TaiGethen made the gateyard.

'Mages only!' Auum called.

He sprinted in, seeing the confusion of the melee around him. Al-Arynaar were backed into small groups, fighting hand-to-hand while enemy cavalrymen charged repeatedly at a larger force of elves led by Rebraal, his face a mask of blood, his eyes undimmed.

Auum nodded at him. Rebraal nodded back and pointed towards the Heart pit. At the same moment, the ground began to shudder and a rending sound of stone on stone vibrated through the college. Immediately, a group of mages broke from cover under the parapet and ran towards the path to the pit. Standing in their way were The Raven.

'With me!' called Auum.

He turned and set off across the gateyard, cavalry wheeling to block his path. They squared up but he was in no mood to fight them. Three paces from them, he leaped high, turning a somersault in the air and carving down with a blade as he passed, taking the cavalryman through the top of the skull. He landed, steadied himself and ran on, blowing out his cheeks as he considered what he had just done without thinking. Behind him, Evunn and Duele had rolled beneath the horses as he might have done himself and were again at his shoulders. Soldiers were closing in on either side. Ahead the mages were pausing to cast and The Raven were running at them.

Auum didn't think they'd make it in time.

'Denser, go!' shouted Hirad. 'See to Erienne.'

They had all heard the chittering and her scream of pure pain but they couldn't turn. Ahead of them, TaiGethen and Claw-Bound had broken into the compound and were heading their way fast. But the sheer weight of the enemy was taking its toll. He saw one of the painted warriors go down with a crossbow bolt in his back, a panther taken in mid leap by a focused Orb. And the Al-Arynaar were being rounded up and slowly cut to pieces.

Behind The Raven, the ground shuddered violently as the

421

Heart began its tortuous progress upwards. Hirad glanced across at The Unknown.

'Pray they do this,' he said.

'They'll do it if we can hold back Xetesk,' said The Unknown.

Mages and soldiers were running at them. Far too many for them to take on. But from behind he saw Auum and the remaining TaiGethen literally leap over cavalrymen and run to their aid.

'Now's the time,' said The Unknown. He tapped his blade once on the ground. 'Raven with me!'

The Raven and the few Al-Arynaar with them broke and ran, hoping to meet the TaiGethen in the middle. Ahead, the mages had stopped and were casting. There were eight of them, enough to wipe out The Raven in one go.

'Trouble, our right,' said Hirad. He could feel that the wound in his chest had opened again, blood was coursing down his body, soaking into his shirt.

'I see it,' said The Unknown. He had dropped his dagger and was hefting his long sword in two hands. Already limping, that style of fighting would add to the pain but for him, as for them all, it was everything or nothing.

Auum was powering towards the stationary mages, Duele and Evunn with him, bows unslung and loaded. The cavalry had turned and were chasing them, eating up the ground quickly. Hirad changed the point of the attack.

'Let's give them some help!'

Nearby, Thraun growled his approval and The Raven closed in, the Al-Arynaar turning to meet the foot soldiers head-on. Hirad felt the time slipping away. The mages would finish casting and the spell, whatever it was, would wash over them. But he couldn't let it affect him. Only thirty yards from the cavalry, he had to be picking his target.

Everything seemed to happen at once. Duele and Evunn loosed arrows, both shafts finding their targets, punching mages from their feet and disrupting the casting for a few heartbeats. In front of him, his target disappeared under the paws of a panther, her partner leaping to snatch another from his saddle. The ground shuddered again, right under his feet and he fell, sprawling to the earth, The Raven all pitching down around him and rolling.

Hirad stood up, a little disoriented, and saw dust and smoke disgorging from the pit. Spells were firing into the air around it. It was Denser, with some Lysternan cavalry mage help, taking on familiars. He heard the shout of warning a little too late and spun, sword up reflexively, the hoof catching him in the midriff and sending him flying backwards to connect hard with the courtyard stone. He fought to sit up but his vision clouded and, with so many closing in, he slipped back, clutching for his sword.

Erienne experienced a unique sensation of pain. She fought hard to gather her concentration, channelling the One force around her body, barely keeping it in check and using her mind to direct it at the blackness that inched inexorably up the Heart. It was blackness that represented a manaless void. Worse, it was the antithesis of mana, an element that none of her learning had told her could exist. Should it cover the Heart, Julatsan magic would be gone forever. She was slowing it, she knew she was, but the effort was draining her so very quickly. She felt the Heart rising and knew she had to cling on.

It was in her mind, taunting her with visions of her daughter running free through meadows and woods. Just let go, it was saying and you can be anything you desire and have anything you desire. You can be the One above all. You can be the only mage. Let me have Julatsa.

It tore at her, the temptation undermining her strength, but she carried on, drawing the cold, bleak dark away from the Heart and into herself where the true One power extinguished it. The toll on her body was tremendous. She was aware her legs were shaking and that she should have collapsed by now but for something holding her upright. She searched briefly for what it was and the charge of knowledge revitalised her.

'You will not have me,' she said to the shadow. 'You will not use my daughter against me.'

She drew more power into her mind and began to force the shadow away.

Denser had left the familiars to the Lysternan mages, who kept them away with careful use of DeathHail and focused Orbs. One of the demons already lay charring, deep in the Heart pit. Denser had seen Erienne swaying, her legs beginning to lose their strength and had run to her, catching her before she had fallen.

'It's all right, love,' he said, though he knew she couldn't hear him. 'I've got you.'

She was dead weight in his arms but what he saw pushed all thoughts of losing grip from his mind.

The shuddering deep within the ground intensified, loose stones on the surface bouncing and skipping, but the mages stood rock solid, each completely in tune with the movement below them. And from the pit came the sounds of stone grinding against stone, and the indefinable feeling that whatever the movement was, it was upwards.

A gout of dust burst from the pit, sparks following it. The ground heaved once more and Denser heard a rumbling, deep and powerful. The edges of the pit fell inwards, cracks forked out across the cobblestones, rippling beneath them, fracturing them, spitting some into the air. And, finally, came the Heart itself. Its casing was a column a hundred feet wide and wreathed in dark smoke. Carvings adorned its outside and they seemed to come to life as the sun touched them.

Denser stared in simple awe as the stone emerged from its grave, shedding dust as it rose, inch by slow inch.

'Come on, come on,' he breathed. 'You can do this.'

He saw the ancient Julatsan runes standing proud on its surface, the intricate friezes of the building of the college, the wars that led to balance and the rise of Julatsan magic. Ilkar had spoken of them many a time. Normally encased in the outer skin of the Tower, they were never seen by mages from other colleges but Denser was privileged.

It climbed, Denser watching it go to a height of twenty feet, the rasping as it came almost musical. And then it paused. Time stood still for a moment and Erienne slumped in his arms, a low moan escaping her lips.

'Come on, love,' he whispered. 'Come on.'

She shifted in his arms, opened her eyes. She saw the Heart and smiled.

'Pheone,' she muttered. 'Keep the faith.'

The Heart edged upwards again. Denser could feel the effort and glanced around at the casting mages. Every one of them wore their effort in their expressions. Arms quivered, teeth ground and tears squeezed from tightly closed eyes.

They would do it. Unmolested they would succeed. Determination radiated like a physical force. But only a few hundred feet away, the Xeteskians were pressing like never before. And Denser wasn't sure the Julatsans and elves would be given the time they deserved.

Chapter 44

Thraun knew he had to save Hirad. He growled loud to attract The Raven who were already running in the direction of the prone barbarian but he was the closest. There were four enemies nearby, each wanting to make the killing blow and earn the right to say that they had killed the legendary Raven man.

He could not let that happen.

So Thraun ran faster than he had ever done before. He felt the smells of the forest in his nostrils, the closeness of the pack and the warm scent of his prey ahead. The sounds of the battle around him dimmed but he heard someone call his name. Or he thought it was his name.

He wanted to heft his sword, to throw it at them all but there was nothing in his hands. He ignored the thought, snarled, snapped his jaws and leapt.

The prey screamed beneath him but he would show no mercy. He dashed a claw through its back and plunged his teeth into its neck, the hot blood pouring into his mouth. Leaving the prey to die he turned on the other three, seeing them back away. With one bound, he was on the next, paws thumping into his chest and knocking him flat. A single claw tore out his throat and he moved again, fangs locking into the calf of the third. And while he yelled for help, the last fell dead beside him, a wound dividing its stomach, another across its face. The one he held fell too, cries stilled.

Thraun let the leg go and swung around. Two stood over him. Not prey. He backed away to the one he had to save hunched to pounce should any threaten him.

He howled.

*

Izack drove his cavalry on at a gallop through the streets of Julatsa for what he prayed would be the last time. The cavalry met no resistance. Chandyr had committed all his men to the battle at the gates now they were down, and his perimeter guard had deserted their posts to join in.

Izack gave his horse its head and yelled a battle cry to clear his mind. Forty men were at his back, swordsmen and mages. He could see those still outside the college unable to get in, the spray of bodies that spoke of an attack by the TaiGethen, and he could see the clouds of smoke rising above the walls and the shattered gates.

The Xeteskians barely saw them until they were attacked. Izack drove in hard, slicing down right-handed, taking the ear off one man, his blade going on to shear through shoulder, ribs and vital organs. He raised his sword again and lashed out, deeply denting the helmet of another, stunning him senseless. A blade came at him but it was blocked by another of his men. More and more pushed into the left-hand side and inexorably, the Xeteskians began to fall back.

But as they did, they fought hard. He saw three of his men taken down by a group of soldiers working together out on the left periphery. Crossbows and arrows sliced through the air, one whistling by his ear to bury itself in the shoulder of a cavalryman behind him.

'About wheel!' he ordered. 'Reform! Mages, give me shields.'

He dragged the reins about, all the time chopping down at his enemies and kicking with his stirruped feet. A blade dragged across his right leg and he saw below him a man who surely should be dead, half his lower jaw missing, still trying to fight. He acknowledged the bravery and ran him through the heart.

He kicked his horse to leap out of the press, his men following him. He galloped away to the edge of the square, turned, gathered and charged again.

The appearance of the shapechanger had caused confusion and panic in Thraun's immediate circle. Xeteskians, Julatsans and elves alike had scattered. His howls had chilled the fraught air of the battle and led to a critical uncertainty that The Unknown was not going to allow to pass him by. Thraun himself was pacing up and down before the prone form of Hirad, daring any to try and take the barbarian's life. There were no takers.

'Leave him,' ordered The Unknown, catching Darrick's arm. 'You can trust him. This way.'

Xeteskian soldiers were trying to force their way through to the Heart pit. Cavalry were behind, being tackled by a group of Al-Arynaar. Rebraal was still there, he could see, still fighting hard. He should have gone to the elf's aid but there were more pressing concerns. Auum was in the thick of the battle for control of the passage to the helpless mages behind and being slowly pushed back. Only four TaiGethen stood with him.

The Unknown flung himself into the attack, trying not to think that Hirad wasn't by his side. He dared not even contemplate what Thraun had done to himself by assuming his wolven form after so long. The Raven were all over the place in the college and he didn't like it. Best he got them back together again.

He tapped his sword once and thrashed it into the back of the nearest Xeteskian, alerting the rest to their peril. There were a good thirty of them, trying to organise themselves and in the confusion, Darrick chopped through the back of another's legs and pushed him hard into his comrades. The Unknown struck again too, his blow biting deep into the skull of the soldier, the momentum of the swing dragging the man from his feet and flicking him across the line to collapse into the arms of one of his comrades.

The two Raven men backed off a pace, the Xeteskians forming up. The Unknown gasped a breath, his hip a furnace of pain. They could see Auum and the TaiGethen, blurs in the late morning, blades whispering through the air, feet and hands employed as lethal weapons. The Xeteskians had no choice but to drive on, those in front of the elves reluctant, knowing only luck would keep them alive. And luck played no part in anything the TaiGethen did.

'Keep close, Darrick,' said The Unknown. 'Angle away, keep an eye on the flanks. Don't be pretty. Hit them hard.'

'Got it,' said the general.

Three enemy moved in, head-on, others moved to flanking positions. The Unknown tried to keep his eyes on them all. Darrick had switched to a two-handed grip, sacrificing finesse for bludgeoning power. He swung in an upward curve right to left, battering the defence of his first man away, bringing the blade back across his face and connecting with his enemy's skull, splitting it like a coconut and careering the body across the short line.

Seeing his chance, The Unknown struck forward smartly, taking an opponent in the stomach. He dragged the blade back quickly and cut across the thighs of another, not quite balanced. Three were down quickly but more came to fill the space. The Unknown found himself fending off blows from two sides, angling his blade up and down, the defence quickly becoming more desperate.

Darrick too was getting hemmed in, forced to jab and cut, the full swing leaving him open to counterthrust. The Unknown changed his tactics. Feinting to catch the next blow as more closed in, he thrust low instead, ducking and shoving forwards hard with his hands, driving a space. Taking the enemy by surprise, he swept his blade up, striking one Xeteskian in the groin and backed away fast, feeling a sword whistle across his head.

He straightened too quickly, his hip screaming pain and threatening his balance, and savaged a blow left to right. He roared to clear his head. It was a sound taken up by animal throats as first a panther and then Thraun stormed into the attack. The Unknown, slightly taken aback, half turned away from a man racing in to strike and couldn't find his position fast enough. The blade was swinging towards his head but it didn't arrive. Hirad's sword cracked it away and his return strike severed the man's head.

'Raven with me!' yelled Hirad.

The Unknown couldn't believe it. He saw the barbarian half running, half stumbling towards the Heart pit, his head covered in blood, his sword held defiantly before him. Thraun was pacing beside him and no enemy chanced getting too close. The Unknown sized up the problem. He and Darrick held the immediate Xeteskian attack on one side and the TaiGethen were whittling them away on the other.

Beyond him, he could see the Heart grinding into the light of the day, smoke pouring from its sides, its runes glittering in the sunlight. But the reason for Hirad's urgency was clear. Seeing the tide of the battle beginning to turn, Xeteskian mages had taken to ShadowWings and were bypassing the block to land in amongst the casting Julatsan and elven mages. Denser and Erienne were in there and they were defenceless.

'Damn it,' he breathed. 'Darrick, let's go!'

He thundered his sword through the guard of the nearest soldier and set off around the attacking group, following Hirad towards the Heart pit. Between them and their friends were enough Xeteskians to delay them too long.

Hirad could barely focus. He felt pain in his head, his chest and his legs and his sword was so heavy in his hands. Every pace he was blinking away blood but still he ran forward. Beside him Thraun, who knew what had to be done, leaped at the back of one of the Xeteskians blocking his way to the Heart pit. The man screamed and those by him moved reflexively aside, unwilling to be the next victim of the wolf.

In front of him, Auum with only one sword in hand now, whipped that blade into the face of his opponent and slammed the heel of his palm into his nose, snapping him off his feet.

'Auum!' yelled Hirad. 'Got to break through.'

He shoved an enemy aside, shouldered into a second and lashed out at a third. Auum had heard him and at a command, the TaiGethen concentrated their attack on Hirad's flank. The enemy folded in front of them. The barbarian roared, struck his blade into the neck of the last man in his way and ran into the courtyard beyond, praying he was in time.

Barely keeping his balance, Hirad headed forward, wiping blood from his face. Thraun bounded past him and disappeared among the casting mages. Everything was confusion. In the centre, the Heart speared upwards. Seventy feet and more of it was above ground now and still it came. Surrounding it, the mages who breathed life back into Julatsa held their arms aloft, pouring themselves into their own salvation. And they were heedless of the enemy in their midst, landed now and taking them down one by one.

Outnumbered, the Lysternan cavalry mages were under intense pressure and dying quickly. Hirad stumbled towards Denser, who still held Erienne, and was looking around him at the Xeteskians closing in fast. They weren't just trying to stop the Heart raise, they wanted to snatch the ultimate prize too.

No way. Following Thraun into the circles of casting mages,

Hirad cracked his sword into the skull of a Xeteskian mage. Three more were heading for Denser. Others killed Julatsans. The Heart shuddered and faltered.

'No!' he screamed 'No! Don't give it up. Push, you bastards, push!'

He didn't care if they heard him but the Heart was moving again anyway. He tried to run faster, tripped and sprawled. The pain was extraordinary. His chest wound split wide, his head bouncing off the cobbles. His vision dimmed.

'Not yet,' he breathed. 'Not yet.'

Somehow, he dragged himself back to his feet. He heard footsteps near him. The Unknown and Darrick came past him, the latter sprinting, the former limping heavily. Both took down Xeteskian mages, leaving his path clear once more. He shambled on. Ahead, Denser had drawn a short blade but could not let Erienne go. She was limp in his free arm.

They were closing on him. Hirad dragged a breath across his chest and pushed himself to a run. The first Xeteskian to threaten Denser felt Thraun's claws through his back. The second took just one more pace before he stepped into Hirad's range. One final time, the barbarian overarmed his sword. It bit into the man's back and sliced out beneath his ribs.

'Denser, there's another,' he said.

But if the Xeteskian attacked, Hirad didn't see him. He sagged to his knees completely exhausted.

The Unknown carved his sword through the waist of a Xeteskian mage and looked down on Denser. He didn't want to move another step. His hip was agony and breath was hard to come by.

'You all right?'

'In a manner of speaking.'

In Denser's arms, Erienne relaxed and sighed a long breath. Simultaneously, the Heart stopped, turned through ninety degrees and was still, the last wisps of black smoke issuing into the bright morning sky.

The Unknown looked around the mages who clearly could not quite believe what they had achieved. Lysternans were moving among them as was Darrick, searching out the final Xeteskian intruders.

Some of the Julatsans had their heads in their hands, some

431

were crying, others just staring in stupefaction. The din of the battle didn't seem to impinge on them at all.

'Pheone,' he said. She didn't turn round. 'Pheone.'

'I . . .' she gestured at the Heart. 'Look at what we've done.'

'It is the most stunning achievement for which you will all go down in history,' said The Unknown as gently as he could. 'But we have trouble in the gateyard. Have you got anything left to give? People are still dying.'

She smiled at him and nodded vigorously. 'The Heart is raised. Our focus is clear. Yes, I'd have said we had something left.'

She didn't have to say anything more. All around her, her mages were returning to themselves and their elven helpers sought the focus of the battle and ran to the aid of the Al-Arynaar.

In the passage between the Heart pit and the main gates, Auum and his Tai still fought. The Unknown just couldn't leave them to it. He patted Hirad on the shoulder, left the barbarian sitting on his haunches, hands on his thighs, and trotted as quickly as he could towards the elves, damaged hip protesting all the way. But at every pace more of the Al-Arynaar mages were coming by him and the spells were already beginning to fly. Focused Orbs took individuals and ForceCones knots of enemy forces. Almost at once, the passageway was clear and Auum's Tai set off to free Rebraal and the rest of the Al-Arynaar.

'Got you,' breathed The Unknown.

He was spent, he knew he was. Behind him, The Raven were in no condition to fight on. Whatever happened now was out of their hands. He leaned on a wall. Thraun's muzzle nudged at his hand. He looked down.

'Gods, I hope you know what you're doing,' he said. Thraun looked up at him, humanity blazing from his lupine eyes. 'You come back to us, you hear?'

From the gates there was another roar of noise and Xeteskians fell over themselves as they were forced into the gateyard. A horse neighed loud and Izack leaped a fallen man and galloped in, followed by his cavalry, his sword dripping blood.

The men that had fallen in before the cavalry and had survived, got up and ran. And they were just the first. All over the yard, Xeteskians detached themselves from battle and headed for the gates. Mages cast ShadowWings and took off, clearing the walls and climbing high from danger.

The Unknown watched them run and nodded to himself. Auum roared a rallying cry and the Al-Arynaar and surviving TaiGethen surged once more. Bottled up by the gate, enemy cavalry and elves around him, the Xeteskian commander yelled for order, for a new attack, but all around him, his men were running. They outnumbered their enemies but with Julatsan and Al-Arynaar mages on the parapets and racing along the stones, casting into their midst, they were broken.

Chandyr bellowed his rage. He turned his head and met The Unknown's gaze. Reluctantly, he nodded, snapped the reins of his horse and rode out of the gates, his men following him. Not satisfied, Izack bellowed his cavalry to order and chased them out, Al-Arynaar elves with him.

The Unknown felt a hand on his shoulder. He looked round to see Hirad leaning against him. Blood slicked his face and dripped from his nose and ears but he still couldn't keep the smile from his face though his eyes were a little unfocused.

'What the hell do you think you're doing?' asked The Unknown.

'Watching us win, I think,' Hirad said.

He wobbled slightly on his feet and The Unknown caught him under the shoulders.

'Come on, old son, let's get you seen to.'

The cheers were ringing round the college. Up on the walls, the elven and Julatsan mages were hugging each other and down on the bloodied ground, Al-Arynaar warriors and mages clasped each other's hands, too tired to do anything else. The Unknown and Hirad were joined in their walk to the infirmary by Auum, who was supporting a bedraggled-looking Rebraal. Duele and Evunn walked beside them, both cut and bleeding. Gods, wasn't everyone?

'We did it,' said Rebraal.

'Did you ever doubt it?' asked Hirad.

'Of course,' said Rebraal.

Hirad smiled. 'Got to learn not to, if you're ever going to be in The Raven.'

Thraun was sitting outside the infirmary and staring in. Hirad unwound himself from The Unknown and knelt by him, ruffling his fur.

'Thanks, Thraun. Saved me again, eh?'

The wolf stared at him, some comprehension in his eyes. His tongue licked at Hirad's face.

'This is some risk you've taken. You can come back, can't you?' He held the wolf's cheeks in his hands and looked at him. 'Listen to me, Thraun. Remember.'

Thraun backed away, yowling in his throat. Then he growled, cocked his head and trotted away.

Hirad stared after him a moment, then let himself be helped inside.

Vuldaroq completed his Communion with Heryst and sat back in his chair, feeling the warmth of the sun on his obese body. He felt a surge of excitement though it had been such a mix of a morning. First, one of Izack's cavalry mages had reported to Heryst that the relief force had been completely wiped out. Only a handful of allied men had been left in the field barring Izack's and they were under Blackthorne's questionable control.

The wait for more news had been interminable and when it had come, just as he was going to turn down an early lunch, it had been better than he could possibly have hoped for. Izack, the elves and The Raven had been victorious. The Heart of Julatsa was raised and the Xeteskians were in retreat.

It wasn't the fact of victory that had so lightened his mood. Indeed, had Julatsa fallen, he wasn't sure that would have been too bad a thing. But it stood and better, the prize remained inside. More than that, Heryst said that he had nothing left to commit. And Izack was not going to be the man to arrest The Raven, that was abundantly clear.

That left Dordover to do, well, do the right thing. Vuldaroq rang the bell by his chair and waited for his servant to appear.

'The reserve,' he said. 'See it is sent to Julatsa with all speed. I will be writing a letter to the acting High Mage, Pheone. We have one of our own that needs to be returned to the bosom of the college.'

Dystran could still not believe what was happening. He stared at the Wesmen army that was organising itself outside his college. Carefully out of spell range, they calmly pitched tents, lit fires and fashioned battering rams and ladders. He shook his head, rested his elbows on the wall, and rubbed his face in his hands.

It wasn't just the enormous numbers of men that were being assembled, it was the mode of their attack. They hadn't, as in years gone by, thrown everything they had at their enemies, only to be beaten back by spell and arrow.

Instead, they'd hurled abuse for a while and now this. They were having a party outside his south gates. It couldn't have become much worse except that his Communion team had just reported the final defeat at Julatsa. His men were routed and fleeing south even now.

'I suppose I should be thankful for small mercies,' said Dystran.

'I beg your pardon, my Lord?' said Suarav.

'At least Chandyr is bringing some people back.'

'We can keep them from the walls, my Lord,' asserted Suarav.

'How many fighting men do we have in the city right now, Captain?'

'Two, maybe three hundred.'

'And how many mages of any real experience?'

'Forty or so, my Lord.'

Dystran could see light dawning over his face. It wasn't a pretty sight. 'They have three or four thousand out there. They fear magic but it won't stop them. If they get over these walls or through those gates, and I don't doubt that they will try very, very hard, they will sweep through this city like a dose of the shits, do you understand? I suggest you go and read up on their normal tactics. It might tell you something.'

'Yes, my Lord.'

'Lucky I've got another dimensional team in the catacombs, isn't it? I wonder when the next conjunction is.'

The mood of celebration had taken hold though it was tempered by the numbers of dead. Sixty Al-Arynaar warriors had perished, along with twenty mages. Another twenty would not make the trip home to Calaius. Commander Vale had died too, in the gateyard. He'd dived on an elf as a spell had struck and taken the full force himself. The Al-Arynaar would respect him for it forever. Auum, Duele and Evunn had survived, a testament to their extraordinary awareness of each other as much as anything.

They were three of just five TaiGethen. And just a single Claw-Bound pair remained. They mourned their fallen alone.

But there remained a feeling of intense satisfaction around the table in the refectory. Hirad sat with his head and chest bandaged, a goblet of wine in his hand. Surrounding him were The Raven minus a sleeping Erienne, Rebraal who had more bandage than skin showing, Auum and his cell, and Pheone.

'Ilkar will be watching,' said Denser.

'He'd bloody well better be,' said Hirad. 'I don't do this sort of thing for just anyone.'

'Feel better now it's done?' asked The Unknown. 'Any of that anger left you?'

Hirad chuckled. 'Some of it,' he said. 'I'm glad it was the Xeteskians we walloped to get here, though. They owe us.'

'They have paid,' said Thraun abruptly.

'I'm almost prepared to believe anything you say,' said Hirad. 'Do you remember any of how or what you did?'

Thraun looked troubled and shook his head. 'Not how,' he said. 'Seemed . . . right.'

The Unknown raised his eyebrows. 'Really? I thought that side was closed to you. What made you do it?'

'No choice,' Thraun said and looked at Hirad. 'Sometimes we must all do that which we fear to save those we must. And we must all come to terms with the pain we carry.'

'What are you looking at me for?' asked Hirad.

'They have paid,' repeated Thraun.

Hirad held up his hands. 'I'll see what I can do.'

'So what's next for the Al-Arynaar and TaiGethen?' Darrick's question turned all their heads.

'Home,' said Auum. 'I hate this place.'

There was not the hint of a smile on his lips but Hirad laughed anyway. 'To the point as ever. You too, Rebraal?'

'Yes. There is so much to do, so much to rebuild. Think of the warriors and mages we have lost. We must rebuild our orders or this will happen again.'

'I doubt it.'

'We doubted it could ever happen in the first place,' said Rebraal.

'Point taken,' said Hirad. 'Unknown, fancy a trip south?'

'Try and stop me, barbarian. I've got a wife and son I have to see.'

436

'Then we should all go,' said Denser. 'Erienne will want to visit Lyanna's grave on Herendeneth. So do I.'

'How is Erienne?' asked The Unknown.

Denser grimaced. 'You know I have absolutely no idea. Has she won her battle with the One? I doubt it. Does she know what she did today? Yes, I think so. But what effect it will have on her when she wakes, who knows?' He looked at them sadly. 'Some parts of her mind are closed to me. To all of us. Like Thraun says, we have to come to terms with the pain we carry. It's her turn now, I think.'

'What was it all about, her and the Heart?' asked Hirad.

Pheone answered for Denser. 'The Heart was . . . infected, if you like, while it lay in the pit. And though mana, in the form of the raising was the only thing that could stop that infection, it also encouraged the infection to flourish. Erienne held the infection at bay, channelled it into herself to kill it, while we raised the Heart. Julatsa is forever in her debt. And yours, all of you.'

'No you aren't. All we've done is what Ilkar wanted,' said Hirad. 'That's enough.' He paused. 'Right then, unless there are any dissenters, The Raven will travel south. And say nothing, General, everyone here wants your head, after all.'

'And yours now, no doubt. I will admit it is an enticing prospect, sleeping without the axe hovering.'

Hirad pushed back his chair and stood up. 'Funny isn't it. We've spent the last, what, six and a bit years saving this ridiculous country from everything that's been thrown at it and all they want to do is kill us. Perhaps we shouldn't ever come back.'

'You would be welcome on Calaius,' said Rebraal.

'In a city,' added Auum and there, at last, were the corners of his mouth turning up. 'I'm not sure the rainforest is ready for you just yet.'

'We'll think about it,' said Hirad. 'Right now, I need some air.'

He wandered out of the refectory, feeling exhausted. It should have been night time from the effort he'd exerted today but it could only be mid-afternoon. He walked across to the Heart casing and looked at its carvings. The column, some eighty feet high, stood proud against the night sky. He felt intensely sad that Ilkar hadn't lived to see his college reborn

437

but he was sure that, in some way, he would know. And Julatsa would remember him always.

'This is for you, old friend,' he said. 'We did it for you. I hope you like it.'

Hirad scratched at his bandages and headed off towards the gateyard, feeling the need to see if there was anything he could do. He didn't know why but it just felt right. Izack's cavalry and the remaining city guard patrolled the walls, and Al-Arynaar filled the gap where the gates had been, just in case of another attack. Somehow Hirad doubted it. Izack had chased the Xeteskians clear out of the city and the last patrols back that night had reported them reformed and heading south, back to Xetesk.

Outside, the city would be coming to terms with the legacy it had bestowed upon itself and that in itself would be worth hanging around to see. Somehow, though, he didn't think the elves would want to stay for the reckoning.

The dull thud in his head eased as if a balm had been spread across his brain. Feelings of warmth and the smells of humid air and cold white stone filled his senses. He could touch the air passing over a wing and feel the touch of a kin after so long apart from so many. And he could hear the distant roars of greeting. A sound he never thought would reach him again.

Hirad smiled and let the sun play over his face.

'Home at last, old friend,' he said. 'Home at last.'